HOT IRON and COLD BLOOD

AN ANTHOLOGY OF THE WEIRD WEST

JILL GIRARDI • OWL GOINGBACK • BRENNAN LAFARO
VIVIAN KASLEY • KENZIE JENNINGS • RONALD KELLY • EDWARD LEE
DREW HUFF • DAVID J. SCHOW • JEFF STRAND • BRIANA MORGAN
PATRICK R. MCDONOUGH • L.M. LABAT
JESSE ALLEN CHAMPION • JOE R. LANSDALE • WILE E. YOUNG

Published by Death's Head Press, and imprint of Dead Sky Publishing, LLC
Miami Beach, Florida
www.deadskypublishing.com

Cover by Robert Sammelin

Edited by Patrick R. McDonough
"It Calls" Edited by Patrick C. Harrison III

Copyedited by Kristy Baptist

ISBN 9781639511396 (paperback)
ISBN 9781639511389 (ebook)

First U.S. Edition September 2023

Contents

Set A Spell, The West Has A Story To Tell: A Foreword

BY RJ JOSEPH

The mere mention of the Wild West conjures romanticized images of open terrain and prairies, dotted with budding and established towns along the road to glistening riches. Strong and hearty people occupy these spaces, performing honest—and not so honest—work to build prosperity for themselves, while helping America fulfill its destiny as an expanded and evolved nation. Humankind wars with, and overcomes nature, breaking the wills of the domesticated animals that aid in these endeavors.

A closer examination reveals this is a vastly simplified picture of a time that included these ideals, yes, but which was also punctuated by sorrow, disease, and horrific living conditions. It is this inextricability—of prosperity and desperation, sorrow and joy—that paints a more accurate story of this space that ultimately mirrors the certainty of life and death.

The Wild West is more than drawls, leather, and ranches. Those of us who live here in the present day, realize other folks may cling to the romance of a time long past, desiring to emulate and report on our lives and culture. But many still do not completely understand what drives us. Those things for which we live and die. The things that bring us joy. The things that terrify us. To truly know a peoples' story is to listen to their souls and hear what they hear, feel what they feel—and to then recognize their experiences as tied to the universality of the human existence.

To embody the Wild West is to revel in our expanses of space, rife with endless possibilities. To witness the spirits of the past permeating the elements, dancing intermingled with the breezes of today—to watch them dissipate into the ethers of tomorrow. The spirits are borne of strength, driven by loyalty, epitomized through tenacity, and bolstered throughout community. These foundational tenets of the Wild West are lain bare through the silence, whispers, murmurs, and clamoring of the stories in this anthology.

Silent strength.

We see just how strong a business owner must be to overcome the opposition when they fight dirty. This same strength must come from within, if one seeks to resist the comforting call of loved ones awash in a beckoning light. The tool of vengeance wielded by a cruel God may wish to deviate from that control, but instead calls on the strength of conviction to carry out obligations. And strength is the only thing left to rely on while steeped in abject loneliness, serving a tortured penance.

Whispered loyalty.

Loyalty and comfort in love supersede distrust and ultimate terror. We see men motivated by pure profit and loyal to gaining it for themselves, innovating to accommodate market demand for special services. A bandit loyal only to self-preservation feels the sting of the spirits in their retribution. A woman and the dark angel sent from her God stand unwaveringly in the face of conflict, loyal to deeply held beliefs.

Murmured tenacity.

An unlikely attacker uses his tenacious cunning to prevail over his hunters. A woman holds true to waiting to enact the ultimate vengeance on her perpetrator. We see a person's true self cling tenaciously through hardship to emerge on the other side. A woman devotes her life to a tenacious embodiment of ultimate power.

Clamoring community.

A group of immigrants finds a recognizable solution from their community to mitigate spiritual invasion. Strangers from the Old World seek community, death, and rebirth within one another. A community concerned about its reputation works to clean up for outsiders. Scientists commune with one another to seek answers to timeless inquiries.

Come, set a spell. Have a cool drink on the porch. Do not mind those voices It is only the restless spirits of the Wild West, channeling through their worthy mediums here. They just want to tell you a story or three...

—Rhonda Jackson Garcia, writing as RJ Joseph
Texas, September 28th, 2022

Ruthless

BY JILL GIRARDI

"GODDAMN IDIOTS!" RUTH SUTTON spat. She tied her roan to the hitching post, alongside several other horses. Across the dirt road, two soused cowhands brawled on the porch of Noonan's saloon. One of the drunkards grabbed the other by the shirt, then hauled back and punched him so hard he flew backward over the steps. His back slammed on the ground with an audible thud, a thick syrup of dark blood streaming from his nose. The winner threw his arms above his head in a triumphant jig, then lurched to the side of the porch and vomited a stream of green bile into the dust below.

Ruth pulled down the brim of her straw hat to shade her face from the boiling East Texas sun. "This is the last settlement before the Llano Estacado and the Comancheria," she muttered. "But these buffoons think whiskey makes 'em death proof."

She stalked across the road, the toes of her cracked leather boots kicking up the dust and turning the hems of her breeches red. When she reached the saloon's swinging door, she paused. She'd gone to the saloon to seek a favor from the proprietor, Billie Noonan. Ruth hated Billie now, as fiercely as she'd once loved her. The thought of having to grovel for help made her guts churn. She slammed her palms against the door, its rusty hinges squealing as it flew open.

The place was full from floor to balcony. Men gulped their gin at the bar, slipping their arms around the saloon girls as they passed, their trays loaded with glasses of Forty Rod and Red Eye. The room smelled of Figurado cigars and unwashed travelers.

"*Qué cabrón!*" A dark-eyed vaquero in a broad-brimmed black hat slapped his hand on the mahogany table, arguing with two men over a game of Three-Card Monte. He stopped mid-swear when Ruth entered, her silver-white hair streaming behind her. Soon the entire bar was in a hush, all eyes on the proud woman in the doorway.

Dennis Noonan glared at Ruth from behind the bar.

"You ain't welcome here, woman."

"I come to speak with Billie, and I ain't leaving till I do it."

"She's in the store room. You got something to say to my wife, you can tell it to me." Noonan accosted Ruth, sticking his face close to hers. He was a big man with a head the size of a blacksmith's anvil. He could have picked her up with one hand and toss her out the door if he desired, but that didn't intimidate Ruth. She leaned into him.

"I can smell the whiskey on your breath, *Dennis*." Ruth fought the desire to move downwind. "I don't blame you for gettin' roostered. Gotta be hard to stand behind the bar while your wife's off blowin' the grounsils with someone other than *you*."

Noonan's hand balled into a fist. Ruth's blue eyes flashed in the glow of the chandelier like light refracting through a diamond. Her hand moved to the Colt revolver strapped to her side.

"You're meaner than a wet polecat, Noonan, but don't be a fool. You know I'll put a dent in your pomade before your arm drops, make that bride of yours a widow."

"Make yourself scarce 'fore I call the sheriff."

"Let her talk, Dennis," said a familiar voice.

Quiet as a phantom, Billie appeared beside her husband. Ruth's heart slammed in her chest, driven by hate and sorrow. She'd aged some, the prettiness of her youth replaced by a hard beauty that still had the power to stop Ruth's breath.

"Quit beatin' the devil around the stump," Billie said. "Say your piece and go."

Ruth glanced around the room, her eyes resting on the vaquero, who watched her with his dark orbs. She shifted, her thumbs laced through her belt loops, reticent in the company of enemies.

"Florence is alive."

Billie's face blanched. Her eyes darted to her husband before she touched a hand to her forehead, then swayed as if she'd fall. The big man caught her, helping to steady her before glaring at Ruth.

"Who are you to come here upsettin' my wife with your lies?"

Ruth ignored him. "I believed you were a good-hearted girl when I took you in," she said to Billie. "A lost woman with an eight-year-old you couldn't keep fed. I gave you a home, loved your daughter like she was mine. And you twisted a knife in my back."

Billie sputtered in protest but Ruth put up a hand to silence her. "Then came the day the Penateka Comanche raided this fort. I was away, just started working for the Paulsons up on their horse ranch. Where were you when they slung your daughter on the back of a horse and rode off? Hiding in a thicket by the river, that's where! You saved your own hide and let 'em take Florence. You're the most spineless woman ever walked this earth."

"The girl's been dead more than twenty years," Noonan growled.

"Cynthia Parker seen her," Ruth said."

The crowd gasped, then began whispering among themselves.

"Nobody'd believe a word she says," Billie piped up. "She's crazier than a rat in an outhouse. Keeps trying to run back to her captors."

"Tom Paulson spoke with her at Parker's Fort last week," Ruth intoned, her eyes narrowed into slits of cold blue steel. "She wasn't any prisoner. The Comanche raised her as a beloved daughter. She married a chief, bore children with him. He got himself killed fighting the Rangers when they tried to take her back. *Protecting her!* What's more, some hunters sighted a group of Penateka on this side of the Brazos, a three-day journey from here. They seen a blond-headed woman with 'em. That's our Florence, I know it is."

"All right, so she's alive," Noonan said. "Nothin' we can do about it. Now that Sam Houston's got his peace talks, he won't send the Rangers out on any more rescue missions. And just 'cause they sighted a group a week ago don't mean they're still there. You know they move camp every few days. Now that you've told your news of the world, you can get the hell out of my establishment."

"It's more my saloon than yours. Was my gold paid for it."

"What are you after, Sutton? You want your money back, is that it?"

"It ain't for me. I need it to go after Florence."

"You going alone?" Noonan laughed. "You'll end up with an arrow in your gut for your trouble. And nobody'd mourn you but that old mare you rode in on."

"I'm going in peace, asking them to let Florence come home. Smallpox has ravaged entire tribes. We gave it to 'em and now the government won't let them have the vaccine. We've killed more than they ever have. I need that money to pay some men to travel with me—I ain't crazy enough to go alone. Now, I didn't come here expectin' you to give up the gold for nothing. I've got four beautiful Morgan horses over at Paulson's, only six miles from here. They're worth two hundred dollars apiece, but you can have 'em for half."

"We got no use for those swaybacks you breed. Paulson needs workhorses. Go do your barterin' with your boss." He turned away, dismissing Ruth.

"We'll go with you."

The well-dressed vaquero stood and walked toward them, his long hair hanging loose under his hat. Ruth wasn't fooled by his dandified appearance. She knew these horsemen could dead-aim a target from the back of a Mustang without even breaking a sweat.

She regarded the two men who now stood, flanking him. One of them was no more than twenty-one, youthful blonde curls edging from the brim of his poblano. He grinned at the nearest bar girl, who swooned into the arms of her giggling friends. The other man was shorter, stockier, with hard, shifting eyes and a Remington lodged on each hip.

"I don't have money to pay you," Ruth said.

"We'll take those Morgans as our fee."

"You're insane, Castillo," Noonan interjected.

"You sound just like my ex-wife," Castillo said, winking at Ruth. "This handsome boy next to me is Dallas Walker. My mysterious friend here goes by the name of Sang Jopah. We're on our way to seek work at Paulson's ourselves."

"Settle your score and meet me there," Ruth replied. "We leave at dawn."

She walked out of the bar without looking back, striding across the road to untie her Roan. Her mind still roiled over the confrontation with the Noonans. Beneath the glowing embers of her hatred, she'd still had some hope, after all. Hope that Billie might have some love left for her daughter—and for her.

"Ruth! Wait!"

Billie dashed out of the saloon, holding up her skirts. Ruth watched her trip across the road in her patent-leather heels. She stopped in front of the Roan, panting as she pressed a hand to her chest.

"I'm goin' with you!"

Ruth let out a mirthless laugh. "You lost your breath running twenty feet. Get on back inside before your man locks you up with the rest of his livestock.

"I don't give a damn what that big meat bag says, and I don't give a goddamn rat's tail what you say, neither. That's my daughter. Come dawn, I'll be with y'all."

"When's the last time your feet were on the ground before noon?"

Ignoring the insinuation, Billie spun on her heels and ran back to the saloon.

Filled with inexplicable sadness, with her heart sinking into muddy rivers of despair, Ruth mounted her horse and rode toward Paulson's.

<hr />

They'd been traveling a day and a half, heading into open territory toward the Rio Brazos. The land this close to the Trinity River was lush, lined with sycamore, pecan, and oak trees. The peaks of the distant hills poked over the treetops like curious birds. Castillo and Ruth took the lead, their horses laden with saddlebags filled with supplies. Ruth armed herself with her revolver and Tom Paulson's Carbine.

Dallas and Billie trailed behind them. Billie had ridden into Paulson's on the back of Dallas's Pinto. Ruth let her use the Roan for the journey. She and the others took the Morgans.

"Dennis tried to stop me," Billie explained, touching the purple welt under her eye. "I put a dose of laudanum in his tonic. It'll be hours before he wakes up."

Dallas provided a steady stream of tall tales of the gunfights he'd won on his travels, brandishing a pair of pearl-handled revolvers, custom-made back East. He handed one of the guns to Billie, who received it with gratitude. The younger man's incessant chatter was a welcome distraction from her anxieties.

Jopah brought up the rear, ever alone, alert for any sign of danger. He preferred it that way. A Comanche family had adopted him after his blood parents died of Malaria. He'd lived with them for fifteen years, learning to hunt and shoot, until Texas Rangers wiped out their camp on a supposed peace mission. Now he worked for himself.

Ruth took a long swig from her canteen, enjoying the feel of the cool water rushing down her parched throat.

"Hot enough to burn the bristles off a warthog," Castillo said, removing his hat. He wiped his forehead with the back of his hand, then glanced back at Billie, who appeared to be wilting in her saddle.

"You think she'll make it?"

"She might outlive us all," Ruth replied. "When I first met her, she wasn't but eighteen, wandering outside the settlement begging for alms. No one knows what she went through out in the wilderness. But she deserves every bit of it for what she done to her daughter."

"Is that why you hate her? Because she didn't fight back when they took her daughter?"

"That among other things."

"She stole your gold?"

"Yep, and my husband, too," Ruth replied, eyes pointing straight ahead. "I don't want to talk about it."

"Tell me about Florence."

The ghost of a smile fluttered about Ruth's lips. "She was as sweet as honey, but nobody could make her do a thing if she didn't think it was right. She wasn't disobedient, just different. Times were, I'd come outside searchin' for her, and damned if it didn't look like she was talking to my horses. She had a strange connection to nature—it was a sight to behold."

They plodded onward, talking less as they passed endless sandstone mesas bordered by emerald green pines. Night fell, and they took shelter in an oak grove. Ruth hunted for jackrabbits, shooting one clean through the head with the carbine. After they ate, the men took turns keeping watch while the others slept. Ruth lay in her bedroll near the flames while Billie curled up next to Dallas.

Their giggling bothered Ruth. She remembered the nights she'd stayed awake, waiting for Billie's goodnight kiss. Those secret kisses, so abundant at first, soon stopped altogether, only to begin anew with her husband while she was working on the ranch. When he died a year later, Ruth found he'd left her penniless, conned out of their savings by his paramour. Now, Billie had returned, slicing open old wounds against Ruth's will.

A lonely howl echoed through the hills, mirroring Ruth's melancholy.

"Hear that wailing?" she heard Dallas whisper to Billie. "That ain't no coyote. That's the war cry of the Nonape, the Little People. They're more fearsome than any gunslinger, with their giant eyes glittering like polished onyx, and teeth sharp as a honed ax. If they catch you, they'll flay you—and eat you while you're still alive! BOO!"

Dallas grabbed Billie and hugged her to him. She squealed, her eyes shining with desire for the handsome grifter.

"You're only trying to scare me," she cried. "That ain't nothing but an old wives' tale."

"They're all around us," Dallas continued as the haunting cries filled the air again. "They'll only let you see them at the last minute, when they're already on you with their spears."

"It's forbidden to speak of them!" Jopah snarled. Dallas ceased his playful talk, chastened by the first words the man had spoken since morning.

Ruth remembered the tales she'd heard as a youth. Folks said the Nonape lived in the caves dotting the hills. These were supernatural doorways they crossed through when called by powerful medicine.

An hour before dawn, Ruth awoke and stoked the fire to heat the last of the jackrabbit. Still on watch, Castillo came to sit beside her.

"You know he's following us?"

Ruth nodded, focusing on her cooking. "I heard him skulking behind the trees last night."

"Reckon he'll be trouble?" Castillo clutched his revolver, running a thumb over the barrel like a lover's caress.

"Noonan's madder than a rabid hound, a fool chasing his fool wife across treacherous country. Might be he gets himself killed and spares us the bullet."

At daybreak, they began the final leg of their journey, reaching the Brazos when the sun reached its zenith. Castillo and Jopah tracked the area, finding signs of a party passing through a few days prior. They followed the trail down into a clearing at the river bottom.

A Penateka lodge rose before them—a conical tent made of buffalo skin, within a ring of cottonwood trees. A string of deer hooves hanging from the door clacked a lonely song in the breeze. Otherwise, an eerie stillness cloaked the solitary dwelling.

Castillo cast a glance at Ruth, unspoken questions between them. Why was there only one lodge when the Penateka traveled in numbers? A lone shield rested on its tripod outside the tent. They dismounted their horses and huddled together, tense and waiting, all ears tuned for any sound coming from inside the tent.

A feral cry tore from the lodge, reverberating through the river bottom. Seconds later, a woman stumbled out, her eyes darting back and forth, her blonde hair unkempt. She fell to her knees, not appearing to notice the group before her. Tears burned Ruth's eyes.

Something wasn't right.

"Florence!" Billie rushed forward, abandoning all caution at the sight of her daughter.

"Wait!" Ruth called. "Billie, stop!"

The pounding of hooves clipped behind them. Dennis Noonan thundered over the ridge, screaming obscenities as he came. Billie was steps away from Florence. She gaped at her mother, and threw up her hands to fend the woman off.

An arrow whistled through the air, piercing Billie's right eye as it drove into her brain. Blood spurted around the feathered shaft embedded in her eyeball. She swayed for a long moment, then fell, twitching on the earth.

"Billie girl!" Noonan leaped from his horse, landing on his feet. He charged the lodge like an angry bull. Florence's hand shot out, seizing the revolver from Billie's holster. She aimed and fired. Noonan's chest exploded. He fell backward, his body throwing up a cloud of dust as it hit the ground. Spooked by the gunshot, his horse bolted over the ridge and disappeared. Ruth's well-trained horses remained ca lm.

A Penateka man lurched out of the lodge like a drunkard, bow in hand, his black hair flying behind him. He attempted to nock another arrow but fumbled it. Ruth drew the gun from her hip and shot. The bullet hit him in the temple, exiting the back of his head. A geyser of bright red blood, brain matter, and splinters of bone sprayed the front of the lodge before he went down. Florence let out an unearthly scream, firing until the empty chamber clicked. She dropped the revolver. She threw herself over the bowman's body and sobbed on his chest.

Castillo trained his gun on Florence, sidling up to her with swift steps. Jopah pulled several strips of rawhide from one of his saddlebags and joined him. Florence gazed at the two men as if dumb, her eyes clouded with anguish. She came alive when they grabbed her, kicking and thrashing as they pinned her to the ground. They bound her hands and feet with the rawhide while she hissed a stream of bitter Comanche words.

Dallas kneeled beside Billie, taking her wrist to check for a pulse. After several seconds, he dropped her arm and blessed himself. He looked up at the group, grim-faced, and shook his head. Ruth steadied herself against her horse as her legs buckled beneath her. The stench of death and gunpowder filled the air. Ruth stared at the mass of gore and blasted flesh that was once Dennis Noonan's chest. There was no need to check for a pulse.

With his gun held before him, Castillo disappeared inside the lodge. Moments later, he poked his head out and beckoned to Ruth.

It was dark and cool inside the lodge. Ruth realized the tent was a home like any other, a jumble of cooking utensils, clothing, and other goods strewn about a central fire pit. Castillo pointed to a corner. At first, it appeared to be a large pile of buffalo pelts. When Ruth looked closer, she saw someone lying atop the pile, wrapped in a large fur blanket. It was a skinny boy about twelve years old, stone dead, his body covered with so many huge red welts they almost concealed his skin.

Ruth pivoted toward the doorway. Outside, Jopah and Dallas were bending to examine the dead man. Behind them, a bound Florence sat on the back of the roan, weeping softly.

"Don't touch him," she screamed. "Smallpox!"

Horrified, the men retreated. Ruth and Castillo left the tent, taking a trowel to dig a grave for the four who'd died. As they passed the bowman, they could see a few small welts on his bare chest. Now, it was clear why the others had abandoned their brethren in this lonesome place. They'd left them there to prevent the spread of infection.

———————◆◈◆——————

It wasn't clear if Florence had contracted the disease. She slumped on her horse, silent and lethargic. She wore no adornments except for a necklace from which hung a large owl feather. From time to time, she raised her bound hands and stroked the token, almost as if she was praying to it.

They continued until evening, camping at the familiar oak grove. The men tethered the horses and built the fire while Ruth hunted. They settled Florence on a log a few feet from the flames. Dallas skinned the rabbit Ruth caught, his face twisted in disgust as he gutted and cleaned it, then used Ruth's hatchet to chop it into small pieces. Ruth tossed the chunks of flesh into the kettle and stewed the meat.

Still riled from the horrors of the day, Dallas forgot the hatchet near the fire. No one noticed Florence edging toward it inch by inch. She lifted her legs, concealing the hatchet beneath her moccasins. When Dallas went to untie her for supper, she snatched the weapon. Dallas was near enough to slash his throat, but she didn't cut him. She slammed her hand flat against the rough log, raised the hatchet, and with a wild cry, hacked off two of her fingers at the joints. Ruth tackled her, wrestling the blade from her grip.

"You fool, girl! What the hell did you do that for?"

She swore as she grabbed the mangled, bloodied hand and inspected it. She cleaned the wounds, then bound the stumps with cloth ripped from the hem of her shirt. As Ruth retied her wrists, Florence sat, listless, her eyes once again glazed over as she moaned with pain. When the food was ready, Ruth offered her a plate. Florence set her mouth in a grim line, refusing to eat.

Trembling with rage, Ruth tossed the meat into the fire. "Billie Noonan wasn't a good woman," she shouted. "She wasn't anything close to a good mother, but she died trying to bring you home. And you're just like her—another ungrateful bitch."

Florence stared into the flames as if hypnotized. Ruth lunged at the woman, her hands balled into fists. Castillo caught her by the arms, drawing her backward.

"The Penateka raised her from childhood," he whispered in her ear. "Did you see how she cut off her fingers? That's a Comanche mourning ritual. *They're* her family. You must try to understand that."

Castillo released her.

Ruth stalked off to see the horses, pressing her face against their sturdy, warm flanks for comfort. She wasn't sure if Florence had understood her words, not having spoken the English language in over twenty years. Her heart overflowed with pity, all her love for the girl flooding back.

Funny how I still think of her as a girl, Ruth thought as she walked back to camp. *Almost like I thought we were rescuing an eight-year-old child. She's a woman who's lived a lifetime outside civilization. And we don't know each other anymore.*

She got out her bedroll and set it in front of Florence—a sacrificial peace offering. The woman ignored her. Ruth shrugged and took the blanket back.

"In time, you'll adjust to our ways again," she said, softer now. Florence turned, regarding her mutely, a hint of recognition in her eyes.

Then it vanished.

———◆———

Bored of keeping watch alone, Dallas stood and stretched. He looked over at Florence, who sat across from him with her back straight as a ramrod. He began to feel unsettled by her relentless stare. Now, through the haze above the flames, he saw her edge her tied hands up her skirt. She tugged at something and drew out a small, black medicine bag. With a thumb and forefinger, she pulled out a pinch of black powder. She leaned forward and blew it into the fire. A cloud of thick, black smoke billowed upward, sweet-smelling and heady, a mixture of cedar and cinnamon.

By the time he realized what was happening, Dallas had already inhaled the smoke. He felt woozy, clutching the side of the log to steady himself. Florence began shimmering in and out of focus. Her head stretched and rounded into a sphere while her nose curved outward, hardening into a beak. Feathers sprang across her face, their brown, white, and gray colors resembling tree bark, with two tufts standing like horns on the crown of her head.

Florence rose from the log, the rawhide strips slipping from her wrists and ankles. Dallas watched, mesmerized, as she began removing her clothing. First, the doeskin top went, exposing her breasts, followed by the fringed skirt. The flames illuminated her body as she stood naked before Dallas. He found himself gazing at the voluptuous body of a human woman with the head of an owl.

She turned and headed into the forest, looking back over her shoulder. Her eyes, elongated and yellow like those of a cat, lured Dallas to follow. He trailed behind her flickering shape, licking his lips hungrily, fully aroused and fueled by animal lust.

They reached another clearing cut off by rock. Moonlight reflected on a small waterfall embedded in sandstone, which opened into a pool. The owl woman climbed the rocks and slowly stepped into the water. She turned to Dallas, starlight dancing on her wet body. He removed his clothing, and scrambled into the pool after her.

Dallas kissed her neck where feathers met flesh, running his hands down her breasts and over the length of her body. She cried like a bird, fueling his desire further. Crazed with lust, he pressed her against the rock, the waterfall soaking their entwined bodies.

An unearthly howl ripped through the night. Dallas reared back. The owl woman laughed at him in a warbling voice, more avian than human.

"Nonape!" Dallas cried. "You called the—"

The spear hit him in the back, its barbed point bursting out of his chest. Senseless with pain, Dallas grabbed the shaft and tried to pull it out of his body. He felt the burning of poison coursing through his veins, quickly paralyzing him. The water soon turned red with his blood. The owl woman threw her head back and screeched.

Dozens of small, dark shapes scuttled out of the trees. They swarmed the pool, their silver spearheads glinting in the moonlight. Through a lens of terror, Dallas watched, petrified, as the Little People converged on him, gazing back with their great black eyes, soulless and starving. The men were two feet high, with round paunches jutting above their deerskin loincloths. They chattered in their shrill voices as they struggled to drag their prey from the water. They pulled Dallas over the grass, binding him to a tree in a sitting position.

He leaned against the trunk, crying out for help though he knew it was futile. They'd wandered too far from the others—they'd never hear him. He breathed in ragged gasps as the little men waddled about on their short legs, gathering bits of wood to build a fire.

When it was ready, the owl woman trilled, a signal to begin the festivities. The Nonape began their ritual dance around the flames. Their stumpy bodies leaped and whirled as they screeched their death song. They jigged close to Dallas, nicking him with their weapons. Each time one of the tribe members cut him, the others cheered in a grotesque celebration, shaking their spears in the air.

Their chief stuck the tip of his spear in the fire, heating it until it glowed red-hot. Tottering over to Dallas, he drove it into his naked thigh. Dallas screamed as searing pain ripped through flesh and muscle like a firebolt from the heavens. The leader sawed a chunk of meat from Dallas' leg, the young man's agony driving him to the point of hysteria. Then the others were on him, stabbing and cutting as they harvested every inch of flesh from his body. Dallas watched as they tore open his stomach like cheap fabric, ripping out his innards like wild dogs fighting over offal. Then darkness washed over everything.

Jopah woke with a splitting headache. His internal clock always roused him at the right time, and now it was his turn to keep watch. He sat up and rubbed his temples, looking around for Dallas, who was nowhere in sight. It was just like the pretty boy to go wandering off instead of protecting his companions. The others were sleeping, except for Florence, who had returned to the fire.

He watched her for a moment as she moved her lips in a silent chant. They'd have been better off leaving her where they'd found her. If he were a speaking man, he could have told Ruth a thing or two about spirit medicine. But why should he tell the hotheaded woman anything? He'd keep silent and take the Morgan as payment. Once they finished the job, he'd put two bullets in Castillo and Dallas and take their horses, too.

Jopah walked out of sight to relieve himself. As he loosened his breeches, he heard a chittering sound coming from his left. He whipped his head around, peering into the darkness of the trees. The noise sounded again, this time from his right. He drew his Remington and walked toward the sound, scanning for any sign of an intruder. Seeing nothing, he assumed he'd heard a night bird calling for its mate. He relaxed and returned to his business.

A short, sharp chitter came from the oak above him. Jopah looked up and saw a small figure squatting on a branch, grinning at him with pointed teeth. There were others, too, at least fifty of them. Jopah recognized the creatures for what they were. Although he knew his gun would do no good, he pointed it upward and fired anyway.

The bullet struck the Nonape in the shoulder. It hissed and rocked backward, almost falling off the branch. Then it hurled itself through the air, snarling as it landed on Jopah's shoulders. It sank its teeth into Jopah's throat. A wet gurgle of a scream escaped from Jopah as blood jetted from his severed jugular. He whirled, giddy with pain, only to come face to face with the owl woman. She raised her hands, her fingers transformed into six-inch claws, and slashed him from chest to navel. His entrails bulged and then slopped out of his body as he crashed onto the ground.

The owl woman poked her beak through the gaping hole in his stomach, pulling out a fat, wormlike organ. The other little men sprang from the branches, using their incisors to tear the man to pieces. One Nonape bit deep into Jopah's nose, wagging its head from side to side with relish, until its sharpened teeth crunched through cartilage.

———————◆◯◆———————

The shriek of an owl on the hunt ripped through the air, along with cacophonous cries that sounded like the high-pitched shouting of children. Torn from sleep, Castillo's eyes darted from side to side. He raced in the direction the sounds had come from.

Using the trees as cover, he crept toward the commotion. He almost yelped when he stuck his head around the bend, rubbing his eyes in disbelief.

The Little People had gathered for a spirited game of Shinny. Two teams raced across the field with L-shaped sticks, trying to bat an object into their opponents' goal. Castillo saw what looked like a large, misshapen ball flying across the clearing. The spectators worked themselves into a frenzy, shouting and slapping their thighs as they cheered. One man slammed the object into the goal, then gyrated his hips in a victory dance. The crowd roared. A fight broke out among them but soon stopped when the players began another round.

The moon peered from behind a cloud, revealing the object they batted across the field. Castillo drew back in horror.

"That's... that's Jopah's head," uttered Castillo.

Something heavy leaped onto his back. It held him with a mighty grip, slashing the nape of his neck into meaty ribbons. Castillo threw himself down, rolling on the grass until the animal released him. He staggered to his feet, his back in bloody tatters, and found himself standing before the owl woman.

He'd seen shapeshifters like this as a boy in Mexico, those who could morph into predators. He drew his gun, aiming it at the demonic woman. She flew at him, slamming him onto his raw, pulpy back. He cried as her talons slashed his eyeballs and blood streaked down his cheeks like red waterfalls. The creature perched on his chest, the breastbone cracking from the pressure. She plucked a crushed eye out of its socket with her beak and threw her feathered head back to let it drop down her throat. Then she went for the other one.

The blind man screamed again. The sound alerted the Nonape, who stopped their game and shuttled over to take part in the carnage. It was, after all, the more entertaining sport.

———————◆◇◆———————

Ruth stirred in the chilly air. The damp grass seeped through her bedroll. She heard someone moving about, but didn't open her eyes. Her head felt as heavy as lead, struggling to lift it from the blanket.

The aroma of roasting meat teased her nostrils. She opened her eyes to see Florence, a woman once again, leaning over the fire. She held a sharpened stick, onto which she'd impaled a dark slab of liver. She pulled the stick back, blowing on the meat to cool it, then bit into it with relish. Alarmed, Ruth sat up too fast. She fought off the feeling of vertigo as the world spun.

"Who untied you?" she shouted. "Where's Castillo and the others?"

Florence didn't appear to hear her. Then she turned her head, juices running down her chin. She spoke in Ruth's language, the abject hatred in her voice chilling the woman to her very marrow.

"They're all dead."

"What do you mean?" Ruth stammered. She backed up several feet.

"I am Death. I am Vengeance. I am the Cannibal Owl."

Her nose curved into a beak and feathers sprouted around her raptor's eyes. The head of the Great Horned Owl rotated in a full circle, returning to glare at Ruth again. She cawed, a piercing call that reverberated off the trees. From out of the shadows, the multitude of tiny figures creeped forth. They surrounded the owl woman, their spears ready for the kill. Florence raised her arms, holding them back with the mysterious power she had over them.

The Nonape bared their fangs and hissed at Ruth, their small bodies rife with tension.

"I gave up everything I had to bring you home," she told Florence. "We were a family, once. Don't you remember?"

"You killed my family."

Ruth's heart sank as the meaning of the words dawned on her, her heart filling with sorrow and regret. Her ignorant beliefs had brought death upon them all.

"By God, you were married to him, weren't you? The boy in the lodge—he was your son."

The owl blinked.

"Forgive me," Ruth continued, her eyes brimming with unshed tears. "All these years, I've been living on hope, believing you were still alive somewhere—that you wanted to come home. *I thought I was saving you—*"

The owl woman threw her arms out, releasing the Nonape. They shot forward, speeding toward Ruth so fast she had no time to retreat. She screamed as they tore into her legs with their teeth, climbing on each other's backs to reach her higher appendages. A little man clambered onto her shoulder and hung upside down, chewing her bicep. Others danced from foot to foot, awaiting their turn to feast on her flesh. The owl woman circled her, hooting in her animal language as she watched the carnage. They'd devour Ruth within minutes, leaving nothing but bone and gristle. Her only hope was to make it to her revolver, which she'd tucked into the foot of her bedroll.

With a mighty effort, she heaved herself forward, dragging the little men who clung to her body by fang and claw. She bent and seized the gun, then whirled to face the owl, who stood before the fire screeching orders to her servants. Ruth knew there was only one way to stop the Nonape. She raised her gun, her arm heavy with the creatures clinging to it.

"Florence!" Ruth wailed.

The gun sang.

The bullet dug a hole between her glowing eyes. She reeled, stumbling backward over the ring of stones outlining the fire pit. She fell on her back, screaming as the flames ate her flesh. The acrid smell of burning skin, hair, and feathers filled the air.

One by one, the Nonape loosed their grip on Ruth. They leaped away from her, shuffling over to the fire to watch the life leave their master's eyes. Her blackened flesh pulsed with torturous pain. Ruth limped forward. The burning body of her beloved girl—whose face had once again returned to human form, tore every tear from her eyes.

The Nonape gathered around Ruth. She raised her gun again, prepared to fight to the death. But the chief only bent and placed his spear at her feet. He kneeled before her, acknowledging her as his new master. The others followed suit, bowing on one knee in reverence to their queen.

"Not on your life," Ruth growled. "Go back to hell!"

She collapsed.

The Little People bound her wounds with strips of cloth torn from her bedroll. She'd survive the attack but would bear the scars for the rest of her life, both in body and heart. As the sun peeked over the hilltops, the Nonape disappeared, melting like shadows into the soil.

Ruth remained where she was, weeping for Florence as she kept vigil over her funeral pyre.

The smoke spiraled upward, carrying the girl's spirit to the heavens.

Texas Macabre

BY OWL GOINGBACK

THE GREAT STATE OF Texas, 1850

William A. A. Wallace had just filled the bowl of his favorite pipe with some fine Virginia tobacco, when he noticed a horse and rider approaching from the east, all hell bent for leather.

Lighting the bowl with a wooden match, he squinted to get a better look. The August sun was rising bright and angry behind the rider, casting a fearsome glare across the valley, shielding his features.

It was not an Indian, for even the warlike Apache, or Comanche, would not be foolish enough to approach a white man's home alone, *especially* someone with Wallace's reputation. He had fought members of both tribes many times over the years, had been especially ruthless after a neighboring band of Lipan Apache broke their treaty with him and stole all his livestock. He and fellow members of the Texas Rangers hunted down the thieves, sending many of them on a one-way trip to the happy hunting ground.

Nor would it be a Mexican bandit that approached. Lord knows there were plenty of bandits operating in the rugged countryside between the Rio Grande and Nueces River, some searching for horses and cattle to steal, others drawn by rumors of forgotten Spanish silver mines. Known as the Nueces Strip, the no man's land between the two rivers remained a place of absolute lawlessness, and the main zone of activity for the Rangers. But the bandits, like the Indians, would not be foolish enough to ride alone.

He heard the land between the two rivers also served as an escape route for runaway slaves, part of what they called the Underground Railroad. He had personally never seen any black people in the rugged wilderness, escaping or otherwise. If he did, he would just look the other way. Wasn't his job to be rounding up runaway slaves, and he knew what it was like to be a prisoner and at the mercy of others.

The rider drew closer, but he still could not identify them.

It would be foolish for William to continue sitting on the oak log he used as a sofa, smoking away, and not properly prepare for company.

"Well, hell. Guess I better roll out the welcome mat."

He set the pipe on the bare ground and stood. Stepping into his wooden cabin through the open doorway, he grabbed the .54 caliber Mississippi rifle leaning next to the doorframe.

"Come on, Sweet Lips. We've got company."

He also grabbed the powder horn, and shot bag, hanging from a nail on the wall above the rifle.

"You too, Old Butch."

William picked up the Bowie knife and sheath lying on a nearby table.

The knife often proved just as important as the rifle, coming in handy when he fought Comanche warriors and Mexican soldiers. It also saved his life against a vicious pack of wolves. He found refuge in a hollow tree that night, stabbing and slicing any wolf foolish enough to stick its head through the opening. He suffered numerous bites, but many a wolf lost its life. Others would spend the rest of their days with scars on their furry snouts.

Stepping back outside, William pulled the wooden plug from the horn with his teeth, pouring black power down the rifle's barrel. He reached into the shot bag and grabbed a patched roundball, and a percussion cap, dropping the ball down the barrel. Seating the ball with the ramrod, he half-cocked the hammer and placed the cap on the rifle's nipple.

Holding the rifle relaxed at his side, knowing he could quickly bring it to his shoulder and fire a kill shot, William squinted and studied the approaching visitor.

"Hoy, Big Foot," the rider called, waving his right arm. And suddenly he was no longer a stranger, for he knew William's nickname.

Everyone called him "Big Foot" Wallace, a name he earned while being held a military prisoner in Mexico City. He was a tall man with big feet, and his captures could not find shoes big enough to fit him and had to have a pair special made. His feet became the source of much amusement to the Mexicans.

The rider slowed as he neared the cabin, and William was finally able to make out his features.

Like William, the man wore leather breeches, a hunting shirt, and a brimmed hat. And though he wore no badge, or other mark to identify himself as a lawman, he too was a Texas Ranger.

As a matter of fact, Creed Taylor was the closest thing he had to a partner, a good man to have fighting at his side when bullets started flying. They had shared many adventures together, and survived quite a few dangers.

"Creed, what brings you out this way in such a hurry?"

Creed came to a stop a few feet from the cabin, but did not dismount.

"We've got trouble, Big Foot. Vidal and his men are rustling again. They must have found out most of the Rangers are off chasing Comanche. Bastard got my prize horses.

"Your big stallion?"

Creed nodded. "Got him too. I was out hunting. Came back and every single one was gone. They hit Flores too. He got a good look at them as they rode off."

"I should have shot that bastard in Mexico when I had the chance," Creed said, spitting tobacco juice.

Creed and another scout captured Vidal during the war with Mexico, the day before his unit of Texas volunteers captured the town of Bexar. Vidal had been a lieutenant back then, but had deserted from the Mexican army. Since he provided useful information to the Americans, they had let him go.

They thought Santa Ana's troops would catch up with Vidal and hang him for desertion, but he managed to escape the noose and become a bandit. Since then, he had been robbing and rustling in the Nueces Strip, fleeing back into Mexico before the Rangers could catch him.

William picked up his pipe, relighting it with another match. Taking several puffs, he looked at Creed through a cloud of tobacco smoke. "You fixing to go after him?"

Creed spit again. "You know I am. Flores is going too. We're going to meet up a few miles from here. Figured you might want to get in on the fun, unless you have something better to do."

"Nothing that can't wait a day or two," William replied. "Just got to grab a few supplies, and saddle my horse."

"I'll wait for you," Creed replied.

William leaned his rifle against the wall and entered his cabin.

He put several pieces of hardtack into his saddlebags, along with a handful of venison jerky, then topped his canteen using a water bucket filled from the nearby Medina River.

He also grabbed his Colt .44 Dragoon, loading the six-shooter before slipping it into its leather holster. No Ranger would think of chasing bad guys without a revolver hanging at his side.

Walking back outside, he circled around to the back of his cabin where the horses were corralled, and picked out his favorite saddle horse, Old Keechie.

The bay mare was sure-footed in rough territory, possessing a natural instinct for picking the best routes through thick chaparral.

"Come on girl, we have work to do."

He opened the gate and entered the corral. Old Keechie stood perfectly still as he put on the bridal, saddle, and saddle bags. Leading her out the corral, he closed the gate and mounted the horse.

Creed was biting off more tobacco from his plug when William rode around to the front of the cabin. Dismounting, he grabbed his rifle and climbed back into the saddle.

"You ready?" William asked.

"Born ready, amigo." Creed said, putting the plug back in his bag. Like William, he was well armed for the occasion, carrying a Colt Walker pistol, and a Kentucky rifle.

"Then let's go get your ponies back."

Creed turned his horse giving him the spurs. William did the same catching up with his partner so they rode side-by-side.

They met up with Flores just west of where Sand Creek flowed into the Medina. It was a hot day, and he waited for them in the shadows beneath a grove of pecan trees. But the rancher had not been idle; he had found the trail left by Vidal and his men, the tracks clearly visible in the rank grass growing along the river bottom.

As expected, the bandits had turned south making their way toward Mexico. They would have to cross the Nueces River and the Rio Grande before they were home safe, but it was mid-August, drought season, and the rivers would be almost dried out in some areas.

"Think we can catch them before they cross the Rio Grande?" Flores asked, wiping sweat from his forehead.

"We can," William replied. "If you can keep up with us."

"They took some of my horses too," Flores replied. "I can keep up."

William spurred his horse following the bandits' trail. The three of them would have to ride hard if they wanted to catch Vidal and his men before they crossed back into Mexico. They may have to ride through the night. That was not a problem for him and Creed; Texas rangers practically lived on horseback, going long periods of time without rest.

William knew he and Creed were up to the task, but he could not be so sure about Flores. Nor did he know if the rancher would be up to the job of killing when the time came. There was no way Vidal and his men would give up without a fight, not when there was a hefty price on their heads. When they did catch up with them, things would get hot and heavy. Lead would fly and blood would flow.

<hr/>

It was late in the day, the three men rode through hill country, passing small valleys where streams flowed through strands of pecan and post oak trees.

They were about to ride past the entrance to a narrow canyon when William spotted something lying on the grass.

"Hold up!" he called out.

The others stopped their horses and wheeled around to face him.

"Find something interesting?" Creed asked.

"Think maybe I did."

William slid out of his saddle and walked toward the canyon's entrance. Lying in the grass was the butt of a tiny cigar; the wretched little "cigaritos" the Mexicans were so fond of.

He picked up the butt and sniffed, wrinkling his nose at the odor. Definite not made with the fine Virginia tobacco he loved so much.

"It's fresh."

Flores looked at the cigarito, then turned his attention to the canyon beyond. "Think they went in there? I don't see any tracks."

William looked around and spotted several freshly-cut, leafy branches.

"I think they erased their tracks," he said, pointing out the branches.

All three men looked up at the hills surrounding them, suddenly worried Mexican rifles might be pointed their way. But they saw no one; the bandits had not posted guards or lookouts.

"I think maybe we should check it out," Creed said. "If they're not in there, then it might be a good place to camp for the night. It will be dark soon."

Creed entered the canyon. He kept his horse at a walk, rifle lying across the saddle with his thumb on the hammer. He did not want to stumble into an ambush, and took things nice and slow. Flores followed him, rifle at the ready, his head on a constant swivel as he watched the canyon walls around them. William brought up the rear, throwing glances over his shoulder to make sure no one was sneaking up from behind.

Twenty-five yards into the narrow canyon, horse tracks reappeared proof the bandits, and the stolen horses, were somewhere up ahead.

The sun had already set by the time they reached the point where the canyon opened onto a wide valley. Up ahead, a campfire burned; the smell of roasting meat drifted on the air.

"Son of a bitches," Creed whispered. "They're roasting one of the horses."

"Better not be one of mine," Flores said.

William could see the shadowy figures of men moving around the campfire. Might be six bandits, might be a dozen. Off to the right of the campfire, the bandits had staked out the stolen herd of horses allowing them to graze in the good grass, while they bedded down for the night.

"What do you think, Big Foot?" Creed asked, turning to look at William.

"They're not expecting company," William replied. "Otherwise, they would have posted a guard. I think we should wait a bit. Full bellies will make them sleepy. Once they've gone to bed, we will give them a little surprise."

Creed nodded. "We'll wait a bit."

The three men turned around and retreated back down the canyon. Dismounting, they led their horses behind a low hill where they would be concealed from anyone looking their way.

Tying the horses to narrow post oaks, William and the others crept back toward Vidal's camp. It was now fully dark, and the bandits would not be able to see them as they crept closer. Stopping their approach a hundred yards away, the three of them settled down to wait.

William and the other men did not speak, not even a whisper, for they knew sounds carried on the night wind. They could hear the bandits, which meant the Mexicans would be able to also hear them.

An hour slowly passed, the camp of Vidal and his men grew quiet. Conversations replaced by the sound of an occasional snore. Even the stolen horses had settled down for the night.

Creed shifted his weight, leaning closer to William's ear and whispered. "What you think, amigo?"

"I think we got killing work to do," William whispered back, slowly rising to his feet.

Creed and Flores also stood, the three of them slowly walking toward the campfire and the sleeping bandits around it.

Fifty yards away, William eased back the hammer of his rifle to full cock. The gun was already loaded, with the percussion cap on the nipple. He heard two other clicks and knew his companions had done the same.

Twenty-five yards from the campsite. The fire had burned down to mostly embers; the glow still bright enough to illuminate the sleeping bandits. William counted seven men but could not tell which one was Vidal.

Ten yards away. They were upwind and a horse caught their scent, whinnying loudly, alerting one of the bandits that something was amiss. He sat up and saw them approaching out of the darkness, tall men with long rifles.

The bandit jumped up and pulled his six-shooter. Creed shot him through the chest; the fifty-caliber bullet knocked him backward causing him to tumble head-over-heels.

"Texas Rangers," William yelled. "Lay down your guns and surrender."

He knew surrender was out of the question. The bandits would not give up without a fight, and the Rangers rarely arrested anyone. Theirs was frontier justice, with shootings and hangings taking the place of judge and jury.

Pandemonium broke out. Bandits jumped to their feet, cursing, pulling revolvers from their belts, and grabbing rifles.

William shot the second bandit that stood. The bullet fired from Sweet Lips struck the man through the left side of his chest, spinning him like a top, causing him to fall face-first into the campfire.

Big Foot switched his rifle to his left hand, and pulled his pistol with his right taking quick aim on another bandit, shooting him twice.

Bullets flew all around, black powder smoke filled the battleground, making it even harder to see.

He glanced to the right and saw Creed and Flores standing side by side, six-guns blazing, giving the bandits a taste of Texas hell. He smiled, seeing the rancher hold his own in a gunfight.

Only two Mexicans still fought, and one of them was Vidal. The leader of the bandits stood defiantly, his legs spread, shooting with a revolver in each hand.

"You bastards will never take me alive. I am bulletproof," Vidal yelled, smiling like a madman.

William heard Vidal's bullet whiz past his head. He raised his pistol and shot back, but the revolver's hammer fell on an empty cylinder.

"Damnit."

William shoved the pistol back into its holster and hurried to reload his rifle. As he did, Flores shot the man to Vidal's right.

"You putas cannot hurt me. I have protection."

Vidal threw one of his pistols away, grabbing the beaded, bear-claw necklace he wore.

The mother of Black Wolf had given William a similar necklace during his brief stay with the Apache, promising it would protect him in battle.

"I will cut off your cojones," threatened the Mexican.

Vidal's necklace might be strong medicine, but it did not make him invincible, or even bulletproof.

Creed fired his revolver, shooting the bandit in the stomach.

Blood spurted from the wound. Vidal cried out in pain.

Creed walked forward, cocked his pistol, and shot again.

Vidal grabbed his chest. "Pendejo, I remember you."

Creed stopped a few feet from Vidal, spitting on the bandit's boots. "Yep. I should have killed you then."

He squeezed the trigger and the hammer fell, but nothing happened. Creed's gun was empty.

Vidal glanced down at his boots, right toe wet with tobacco juice. "You will die for that."

The Mexican raised his revolver, pointing at Creed. But before he could pull the trigger, the roar of two long rifles split the night.

William and Flores fired at the same time, two heavy roundballs striking Vidal in the center of his chest.

The bandit fell dead, staring up at the night sky with open eyes, a look of shock etched upon his face.

Creed turned around and looked at the other men, frowning. "Damnit, Big Foot. He was mine."

"Sorry about that." William stepped forward. "I'll let you kill the next one."

"Where do you think he got that?" Creed pointed at Vidal's necklace.

"Maybe he bought it from the old Apache woman who lives out past your place. People say she has powers."

"Powers?" Flores laughed. "That heathen trinket didn't save him."

"I want to make an example of him," Creed said. "A warning that will scare the hell out of other bandits."

William smiled, pulling Old Butch out of its sheath. "I know just the trick. You two go gather your horses; this won't take long. And bring me a saddled horse for our friend here."

While the others went to get their horses, William kneeled beside Vidal.

"This won't hurt a bit."

William drew the blade across Vidal's neck, slicing deep, blood gushing from the wound. As he did, he heard a moan.

What the...

He stopped and looked around, thinking he had heard one of the other bandits. But they lay motionless, all of them quite dead.

He looked down at Vidal.

"Did you say something, amigo?"

He studied the bandit's face for signs of life, but the man's eyes were glazed over. If he had made a noise, it was only air escaping, a final death hiss, and nothing more.

Quit spooking yourself, and get on with it.

Leaning forward, he sliced the knife across the bandit's neck a second time, the blade cutting through muscles, tendons, and vertebras.

One more pass with the blade, and Vidal's head separated from his body.

"I told you it wouldn't hurt." William laughed.

He cleaned the bloody blade on the bandit's shirt before slipping it back into the sheath.

Creed returned leading a mustang, saddled and ready to ride.

"He looks better," Creed said, seeing the headless body.

"Give me a hand getting him up on the horse."

William and Creed lifted Vidal onto the saddle, tying him in places with several lengths of rope. They lashed him tight making sure he would not fall off.

Once the body was secure, William hung the severed head from the saddle horn.

Knowing bandits did not go anywhere without their hats, Creed tied Vidal's black sombrero to his head.

They both laughed when finished. The dead Vidal sat straight in the saddle, bridle reins tethered to his hands, head hanging beside him.

"I give you the Headless Horseman of Texas," William said, laughing. "The terror of no man's land, guaranteed to strike fear into the hearts of bandits and savages alike."

"And anyone else who sees it," Creed added.

William turned the horse so it was facing the canyon's exit, raising his right hand to give it a healthy slap on the butt.

But as he started to bring his hand down, he heard a voice causing him to freeze.

"You pinche bastards! I will get you for this."

The severed head of Vidal slowly turned to face him, the bandit's eyes fixing him with a hateful stare, mouth twitching in anger.

"I will get you. Just you wait," Vidal said.

Creed jumped back. "That's impossible. You're dead."

But Vidal's spirit had not crossed over, nor occupied a special place in hell enjoying coffee and beans with Lucifer. It was still in his body. Somehow, the Mexican still lived.

William's gaze went from the severed head to the body sitting tied in the saddle, seeing the Indian necklace around the dead bandit's neck.

I am bulletproof.

"Quick. Grab the necklace!" William yelled.

But before they could move, the headless body of Vidal spurred the horse causing it to lunge forward. They had fastened the bandit's body to the saddle, tied his arms, but had not secured his legs.

The horse galloped away into the night, leaving the two Texas Rangers standing there dumbfounded.

———— ◄O► ————

The Apache woman's name was Nascha, and she might possibly be the oldest woman alive. Her face was dark as ancient leather, crisscrossed with countless lines like rivers in the desert. Her hands were also aged, and wrinkled, but her eyes were bright and filled with intelligence, and cunning, like those of a wolf.

They had come to her wickiup out of sheer desperation, searching for days before they found its location even though the tiny structure of sticks and dried grasses sat in plain sight. It was as if the modest dwelling, and the woman inside, existed under a magical shadow and could not be found unless she allowed it.

Flores refused to come with them frightened by stories about the old woman, fearful legends of witchcraft and terrible powers. Even her own people were scared of her and stayed cleared. But some believed she also had healing powers, and brought food and tobacco in exchange for rituals and herbal cures.

The leather pouch of fine Virginia tobacco William had brought sat before her on the dirt floor. She had not picked up the pouch to examine its contents, or given it more than a passing glance. Instead, she sat quietly and listened to their story.

They told her about Vidal, and how the headless bandit rode the countryside, dead but still alive, terrorizing both Texans and Indians, causing villagers to flee and ranchers to pack up and move to another location. They admitted it was their fault, asking for help to kill someone who should already be dead.

"He wears one of these," William said, pulling his Apache necklace out of his bag and setting it on the floor in front of her.

Nascha looked at him for a moment then picked up the necklace, running her fingers over it.

"Strong medicine," she said, her voice like autumn leaves rustling in the wind. "The one Vidal wears, he stole from me. He also stole my pony."

"He stole from you?" William asked, surprised.

She nodded, setting the necklace on the ground before him.

"What can we do to stop him?" Creed asked. It was the first time he had spoken since entering the wickiup.

"Not you. Him." She nodded at William.

"It is your bullet that killed him," she said. "You who removed his head. You must be the one to stop him. But you must hurry, for Vidal's power grows stronger each night. You may already be too late."

"What can I do?" William asked.

"You must first remove his necklace."

Nascha reached behind her back, producing a hooked needle and a roll of sinew thread.

"You must sew his head back on, with this." She handed William the needle and thread. "And then you must kill him again."

"Will that stop this madness?"

She nodded. "Only if you give him a proper burial."

She reached into a beaded leather bag, and pulled out a small, glass bottle with a cork stopper. There was clear liquid in the bottle.

"Sprinkle this over his body." She handed the bottle to William.

William took it, looking at its contents. "Holy water?"

"Very sacred," the old woman replied, a smile touching the corners of her mouth.

———◆◆◆———

William and Creed searched for Vidal in the no man's land between the Nueces and Rio Grande rivers, but a week had already passed and they still had not found the living-dead bandit. But they weren't discouraged, because they had spoken with numerous people who had witnessed the Headless Horseman of Texas and knew they were closing in on his trail. A small hunting party of Comanche even claimed to have shot the bandit full of arrows, puzzled why they had not dropped him from the saddle.

It was nearly midnight, a full moon hanging bright in the night sky, when they spotted a horse and rider moving through the scrubland.

"That's him," Creed said, pointing.

"How can you be sure?"

"Who else would be riding in bandit territory at night?"

Creed spurred his horse, chasing after the bandit. William did the same.

"I have to be the one to kill him," William shouted to his partner.

Creed nodded. "You can kill him all you want, but I can help catch him."

Vidal rode at full gallop, dodging prickly pear cactus and patches of chaparral.

As they drew nearer, they could see the rider was indeed headless. Several Indian arrows stuck out of his back.

Vidal's head still hung from a rope tied to the saddle horn, bouncing around as his horse galloped over rough terrain.

They were still about twenty yards behind him when Vidal's head bounced and turned to the rear, his eyes going wide with surprise.

"I see you," yelled the bandit.

Creed raised his rifle and leaned forward in his saddle, taking aim.

"You can't hurt him," William said, seeing what his partner was doing.

"Not him," Creed said. "His horse."

Creed took quick aim and fired, the flash of the fifty-caliber rifle illuminating the night. The bullet struck the horse behind the front shoulder, dropping animal and rider.

They quickly closed the distance and dismounted, reaching Vidal's side before the dust cleared. His horse was dead, and the bandit still tied to the saddle. Luckily, the horse had fallen on its left side and not on top of Vidal's head.

"Stupid pendejos," Vidal cursed, spitting dirt. "You cannot hurt me."

"That remains to be seen, amigo." William stepped forward and removed the bandit's necklace.

"Give that back, you thief. It's mine."

"I know an old Apache woman who says otherwise." William tossed the necklace to Creed, who slipped it into his bag.

Vidal looked shocked. "The old woman? What did she tell you?"

"She told us lots of things." William pulled the curved needle and sinew out of his bag, threading the sinew through the eye of the needle.

Untying the rope from the saddle horn, William picked up the bandit's head.

"What are you doing?" Vidal asked, snapping his teeth in a threating manner. "Come closer, I will bite off your nose."

"Now, now. None of that."

William placed the severed head against Vidal's neck. The bandit's body twitched and strained against the ropes.

"Stop that," he said, kneeling on Vidal's chest. "Or I will sew your head on backwards."

The threat seemed to work. Vidal settled down and kept still.

"That's better."

Holding the hooked needle between thumb and forefinger, William forced the point through Vidal's flesh, connecting head to neck stump, one loop at a time, pulling the thread tight with each pass. When finished, he tied a knot in the sinew and cut free the needle.

It was not the fanciest sewing job. In fact, it was rather rushed and sloppy, and none of the veins, muscles, or vertebras were reattached. But that did not matter. Vidal was back together in one piece, just as mean as ever.

"Now, untie me and let me go."

"No problem, amigo." William pulled Old Butch from its sheath. "Hold still while I cut these ropes."

William cut through the ropes holding Vidal to his saddle. He stepped back, putting his knife back in its sheath.

Vidal jumped up fighting mad, spitting, cursing, and kicking dirt. He snatched up a rock and threw it at William but missed.

"You puta!"

"Now, is that any way to thank me?" William asked.

"No, it isn't," Creed answered, tossing William his rifle.

Big Foot Wallace raised the rifle and fired in one quick motion, shooting Vidal in the heart and putting an end to his complaints.

The bandit fell backward, hitting the ground hard.

William stepped forward and kicked Vidal in the leg, but the bandit didn't respond.

"He looks dead to me."

"Well, let's get him in the ground before he can change his mind," Creed said.

Using a small pack shovel, they dug a shallow grave. Before tossing the bandit in the hole, William pulled out the glass bottle Nascha had given them.

"I'm surprised an Apache witch would use holy water," William said, pulling the cork from the bottle and sprinkling the contents over the bandit.

"Doesn't smell like holy water," Creed replied, wrinkling his nose.

"No, it doesn't," William agreed. He dropped the empty bottle next to the hole.

"At least there will be no more headless horseman stories."

Both men lowered Vidal into the grave, covering his body with dirt and rocks. They did not give him a marker, or say a prayer, certain the bandit was already atoning for his sins in Hell.

Climbing on their horses, they rode off in the direction of home.

Had they waited a little longer, or even looked back, the Rangers would have been surprised to see the bandit slowly pulling himself from the grave, rising up to stand on two legs, shaking an angry fist at them.

"I will get you for this!" Vidal yelled.

He stopped, suddenly aware his clothing was wet.

"What did you do?" He touched his shirt. "Why am I wet?"

He sniffed his fingers, coughing.

"This is piss!" You pissed on me!"

He stomped the ground, hopping mad. Turning, he saw the empty bottle lying beside the grave, and heard the laughter of an old Apache woman deep inside his mind.

"Wait. I know that bottle." Vidal sniffed his shirt. "This is her piss... the old woman."

"Puta Madres!"

Furious, he turned and kicked a large rock, hitting it so hard shockwaves shot up his leg and through his body, causing the thin sinew thread in his neck to snap in two and unravel.

Vidal's head tilted backward and separated, the thread pulling free from his body.

The head hit the ground and rolled, coming to a rest beside the very rock he had kicked, sitting perfectly upright, and allowing him to watch his body stagger blindly into the Texas night.

"BASTARDS!"

Holes

BY BRENNAN LAFARO

LIKE EVERYONE ELSE IN Buzzard's Edge, Johnny Mabry heard the tales about the new sheriff. Elijah "Hellfire" Sparrow. Typical of this shitty little place. Building up a myth around its newest lawman to scare off the brigands who'd previously declared open season on the town.

Yeah, Johnny Mabry knew the stories and wrote them off as bullshit, until the moment he sat tied to a stake outside the town, hands knotted behind his back with Elijah Sparrow staring down at him. The sheriff aimed a Colt pistol not at Johnny's head, but at the ground next to him. A line of stygian black gunpowder slithered out from underneath the notorious outlaw like a rattlesnake fleeing across the scalding desert. The sand was hot enough under Johnny's ass that the gunpowder might take mind to go up on its own.

"What you want from me?" Johnny choked the words out through a sob. Death often plagued his mind, yet he hoped he would meet it with more gumption than this.

"Want you the fuck outta my town." Elijah stared at his gun. Didn't deign to meet the eyes of the man begging for his life.

"Fine. Cut me loose. I'll ride west and you'll never see me again, I swear it!"

"Not good enough." Elijah took a few steps back. He knelt at the end of the sleek, dark line of gunpowder and lowered his pistol. With a deafening bang, the trail of gunpowder sparked, blazing to life and racing toward its intended.

Johnny had no time to cry out before the dynamite packed tightly under his ass blew him to smithereens, raining chunks of Mabry from the sky. Shit, some of him maybe even landed back in Buzzard's Edge. Only on the outskirts, though. That was alright, the bloody precipitation wouldn't bother the people who paid Sparrow's salary.

The first hole appeared outside of Elijah Sparrow's cabin, no bigger around than a silver dollar. What it lacked in width, it seemed to make up in depth, far more than just an indentation. Although that was only a guess. He didn't hold any great desire to go sticking his fingers down there to verify. When Jeb first sniffed out the hole, Elijah cursed the mangy mutt away from it. Last thing he needed was a snakebit dog collapsing on his land. Lord only knew where that beast had got off to now.

With the vinegar gone from his lips, Elijah softened a bit, guilt bubbling to the surface. Dumb as a post the dog might be, and half coyote to boot, but Jeb remained his sole companion after the town of Buzzard's Edge abandoned him. Or he abandoned them. Depended on the vantage point you chose.

Elijah. A whisper, riding on the breeze, catching him by surprise.

"What you lookin' at, Mr. Sparrow?" The voice asking was light but with enough husk to carry and always contained a smile.

God damn. Was it Tuesday already?

Renny approached, wearing little more than the groceries that hung by her sides and just enough cloth to cover her unmentionables. She visited old Elijah at least once a week, however, and being spotted in that state of dress had never proved a problem before. The land surrounding the desolate cottage gave way to harsh conditions and flat plains as far as the eye could see, encouraging any self-respecting towns person to steer clear.

"Ain't nothin'," Elijah spat through his droopy mustache. Tobacco had tinged his facial hair an unsightly shade of yellow, not far off from piss. He turned his back on the hole to study Renny from head to toe, hoping she wouldn't try too hard to peer around him. Something about the little tunnel to nowhere made the hair on his neck prickle. He couldn't nail down what exactly, but the hole seemed too dark for daytime.

By God she looked beautiful today, Elijah thought, as he drank her visage up. Her legs stretched out so long, surveying them made Elijah's eyes tired by the time they reached her thighs. A great set of tits lay hidden underneath a swathe of cloth that barely passed for a shirt; big enough to give a man a handful, but not so boisterous they might cause a woman to lose her balance. Although Elijah's eyes lingered on the body, it was Renny's face he most looked forward to during these visits. Warm, kind eyes and a genuine smile that bespoke that old hooker with a heart of gold cliché, and an untidy mop of brown hair that some men might call too short, but Elijah thought suited her to perfection.

She raised an eyebrow in a playful gesture as she drew closer. "Just outside inspecting the dirt then, is that it?" Renny climbed to her tiptoes, struggling to see around the former sheriff, but she wasn't tall enough to get a good look.

"Just a hole some vermin dug. Never you mind," he said, but made no move to reveal it. Elijah knew her buying that weak excuse was every bit as likely as getting a horse to waltz, so he quickly changed the subject.

"What you bring me?" He gestured at the canvas bags dangling from Renny's long fingers.

The girl shrugged. The bag clinked and sloshed, providing the only answer Elijah needed. "Nothin' special. Just a couple items from McGregor's to tide you over a while."

The same exchange every week, like a dance; Renny playing coy and Elijah eagerly anticipating the next step.

She held the bag out, eyes still searching the ground that stretched out behind Sparrow, the mysterious nature of his yard a long way from forgotten. "Where's Jeb?"

Elijah scratched the back of his neck and looked around. Renny nearly made him forget the dog's existence. "Run off somewhere, I guess. He'll be back. Always is." He took the bag and dug through his pockets, fishing out a few silver dollars that called to mind the impenetrable darkness of the hole. Dropping the coins into Renny's outstretched hand, he mumbled something about keeping the change. Only after the girl made the money disappear did he realize he didn't know one way or another how far a dollar would fare in a general store these days. Renny offered a half-hearted grin, her face not betraying the answer to Elijah's unasked question.

"Like to come in?" Elijah's cheeks reddened in a way unbecoming of his Hellfire days. One of these times, she would say no, and he didn't think he could stomach that.

"Love to, Mr. Sparrow."

"Elijah, please," he said, heeding her smile. The embarrassment written on his features had not escaped her notice.

He tried not to think too hard on it. Best to let sleeping dogs lie. Speaking of sleeping dogs, he scanned the deserted yard once more, listening carefully for any sign of Jeb's whereabouts, but the land remained silent. Not so much as a whisper.

As Elijah turned to go inside a pinprick of darkness caught his eye. Another hole. Unease clenched his stomach as he realized, even at a distance, this one would have housed a silver dollar with room to spare.

Shit hole is overrun by pests. Got us an infestation, he thought, detecting a tremor even in his internal speech. He followed Renny in and slammed the door behind him; a clamor that he expected must have echoed all the way to the nearest neighbor.

⸻◆⸻

Renny's clothes dropped to the floor. There she stood, naked as the day she was born, and in his parlor, no less. Her head low, as if searching for the confidence that usually came with putting oneself on display, but she wore an inviting smile. Elijah wondered what he'd done to deserve such a bounty, but the thought quickly fled from his head alongside the blood flow needed elsewhere.

The groceries hit the floor with another clink, muffled this time, and he approached her lithe form, unbuttoning his shirt as he crossed the room. Renny retreated, an impish look plain upon her face as she led him to the bedroom. He found her there, splayed upon the mattress, eager and ready for him. Once she bit down on her lower lip, Elijah's pants refused to contain him any longer.

It had been a long time since he'd fucked a woman without paying for it and if the notion of foreplay had ever existed within his mind, it was buried somewhere in the back now. Prostitutes never kissed, but he believed if Renny were to allow any man's lips to grace hers, he'd be the one. A mischievous twinkle made his heart jump as he gazed into her eyes and trailed a weathered hand up and down her body. Her pale white skin, never tanned even under the Arizona sun, felt smooth as the finest China silk. She gasped at his touch, lowering one hand to unbutton his pants.

Unable to wait any longer, he plunged inside her. Warmth consumed him, gripping tighter with every thrust. As Elijah bucked away, taking care to find something resembling a rhythm, Renny dug her nails into his back, tracing the scars earned from previous battles. Elijah grimaced at the pain.

He closed his eyes as he drove himself into her, lost in her cries and moans.

BANG!

A gunshot split the head of Anderson Downs, an accused cattle thief who would never stand trial. The top of his skull vanished, as if part of a magic act while flaps of skin draped down in a pathetic attempt to hide the damage. His body stood for nearly five seconds before receiving the message that it was dead and should, therefore, make acquaintance with the ground.

Sweat gathered on Elijah's brow as he tried to shake the image.

Jeffrey Livingstone pleaded for his life, tears lining his puffy red eyes. "I've stuck up my first and last bank," he cried, right before Elijah drove a serrated knife into his stomach, ripping the lining to shreds and spilling reddish gray coils of innards among the sand, unnaturally bright against the dull desert.

In and out went the knife. In and out.

Renny's passionate cries mingled with the screams in Elijah's head—frequent visitors he alone was doomed to hear. On the first occurrence, he'd gone soft as a foal's down and apologized profusely. Since then, he managed to push through it, extracting as much joy as the meager bit of life left to him would allow.

Faith Dunn stared over his shoulder, ice in her eyes, as her body rocked back and forth beneath his. The woman felt no remorse for drowning her babies in the bath tub, so why should he feel shame for delivering comeuppance? Justice. He stole her last remaining bit of warmth and then filled her with his seed, before leaving her bound in the middle of the desert as the night grew cold.

Elijah opened his eyes as he climaxed and terror wrapped cold tendrils around his heart as he met the dead eyes of Faith Dunn, imposed upon Renny's face. She pulled him tight as the final spasms took hold, a convulsive death grip to prevent his escape. Relief only set in as Renny's face returned to its sweet, comforting normal.

Elijah rolled to the side, wiping himself off with a crusty sheet. Renny shot him a concerned look, but didn't allow it to dally. The two lay in bed, their labored breathing the only sound. Their tryst hadn't lasted any longer than a man like Elijah—not yet old, but prematurely aged—could maintain, yet the sunlight streaming in the bedroom window had changed positions, sinking a little further toward the horizon.

"Guess I'd better get back to town," said Renny, without making a move.

"Yeah, I guess you better." Elijah's voice was distant. His eyes remained fixed on the ceiling, studying something that wasn't there. Somewhere beneath the bed, a scratch sounded against the floorboards. So faint, it was easy to ignore.

———◆———

The silver dollars clinked together as Renny stepped out on Elijah's porch with an unsteady gait in the cooling desert air. He appeared almost comatose as she abandoned him, but she expected he'd be situated with a glass of whiskey in his dank, disheveled parlor by the time her feet met the sand.

The former sheriff of Buzzard's Edge wasn't much to look at, wasted away after having spent the past few years drinking himself into oblivion, but he still radiated a sense of power. If pressed, Renny expected that was why she still made a weekly trip out to the middle of nowhere to throw him a fuck. Some misplaced sense of adoration and puppy love. That and he paid well. So well in fact, she suspected all those rumors of corruption and violence that followed the name of Sparrow like flies after a horse's ass, must hold some water.

"Necessary evil," she whispered as she got her bearings and squinted in the direction of Buzzard's Edge. That's what the people said about him. He cleaned the muck off the town's boots that his predecessor was too afraid to touch. It was only after Sparrow's single failure that the murmurs began about how terrible he'd been. When he made every attempt to execute a local hellion known as Noose Holcomb, and inexplicably failed in his duties because the outlaw refused to up and die at the end of a hangman's rope.

She might be the only person who knew that when Sparrow fled west, he hadn't actually left the town's borders.

Caught in a reverie with a grin on her face, Renny hadn't taken a single step away from Elijah's porch. Something else niggled at the back of her mind. He'd blocked her view when she arrived. But what had been hiding?

The sun dropped lower every minute, yet still provided enough light to study the ground. At first, Renny saw nothing, thinking the old man had finally lost it, then she noticed the holes in the ground. A multitude of them, no less than twenty, and all large enough to catch a man's ankle and give it a nasty sprain. Renny fell to her knees, placing her hands against the sand that still retained the sun's heat. It stung her palms as she stared into the closest hole.

An odd shimmering blackness returned her gaze. Renny's stomach took a tumble as her brain attempted to translate what she saw; the darkness one anticipates inside a small tunnel, but only because that's what she expected. The blackness covering the top of this hole appeared as though something had placed a cap over the crevice, shielding the viewer from the horrors contained within.

Renny reached a hand out to touch it, positive the darkness would have substance, then jerked it away before making contact. Probably not a wise idea to plunge her hand into the unknown. A whisper reached her ears. Renny stood straight up as though a freezing cold hand had goosed her backside.

Not a whisper. Whispers.

Voices held a certain quality when they talked about a person, rather than to them. These murmurs issued from every conceivable direction—above, below, behind, and even right in front of Renny's dumbstruck face, as absurd as that notion was. The mixture was so muddled, Renny couldn't decipher a single word as the susurrus continued to condescend. Each syllable sounded familiar as though if she were able to focus on just one voice, the meaning would become clear. But that didn't happen. Renny grew red in the face, going from frightened to pissed off in the space of a heartbeat. She opened her mouth to scream out in frustration when an ungodly pain chomped down on her foot.

The scream turned into a quick yowl. Tar-like blackness seeped from the hole, wrapping Renny's foot in an icy embrace. Freezing cold needles stabbed by the thousands and each one hit a nerve and pierced tendon and flesh.

Renny squeezed her eyes shut, forcing tears from the corners and gritting her teeth so hard she expected one to shatter. She screamed once more, but it offered no relief. When she tried to look down, she knew what she would see before her eyes took it in. The substance had sucked her leg in up to the knee, not climbing so much as yanking her into the depths. The frozen shards of pain returned as she simultaneously heard and felt a bone snap in her leg.

"Elijah!" Her voice was little more than a mewling squeal, not even powerful enough to reach the house a stone's throw away. Sparrow might not be able to stop what was happening, but he could try God dammit!

Renny's right leg sank to the crotch as talons severed the flesh from her inner thighs. Razor sharp claws sliced into her pelvis and for the first time, she felt thankful she couldn't see what was happening within the murk. Her left leg, perched on the ground away from the miniature abyss, rose at an unnatural angle. Tendons pulled and popped when they reached their limit, and her ankle ascended over her head. The hole gave no quarter, sucking Renny's stomach then chest into the pit. It hadn't been large enough to accommodate her body at first, but ribs snapped and internal organs shifted to new shapes and locations as Renny disappeared little by little.

When all that was left above ground was her head and neck, she wondered how much of her still existed in some capacity. Freezing cold fire ate at all her extremities and shards of broken bone poked into the soft parts of her body, but her mind retained a perfect clarity even as she wished to black out. Some otherworldly force wanted her to experience her own end. Twenty-two years old and this was as far as she'd get. Frigid hands closed around Renny's throat and just when she thought she had found the strength to scream once more, she went under.

Though Renny knew no more, she felt everything.

———◦◦◦———

Elijah had a drink fixed less than a minute after Renny walked out. Wasn't no mixing to the way he took his liquor. Pick up the bottle and serve. How the fuck else were you gonna forget all the bullshit that cycled through your head when you were trying to know a woman in a biblical sense?

The remaining liquid sloshed noisily against the glass bottle as Elijah half sat, half fell into his favorite chair. Maybe not the most comfortable, but it suited him fine. He breathed deep and heavy, staring fixedly at the wall, when a howl broke his concentration. Some damn coyote or something. Or maybe Jeb returned. He perked up at the thought, but remained lodged in the wicker chair. Despite pretending to be cross with the mangy beast earlier, he hoped Jeb was okay. In truth he always looked forward to the dog's company. Renny's too, though any interaction from townsfolk that didn't end with him being called a murderer or a coward, two very different sides of the coin, was okay with him.

As if reading his thoughts, the gold sheriff star on the table caught a passing glance of light. Almost as if to say, I remember the times, Sheriff Sparrow.

Hellfire.

I remember what those ungrateful motherfuckers choose to forget.

He sank deeper into the chair, reveling in the lingering scent Renny had left on him. Love wasn't a word that described what they had, but it didn't entirely miss the mark either. At least from his point of view.

Elijah, a voice whispered, causing him to stiffen and eschew any notes of drunkenness he had accumulated in the last few minutes.

The drab hollow of a parlor remained as devoid of life as ever. Nothing moved, not even a flicker of shadow. He raised the bottle again, shaking his head as he brought it to his lips and took a generous pull. Liquid fire to drown out the unnecessary noise the world provided, whether you wanted it or not.

Skrit, skrit, skrit.

Three sharp staccatos burst under his feet, soft but unmistakable. Something trying to claw its way out.

Rats, he reasoned, not believing his own bullshit for even a moment. Rodents abounded in the desert, but Elijah had inhabited this cabin for some years and never had to contend with vermin moving freely under the floorboards in the past. Placing the bottle down with uncharacteristic tenderness, he eased to the floor and placed one ear against the wood. The blood pounding in his ears reverberated against the dusty boards and the groans his body produced roared in the comparable silence.

Maybe he'd imagined the scratches. A foolish grin formed at the corner of his mouth when the sound came again. More frantic this time, the noise sent Elijah scattering. His arms failed to save him from landing on his ass. He scrambled away from the source of the noise, but it followed, slinking beneath the house.

A light rumble shook the floorboards and Elijah pictured a horrific monstrous serpent, writhing through the sand. Cold sweat gathered on his forehead, quickly spreading to the rest of his body and unleashing the acrid stink of fear. It overwhelmed any remaining aroma that Renny had left behind. Squeezing himself into a corner as a means of retreat, Elijah's heart pounded as the scratches closed in on his position, and tore at the underside of the house. The monster's manic pace crescendoed, resonating through the walls until it surrounded him. Elijah cupped his hands over his ears, but it did no good. The floor trembled beneath his feet, nearly knocking him over once again.

Sparrow.

Whatever beast thirsted for his blood. They had sent it.

Faith Dunn, Anderson Downs, Jeffrey Livingstone, Johnny Mabry, and the others. So many others.

Their names careened around his bedraggled mind, his put-upon mind, at the speed of light, creating a desperate whirlwind of whispers and clawing. The tempo increased, the beast below was almost through. The shoddy flooring could not hold its fury at bay much longer.

Then, at once, it stopped. It all stopped. The noise, the names, the movement. The cozy, isolated cabin on the outskirts of Buzzard's Edge regained a sense of tranquility. Elijah slid down the wall and cradled his head in his hands. He was tired all of a sudden, so very tired.

A new noise caught his ear, but not one to make his heart beat clear out of his chest this time. A small yelp, distant, but within reach. It echoed from beneath the floor as though traveling through a long-forgotten series of caves.

"Jeb." Delight crept into Elijah's voice. Of course, the dog wound up under the floorboards. A chuckle escaped his lips at the insane notion of a great scaly beast traversing the sands underneath him to exact some sort of revenge. What had McGregor topped the bottle off with to make him believe such fucking nonsense?

He pulled himself to his feet and plucked a wool coat off the back of the chair to go and search for his companion. Throwing open the front door, the first thing Elijah noticed was how quickly the sun dropped. A line of brightest orange spilled enough light to make up for the lack of the moon's glow, caught halfway between day and night. The second thing he noticed stole every blustery bit of confidence from Elijah.

The holes covered his yard, dozens of them. Some no larger around than the first—*a silver dollar*, he thought—some massive enough to devour a horse. Elijah stood still as a cactus on a calm day, studying the new landscape. The darkness within each hole undulated against the light, but absorbed that beautiful orange rather than reflect it.

Elijah, a voice whispered. No. *Voices.*

He couldn't be sure, but it sounded as though every hole spoke. A variety of timbres, combined to create a symphony of the damned. High, low, loud, soft, and every imaginable interval between, chattered in a ghastly unison that forced the hair on his arms to stand at attention.

"You *have* come for me, then," said Elijah, unable to keep from trembling.

"Not you." To his left, the darkness filling one of the craters formed the dead-eyed, hateful face of Faith Dunn. It spoke in her familiar dulcet tones, stating facts without emotion. Taunts filled the air, stemming from each and every trench that now honeycombed the landscape of Elijah's yard. The words cut like a freshly stropped blade before joining together in a convoluted chorus. The voices seemed to speak in an unknown tongue, something equal parts ancient and terrible.

"Wouldn't dream of ending your suffering, Sparrow." The playful tone belonged to a man. It stood out crisp and clear against the muddled chants.

Elijah tore his gaze from the Faith-hole to see a gaunt, fish-white hand emerge from one of the larger pits, clawing at the surrounding sand. Painstakingly, the hand dragged itself forth, the body of Johnny Mabry attached to the other end. When Elijah last saw Johnny, a concussive explosion blew him to so many bits, he couldn't fill the stomach of a vulture. The ghoul clambered to its feet, not so much an image of the man before, as an unholy mass of skin stitched back together by the type of magic men feared. The kind of dark magic that had saved Noose Holcomb from the hangman's rope and cost Elijah Sparrow his dignity.

Mabry stood to his full height, his patchwork body creaking as he moved, even when his lips pulled into a hellish grin. The choir didn't disseminate, but sank to a dull roar.

Mabry tipped his hat, loosing a few maggots. Elijah watched them scurry across the hard-packed sand and squirm into the roiling dark they'd ridden in from.

"Like the lady said, we ain't here for you, Elijah. Not here to kill you anyway."

"Then why have ye come? Just to put a fright in me?" He spat on the ground, tasting bile as it left his lips, and summoned more bluster than he thought possible. "It won't work."

"Here for vengeance, Mr. Sparrow." Mabry grinned, letting the words hang.

The cold sweat returned as confusion set in.

"Elijah," called a voice, more fear than malice in its tone. He recognized it immediately and his heart missed a beat.

"Renny," he whispered.

It called again twice more, softer each time. It might've called a third, or that could have been the wind breathing across the plain. As he strained to listen, he thought he heard a dog bark in the distance. It didn't come from under the house this time.

"Hellfire, they called you," said Mabry, watching the tears cut through the grime on Sparrow's cheeks. "You know nothing of hellfire, sir. Surely you will someday, but death would be too easy, too quick, for the likes of you."

"If not kill me, what do you aim to do?" Any trace of fire in Elijah's words had disappeared with Renny's pleas. His pathetic whispers could not have crossed a silent room.

"We aim to cut you off. Seal you up in this hovel like a tomb and make sure you spend every miserable fucking second alone. Anyone or anything who tries to give you comfort will know pain and suffering the likes of which words cannot do justice." He paused, as if expecting a retort from Sparrow, but received none. "She loved you, you know. I expect you'll have to live with that. With your sins."

Once again, Mabry found only silence in the cool desert air. He filled them with his parting words. "Remember Sheriff, we'll always be with you. Every flicker of the wind, every inexplicable bad feeling, every scratch at the floor…"

Mabry seemed poised to continue, but instead kept his eyes fixed on Elijah. A bubbling black oil-like substance enveloped his pale visage. Tendrils wrapped around him lovingly, and drew him back to the dark hole. The menagerie of voices diminished to nothingness, as one-by-one the holes contracted until they ceased to exist altogether. Less than a moment after standing face to face with a man he'd blown to smithereens, Elijah watched the land return to its familiar appearance. The last vestige of sunlight dropped below the horizon, and coarse sand shone under the emerging moonlight.

With the last of his strength drained, Elijah Sparrow fell to his knees. The stream of tears coursed down his face like a mighty river. His chest hitched, whether for Renny, the dog, or the future, he couldn't rightly say.

A touch of whiskey might help ease the hurt, but he needed to conserve his stores. Lord only knew if or when he'd be able to leave this place again.

Soiled Doves

by Vivian Kasley

DAPHNE USED ONE HAND to cover her mouth, and the other to usher the burly butcher out of her bedroom, then she raced over to the wash basin and spewed the contents of her stomach. She hadn't been feeling good as of late, and kneeling before the butcher had been the last straw. Lifting the sling of his sweaty belly to take him into her mouth had caused her to gag. He'd smelt like the undercarriage of a buffalo with the backdoor trots, and even though she needed the dough and knew Madam Jennie would be as mad as a hornet, she couldn't do it. She wiped the froth from her chin and eyed the tiny silver pillbox on her vanity. It contained the special powder that'd get rid of her unwanted problem. If she was to continue to work, she'd have to take it before her abdomen began to swell. There was no other way.

—◆—

Daphne awoke when she heard the knock on her door. She lifted her throbbing head and tried to get up, but found she couldn't move without agonizing pain. It felt like a knife fight was taking place in her abdomen, and that her bowels were being flayed to pieces. *What was in that powder?* she wondered. She clutched her stomach and moaned, prompting Luella to open the door.

"Sakes Alive! What's the matter, Daphne?" Luella stood in the doorway, dressed in only a corset, net stockings, and kid boots. She wrinkled her nose when she saw the vomit in the wash basin, then went to Daphne's bedside. "Madam Jennie's got bees in her bonnet over you tossin' out Ol' Mr. Porter. I reckon you had good reason, I know he can be a hard case."

Luella winced when she caught sight of Daphne. She looked green, and even though all she wore was a chemise, she panted like a dog laying in the hot sun. Her long golden hair was plastered to her head and neck with sweat and you could hardly tell her eyes were blue due to her pupils being so large.

"I think I'm dyin', Lu," Daphne rasped.

"Horse feathers, you ain't dyin', you can't! Yer one of the best we got here at Pretty Kitties. You can't go dyin'! Who else'll play piano in the parlor and sing all them songs you sing?" But Luella wasn't sure how bad off Daphne truly was. She was gonna have to go get Madam Jennie, and fast.

"I-I can't hardly breathe, Lu... my whole body's on fire. It's like flames is lickin' at my flesh!"

"Lemme go get Madam, she'll know what to do." Luella strode from the room, worry in her eyes.

Madame Jennie was annoyed when Luella told her the news. Eleanor, Laura, and Julia had customers in their rooms, and she didn't have time to fuss with no nonsense. Daphne had already tossed out Roy Porter, which only meant he'd go across town to Etta's Doll House and spend his dinero there. If her best girl was ill, it'd put her at a disadvantage. Ever since Etta's opened, the competition was proving to be problematic. She'd have to hire a couple more girls, and maybe spruce up the parlor. Two brothels in their small dusty town were two too many. She sighed as she climbed the creaking stairs, the bustle of her blue satin dress whooshing behind her.

<hr />

Madam Jennie instructed Luella to fetch some fresh water and rags. She walked circles in Daphne's room, the heels of her boots like a ticking clock. She'd never seen anything like this before. None of the sicknesses she knew of caused what she was witnessing. Daphne's skin was turning the color of someone who'd been dead for days, and the smell of her was even worse. She walked over to the bedside and groaned as she inspected the black veins beginning to streak over Daphne's body.

"What'd you go and get into Daphne, you gump?" Madam Jennie asked. "I sure hope it ain't the French Pox. Or worse—consumption! It'll wipe out the whole house! Have you been being over-careful like I told you? I know I ain't got none of them condoms, but I do check out the men who come in and make sure they look presentable fer I let 'em near you."

Daphne tried to speak, but found she couldn't form coherent words. She wanted to tell Madam Jennie everything, about the powder she'd taken and where she'd gotten it from. Besides feeling like her innards were being boiled from the inside out, it also felt like an invisible force was sitting upon her chest, crushing her ribcage into her lungs as it wrapped its greedy hands around her neck and choked her. She tried to take a breath, but it was almost impossible. As her air dwindled down to zero, panic gripped her. She clawed at her neck, long fingernails tearing through the delicate flesh there. Any hope she had of fending off whatever was stealing her breath, was lost as soon as she began to shak e.

She shook so violently, that the bed shook with her. When the shaking stopped, her body went rigid, as stiff as a board. She struggled to move her fingers or even wiggle a toe. An artic chill climbed her feverish body, slowly at first, and then rapidly, until it settled in her skull, turning her brain into what felt like a solid block of ice. Her bowels release and she managed to let out one last choking sob, and by the time the rank odor of her own shit and piss hit her nostrils, her eyeballs rolled to the back of her head and her thoughts went completely dark.

Luella ran into the room with rags and a pale of water. She yelped when she caught sight of her friend. Daphne was covered in blood. It looked like it had oozed from every orifice on her body. Madam Jennie yanked a rag and the bucket from Luella's hand and began to wipe clean Daphne's face.

"Don't just stand there, Lu, help me," she barked.

"W-What h-happened to her?" Luella asked. She gently pressed a rag to Daphne's neck to soak up the blood still trickling from her ears. The scent of her friend's hot sticky fluids mingled with the smell of her shit and piss was overwhelming and forced Luella to gag. The gags became as constant as hiccups as she watched blood from the saturated rag run down her forearm, and drip from her elbow.

"I don't know…" Madame Jennie murmured. She was afraid, and beside herself with bewilderment.

"Maybe we should fetch the doc," Luella cried.

"Too late fer that, Lu. Ain't no doc 'round here gonna know how to cure whatever the hell this is."

Both women jumped back and screamed when Daphne sat up and sprang from the bed like an animal. Blood rained around her, forming a dark red pool around her dirty bare feet. She stood as still as stone, and stared with cold vacant eyes at both women as if they were strangers. The screams brought Julia, Laura, and Eleanor in from their rooms, followed by the men they were entertaining. Two of the men scooted back out with their wool pants around their ankles when they caught sight of the blood-soaked woman, but one remained. He fastened his own pants, then quickly jumped in front of the three ladies, putting his arm out to stop them from entering the grisly scene in the bedroom. Laura ducked under the man's arm and rushed in to meet Luella and Madam Jennie.

"What in the tarnation…" the man mouthed.

"Madam, what's happened to her?" Laura asked. Eleanor and Julia sobbed into their hands and turned away, unable to stomach the horrific sight.

Madam Jennie didn't answer. She kept her eyes trained on Daphne, afraid that if she spoke or moved an inch, Daphne would strike like a rattlesnake. Luella trembled and whimpered beside her, bloody rags in hand.

Again, Laura cried, "Madam, please, what's happ—"

Daphne screeched and then with lightning speed, leapt onto Luella, knocking her to the ground. Her teeth sunk into Luella's throat, jerking her head back and forth like a rabid coyote.She hungrily gnawed on her larynx, turning Luella's screams to a gurgle. When Luella stopped twitching, Daphne continued to feast. She crunched on bone and nose cartilage, and then savored the fat from one of her cheeks.

Laura found her footing and tried to pull Daphne from Luella, but this only made Daphne turn on her, her gruesome face full of rage as she chomped down on Laura's shoulder.

It was a struggle to wrench herself from Daphne's jaws, and she slipped in all the blood. Before she could attempt to escape, Daphne buried her teeth into the side of her neck, spitting away chunks of flesh and gnawing into the ropey neck cords before moving to her jowls. Laura's screams of anguish at being eaten alive brought a petrified Madam Jennie back to the surface.

Madam Jennie shrieked, fell backward, then crab walked from the room, grabbing the hands of the shocked man and ladies in the doorway to help herself up. After she caught her breath, she hollered, "Get downstairs... now, goddamnit!" Then she slammed the door to Daphne's room, muffling the sounds of carnage within, and quickly followed behind them.

In the parlor, Madam Jennie downed two shots of her best bonded bourbon. She grabbed her revolver, then handed the bottle of bourbon to the man, who took it with a trembling hand. He took a long pull, wincing as he swallowed.

"Madam, w-what're you gonna do?" Julia asked, tears streaming down her cheeks.

"What's it look like?" And with that Madam Jennie ran up the stairs.

Six gunshots rang out and moments later Madam Jennie appeared at the top of the stairwell, tendrils of smoke still floating from the gun's barrel. "She's... she's dead," she croaked. "Had to use all six slugs, but the last one hit her square in the forehead and struck her dead. She's finally gone..."

Madam Jennie told Eleanor and Julia to draw the curtains, then she marched outside and pulled down the red lanterns she'd hung under the eaves of the Pretty Kitties mansion, along with a hand painted sign that read, "*We Don't Bite Unless Asked, But We'll Always Make Y'all Purr.*" She didn't want any more visitors for the night, and hoped that'd be enough to let people know they were closed.

Back inside, she sat in a chair in her blood-drenched dress and cried. Eleanor, Julia, and the man sat on the sofa, passing the bottle of bourbon around in silence.

The man rubbed his Adam's apple, then cleared his throat. "Name's Wesley. I ain't never seen nothing like that 'fore in my life, and I done seen a lot. I'm real sorry, Madam, 'bout what happened."

Madam Jennie nodded, and blew her nose into a handkerchief.

"Madam Jennie... I thought I saw something... when I glanced into Daphne's room I mean, I saw she'd might've taken, well—"

"By Gum! Quit blatherin' Julia and spit it out yer bazoo! You saw what, girl? What'd you see?" Madam Jennie probed.

"I'm sure as a gun I saw an empty pill box on her vanity. 'Cause, well, I got one similar." Julia's face turned almost as red as her strawberry hair.

"What's that got to do with anythin'?" Madam Jennie asked.

"Well, I... I don't know, but—"

"So help me God Julia, I'm gonna beat you raw with a hickory switch if you don't spit it out!" Madam Jennie's left eye twitched, with an evident snarl on her face.

"Oh, Madam, we thought we were pregnant!" Julia sobbed. "It was a coupla weeks back. I'd told Daphne I thought I might be, and she told me that she thought she might be too. We was at the general store gettin' stuff for a douche to help get rid of"—she leaned in then and whispered—"*you know*."

Both of Madam Jennie's eyes twitched in tandem, her teeth now fully bared as Julia continued.

"Then, Madam Etta, she saw us, and said she knew what we were up to. So, she reached into her reticule and pulled out these two tiny silver pill boxes.

"She said she gave it to her own girls when they needed it, and that it'd take care of our problem right away. But I never took mine, 'cause I started bleedin' not soon after, but Daphne, she mustn't of. Madam Etta said it wouldn't hurt us! I'm sorry, Madam Jennie, but I know how over careful you tell us to be, to use the rhythm method, and I was afraid to tell—"

"Shut yer trap, Julia! I need to think." Madam Jennie closed her eyes and rubbed her temples.

Eleanor hiccupped, brushed her brown curls from her face, and drank down more bourbon, waiting for Madam Jennie to tell them what they were gonna do.

Madam Jennie knew in her gut, that the scallywag Etta was somehow behind what happened. Losing her best girls in such a shocking way would certainly mean

Pretty Kitties would have to shut down, which would give all the business to Etta and her Doll House. She was no gump and she sure as hell wasn't gonna let that no good bitch ruin what she'd worked so hard for.

Ever since her family moved from the East to farm buffalo, Jennie had wanted to get out of Arizona, cut dirt and leave behind the dry and barren hell of the one-horse town she'd been in since she was a little girl. She dreamed of meeting a bearded cowboy, jumping the broom, and heading to the Black Hills of Dakota, the hills of gold. But life don't always go as planned, and she ended up working as a saloon girl. She made good money dancing and getting men to buy drink after drink, but her once perky bosom sagged, and she aged out.

Single and out of work, she'd bought a mansion with the money she'd been so careful to save and opened up Pretty Kitties. It was funny really, there was a time when as a saloon girl, she wouldn't be caught dead talking to a girl on the line, and now *she* was a Madam!

Even as a Madam, she was respectable, and seen as an enterprising woman. She lived in a big beautiful home with her girls, who each had their own lavishly furnished room. Sure, the women rented their rooms and paid her fifty percent of their take, but still, they had it good. They ate well, and dressed even better. She took care of them. She also took care of the town, and became known for her philanthropic work. She had put up the money to build a school and a church. And what had Etta done? Besides strolling into town and opening up her honkytonk bordello? She'd done nothing but try and take away her business by any means possible, and now, she'd gone too far. Too, too far.

Madam Jennie opened her eyes and looked at all of them. She inhaled, holding her breath, then exhaled slowly. She repeated that action two more times before she spoke.

"Listen here. We're goin' to Madam Etta's," she said.

"Tonight?" Julia asked.

"Yes, tonight."

"But, Madam, we can't just—"

"*Julia*, you said where that powder came from. And you also saw firsthand what happened up there. I got three carcasses in my house, and someone's gonna pay. I ain't askin'ya, I'm tellin ya, yer both comin' with me tonight to settle the score. I got pistols and pig stickers, so pick yer weapons." Madam Jennie took a swig of bourbon, burped, and wiped her mouth with the back of her hand.

"'Pardon me, Madam, but do you mind if I join y'all on this venture?" Wesley asked.

Madam Jennie raised her eyebrows. "You sure you wanna do that cowboy? Could bring you more trouble than you asked fer."

"I'm a road agent on the run. Ain't no more trouble than I already fell in." Wesley held out his hand for the bourbon, and Madam Jennie handed it over.

"Alright, cowboy, yer in," Madam Jennie said.

Julia looked at Eleanor, who looked at Madam Jennie and shrugged. "I'll take a pig sticker," she said.

"Eleanor, are you outta yer mind?" Julia asked.

"Laura, Luella, and Daphne were our friends. My mind's just daisy," Eleanor said, her eyes wide and bright. She hiccupped, then burped, and a mischievous smile crept across her booze-flushed face.

"Alright then, it's settled. Go and put on somethin' easier to move 'round in. I gave you each a calico dress when you came here. We're walkin', not ridin', so them'll do just fine, I reckon. And bring down the cowboy's hat. Every cowboy needs his hat."

Wesley nodded. "Thank you, Ma'am."

"Are you gonna change, Madam?" Julia asked.

"Don't need to," Madam Jennie said, then turned to Wesley. "You packin' iron, cowboy?"

"Sure am. An 1851 Colt Dragoon, but I call her Betsy. She was my Pa's. He named it after my Ma, 'cause she was always shooting off at the mouth," Wesley said.

"Swell... that's swell," Madam Jennie said.

While the girls were changing, Madam Jennie reloaded her revolver. She stuffed one of her prized jeweled daggers from her saloon days into the top of her boot and concealed another between her breasts. She didn't know if they'd run across anyone on their way to Etta's, but if they did, she'd be ready for 'em. It'd been years since she'd worn her hair down, but she undid her bun and let her sleek chestnut hair tumble over her shoulders.

"You sure're somethin'," Wesley said, as he took in all of Madam Jennie.

Madam Jennie winked. "You ain't too bad yerself, cowboy."

The generous yellow moon lit up the night making it easy for them to make their way in the dark. No one spoke and the only sound was the crunch of Arizona clay under foot and the clink of the spurs on Wesley's boots. They passed the sheriff's, the bank, the general store, the school house, and the saloon. Other than a string of horses, and a few stumbling drunks, no one stopped them or asked where they were headed. Etta's was just across from the seamstress, and they were almost there.

The bold red lanterns that hung beside the entrance of Etta's Doll House shone bright, and Madam Jennie scowled when she saw them. They stopped at the bottom of the steps leading to the house, waiting for Madam Jennie's command.

"Here's how it's gonna go. We walk in, and I state my business with Madam Etta. When you see me raise my right hand, it's gun's a blazin'! Got it?"

"Got it," they said in unison.

They walked up the creaky steps and through the double doors. There was a bare-chested young woman playing a piano, and a little more than a handful of men and working girls sat around the parlor drinking, smoking, singing, and laughing. Etta stood beside the piano, clapping in rhythm to the music. When she noticed them, she continued to smile with her mouth, but not her eyes.

Etta stopped clapping, and the young woman stopped playing, and with that the laughs and singing, ceased too. Every set of eyes in the place were laid upon them, waiting for what was about to unfold.

"Yer as crooked as a dog's hind legs, Etta Dalton," Madam Jennie hollered. "You know it and I know it. Best you acknowledge the corn."

"I haint got no idea—"

"Can it, Missy. The jig is up! First you tell tall tales 'bout my girls spreadin' the pox, and I let that go, but now, now you've gone too far. You know what you did to my girls! I got three that's buzzard food as I speak. I don't know what you gave 'em or where you got it, but I'm gonna find out!"

The men and ladies sitting down, stood up and walked behind Madam Etta.

"I haint gave nothin' to nobody! What yarn're you tellin'?" Madam Etta asked.

"What's that powder made of Etta? Where'd you get it? You know what it does?" Madam Jennie asked. "It turns people crazy enough to eat the Devil with horns on! One of my poor innocent girls took that powder and then she… " Madam Jennie choked back a sob before she could finish. "She killed and attempted to eat two of my other girls!"

Everyone gasped.

Except for Madam Etta. She laughed. She held her side and laughed so hard, she turned purple, then she spat, "If yer girls weren't such coots, they'da been more careful! Now, I suggest you and yer lot make tracks, 'fore there's trouble."

"No can do. What the blazes was in that powder Etta?" Madam Jennie demanded and stepped forward.

"How should I know? I got it from some bitter Chinese immigrant. No tellin' what's in that Devil's magic."

"But you had to know what it did. You had to know it'd hurt them!"

"I may've given it to a coupla saddle bums, to see what it did." Madam Etta shrugged.

"And then you gave it to my girls, who ain't done nothin' to you. Why?"

Madam Etta smirked and said, "Good for business."

"Tit for Tat!" Madam Jennie growled, then pulled her revolver and shot the topless pianist right between her breasts. The young woman looked down at the pulpy hole between her breasts, then let out a tiny yelp before slumping onto the piano's keys, sending a barrage of ugly notes into the air. Wesley, Eleanor, and Julia took that as signal enough and began their own assault.

Wesley shot three men down before they could unholster their own guns, and cracked a fourth in the skull with the butt of his Colt when they grabbed him from behind.

Julia screeched as she grabbed a girl by her hair and shot her under the chin, then shot two more girls in the back as they tried escaping up the stairs. Eleanor grinned and bared her teeth as she snatched up a girl hiding behind the sofa. She jammed her knife into the girl's heaving bosom and dragged it down, shredding the girl's dress and corset until her guts spilled forth, plopping onto the floor. Madam Etta watched in horror, then tried to run away from the onslaught in her parlor.

Even with all the chaos around her, Madam Jennie only saw Madam Etta. She didn't want to shoot her, that'd be too quick. She wanted to mutilate her. She raced after her and caught her by the bustle. Madam Etta turned and slashed at Madam Jennie with her claw-like nails, but Madam Jennie slammed her fist into Madam Etta's face shattering bone, causing teeth to fly like bits of shrapnel. It was only when her knuckles split and slid in the viscous mixture of their blood, that Madam Jennie drew her dagger from between her breasts. Snot ran from her nose and spittle sprayed from her mouth as she plunged the blade into Madam Etta's stomach, over and over, cursing her name and stirring her entrails like a pot of sonofabitch stew.

With all the hullabaloo, no one noticed the naked skeletal man running down the stairs gnashing his teeth. There was rope trailing behind him, wrapped around his waist and wrists as if he'd been tied up. Black veins mapped his gore-encrusted body. The naked man sprinted and leapt onto the back of Wesley then bit into his ear. The man growled like a rapid dog, shaking his head back and forth as he tried to gnaw free his prize. Wesley screamed and tried to throw the wild man off, but the man held tight, squeezing his legs around Wesley's midsection, and biting into the back of his neck. The pain was severe, and when his teeth pierced Wesley's jugular, he dropped to the floor.

Blood sprayed like a geyser. Wesley let out a wet wail, alerting the others. Even as Wesley rolled about like a dying lizard, the man clung to him, ripping at his clothes, biting off and swallowing fingers whole, and chewing more holes into his flesh. Eleanor, Julia, and Madam Jennie could do nothing to save their cowboy friend, but they knew they had to kill the deranged man that was eating him.

Madam Jennie tiptoed toward the man making a meal out of Wesley. She put her finger to her mouth and motioned for Julia and Eleanor to stay back. The naked man paid no attention as he gobbled down more hunks of meat. When Madam Jennie cocked the revolver, the feasting man stilled. He sniffed at the air like an animal, then turned his head toward Madam Jennie, his vacant eyes as black as coals. She didn't wait to see what he'd do next; she pulled the trigger and fired until the only sound was the *click-click-click* of an empty chamber.

Thick dark curdled blood poured from the holes in the naked man's forehead. Madam Jennie, Eleanor, and Julia looked around the room, and waited to see if anyone else would come charging.

When they didn't, they searched the house. In Madam Etta's room, Madam Jennie found a small wooden box filled with a puce colored powder. She picked it up and brought it with her downstairs.

—◆—

"Find anyone?" Madam Jennie asked.

Eleanor and Julia shook their heads.

"What do we do now, Madam?" Julia asked.

"Thing we gotta do now is, get our stories straight 'fore we go to Sheriff Willoughby. Mostly we tell the truth, but also leave out some stuff."

"Like what?" Eleanor asked.

"I'd reckon the part where we came here to slaughter people."

"What's in the box, Madam?" Julia asked.

"That dang no-good powder."

Julia cringed. "What'll you do with it?"

"I ain't sure yet. Burn it. Bury it. Or maybe keep it in case I need it fer somethin'."

"What on earth would you need it fer?" Eleanor asked.

"Who knows?" Madam Jennie said. She thought about that as she looked at the state of herself and of her girls. All three of them, soaked through with blood. She'd always hated the phrase soiled doves, but now, here they stood, actual soiled doves. She couldn't help herself, and chuckled in spite of everything. "What I do know girls, is that no one else better mess with the soiled doves at Pretty Kitties. Alright then, c'mon and let's get goin'."

Madam Jennie sucked her teeth as she picked up Wesley's hat and put it atop her head, then she held out her hands to Eleanor and Julia. Hand in hand, all three women left behind the massacre at Etta's Doll House, headed to wake the sheriff.

About Her Given Name

BY KENZIE JENNINGS

THE BLOOD TRAIL LED her to the giant oak.

What little left of him hung there, slowly turning in the wind like a macabre ornament. His eyes were carved out. His face was swollen and purple. A fat slug of a tongue protruded from his raw lips. His arms and legs had been ripped from his body, the meat shredded and dangling from the sockets.

Someone hung a sign around his neck that had the word "REPROBATE" painted there. At the time, she didn't understand what it meant, but it didn't matter.

It simply didn't matter.

The mere sight of him with a black mass of flies swarming around his remains told her plenty enough what she had to do.

———◆———

It would be her last visit to the cabin at the center of the forest, and by the time she reached its front door, the tears came. She'd been conditioned not to cry. After all, crying was for the helpless, the forgotten, and she was much too privileged to even consider crying. However, there was no one there to reprimand her for it.

When she wept, she cried until it hurt her insides, and she knew something in her had broken.

Once inside, she sat in his rocking chair. He'd told her never to light a fire when the forest was alive with noise. It meant interlopers were present somewhere. The reckless part of her wanted to send a signal to the ones who'd butchered him, but her practical side wouldn't hear of it. She needed to collect her thoughts and plan carefully.

Besides, there was only one person who was ultimately responsible.

The sound of the wind whistling around the house brought her comfort and clarity. Otherwise, everything out there was quiet, as if slumbering.

If you ever find yourself alone, he'd said to her, *it will be a time of great patience and will for your reckoning, little robin. Listen to the whispers of your soul. They'll tell you when to strike.*

Her soul whispered something terrible.

And she listened to its every word as she rocked back and forth, back and forth, with his bowie knife in her lap.

TWENTY YEARS LATER

The inn was bustling with patrons much to the dismay of one Mrs. Ernestine Crowley, the brick-jawed, iron-and-gristle head of housekeeping. While she'd stepped in a mere two weeks prior, the woman had already taken her duties so intently. She had since intimidated not only the other employees, but even the most steadfast guests as well in such a short period of time. If she was unable to anticipate and accommodate the Colonel's needs, she took her anger out on her staff, having them clean until every square inch of each room and hallway was dust-free and gleaming.

She had been on one such mission on the second floor, reciting perfunctory orders to the poor maids who had been on their knees, frantically scrubbing the floorboards that were caked with dust. When she knocked on the last door of the hall, it opened barely a crack. A stately woman in a crimson dress stood in the doorway, her gaze cutting.

"Beg your pardon, Miss Northway. How is your room? Is everything to your approval?"

The lady in red offered a polite smile. "The room is lovely, thank you. Please give my thanks to the Colonel for his hospitality as well, and I look forward to supper."

Something made a slight squeak of noise beyond the door, and before Mrs. Crowley could react, the lady in red had shut the door and bolted it, the action of which rendered Mrs. Crowley speechless. From one end of the corridor, one of the maids snickered. Mrs. Crowley spun, catching the young woman mid-giggle with a hand to her mouth.

"What did I tell you about such behavior?" she snapped. "Perhaps some time cleaning the communal privy will set you right again!" Mrs. Crowley then turned to the other maid who was still on her hands and knees, scrubbing frantically at a stain ingrained in the wood. "I want you to report the lady's comings and goings to me, every movement, but nary a word about what you're doing," she said just above a whisper before she left.

She would've stayed, hovering there, but there were other matters to attend to, other matters that needed enough time to covertly devise before the night was over.

<hr />

The Bowie knife spiraled end over end, towards the head of the curly-haired gent from Kansas City. It missed his left ear by a pinch, the blade piercing into the grain of the wardrobe door. His eyes shot open, his breath catching in short puffs. He managed a weak half-smile, his eyes steady on the lady in red who'd thrown the knife at him.

"Didn't anyone tell you it's rude to kill the messenger?" he said, his voice quavering.

"I warned you not to make a sound," she hissed, as she yanked the knife from the wood. "The reason I permitted you in was because *you* offered information. This is *your* doing."

"My *un*doing," he said with a nervous titter.

She tapped his nose with the blade's tip. "Out with it then."

"If it's all right with you, I'd like to keep my nose, ma'am. I find it useful."

She tossed the knife on the bed amongst her belongings and then turned back to him. Her hand cupped around his Adam's apple, a warning. "I've been waiting here for three days. *Three*. My fiancé is likely in a state, worrying for my wellbeing, but I've not heard a word from him. There's no excuse for this."

"That's precisely why I'm here, Miss Northway," he squeaked as her hand gently squeezed. "Regarding your fiancé, the Commodore," he blurted. "I won't be of much use if you deprive me of air."

The lady in red released her hold, and he gasped, bending, his hands on his knees.

"Well?"

He held up a finger, taking a moment before he gathered himself and straightened. "As I was saying, I'm here on behalf of interested parties pulling me this way and that. On the one hand, there's Commodore Darrow. Demanding fellow. Bit of a brute. I confess, at first, I didn't understand what drew you to the other." He managed a cocky grin. "Now I see it plainly. So temperamental, the both of you."

"And?"

"And what?"

"Oh, for heaven's sake," she said around an exasperated sigh. "You're quite eager to be stabbed today, aren't you? What's the message he's had you relay?"

"Ah, yes, but that's the quandary you see. As of today, I'm now here on behalf of the interested party that has since usurped the Commodore's authority over Idlecreek." The curly-haired man's tone had grown cold, his grin tugged into a sneer. "She said I may do with Miss Northway as I see fit," he said. "And truth be told, I'm not fond of threats, particularly from a lady."

"She?"

That sneer.

The chilly stare.

Something lingered there and played with his tone. He clicked his tongue, once, twice, three times, and pointed at his eye.

It was like the sound of a clock ticking away the seconds.

The hairs prickled on the back of Miss Northway's neck. She caught the slightest bit of movement coming from the hands of the man, something slipping out from his sleeves into his palms. With a quick flick of his wrists, blades snapped open from their sheaths, and he suddenly scuttled forward, swinging the blades this way and that at her. She parried each strike, her focus on him, then around the room, visually calculating, measuring.

Their deadly dance ended when Miss Northway tipped back onto the bed, one arm trapped beneath her, and just as the man bent over the bed, readying to slice her throat, his abdomen met the blade of the Bowie, the handle of which she had in her grip. She let go of the handle and quickly shoved him off her. He staggered backwards, dropping the blades onto the rug. The man squawked at the sight of the knife embedded in his gut. Miss Northway pushed herself up and sauntered towards him.

"I say, I think you..." He trailed off. He seemed about to pull the knife out but then quickly realized that lethal mistake. "Well, this is a nasty piece of business, isn't it?' he said with a chortle.

She put a hand on the man's shoulder, squeezed it. "Who else is here for me?"

"I'm afraid I've no idea—"

"Oh, hush your lies," she said, shaking her head. "Who else has she sent to relay her little... *message*?"

He let out a bark of a laugh. "You won't leave here alive."

Miss Northway curled her hand around the handle of the Bowie, pulling him to her, her lips close to his ear. "We'll see," she whispered, before yanking the knife to the side and out, ripping his shirt and flesh wide open.

The man's innards tumbled out, plopping wetly in a gooey pile on the rug. The man himself followed suit, collapsing to the floor, his head thunking hard against the wood.

The lady in red winced at the mess and stepped back. The hide of her boot had caught some of the gore, so she wiped it off on the man's trousers, nudging the body as she did.

———◦———

One of the chambermaids was cleaning the room across the hall when she turned right into the lady in red, who was looking rather harried.

"I'm in need of assistance. Can you possibly provide it for me?" Miss Northway quietly said, standing there in the doorway. She held out a hand towards the chambermaid. A necklace bejeweled with gleaming garnets dangled in her grasp. "For your discretion."

The maid, wide-eyed and speechless, simply nodded, set her broom against the doorframe and scurried over to the lady's doorway. She stole a glance in either direction, double checking the hallway for people, before she took the necklace and let herself be ushered in just before she shrieked and was promptly shushed.

"*Discretion*!" Miss Northway said, as she shut and locked the door behind them.

After all, she had to maintain her reputation as a lady.

TWENTY YEARS AGO

"If you stray to the edge of the forest, you will not be permitted to sleep. For every instance you've been insolent, you will find that sleep will become what you most desperately covet. Your mind will rot, and your body will cease to function as a result."

With every other word, the Governess focused on the face of each girl standing there in a row. Her chilly gaze rendered their faces red with shame. She stopped in front of the girl with the wild chestnut locks sprouting from her plaits, the very same girl who had been fixedly watching her pace. The girl's eyes were usually full of mirth and mischief, her cocky grin notorious amongst her peers, but when the Governess addressed her directly, she matched the woman's scowl with a defiant glint of her own.

Such girls needed much more than mere sleep deprivation. The Governess, however, had tried every disciplinary measure allowed. Nothing seemed to shake the insolent girl's resolve.

"Rose, is there something you wish to say?"

"No, Governess," said the girl, her grin narrowing into a smirk, "unless you define 'edge of the forest' as the point where the grass turns to weeds and the sun hides from its chores."

"You know where the barrier is," the Governess snapped. "You don't get to decide *where* it is, child. That area is determined by the Head of House, and if *any* of you girls leave the premises—"

Both the girl and her copper-haired, freckled companion standing beside her, cupped their hands over their mouths to smother their giggles.

The Governess slapped their hands down with a hard smack each.

But it was too late. The pair's tittering had spread its contagion. The giggling rippled though the line.

"Stop this wretched behavior!" barked the Governess. "Stop it right now!"

"Head of HOUSE!" shrieked the redhead. "It's a giant head... Just a HUGE head... floating by... bellowing orders!"

"Oh, floaty Head of House," her friend chanted, "kindly explain the barriers of the grounds for us lowly, loyal plebs. For we know not of what the Governess speaks!"

That tittering ripple grew into a tidal wave of girlish laughter, echoing throughout the halls of Everly House.

The Governess' expression went flat, her silence a warning that all of them instantly understood. The laughter ceased.

Before the two troublemakers could protest, the House Quartermaster handed the Governess her punishment tool of choice, one that caused the littlest ones to wet themselves and the middle girls to go grey all over.

The eldest ones, however, especially the mischievous pair, had grown acclimated to such forms of corporal punishment. It was no more than the promise of another day of abuse, the same as it ever was.

Before the girl with the chestnut braids could say another word, the Governess pulled at the girl's arm and struck her forearm sharply five times with the reed, leaving bright pink welts that teared red. Then the Governess did the same to the red-haired girl's forearm.

The duo had taught themselves a trick for bearing the pain, one that entailed further pain that served as a distraction, a hard bite to the inside of the cheek. That day, however, it hadn't worked well to distract from the searing agony of the welts.

<hr />

"I wish we could set her hair on fire," whispered Dahlia—the copper-haired girl—to her friend.

They had all settled down for the night, tucked in their beds in their sleeping quarters. Rose, the girl with the chestnut locks, pulled the blanket aside for her friend to join her, for the two had long since vowed never to let the other sleep alone when hurt.

Rose snickered. "She loves her hair," she whispered back. "Her head would be as bald as a crow's egg."

"*Any* egg."

"Yes, but crows are meaner."

A tiny voice piped in, cutting into the girls' secrecy. "You mustn't speak ill of the Governess, Dahlia."

"Eat a blade, Daisy," growled Dahlia.

There were audible gasps from across the room. Rose and Dahlia giggled at the sound and then grew silent once more. Dahlia squeezed her friend's hand and shifted around to face her.

"When are you taking me to see the Bear?" she whispered, ever so softly. Rose wiggled closer to hear her.

"We'll leave when the moon is ready," Rose whispered back, "and you'll learn that we *can* see our way in the dark."

⸻⬥⸻

The two girls reached the apex of the forest, their path illuminated by the blue glow of the moon. Rose led the way, her hand around her friend's.

The ramshackle cabin gave itself away, by the plume of black smoke blocking a section of starry sky. Its shadows spread an inky darkness over the grassy clearing. There was little light emanating from either of the cabin's windows, apart from an orange flicker that created cracks in the shadows, appearing, then disappearing.

Appearing. Then disappearing.

Rose pushed the door open and whispered, "Papa Clyde?"

The floorboards groaned in protest under heavy footsteps, announcing the arrival of a mountainous dark mass of a man that appeared before them. His wooly beard was streaked with grey, the hair on his head long and unkempt over his shoulders. He wore a union suit that had seen better days according to the mismatched sewn patches covering the holes.

"And who's this, little robin?"

Dahlia was anything but shy. She thrust a hand in the giant's direction. "Pleased to meet you, Mr. Bear, sir. My name's Dahlia."

The mountain man eyed the girl's hand before he let out a laugh from deep within his big belly, a roaring chortle that rattled the cabin's rickety frame. Just before he pulled Dahlia into a hug, he said, "You *are* a real lady of the house, aren't ya? Or are we having a gentlemen's agreement with the handshake?"

Dahlia, swallowed up in the giant's hug, croaked. "I'm not a lady!"

The giant let Dahlia go, laughing at her startled expression. "Well, if you're not a lady, what are you then?"

"I'm an Everly girl, and I wear that honor with the pride I'm afforded."

"They wouldn't have it any other way, Miss Dahlia."

Dahlia glanced skeptically at Rose, but her friend already plopped herself in front of the fire that was on its last legs, wilting to a small band of flames. Dahlia made herself comfortable beside Rose on the pitted wooden floor.

Rose finally piped in. "Papa Clyde used to be the stable master."

"I *know*," said Dahlia. "And they banished him."

"It's not like that, Dahlia. He left on his own. Oh, and don't call him 'Mr. Bear'. His name is Clyde."

"Oh, now. Whatever nickname keeps unwanted company away is welcomed by me. As for what happened at Everly House, that was a long time ago," said the giant. "I worked there when the elder Everlys lived at the house. Good people. Their sons didn't care much for me though, and when their parents left this world, and *their* sons and their families took charge of the house and its legacy... well..." He sat down in the rocking chair by the girls. "I didn't care for their methods of running the affairs that our countrymen expected of them. There were rules they'd not been keen to follow, so they created their own, and you know very well what came after. Didn't care much for that."

"Papa Clyde once gave an Everly boy a whipping for laughing at one of the girls who fell off a horse," Rose said. "That boy couldn't sit properly for weeks!" She snickered into her palm.

The giant shook his head disapprovingly at Rose. "There was nothing humorous about that incident, little robin. You know now their mark's been a blight on that house."

"Sorry, Papa Clyde."

He smiled and patted her head, a tender gesture that often signaled he accepted her apology. "And that was the last of my presence there," he murmured. "Now I live out my days here."

Rose then turned to Dahlia. "Whenever I'm here with Papa Clyde, I do everything we're not allowed at Everly House. I can throw axes and fish with my bare hands and—"

"You know all of that," Dahlia said. "Governess has us train and hunt and use axes—"

"Not so! We can cut wood and skin a rabbit, but we don't know how to—"

"We know EVERYTHING!" Dahlia shrieked. Red spackled her cheeks and neck. "We must be *grateful* to our House," she recited. "We are indebted because without our House, we have no purpose. Everly House gives us purpose!"

"But, Miss Dahlia," the giant said softly, "you've *always* had purpose. It's not for a house to decide what that may be."

By then, Dahlia's outburst had given way to tears. "They took us in when we had no one. Our own mothers and fathers didn't want us. We were left alone and hungry, and they gave us meals to soothe the anger in our bellies. They gave us beds where we can sleep in peace, and no one dares hurt us."

"Except Governess," Rose said. "And we're now burdened by our debts to Everly House—"

"Little robin, don't interrupt your friend. She needs to release her anger."

Dahlia shot up to her feet, fuming. "I'm NOT angry!" She faced Rose with her hands balled into fists. "You're just a plain girl who hides here with a big, ugly *bear* whenever her pride is punished." She then directed her anger back at the giant. "And you're just a wretched old man who's only company is a *girl*. What do you think Governess will do when she learns that one of her wards disobeys the covenant of purity and spends her nights with an old man in the woods?"

"Dahlia!" Rose wavered to her feet, eyes wide in shock. "Don't EVER speak to him that way. He's my friend!"

"*I'm* your friend! He's just a... a filthy man with vile intentions!"

Before Dahlia could say another word, Rose smacked her hard across the cheek. Dahlia gaped at Rose, her hand over the injured cheek. However, Rose wasn't finished. She grabbed Dahlia with one hand at her throat and started to squeeze.

"That's enough, robin."

Rose wasn't about to be deterred, though. Her other hand wrapped around Dahlia's neck, strangling the girl. Dahlia clawed frantically at Rose's hands.

Rose said through gritted teeth, "I would've taken my own life if Papa Clyde hadn't found me, starving and cold out in the woods. Governess did *that* to me."

"You were being punished for stealing food for the stable boys," Dahlia sputtered.

The giant pried Rose's hands away from Dahlia's throat and grabbed Rose around the middle, lifting her before turning and setting her down to create space between the girls. "If you use your anger for the wrong reasons, you know your way back through the woods, little robin," he said. He held her head between his big hands, keeping her gaze steady on his own. "I've taught you better than this."

It wasn't Rose who intended to leave. Dahlia tromped over to the door and opened it, and just before she headed into the night, she turned to glare at them and said, "She can do what she wants, but *I* won't be getting in trouble." She pointed at Rose. "*She'll* be sent to Northway House where the wicked girls go!" The giant seemed to just about say something in protest, but she held out a hand in his direction, palm out. "I can find my way back. That's what the stars are for."

With that, the red-haired girl left the two there in the smoky, little cabin. Rose looked sheepishly up at the giant, who moved around her to stoke the fire. She went over to him and hugged him from behind.

"I'm truly sorry, Papa Clyde."

"You should be apologizing to your friend. She feels betrayed, little robin. Remember what I've taught you. Betrayal breeds trouble and makes enemies out of friends."

"I know, but Dahlia's always angry about something. It's her way."

The giant turned to look at Rose, his deep brown eyes unreadable. The sudden absence of mirth was jarring. "Now you catch up to her out there, and the two of you reconcile before you reach the grounds. You cannot afford to be alone in this world."

"But I'm not alone! I have you!"

"I'm getting up in years, little robin. It won't be long before they send you out in open country, repairing men's souls and hearts, keeping them from their predictable acts of cruelty."

"It's my duty above all else," recited Rose, her gaze trailing off.

The giant ruffled the girl's hair. "It is indeed."

Before she left, she gave the giant one last hug, wrapping her arms tightly around his middle.

That would be the last time she saw him alive, her only protector.

Her only true friend.

———

It wasn't the chimes of the early breakfast bell that woke Dahlia from her slumber, mere days after the Governess had ordered the giant man's death. Dahlia opened her eyes at the sudden movement in her bed. She tried to move, but something bent low and pinned her down, trapping her arms and torso.

"You had him killed, didn't you?" Rose whispered, her breath hot against Dahlia's cheek.

Dahlia stopped squirming once she realized who had her pinned. "He's not your friend. He's just *vile*."

It was in that moment when Dahlia caught the flash of something in Rose's hand, the Bowie's blade, sharp and angry. Before Dahlia could scream, Rose stuffed a rag into Dahlia's mouth.

"They cut out his eyes, the windows to his soul." Rose scratched the tip of the blade up from the bottom of Dahlia's cheek to the corner of her eye. She then pulled the lower eyelid down using the blade's tip, poking the skin and tissue with it. A trickle of blood wiggled down Dahlia's cheek. "I wonder how you'll be without this eye. Not like you have a soul that'll fly away."

Dahlia squirmed, trying to twist about and force Rose off her. Rose shifted, scooting closer to Dahlia's neck. The sudden movement caused Rose's knees to dig down against each of Dahlia's arms.

"When I'm done with your eye, I'm going to cut up your pretty face," Rose said. "Everyone will know you're guilty of something terrible, but we won't tell them, will we?"

By the time Rose carved her way through one side of Dahlia's face, creating half a mask of raw meat, she became numb to the world. Her focus honed and savage, the rage blinded her as it had taken control. It took three adults—the Governess and a couple of brawny staff—to pull Rose off Dahlia and drag her away, as she kicked and screamed, slashing the knife at any convenient target within arm's length.

"I'll KILL YOU!" Dahlia shrieked.

The last words Rose heard before she blacked out from the hard blow to the side of her head were uttered by the Governess:

"To Northway House you go, *devil* child."

TWENTY YEARS LATER

"Mrs. Eldridge, I must say... absolutely divine," said Miss Northway, as she dabbed at the corners of her mouth with a napkin. "You have been a most gracious hostess, and the supper... Sublime."

Mrs. Eldridge blushed pink and pretty in the glow of the candlelight. "Oh, you are a dear. But it's not as if you'll get any kind of comparable sustenance while suffering the journey to Idlecreek. Stages are ghastly."

The Colonel chortled and reached over to squeeze his wife's hand. "You're still haunted by our journey here."

"Out there in no man's territory, eating nothing but dried provisions and tinned pork and beans. Nothing quite like nights of flatulence and foul language, sleeping on rocks, choking on dust." Mrs. Eldridge said with a shudder. "Men out in wide open spaces can be such awful creatures, forming their bond with the great wilderness, so rough and boorish."

"Caroline, come now!"

"Well, honestly..."

The lady in red laughed at her hosts' banter. "It's not that bad," she said between chuckles. "Besides, the Colonel has informed me we've a designated stop at a home station. That should keep us from having to spend an evening among the snakes and bandits."

"Oh, I'd forgotten about the snakes!" Mrs. Eldridge turned to her husband. "Do you remember the shotgun, the rude one with the mustache that looked like straw...? That rattlesnake stew of his..."

"Yes, yes! He'd not said a truthful word about it, not until *after* we'd eaten it!" The Colonel howled, patting the corners of his eyes with his napkin. "Insisted it was wild hare or something of the sort. And he never laughed. Like the humor had been sapped dry from him... but the stew! He'd laughed at us when he saw our expressions."

"Of horror. Expressions of horror," Mrs. Eldridge added.

Miss Northway's mouth curled at the ends. "Well?"

"Well, what now?" The Colonel said, stifling a stray burp behind his napkin.

"Was it any good?"

Mrs. Eldridge leaned in, her tone low, a twinkle in her eye. "It was *delicious*!"

"Like a prickly chicken stew," the Colonel added. "Tingled the tongue, but that may have been the peppers."

Mrs. Eldridge shuddered. "The *peppers*."

"Bowel hell for the remainder of our journey, the lot of us."

"Just ghastly. We won't be traveling by stage again," Mrs. Eldridge said.

"It gets better, my dear," the Colonel continued, settling back in his chair. "Miss Northway won't have anything of the like to regale her guests once settled in Idlecreek. However, the boy who'll be driving the stage told me the very same shotgun is joining them on their journey."

Mrs. Eldridge looked at him in disgust. "Dreadful man."

"Oh, he does what he does well. Good aim. Good eye."

"Beastly cook."

"Shush now. You'll worry our guest." He turned back to the lady in red. "Rest assured, Miss Northway, you'll be safe. Just don't eat anything suspect," he said with a nod and a knowing wink. "Although with any luck, you'll have a pleasant supper waiting upon your arrival at the home station. One can hope."

Once their little dinner party had ended, the lady in red made her way up the staircase to her floor. The corridor was eerily silent, a sign that something was certainly amiss, a shifting in the air that she readily recognized.

It was waiting there for her.

She crept down the hall, taking care to keep the weight of her steps from creaking the floorboards. When she reached the door to her room, she chided herself for being so foolishly unarmed, her usual weapons having been left in her luggage in the room. The garnet-adorned hairpin that held her updo's strays in place would have to suffice. She slid it out and then opened her handbag. The tiny bottle of venom she often carried on her person while out would finally be useful. She uncorked the bottle; dipped in the sharp end of the hairpin, swirling it around before she corked the bottle, and then dropped the bottle back in her handbag.

The soft glow of the room's gas lamp flickered once Miss Northway slipped inside. Only the shadows moved. She quietly set her handbag down on the chest of drawers. Her other hand gripped the hairpin, readying to strike.

Gunshots suddenly cracked the night open, the noise coming from outside the tavern across the road. Startled by the sound, she peered down from the window only to catch sight of a gang of brawlers in the middle of a violent altercation.

Just as she turned back around, Mrs. Crowley rushed her, having emerged from the wardrobe where she'd been hidden. The stocky woman clutched the bowie knife she'd confiscated from Miss Northway's belongings and swiped it, aiming for Miss Northway's face, but the lady in red was quicker, sidestepping the swings this way and that.

"You won't leave this place alive..."

The lady in red snapped to, grimacing, and grabbed Mrs. Crowley's arm. She yanked the woman in towards her and head-butted Mrs. Crowley so hard, the two women audibly gasped at the crack of searing pain, causing them to stagger backwards. Mrs. Crowley toppled and fell against the edge of the bed, while Miss

Northway wavered on her feet and grabbed at the window curtain, getting tangled up in it as she took a tumble, and the curtain and rod went down with her.

During the fray, the hairpin slipped from Miss Northway's fingers, so she crawled around the floor, searching for it, pushing the pile of curtain out of the way. Right when Mrs. Crowley had gathered herself up again, Miss Northway had given up looking for the hairpin. Instead, she reached for the rope tie back that had kept the curtain open. As soon she had it, she spun around and parried Mrs. Crowley's downswing of the blade, causing Mrs. Crowley to stab a floorboard instead. The Bowie blade, embedded there, refused to budge, and by the time it dawned on Mrs. Crowley that the knife would no longer be useful, she was already on her knees, allowing Miss Northway to swiftly wrap the tie back around Mrs. Crowley's neck.

The lady in red pulled on either end of the rope, one foot braced against Mrs. Crowley's back. The tie back garrote bit into the big woman's neck, strangling her as Miss Northway pulled with every ounce of strength she had. Mrs. Crowley flailed at the rope, her fingers plucking uselessly as she wheezed, desperate for air.

Miss Northway yanked Mrs. Crowley against her and whispered in her ear, "A bit insulted she sent a couple of simpletons to do me in. Just pathetic."

Mrs. Crowley's body sagged against Miss Northway who then slid back, letting the big woman's lifeless form thunk against the floor, her heavy head smacking the wood. In the corner on the floor, beside the dresser, something sparkled in the light. Miss Northway got herself together and went over to pick up the hairpin—

—just as Mrs. Crowley sat up, coughing, rubbing her neck.

Miss Northway spun around in a whirl of red satin and plunged the hairpin down into Mrs. Crowley's eye.

It took seconds for the big woman to slam back down, her eye dissolving in her skull until there was nothing left but a thimbleful of blood in the socket.

There, in the welcome silence of the room, the lady in red peered back out the window, glancing down at the commotion that still ensued below. There were only stragglers left, and she wondered which of them she could possibly bribe for yet another cleanup...

... and if she'd have to continue that sort of tediousness throughout the remainder of the night.

"Up and vanished. No one's seen her. Just a bad bit of business," the Colonel mused as he escorted Miss Northway to the stagecoach the next morning. "One of the staff mentioned she'd had a penchant for gambling, which might be motive. Owed debts. Had I known, I wouldn't have hired her to take Essie's place as head of housekeeping. She'd been in my employ for barely a fortnight."

Once they reached the stagecoach where the young, sunny-faced driver and the surly shotgun waited, the Colonel turned to Miss Northway. "This is where I leave you. I bid you safe journey, Miss Northway, and wish you all the best with your nuptials. If you ever tire of Idlecreek, you're always welcome here."

The driver wandered over as they shook hands. "Miss Northway, I'm guessin' by the finery and grace... May I take your bag?" he said.

"You take care of her, Mr. Evers. Limit your vulgarities and drink."

The driver's freckled face broke out in a wide grin. "That's all for the devil's kin, an' we ain't related. Anyways, we'll have her in Idlecreek tomorrow when the sun takes leave, rest assured, sir."

Miss Northway and the Colonel exchanged a final goodbye as the driver gave her bag to the shotgun, who cursed under his breath as he packed it in the boot.

"You'll be sharing the ride with a couple others. No hangers-on though, which will have our journey good and light. Watch your step, Miss Northway." The driver held out his hand for her as she stepped up into the coach.

"The Adlers will be our hosts for the evenin'. Good folk, if set in their ways. We'll be there before the storm hits. Don't you worry none," he said, as he shut the passenger door.

Miss Northway leaned out the window. "Storm?"

"When you're out there in wild country, you can smell a storm comin'. It weighs down the air somethin' awful." The kid cleared his throat, hesitating, and then softly said, "Ma'am, may I ask you somethin' that someone of your station might think too forward?"

"By all means."

"It's about your given name. Kinda odd for a lady of your standin'..."

———◆◇◆———

A tall, bespectacled woman in a simple dress and stiff stance, stood at the entrance of the manor house, an imposing structure that would've overshadowed Everly House. The carriage came to a halt beside her.

Rose went grey at the sight of the place and the woman who'd been waiting there. As soon as the woman locked eyes with hers, the woman's thin lips spread into a welcoming smile.

It wasn't the smile that eased Rose's anxiety, however. It was the skin around the woman's bright blue eyes, softened around the corners, revealing laugh lines around the edges. They were the eyes of a woman who loved deeply and true.

She helped Rose out of the carriage as a servant carried her belongings inside.

"Welcome to Northway House," the tall woman said. "Your destiny here is your own to shape, so..." She crouched down in front of Rose so they were eye-to-eye. "What is it you wish to be called?"

For the first time in all of her nine years, Rose realized what had been in her heart all along.

"Call me Clyde," she said.

The Night of El Maldito

BY RONALD KELLY

IT WAS THE SUMMER of 1884 when Death stalked the Triple-D.

Sam Dugan lost his first head of cattle – a white-faced Hereford bull from a strong bloodline – on a hot, moonlit night in June. He, his two sons, Trey and Bob, and several ranch hands awoke to the most godawful commotion. It was a horrible bellowing, brimming with agony and fear, from the south pasture; the sound of an animal being slaughtered, but while it was still alive and kicking.

By the time they pulled on their boots, grabbed their rifles, and saddled their horses, it had come to an end. An unnerving hush had fallen over the land. The Hereford had ceased his cries of torment and the other cattle stood about the broad pasture, frozen in silence. Nary a one stirred or uttered a sound. It was clear to see that something had spooked them into petrified immobility.

They rode to the outer boundary, near Shale Stone Creek, to find the bull scattered across the length of a half-acre. His massive, glassy-eyed head lay in one spot and his upper torso in another. The other half was never found, although grass – blood-stained and trampled flat – showed where the cow's lower spine and haunches had been dragged, across the creek, and into a stand of dense pines. The Dugan boys wanted to go in after it, but their father refused to let them. It was pitch dark in the grove and Sam feared they would tangle with something they couldn't handle. Something strong enough and mean enough to rip a two thousand pound bull into pieces.

Of course, it didn't end there. The following night, three head were dispatched just as violently as the first. These had been taken down swiftly, fast enough that the animals hadn't found time or opportunity to make a single sound. Come dusk of the next day, the cattleman had three hands riding the ranch's boundary. The moon was bright and full, as it had been the previous two nights. But no cow fell victim to the unknown predator. Instead, five miles away, a good sized grizzly had wandered down from the Tetons and had been torn asunder and partially devoured.

Then there was a long lull in the nightly attacks, until a month had passed and the Wyoming moon had passed its full cycle. Four head of prime Holstein and Angus died the first night, then six the next. On the third, only two had been slaughtered. But the critter had grown bold and jumped Luke Melford as he sat watch atop his dapple gray. The horse was unharmed, but Luke was nowhere to be found... well, most of him. Only a small piece of him remained. His right hand, still clutching his .44 Schofield with its cold fingers, lay near the edge of a watering hole. Three shots had been fired from the revolver, but two of the slugs were found deep in the earth; apparently discharged as the cowboy's twitching, severed hand acted out of reflex, rather than conscious will.

* * *

A month passed, again without incident. But Sam Dugan knew the calm would soon come to an end. He planned to drive four hundred head from Jackson Hole to Billings during the week of the next full moon. And a lot could happen in two hundred and eighty miles, especially if that murderous creature decided to stalk them along the way.

Sam sat in the library of the big house that he shared with his two sons, when a timid knock came from the door. He had been sitting there, mulling over his options, with a cigar and shot of Kentucky whiskey. He had about decided to wire a man he had heard lived in Greybull; a tracker of some notoriety named Timber Gray. It was said that he had hunted down and killed more mountain lions and bears than anyone in the territory. He had even tracked a pack of fifty timber wolves across the Bighorn Mountains the winter before last, of which he had bagged forty-nine. The only one that had eluded him was the ancient and legendary Old Clubfoot.

He was about to take pen in hand and write the missive, when the knock drew his attention. "Come in," he called.

When the door opened, he was surprised to find his cook, Mateo Delgado, standing there. The elderly Mexican man was grizzled and gray, well over seventy years in age. But, he could cook like an Amish grandmother; steak and chicken, beans, sourdough and cornbread, and gooseberry pie that a man would ride a far piece for. He was a treasure to have on a cattle drive, and when Dugan called for extra hands, he got his quota from the promise of Mateo's morning and evening meals alone.

"What is it?" asked the rancher. He sighed, returned his pen to its ink well, and regarded the old man with impatience.

"Pardon the interruption, Senior Dugan. But we must speak."

"Whatever about?"

Mateo's dark eyes narrowed. "About the beast."

Sam could tell by the man's demeanor that he was of a serious frame of mind. "Come in... and close the door behind you."

The cook did as requested. Soon, he stood before the rancher's big mahogany desk; the one that had come by train clear from St Louis. The old man's eyes lowered toward the blank piece of paper. "No need for you to seek help. I know what to do to stop this. You must simply trust me and do as I say."

"What do you know of this creature?" Sam's remark came more as a demand than a question. "Have you encountered its kind before? Across the border?"

Mateo nodded. "Many years ago, in Saltillo near the Rio Grande. Cattle and horses were taken and devoured... and women and children as well. I was a child then, a small niño, but I remembered the tales the old ones told. *El Maldito* they called it. The Accursed. A savage beast who sprang from the form of man when the luna was full and high. Full of fury and ceaseless hunger, cursed to roam for eternity."

Sam Dugan considered the man's words. He had heard such tales as well, but from his Irish grandmother. He recalled how she would sit before the hearth when he was a boy back in Boston and tell him of creatures in sweet Erin that changed by moonlight and hunted the moors. The one that had unsettled him most was a savage nobleman that reigned terror upon the Emerald Isle in the nineth century; a bestial tyrant known as *Arget Bethir*. The Silver Beast.

But the rancher was a good fifty years older than he had been back then, and such stories failed to hold as much credence as they once did. "Are you trying to tell me that a damn werewolf is eating my cattle?"

Mateo nodded. "Yes. And poor Señor Luke, too." A sly grin suddenly split his weathered face. "But we can end this and soon, for I know who the culprit is."

Sam regarded the cook with interest. "Really? How so?"

"There is a man in your outfit. One who hasn't been present during or after the slaughterings. In June, he was nowhere to be found when your hands found your prized bull torn into pieces. He failed to be among them. In July, he spent the weekend in town, drinking and whoring... or so he claimed. And the last time you and your men hunted the beast, where did its tracks lead you? Back to the Triple-D, vanishing in the yard between the corral and the bunkhouse."

Sam sat back in his leather-bound chair and contemplated what the old Mexican had told him. He also recalled the old Irish tales Nana Dugan had told him and began to wonder if there was some truth to it all. "And who do you suspect of being our killer?"

Mateo glanced out the side window of Dugan's study. The cowhands of the Triple-D were perched along the corral fence, hooting and hollering, as a lanky man attempted to bust a brown and white appaloosa pony. His gloved hand gripped the rope tightly, stubborn to not let go of the angry horse, bucking like a wild beast beneath him. He held fast and soon the animal was tamed and docile.

"Harley Tucker."

Sam Dugan couldn't help but laugh. "That old saddle tramp? Harley wouldn't hurt a fly. He's a good hand, especially with horses. And, you're right, I recall that I lambasted him something awful for not being around when the bull was killed. I just figured he was still in his bunk asleep while the others were out hunting the confounded beast."

"Ah, but remember? He was hired on at the end of May, just before all this began. Just came riding in out of nowhere on that buckskin roan of his. A wanderer with no ties or past to speak of."

Sam nodded. "I'm beginning to believe what you're telling me, Mateo, no matter how unthinkable it seems to be. And those tracks leading back to the Triple-D, would suggest that the critter might be someone right here on the ranch." He sat and thought about it for a long moment. "My nana once told me a creature like that is impossible to kill... except with silver."

The cook nodded. "Yes, but I can provide the means with which to destroy him." He reached to his belt and removed a large cooking spoon. "This was my dear madre's. It is made of pure silver. We will melt it down and cast a bullet or two. They should bring Tucker down with no trouble at all and you will be rid of this devourer of your herd for good."

"But we can't just walk out there and shoot him down in front of everybody. Even if we did it somewhere out of sight, word would get around. The judge in town doesn't give a damn about folklore and superstition. Killing a man in cold blood is a hanging offense, whether he's a shapeshifter or not."

"It can be done during the drive," suggested Mateo. "We will be well into the Yellowstone when the first full moon rises. Have him keep night watch on the far side of the herd, away from camp. Isolated from the others. So, who will do it? You?"

"No," said Sam. He flexed his right hand. It was stiff and knotted with arthritis. "It'll take nerve and a steady aim. My boy Trey will do it. He's about as cold-hearted as they get and he could plug a blow fly betwixt the eyes at twenty paces." Warily, he stared the old man in the eyes. Mateo stared back, unflinching. "You know, if you're wrong about this, we could all three hang for killing an innocent man."

"I know," replied the cook. "But he isn't, and we won't. And you'll not lose another head of cattle to that murderous demon."

<hr />

They were four days into the drive when the night – and the opportunity to act – presented itself.

As the evening shadows began to gather and Harley Tucker and several others were sent to their individual watch points, Sam Dugan and his eldest son met, out of earshot, behind the chuckwagon.

"Here," said Sam, digging a single bullet from his shirt pocket and laying it in Trey's palm. "Don't let anyone see you ride out. After you do it, take Tucker's gun and fire a few rounds. They'll hear the gunfire for sure, so there'll be no stopping them from heading out to find out what's going on. Your brother and I will stall them, give you time to make it back to camp. Then we'll all ride out together. When we find him, it'll look like he chased off rustlers and got hit with a parting shot. If we do this right, no one should be the wiser."

"I'll get it done," Trey told him. He loaded the bullet into his revolver and returned it to his holster. "I'm taking his horse, though, for my trouble. That's a prime piece of horseflesh, that buckskin of his."

"You leave that horse where it stands," his father told him. "I know you and Tucker have had words and that you don't give a damn about the man, but don't get cocky and greedy. Just do what needs to be done and get back here."

Trey grinned and nodded. Then he mounted his horse and headed off into the darkness, out of sight of the men around the campfire.

"I'll be riding out, too," came the voice of Mateo behind the rancher. Sam turned to find the old man swinging atop his gray mule. "But I will be back by morning, in time to cook breakfast."

"What are you up to?"

"I am going to pray," the Mexican told him. "Pray for that poor man's tortured soul. And I always do my best praying alone."

"Say one for me, while you're at it," Dugan told him.

The cook nodded, then spurring his mule, melded with the darkness of twilight.

———— ◆◇◆ ————

Trey came upon Harley Tucker quietly. He was surprised to find the cow-hand amid a copse of birch trees, standing next to the buckskin roan.

"Whatcha doing off your horse, Tucker?" he said aloud.

The lanky man was startled by his voice. Harley turned, his eyes suspicious.

"What are you doing out here?" He stared not at Trey's face, but at the gun in his hand.

"I've been sent to right a wrong. We know you're the one who's been killing our cattle. And the one who murdered Luke Melford, too."

"You're making a mistake," Harley said. He stepped away from his horse and faced Trey Dugan. "I'm not the one who did it."

"Well, my father and that old Mex cook seem to believe you are," said Trey. "Don't make no never mind to me. I'd just as soon shoot you than spit on you, for no good reason at all." He cocked the hammer of his Colt and took aim.

Desperation shown in Harley Tucker's eyes. "You do this and there'll be no saving you. You'll end up dead... or worse."

Trey shook his head and laughed. Then he pulled the trigger and put the silver slug three inches above the bridge of the cowhand's nose.

Harley fell backward and laid there in the tall grass, as dead as a snuffed candle. "That was easier than I figured," Trey said to himself. Following his father's instructions, he raised his revolver skyward and fired a couple of rounds. Afterwards, he swung down from his horse and walked over to the dead man. He shucked Tucker's sidearm from its holster and fired four shots into the darkness beyond the trees. Tossing the revolver to the ground, he turned and regarded the buckskin roan. "The old man be damned. I'm having this horse."

He mounted the animal and sat there for a moment, getting the feel of him. The roan was strong and true. *Yes, a mighty fine piece of horseflesh,* he thought to himself.

"Gotta ride back to campfor a while," he whispered. "But I'll be back for you. Tucker had no next of kin, so I'm claiming you for my own."

He was about to dismount, when a bank of clouds shifted with the wind. The horse snorted and grew skittish.

"Calm down, ol' boy," Trey said softly. He leaned forward and ran a hand soothingly along his neck.

He felt scars beneath the animal's hair.

As the clouds fell away and the moon revealed itself, full and bright, the horse beneath him began to tremble.

———◦———

As Sam Dugan expected, the gunshots roused the men from their bedrolls. It wasn't long before they had their mounts saddled, biting at the bit to ride.

"Let's not go off half-cocked now!" Sam told them. Worried, he looked over at his younger son. Bob Dugan simply shook his head and shrugged. *Where the hell is that boy of mine? He should've been here by now!*

He didn't have to wait very long to find out.

A deep growl rumbled out of the darkness, causing the cowhands to freeze in their tracks. Their horses stood tensely, nostrils flaring and eyes rolling in sudden fear.

"What the hell was that?" said a man named McLandry. He shucked a Winchester from his saddle and worked the lever.

It was at that moment that something moved swiftly across the earth from out of the night. All eyes were upon it as it rolled, scalp over stump, and ended up in the center of the campfire. From amid the flames, the slack-jawed face of Trey Dugan stared at them, glassy eyes full of terror and confusion.

Before they could react, the one responsible came tearing out of the darkness.

"Good God Almighty!" exclaimed the rancher. But the creature that was revealed by the glow of the fire had nothing whatsoever to do with the things of Heaven.

It was a horrible hybrid of horse and wolf. Thirty hands high from its twisted, iron shoes to the tips of its ears, and a good nine feet in length from chest to tail. Its limbs were thick and brawny, its back arched with the bones of its spine showing in stark relief through its coat of buckskin beige fur. The monster's massive head was long and slender. The wide-set eyes were dark and full of bestial fury... the muzzle bristling with jagged fangs, each as long and sharp as a Bowie knife. The bone and cartilage of the were-horse's hooves had split into four spiky claws, wickedly hooked and each tapering to a point like the edge of a broad axe.

Two cowboys standing at the boundary of the campsite could only gawk as the creature attacked. One was carved away, head and limbs careening in a shower of blood and gore as the deadly hooves flashed and flailed savagely. The thing's mouth widened, the jawbones crackling, as it bit into the throat of the second man, mangling flesh and muscle, pulverizing the bones of his neck, then casting him away like an abandoned rag doll.

The others frantically drew pistols and rifles and fired. However, the lead they expelled was impotent and of no consequence to the creature that barreled toward them. The wounds wept dark blood, spitting out slugs, then closed and healed. As the horse-critter reached them, gunmetal was mangled and flung away, leaving the men exposed and defenseless. Eight strong and strapping men were mowed down like wheat beneath the blade of a scythe. Soon, their bodies lay in heaps about the campsite; bones shattered and jutting, flesh and muscle torn asunder.

Bob Dugan screamed and turned to flee, but he got no more than six feet. The behemoth reared and brought its front hooves down, splitting flesh from the base of his skull to his tailbone. Fangs gripped the bloody column of his spine and shook the man violently until the chain of bones broke free. It flung the backbone into the darkness, leaving Bob no more than a flaccid husk near the front of the chuckwagon.

The boom of a scattergun split the night air. The side of the creature's head opened like a rotten melon, then immediately began to mend itself. It turned and grinned at Sam Dugan with jagged teeth, caked with shredded flesh and tatters of clothing. One of the incisors had impaled someone's eye during the fray. It stared at the rancher in accusation. Sam knew then that he should have never listened to the old cook. He would have gladly sacrificed his entire herd at that moment. Instead, it was him who would pay the price of atonement... with his life.

Mateo Delgado returned at daybreak.

As he slipped from the back of his mule and planted his feet on blood-soaked earth, he regarded the carnage. There was no shock or surprise on his ancient face at all, only a grave satisfaction.

A low moan drifted from a few feet away. He walked over and stood over the ruined body of Bob Dugan.

"Help me," the young man pleaded. His round face was bloody and etched in pain. "Please... do something."

Mateo smiled and nodded. He took a pepperbox pistol from beneath his vest and shot the man in the back of the head. He stared at the ugly black crater that ran down his back. "Spineless gringo."

He turned his eyes to the center of the campsite and found the one he expected to find. Harley Tucker's buckskin roan stood there, splattered with blood, shivering, its head hung earthward, as if in shame.

The old man walked to the chuckwagon and retrieved a bucket of tepid water and a sponge. Gently, he bathed the animal; washing away the crust of dried blood and bits of tissue and bone, soothing the horse's rattled nerves.

"Be easy, *afligido uno*," he whispered in soft tones. "I am here now. To care for and protect you. To guide you."

The horse's trembling muscles settled, and a calm came over the animal.

"Like your former master, I am a wanderer... a saddle tramp... roaming here, there, and yonder. Like you, I have no home. Mine was taken from me many years ago. My madre and padre, brothers and sisters... all slaughtered by those who oppressed us. Banditos, federales, the soldiers of Santa Anna. They caused me to fear, to weep countless tears of sorrow and loss. There was nothing strong enough or savage enough to oppose them." He dropped the sponge into the bloody water of the bucket and leaned forward, until his forehead rested against the forehead of the roan. "Until now."

The horses of the slain cowboys stood around the campsite, as though in reverence rather than fear. Mateo searched for the finest saddle of the bunch. He found it on Sam Dugan's chestnut bay. It was fancily-embossed and decorated with silver conchos, and fit the buckskin perfectly.

He gathered what gold and possessions he could find among the dead, then left them for the maggots and buzzards.

Mounting the roan, Mateo Delgado ran his aged hand through the creature's dark mane. The scars beneath the hair were hidden, but he felt them beneath his fingertips, and he nodded.

"Let us go home now, *el maldito*," he said, reigning the animal southward, toward the territories of Utah and Arizona, and the border just beyond. "Let us find the oppressors and deliver to them a taste of Hell. Let them fall to their knees and plead for mercy. Let them cower at the infernal fury of *Lobo de Caballo!*"

The Deviltry of Elemental Valence

BY EDWARD LEE

MARCH 15, 2000

It was a Parson's Model F144 power-trencher that Ryan Cooper climbed onto; no frills and no canopy, just four wheels, a seat, and 750 horses on the digging blade. Cooper, a wiry guy with tattoos and too many death-metal ballads in his head, lit a Winston and expertly jinked the cutter over the grave.

Fuck me six ways till Sunday, he thought. A norther was coming in; the air had teeth. But his boss at Horace B. Knowles Funeral Home has offered him under-the-table doubletime to do this job today. No taxes taken out.

Fuck.

That was righteous bucks. Four-hour job. And that meant...

A solid night of Johnny Black at the Ruff Stone on Metcalf and then a blow-job on Allens Avenue. Ryan cut a grin. *Fuck. Maybe two blow-jobs. The whores are always more desperate in the winter. Ten, fifteen bucks...*

Fuck. I'm there.

Those dizzy crackheads could smoke a pole like nobody's business.

Coop whistled Slayer's "South of Heaven" when he throttled the cutter down. He'd done this job long enough that he could sense depth. This plot was a "three-stacker," and Cooper's concern was top of the stack. He dug back and forth until the burial perimeter was thoroughly tilled, then he pulled a neutral steer, traversed the guttering trencher 180 degrees, and began to take out the earth with the scoop.

Biohazard, Pro-Pain, Machine Head, Vader– filled Coop's head; he dethrottled to idle for a smoke break when–

"Hi, there..."

Coop cast an intolerant glance down from the high seat. Looking back up at him was some gussied up fat guy, mid-fifties or thereabouts, dark suit and tie, Burberry overcoat that probably cost more than Coop earned in a month. He turned up a fruity smile.

"I see the transfer's right on time," the man said. "This is plot 64E-031537, I take it?"

"Yeah," Coop sniped back. "Some asshole paid fifteen grand to have the corpse moved to the west end with its own stone."

The visitor's bulbous face twitched. "Then I suppose that means I'm the 'asshole.'"

Cooper shrugged. It never occurred to him to apologize. *Fuck. You wanna drop fifteen large to move a stiff that's been in the ground since Prohibition? Knock yourself out.* "Family member, huh?"

Another fruity smile, belly sticking out like a bushel basket under the overcoat. "You could say that. You don't mind if I watch, do you? I'm Dr. Oleg Fichnik."

That's a name? Cooper wondered. *Did he say fishdick?*

"And I have a copy of my receipt from Mr. Knowles."

"Keep it," Coop said. "You wanna watch me move a stiff, that's okay by me." It was probably this guy's great grandpappy he was digging up, and the fat swish was here to make sure Coop really did the job. Lotta scandal in the grave business nowadays; Coop had taken a few kick-backs himself to dig a hole and cover it back up, sans casket. Resell the box, cremate the body, flush the ashes. Nobody knew.

He flicked his butt and got back to work, revving the Parson's engine and lowering the scoop on the back. In minutes he had expertly removed a perfect rectangle of earth and piled it at the foot of the plot.

Dr. Fichnik glanced intently into the hole.

"Keep your silk shirt on, professor," Coop said when he cut the engine and hopped off. His head thrummed with "Dead Skin Mask." He grabbed a shovel. "Any idea if the casket was metal or wood?"

"Veneered mahogany," the odd fat visitor replied. "The Brundage 'Serenity' series, guaranteed to be waterproof and to resist decomposition indefinitely. I have an original advertizement from the local newspaper of the time. Would you like to see it? It says guaranteed."

Coop chuckled smoke. "Good luck suing the manufacturer if they're wrong. Look, man, if the casket's intact, I pull it out by sway-bars, but if it's collapsed, then the regs say all I gotta do is scoop out the dirt, put it in a hopper, and then dump it in the new plot you bought."

"I...understand," Fichnik intoned, peering closer.

"Just wanted to prepare you," Cooper obliged. "You might not want to watch me scooping up a bunch of dirt full of your relative's bones."

"Don't worry about it," the doctor said. "Please, just...dig."

Coop barely heard him. He wanted this job *done* and his dick in *whore-mouth* ASAP; he could be digging up George Fucking Washington for all he cared. Now it was Legion of the Goat's, "Slain and Lain," a upbeat little number about necrophilia, in his head as he tested the skimmed grave with his shovel and did indeed find an intact coffin down there. *Suck my ass!* he thought. Now he'd have to pull the whole thing, which was a major kick in the cock. He'd have to hammer in the sway-bars and torque the blades closed. But...

All in a day's work at Swan Point Cemetery.

Out of my way, Fishdick, he thought, grabbing the tools and getting to it. Fichnik watched over his shoulder like an executive chef supervising his apprentices as Cooper hammered the bars down along the casket's side and torqued them up with a box wrench, more death metal beating behind his skull. It wasn't long before he'd hooked up the pull-chains and was lifting the casket out of the ground with the trencher's winch.

The engine chugged as the casket dangled.

"Put it down!" Fichnik shouted over the diesel noise.

Coop winced. "What?"

"Put it down! Please!"

Coop lowered the box and dethrottled. "What the fuck for?"

Dr. Fichnik sheepishly approached the trencher. "If you don't mind, young man, I'd like to open the casket."

Cooper lit another Winston. "Yeah, and I'd like to fill Gillian Anderson's belly-button with cum. But it ain't likely either'll happen."

"I merely would like to inspect the structural state of the cadaver before it's moved."

"Dream on, pal. I can't let you open the coffin. It's against the law without a warrant or an order from the medical examiner."

Like a card trick, a $100 bill appeared in Fichnik's fingers.

"Or a $100 bill," Coop amended. He snatched up the bill. *Whole lotta blow-jobs tonight,* he thought. Shit, with this kind of green he could rent a motel room and turn a bunch of junkies' cunts inside-out; they'd be walking bow-legged back to their pimps. *The fuck do I care? This turd-burglar wants to eyeball a skeleton, well...* He slipped the bill into his pocket. *Whatever tickles his stick.* "Here ya go, Rocky." Cooper passed the rotund man a crow bar.

"Really, I..."

"Oh, a long time since your last workout?"

"Well..."

"For another hundred, I'll open it for ya," Cooper was charitable enough to offer.

No objection was made as another $100 bill was purveyed. Cooper took it and hopped off the trencher. *Now we're talkin'.*

He wedged the crow-bar under the coffin's lid, leaned down.

No give at all.

Damned thing's shut tighter than a 12-year old's asshole, he thought as he grabbed his hammer, tapped the crowbar in deeper. One thing Coop knew about coffins was that their locking mechanisms were all different. *Come on, you little bitch...*

Fichnik seemed amused. "How's it coming...*Rocky?*"

How about I stick this crowbar up your ass, Liberace? Bet I'd pull out a bunch of used rubbers and a butt-plug or two. But Cooper, in spite of his overall societal hostility, would not be dissuaded. He moved the crowbar further down the lip, hammered it in, then stood on it.

He began to rock his full body weight against the bar.

"Be careful!" Fichnik exclaimed.

Shut up, Cooper thought. He began to bounce to the rhythm of Suicidal Tendencies "Waking the Dead." Carefully balanced with both feet on the bar, Coop bounced harder--

"Be care–"

CRACK!

Wood splintered. Decades' old locking teeth tore out of brass bolt slots.

The coffin's lid flew open, and–

Hoooo!

–Cooper plummeted. He landed hard on his back before the gravestone, then actually tumbled over once and fell directly into the opened grave.

Luminous stars burst before his eyes, an interesting accompaniment to the Suicidal song. It took a moment for him to retrieve the wind that had been knocked from his chest. When he finally managed to crawl up from the hole...

Dr. Fichnik was looking down into the casket, his wide back to Cooper.

"Oh...oh my," the man croaked.

"What is it, Dr. Fishdick?" Cooper asked, crawling out of the hole.

"I knew it. I knew it."

Cooper finally got to his knees in the surrounding mounds of dirt. He wasn't in the best of moods.

Fichnik quickly faced him, grabbed his shoulders. "I knew it," he whispered.

Cooper looked down into the opened coffin and saw--

<hr />

March 15, 1877

Brock's eyes squeezed shut as if pained. He felt his jism jump into the hot slot between the whore's wide-spread legs. His hips pounded the back of her buttocks almost violently. *No, oh no,* he thought. *Forgive me, Lord. I just can't help it...*

He came so hard the frame of the little jack bed nearly fell apart.

"Gracious, sugar," came a lilting voice. "That was fierce as if you ain't had a woman's company in a year..."

The whore's name was Mary, but then a lot of whores were named Mary, since the Magdalene was forgiven. This one was Brock's favorite–ample-bosomed and blond--with noon-blue eyes and a soft voice that made a man feel like he was with someone wholesome. Brock liked the appearance; it didn't matter that all five of Suttonville's trollops were little more than pretty spittoons for a man's need. A shot of Kansas whiskey and a Jennings Bryan half-dollar was all it took. Each of the girls had their own little sodhouse out behind the Short Branch saloon. Brock didn't want this type consorting in the public house, lest Suttonville gain the same reputation as Wichita, Ellsworth, or Dodge.

Brock was Suttonville's sheriff.

He struggled for breath. He left his cock stuffed up in her, let it limpen and eventually fall out. Then he collapsed to her bosom, exhausted.

She was exhausted too, from the frenetic working over he'd just given her. Three times in less than an hour. His cock hurt; he could only imagine how *she* felt.

But in his exhaustion, he shivered.

"You're not catchin' sick, are ya?"

"No," Brock mouthed into the hot skin between her breasts. Instead, he was simply horrified.

The little sodhouse stank: of sweat, sperm, and the daub of pig fat burning in the betty lamp. Her breath stank, too; her teeth had gone to rot. Yet Brock felt soothed as her long pretty fingers slid through his hair. "What'choo so pent up about, honey?"

Brock didn't answer–he just lay there on her sweat-slick flesh like a baby suckling. No, it wasn't any surge of lust that had brought him here (Brock routinely fucked at least every other day), it was diversion.

Brock needed to be distracted from the memory of what he'd seen this morning. The images shouted at him whenever he closed his eyes.

God in Heaven...

He wondered if he'd ever be able to sleep again.

"There's rumors goin' round," Mary posed.

"Oh yeah?"

"Virgil at the Short Branch said he saw you'n Clyde Nale bring in a dead man this morning in Clyde's wagon."

"It wasn't a dead man," Brock's voice grated back. "Doc says he's unconscious, in a coma."

"A– What's that?"

Brock couldn't get the strange man's face out of his head. "Never you mind. That's all fer the rumors?"

"Naw, somethin' about the Bowen Place. Virgil said he heard they was all kilt."

Brock squeezed his eyes shut hard.

She nudged him. "Well? Is it true?"

Then the rest of the images followed. Those people. The child.

And all the blood.

"Never you mind," Brock whispered.

———————◆———————

Back in his boots and buckskins, Sheriff Brock walked down Front Street, the high sun at his back. Several wagons owned by skinners sat hitched before the Short Branch, their owners hooting up a good day's work beyond the swing doors. Old Man Harding leisurely chewed a plug from his rocking chair in front of the Overland Telegraph office. Men strode in and out of the wainwright's shop, and the barreler's, the smith's. Children frolicked about the general store, rejoicing over fat sugarcones, pinafored girls working whirligigs and overalled boys spinning their teetotums in the earthen street, pretending to be gamblers. Dogs lolled in the sun; women bickered over lye and sorghum prices.

A nice normal town.

My town, Brock thought.

Since the Homestead Act, Suttonville had boomed from a typical cow town to a bustling trade point for the government and the treatied Indians. At first, Brock feared that all the extra commerce could turn Suttonville into another Dodge City, the Gomorrah of the Plains. Not even the hot guns like Earp and Masterton could keep a rein on that hell-hole. But this close to Fort Benteen, Suttonville kept its true face. Sure, Brock would get some trouble now and again, a little rustling, a bad lynching or two, a panner trying to pass pyrite as gold. There were plenty of Saturday night fights, too, but Brock had never had a problem handling any of it. Indeed, Suttonville was as fine a town as he could ever hope for.

Until this morning.

He'd seen his share of atrocity in his time. First, the War, of course. After his discharge, he'd worked for Pinkerton's, and there'd been that dock strike in Portsmouth. Five men hung upside-down from trammels, their bellies opened by a hay knife. The smell was extraordinary, and the way their innards looked lying on the floor defied description. Brock had also witnessed a number of lynching victims days after the event: bodies the size of cattle via gas distension. Then there was the time when Brock served as a Centralia deputy sheriff in the Missouri Territories; he discovered a range brothel where all the women had been branded to death. *Just for the hell of it,* Brock realized. They'd each been tied down, breasts and faces cooked off, red-hot pokers teased into vaginas and rectums. Brock stood appalled as the lingering stench of baked shit swept into his nostrils. *Madness...*

When he'd caught the men responsible–two escapees from Gallatin federal stockade–he'd gut-shot them both with his Winchester '73, let them lie there and caterwaul for an hour till they died.

All that...

But now this.

Brock had never seen *anything* like this.

All his life, he'd believed in God. Now he believed in the Devil. Only the Devil or one of his acolytes could have ministered to that which Brock witnessed at the Bowen Place this morning. One of Nale's boys had come to fetch him. When Brock had walked in...

The images assailed him again. He nearly collapsed to his knees in the street.

He couldn't think of it.

Should he go back to Mary and her sodhouse pungent with the malodor of old sperm? But if he did, how long would the reprise of distraction last? *Minutes,* he realized. Or perhaps he should go to the saloon and blanch his memory with whiskey. But he couldn't do that either, in case Doc called for him.

There was no escaping his memory...

No getting away from it. I have a job to do, and good people depending on me.

Dust rose behind his rawhide boots as he strode for the jail.

———◦———

The man he and Clyde Nale had found in the Bowen Place now lay perfectly still on the rope cot in the first jail cell.

Brock's vision seemed to shift as he peered in.

The man looked just plain...odd.

Brock got a chill–and an impression that he was looking at a corpse.

Almost as skinny as some of the men Brock had seen at Andersonville. Short hair and a long thin face. Trousers and shirt made of a funny-lookin' fabric that made Brock think of city folk.

"Still nothing," Doc Hall said, coming down the jail corridor. "No movement, and not a word."

Brock continued to gaze fixedly through the bars. "You sure he ain't dead?"

The lean doctor ran a finger through one of his great muttonchop sideburns. Perplexion drew runnels across his bald pate. "He blinks, and his heartbeat's normal. Normal respiratory expansion and pupillary dilation. It's the strangest case of catatonia I've ever seen."

Brock smirked at the doctor's lexicon. "Come on, Doc. All that fancy medical talk don't do me no good. What'cha reckon happened to him?"

"It's impossible to say, Sheriff. During my internship in Boston, we'd make weekly rounds at the sanatorium, to examine the most immoderate mental cases. Some of the elderly victims of what's known as dementia praecox would often lapse into comas–but nothing like this."

Brock smirked again. *WHAT? Dementia peacock?*

"The heart rate would plummet, autonomic responses would drop to practically nothing. What I'm trying to tell you is that, based on my examination, I can find no clinical reason for this man to be unconscious."

"And you say he could be in this here *coma–*"

"For years," Doc Hall answered.

"Years, huh? Well, I ain't got years and neither has justice." Brock looked Doc Hall square in the eye. "You and I both know that the man in that cell is the one who kilt the Bowens, and there ain't a judge in the entire country who'd see otherwise. There ain't gonna be no waitin' *years* for that skinny murderer to git what he deserves."

Hall raised a brow that might be considered a gesture of criticism. "You don't know that, Sheriff. And if ya want my medical opinion, I don't see how a man–'specially a man as slight as him–could've done those things to them people. Don't see how *any* man could."

Brock's memory drifted back to the scene he'd witnessed hours earlier when he'd walked into the Bowen house...

Chester Bowen–a well-respected farmer in his forties–lay sprawled on his back before the family's cherry wood hope chest. He was fully naked. From his mouth hung a long plume of some unidentifiable material, glistening wet. Doc Hall later ascertained that this "material" was Chester Bowen's innards: stomach, heart, lungs–everything. In addition, his sexual parts were not in evidence betwixt his legs. Ripped right out of his groin, it seemed. It was Clyde Nale who later noticed them in Bowen's own clawed hand.

Mrs. Bowen was worse–far worse. At first, neither Brock nor Clyde Nale could speak when they saw the perfectly clean skeleton settled in the corner by the pot-bellied stove. If it were Dora Bowen, she must've died months ago for that's how long it would take for a corpse to decompose so completely–yet Brock had greeted her himself just two days ago buying a trivet and some treenware at the general store. When Clyde had glanced behind the grinding quern...

That's when he'd run out of the house, shouting for God's protection.

Brock had taken a glance himself, and just gaped.

Two eyes sat atop a stagnant pile of flesh, something like a stretched face settled in the middle of the mass.

The shock and revulsion pinned Brock to the tabby-brick wall. He would've run out of there himself but...

The girl, he remembered. *The little girl...*

The Bowens had a daughter–Kelly Ann, not but six years old. Brock knew he was no man at all if he ran out now. *I've got to find her,* he vowed, even as his stomach convulsed. *She might still be alive...*

Brock found her in the loft.

She was not still alive.

She'd been splayed out naked on the floor, her breastless chest the hue of candle wax, her little legs parted so extremely that the hip joints must surely be dislocated or broken. Her small jaw, too, appeared dislocated as if pried apart in order to force something huge down her throat. And her privates--

Brock cut off the rest of the memory, biting his lip till he tasted blood, his eyes squeezed shut.

When he opened them again, he was looking back at the bizarre man unconscious in the jail cell.

What had Doc Hall been saying? *I don't see how a man-'specially a man as
slight as him-could've done those things to them people. Don't see how any man
could.*

"No, Doc, maybe not a typical man," Brock returned to the conversation. "But
how about a man in league with Lucifer?"

Doc Hall frowned but bid no comment.

"Come on, Doc. You saw them bodies. You saw what he done to 'em. It's the
Devil's work if there ever was." Brock jabbed a finger at the jail cell's motionless
occupant. "And that fella there? He's surely an acolyte of the Devil."

They sat up front in the sheriff's room, sipping coffee from tin cups, Brock
ringing the spittoon every few minutes. He knew Doc Hall wasn't pleased, just as
he knew the Constitution and the Bill of Rights were noble pieces of work which
granted that all men, 'cept niggrahs, was created equal and due certain inalienable
rights. Brock, in fact, believed that niggrahs was too, just like President Lincoln
had said, and he strongly disapproved of lynchings.

All men accused of a crime were entitled to a trial by a jury of their peers.

But not Devilers, Brock thought.

"If he doesn't come out of the coma," Doc Hall broke the silence, "then ya
don't have to worry about it. He'll starve to death by the time ya report it to the
governor's office. Ya only got to worry about a trial if he *does* come out of it. Just
as I was sayin' earlier, some comas last for years. But some only hours."

"Hours, huh?" Brock spat another plume of juice into the spittoon. "You
don't get it, do ya, Doc? I ain't sittin' here waitin' for him ta wake up. I'm just
waitin' for sundown. Coma or not, once it's dark, I'm ridin' him out to Tunstall
Gulch-" Brock raised his Colt Model 62, 44-40-"where I'll shoot him proper'n
leave him fer the buzzards."

"Ya can't do that, Sheriff," Hall warned. "It ain't right."

"Tell that to the Bowens. Tell that to that little girl."

"He deserves a fair trial!"

Brock rested back against his chair, his rawhide boots up on the desk. "He's a deviler, pure'n simple. Folks'd ask questions if there was a trial. That's why I got my deputy and some men buryin' the bodies right now. We'll say it was typhoid."

"But it *wasn't* typhoid!" Hall yelled.

But Brock yelled back, louder, "To give that man a fair trial, I'd have to ride clear to the Collier County seat to fetch a judge! And a trial like this? The town'd be cursed. Just like Salem! We'd never live down the rumors of deviltry. Folks'd move away, to California or down south. There'd be nothing left. We'd be a ghost town in a year!"

The two men stared each other down.

"So that's the story," Brock said more quietly. "Typhoid is what kilt the Bowens. And you'll verify it ta anyone who asks."

Hall simmered. "And if I don't?"

"If you don't, I call in the U.S. Marshals from Springfield. They'll be very interested in what'cha been doin' on the side. What's the word? Abortion? Same as killin' babies is the way the government sees it. Don't think I don't know about that, Doc."

Hall's face paled.

"Best we just stay friends'n you see things my way, huh?"

"Typhoid, yes," Hall muttered. "A family out in the hills, no chance of contagion to the rest of the town. Expeditious burial...was the only safe course of action."

Brock nodded, took another bite out of his plug. He set a bottle of sour mash on the desk and two glasses. "Now while I'm pourin' us a drink, why don't you go take a peek in on our guest? See if he's still in this coma're not."

Deviler, he thought

Kansas whiskey wasn't nothing like what they made in Kentucky and Tennessee, but it was good enough for Brock. He belted three neat shots in a row to help take some of the edge off of the day. Half drunk, he figured, was a fine state to be in when he wagoned his convict out to the Gulch and gut-shot him, watched him bleed out slow, *real* slow. In the War, Brock had seen many a man die in howling agony from gut-shots; they'd shriek in the field for hours. That's what Brock would do to this man. Then a final 44-40 shot to that gaunt face.

Job done. Justice served.

And God avenged.

Deviler...

There was no place in the Lord's domain, nor in Brock's town, for such an emissary of evil. Brock's gun would do God's work.

He was about to pour himself another shot when...

Holy–WHAT!

A smell, quite rich, drifted into the room. Brock's nose crinkled when he sniffed.

Smells like...shit...

And the smell was coming from the jail room.

Brock was up and striding across the floorboards, thoroughly addled. When he stepped into the hall and took another sniff, his suspicions were confirmed–doubly. The odor of fresh excrement slapped him in the face. "Hey, Doc!" he called out. "What's going on back here? That fella in the cell up'n shit hisself?"

This seemed the only logical explanation...but when Brock turned the corner and faced the jail hall, what he saw was not logical at all. It was insane.

It was deviltry.

Doc Hall's trousers had been ripped clean off, and he was being pressed face-first against the wall. What was pressing him, though, was a long, fat hoselike thing which had reached through the bars of the jail cell and had girded about the doctor's waist. Brock, in spite of his horror, knew what the *thing* was.

A demon's tail, he thought, staring.

The tail of a serpent from Hell.

He only saw it for a moment but a moment was enough. Doc Hall, in a second of deranged realization, looked over his trembling shoulder to glance helplessly at Brock.

But the doctor's eyeballs had already come unseated from their sockets. They dangled against his cheeks by nerves.

Hall's excrement was freely dropping from his anus to the floor, where a considerable pile had already amassed.

Brock had no choice but to conclude: *A-A-A demon's got its tail wrapped 'round the Doc's belly'n it's squeezin' all the shit out of him!*

In the next second, the tail constricted more tightly, and when no more feces could be squeezed out, out came the doctor's entire intestinal tract. And in the second after that, Hall was released, collapsing dead to the dusty floor as the tail withdrew back into the cell.

Brock's psyche shattered. He could not much calculate beyond the basics of observation. There was deviltry afoot, all right—just as he'd suspected—and he knew that when he looked into that cell, he would find a devil.

He drew his long Colt pistol, cocked the hammer. Then he stepped fully into the hallway and turned to face the first jail cell.

"My period of inactivity, quite aimlessly mis-diagnosed by the good doctor, was not an aspect of catatonia at all," a snide snippish voice told him. "It was instead a necessary component of sensory transfer based on, one, the limitations of the human body and, two, the accommodating time-effect of such a transfer of information."

Brock stood stock-still, staring in. He expected to find a demon in full incarnation: horns, fangs, taloned hands, and the great python-like tail. But all that faced him, standing now, was the thin oddly dressed man he'd locked up in there several hours ago.

Brock was speechless.

"My master is quite smarter than yours," the gaunt-faced man said next. "It's merely an assimilation of informational synergy as a form of resolute action. It's all transitive mathematics, in a sense, and elemental malleability. Identifying a transpositional point of valence is rather simple; it all boils down to the exploitation of a particular atom with the capacity of forming a single bond with hydrogen, which then allows a *transposition* of time with regard to a selected physical mass—such as a human body. Past, present, and future, then, are wielded as effectively as a juggler's pins. Do you understand?"

Brock did *not* understand. All he understood was that a devil stood in his midst. "Demon," he croaked. "Get thee behind me." Then he raised his Colt pistol.

The man in the cell smirked. "You're not listening. I've just told you that time can be manipulated. Hence, so can energy. See? Brainwaves function via energy, and that colloquial force we think of as human will is derived via the function of brainwaves." The man's shoulders shrugged. "Time travel, immortality, physical transfiguration–it's all elemental physics. If a proton ceases to move at the speed of light, the proton ceases to exist."

Brock's finger began to squeeze the trigger, but before the action could be completed, the pistol turned into something like black vapor, and had disappeared in a fraction of a second.

Then the cell's iron bars disappeared too.

Brock stuttered, "Yea, though I walk in the valley of death, I fear no..."

"What you perceive of as sorcery is actually only simple science," the prisoner said. "But all beings evolve at their own rate. You're right about one thing, however. Evil, though you pray not to fear it. It's the only one thing that's relative everywhere."

Brock swallowed hard.

"Evil," the man said. He stepped out of the cell. Brock wanted to run but now found himself completely immobile.

"God, save me," he prayed.

"Not God," the man said. "Yog-Sothoth."

———————◆———————

March 15, 2000

Cooper looked down into the opened coffin and saw–

The fuck?

–nothing.

The coffin was empty.

"It's true," Fichnik said. "It's all true."

Cooper was pissed; he didn't like not knowing what the fuck was going on. Empty coffin? Big money paid to move it? Where was the body?

H crawled up in the dirt. Hadn't Fichnik said he knew something about the deceased? Cooper, in his lackadaise, had forgotten the name of the decedent. He kneed back over to the stone, and began to push the machine-tilled dirt away from the base.

Dates began to appear in stark gothic numerals: 1890-1937.

Then he brushed more of the dirt away, and letters appeared: HOWARD PHIL--

But Fichnik's next outburst tore Cooper's attention away from the stone before he could read it all.

"It worked! It worked!"

Cooper stood up from the dirt and glared. "What are you talking about? There's a body missing from this box...and I got a funny feeling you know something about it. So start talking, or start getting your fat ass *kicked*."

"But of course, you don't understand," the portly man asserted. "He was the senior envoy of our plight. It's not a plight by *choice*. It's by design. Don't you see?"

"All I see," Cooper said, "is a fat twinkie about to get his cream filling knocked out of him."

Was it a sudden movement of cloud cover, or did Fichnik's face physically darken? "Your God seeks reverence. Ours merely seeks experience, the excitement of the spectacle of agony, of horror and despair—the human species at its truest. They'll be here soon, and they're using us to scout the land, so to speak."

Cooper cocked a funky brow.

"Our gods want to taste your world," Fichnik said, "...and we are the tongues."

"I'm calling Providence PD," Cooper assured. "Let them figure this out, ya fat whack."

"No, son," Fichnik said, casting a revered glance down to the opened grave. "All times, all places—that is our sojourn. The Old Ones were, the Old Ones are, the Old Ones shall be, not in the spaces we know but *between* them. It's all about this: the exploitation of a particular atom with the capacity of forming a single bond with hydrogen, which then allows a *transposition* of time with regard to a selected physical mass–such as a human body."

Cooper stared--

–and suddenly he was being strangled. Just as his breath ran out, he calculated what he'd seen. A great trunk-like thing had ejected from Fichnick's mouth and had wrapped around him, and now that same thing was slipping down to Cooper's waist.

No more death-metal rang in his head. Just death.

His final thought was that the trunk-like mass seemed like the tail of a demon. But as he died, vomiting and defecating his internal organs–and was then thrown into the opened casket–he realized it was more like a tentacle.

Old World Birds

BY DREW E. HUFF

SPARROWS WRITHED THROUGH HER guts as she opened the door for her next customer, birds squirming behind her corset, pecking at the corset's whalebone bars, always hungry. Always.

This one had auburn hair and reeked of whiskey.

"I paid. There more?"

Her mother tongue tainted each word of English, hardened the consonants, and slurred the softer letters, but still she spoke. "The barman's downstairs. Perhaps you'd like another lady?"

"I asked for you," he said, and stumbled closer. "Show me."

"I don't have any bread for them, sir."

"I brought some," he said.

Too eager, but better than nothing. The eager ones might hurt her. The disgusted ones paid, gawked, and left. She might touch them. Nobody dared to touch her. Only her birds, nestling in their bloodless cavity.

She pulled him into her room and shut the door behind them. An oil lamp burned on a battered roll-top desk. Her light hair swirled around her shoulders. Firelight gilded it. Stress lines aged her palms.

Undressing. Same clockwork motions.

He sat on her rickety cot and asked the same questions as the others. New World questions.

"Where are you from?"

"Far away. The Old World."

His gaze travelled down her pale thighs. "Have they always been there?"

"No."

"How long?"

She sighed. "You brought them bread? They adore it."

He had the blank eyes of a callow pup. She folded her day dress. Padded in front of him. Fumbled for her corset laces, found the end.

"The bread, sir?"

He blinked. "Oh. Yes."

She loosened the laces. He dug around a leather satchel on his hip. Something ripped in her chest. Hungry birds. They clawed each other.

Chitter-chitter-cheep—

"God in heaven," he said, face paling.

"Would you like your money back? The barman will return it. You may leave."

He swallowed audibly, shook his head, and handed her a hunk of bread wrapped in white cloth.

Chemise only. Fabric rippled.

Chitter-chitter-chitter.

She picked up a penknife from the desk and sliced open her thumb. Blood dribbled out, but the man sat, expression rapt.

"They'll like you," she said.

She daubed the bread in blood, crumbs pattering to the floor.

Chitter-cheep-cheep.

Grabbed the edge of her chemise. "You can touch them, sir."

Pulled it up and off.

Sparrows burst out of the long-ragged hole in her torso. They soared in circles around the room, dripping visceral fluid. Most remained. They surged within her. Hungry. Always hungry. She crumbled bloody bread between her fingers. Several birds lit on her arm. Lice swarmed and dropped onto her callused skin, caressing it in little itches. Oh yes. She indulged them for a half-second, and they bit, sucked, and glutted themselves on her, before burrowing underneath flesh. A tingle. Her body reabsorbed the lice, as always.

The young man gaped. He sat, stock-stiff, hands white-knuckling each other in his lap like an idiot schoolboy.

She thrust handfuls of crumbs into herself.

Birds flurried home. Frenzied in a dusted rush.

"God in heaven."

"God dwells as he chooses," she said. "Would you like to try?"

"Try?"

He wasn't as eager as he'd seemed. But harmless enough. He hadn't called her anything, or demanded to be touched, and he'd paid for that.

"So," she said, in a sweet, schoolteacher voice. "Would you like to feed the birds?"

It took coaxing, but he did.

He left without touching her. She went to bed, doing it herself. One hand stroked sparrows. The other crept lower. A teetotaler's cure for prairie-sickness.

They never asked for her name. Nobody ever did. She was only the Bird Lady.

———— ◦◯◦ ————

"Reckon you oughta go on the trail again?"

She looked up from her plate of boiled tongue. "Pardon?"

The barman polished another glass, underlip in his teeth, not looking at her. She hunched at the bar, over her breakfast and a mug of weak beer. Chatter hissed in the air. It smelled like varnish and spoiled, spilled alcohol. Early morning sunlight brightened the oiled paper windows.

"The McCartys think you oughta," he said.

Only two weeks here. They wanted her gone. Fine. This was better than that dusted ruin in Oklahoma, but not by much. What was the name again? Huntley? Harlon? Something with a soft h. Too many names to recall. Too many scrubbed lands under endless sky.

"Thank you, sir," she said.

"Mule still stabled at Earl's?"

"Should be. Why?"

He reddened. "I didn't have nothin' to do with it. You hear?"

She put her fork down. A sick *pulsepulsepulse* started in her ears. Her face burned. *Calm. Soft voice.* Birds rustled once. Then went still. She patted her stomach. *Good birds. Be calm.*

"Is it well?"

He didn't respond.

Her voice cracked, despite her best efforts. "T—they expect me to leave without a mule?"

"Want you to walk," he muttered.

"I can't."

"Sure you can. Just not for long, miss."

She stood. "Thank you, *sir.*"

"I told you, didn't have nothin' to do with it."

"I'll gather my things. I'm paid through," she said, "Keep the rest."

He moved the rag around the same glass. Over and over. Still not looking at her. She waited. The glass sparkled. He kept polishing.

Finally, she trudged upstairs, folded her few trinkets and money into a kerchief, and left.

Sun fried the land. Heat broiled the air. Too much sky. It hung over her like a guillotine. Dust clung to her shoes and billowed with each step down the lone road that cut through town. Bleak wooden structures squatted alongside it. Her nose stung. She blinked away tears. Bird Lady. The barman had wrapped a rag around his hand before he touched her used dishes.

It might've been a threat. An early warning. Perhaps the mule was fine.

She leaned behind a store, its boards long desiccated into splintered rot. Nobody in sight. Flat land. A dust cloud curled up on the horizon like a lover's hand.

She hitched her skirts up. Wormed a hand underneath her corset. Found the hole. Wet warmth. Muscle. Organs thrumming life. Feathers. Sharp little bird beaks. She opened her hand, closed it, and brought out a mostly dry sparrow. It chirped in protest.

"Go on. Find the mule," she said.

It fluttered once. Didn't fly.

"Blood for you if he's dead," she said. "And bread. Go find him, *rebenok.*"

It blinked. Flew off.

"Clever little thing, ain't he?"

Oh no someone saw—

She whirled, smoothing her skirts down. "The birds. I train them, sir."

"Do you?"

The man had a honey-smooth drawl, and a back twisted into ruin. He hunched by her, burly and half-groomed, bits of foreign lichen threaded through his patchy black beard, and adjusted his hat. Normal enough. The rest was lunacy. Dust-clotted rags clothed his arms and chest. Dried blood crusted his bare hands. New boots. Stained trousers. A leather pack rested on his hip. A flyspeck of blood dotted his cheek.

He grinned at her. "You like this place, ma'am?"

"I need to move on," she said.

"Wasn't the question. You like it?"

"No."

It felt too good coming out of her throat. "No. Beg pardon, sir, but what's your name?"

In the sky, a dark dot approached.

"Sometimes I git called Shiner," he said.

The sparrow lit on her hand, smearing blood. Blood beaded off its feathers. It chittered. *Happy. Blood. Dead.*

Dead. It hadn't been a threat. *Go walk into the desert, Bird Lady. Walk until you can't no more.*

She stuffed the sparrow back home.

"Lookin' real pale, ma'am," Shiner said. "Can I—"

"Do you have a horse? A wagon? I had a mule, but it's dead. I need to leave town."

He cocked his head. "You seen it die? Maybe it ain't dead."

"They killed it."

"I got a camp outside of town. Reckon I can fix it," he said, and wrinkled his nose. "But, I need somethin' from you."

She laughed, a harsh little twitter. "No wife, sir?"

"A man can't have wants?"

His callused grip strangled her arm. Squeezed once.

"What can you lose, Iliana?"

Iliana.

Her mouth went dry. "That's an old name."

"Yours. Ain't it?"

She pressed her lips together, nodded. He released her arm. Started scuttling off. Sweat glittered on his forehead.

Iliana. Such a nice name. Like a princess, or a bride, or anyone not plagued by sparrows. How long had it been? How did he know?

How does he taste?

Hungry. Always hungry.

She followed him into the desert wastes.

"Can you get hungry for a name?" Iliana asked.

He lay next to her, unwinding the cloth that was once a shirt. "Don't remember the one they christened me with."

Canvas tent enwombed them. Furs carpeted the floor. Heat and dust and the thick smell of whiskey swirled in the hot air. Heavy breathing. Dim light. She'd removed her brown day dress.

Outside, sky and land vied for dominion—flat brown expanse and merciless blue maw. Older things than either her or him. More permanent, marred occasionally by tufts of tumbleweed and sage grass, and clouds. A bowl of sky to fall into. Slip away.

Chitter-chitter-cheep.

She rubbed at her corset, felt thrashing between its whalebone bars. "Would you like to feed the birds?"

"They really try to put you outta town?"

He was down to the last layer, eyes half-lidded. He sat up. Turned away.

"It happens," she said.

"Eat 'em."

"Excuse me?"

"If I git your mule up and runnin', will you do somethin' for me?"

Always something with people. Perhaps he wanted a bird. So give him one. It'd wither and die within a week. *My God, when did I become so bitter?*

"What may I do?" Iliana asked.

The gnarled curve of his backbone twisted down, a column of crooked buttons. She caressed her hand down it. Soft skin. Warmth meeting warmth.

"Please," he said softly, "Please don't run."

He turned.

Knit flesh.

Same ragged mess of a torso as hers. But no birds. Skin twined into flesh-yarn, looped, and knotted into living fabric over the hole. Organs glistened through the weave. Stockinette stitch.

Touch. I hunger for touch.

Her breath caught. He froze.

So very hungry.

And the low sweet ache pulsed between her legs. Slickness. Heat. Her birds stilled.

She touched his weave of living flesh and groped at the waistband of his trousers.

"Can I?"

He caught her hand, placed it on herself. "Can *I?*"

"You came from the Old World?" Iliana breathed.

Rubbing. Rough callused fingers. Grit and blood under his nails. Pleasure—*oh yes oh yes he wants to touch ME ME not these damned birds HE IS touching me oh yes*—she pressed her lips against the blood spattered 'cross his cheek, tasted salt.

"I unravel," he said.

"Yes. You do."

Faster. She ground into his hand, white-hot, burning. *ME I am being touched*—

"No birds," he laughed, "Y'know I saw you from aways and I bought the fancy hat to impress you, Iliana."

"Say it again."

"Iliana."

They burned under hot canvas.

He eventually said, voice thick with sadness, "Ain't I a real man?"

She reached for him again. Met fabric. Only fabric. No bulge? No flesh?—

"Oh, Lord. Don't."

She let him pull away. "Show me."

"Only from the waist up, Miss Iliana."

His gaze chilled. "Check on that mule."

"But—"

"Might see you the next town over."

He'd hit his limit. Clearly. Of birds, of her, of Old World Iliana. Her face heated as she dressed. *I found someone like me and he still didn't want me.*

"Wasn't I good enough?"

"Better. I'm sorry," he said.

She was already halfway outside. Shiner watched her leave.

⸺◆⸺

The mule brayed as she neared.

Vultures ringed it, faces matted in gore. Reeked of sunbaked rot. A spavined shack canted, chickens scurrying around it. She cooed at the mule. It clomped over. No blood. Maggots dropped off it. No wounds. No screwworms, no rot. She combed vulture feathers out of its mane.

Rot in the air. Shit. Not mule dung. The Sun blared in a white-hot disk. Acid crept up her throat.

A woman in homespun guarded the shack. *The wife.* Raised her head. Thin lips set in a hard white line. She smothered a toddler into her skirts. Slowly dug a revolver out of her apron. It glittered in the sun.

No closer, she mouthed.

Fine by her. The vultures circled around something new. Iliana the Bird Lady saddled the mule. A dried circle of blood marred the ground, wider than a dinner table.

Something wet glistened in the sun.

Just to her right, a few paces off, something akin to rope—*rope, that damned stableman had rope and it got bloody when he killed my mule earlier*—but too smooth for rope, wasn't it? Not all of it red, so she mounted the mule and drove it closer to the gleaming rope pile—*the smell's worsening?*—nudging past two fat vultures and why oh why was there an eye in the pile of rope?

I unravel.

The stableman, Earl Garrett, lay unraveled in dust.

What remained of him laid rendered into obscenity.

Flesh rope, twined, thick around as her thumb. A retina joined the twist, beading rope with one eyeball. Organs knotted together, red, raw, all of it meaty and crawling with flies, feasting droning flies—*he's paler near the bottom of the pile because it started from the outside in*—but fine, fine, all of it fine—

Sparrows slipped out. Five clustered on her shoulder.

She gagged. *The smell.*

Flies tickled her face. *Go walk in the desert until you can't no more, Bird Lady.*

We'll kill your mule.

Not again they wouldn't. Time to move on. She smiled.

"Rebenok," she said, "Glut yourselves on blood, my darlings."

Sparrows joined vultures.

<hr/>

It only took a week before the warnings started.

The general store wouldn't take her money. The rest of the new town—*Showna, Shanla, something with an s*—followed suit. Pebbles stung her back as she walked down the street. She asked for the use of a local well and received silence. Everywhere, the tension. Energy like the uncertainty of a jammed shot. A traveling salesman paid her three times as much to feed the birds, his brow wrinkled.

He'd said, "They really ain't fond of you, are they, miss?"

"I won't be here long."

"Take this and leave. From a friend," he said, and overpaid.

Now she laid on another bed, scratching bedbugs, in another sun-bleached rotted place dying slowly. Touching herself. Hungry.

A knock.

Time to feed the birds. She padded over and opened the door.

"Oh!"

"Said I'd be back, Iliana."

Shiner was cleaner, and his shirt was no longer rags. He wrapped his arm around her waist. Leaned in. She stepped back. Maneuvered him through the d oor.

"Do somethin' for me," he said.

"You're a very vague man, sir."

"You would. I reckon. But that's it, ain't it? Can only reckon," he said, twisting his shirt in his hands. "Bodies are a hell of a thing."

She considered for a long moment. The Old World. Puberty. Birds, gestating and growing till they burst out, cawing. Blood-covered *rebenok*.

"They tried to kill me over mine," she finally said.

"Here? Now?"

"Feed the birds and I'll tell you."

His hand, warm and soft in hers. She led him to the cot.

"Thank you," she said, as he stripped his shirt.

"I'm sorry," he said.

Why? Why does he keep—

But he pressed his lips to her neck. Sweet honey warmth arced down, burned, burned low and deep—*lower, lower, Shiner*—and he trailed down. Mouth working.

Burning.

I will never be hungry again.

———◆◇◆———

You're a young girl, and you grow like a canker.

Sasha thinks you're getting fat. Where's your store, Iliana?

Birds and bursting open horror. Like fruit long-rotted, you split open. They lead you away gently when the Christendom fails. When the sparrows attack the priest. Dole the sad girl a repurposed shed, pray, and leave food. You grow into a woman-shaped monster. Your birds bring back scraps of marchpane for their Mama. You embroider, enwombed in make-believe safety until one night Sasha knocks on the shed—already married, his new wife already with child—rag wrapped around his hand so he doesn't take your *wrongness* home, and shows you the clearing in the forest where you're supposed to die. Shows you the sharpened knife. The silent wafers of Host.

Run, Iliana, he says.

Can't you halt them?

And all Sasha repeats is, *Run.*

You run.

In the dim oil-lamp light, Shiner rubbed a spot on his cheek. Swallowed.

"I'm sorry, Miss Iliana."

"It's in the past. I don't brood."

"Loved a girl. I showed her...me. When she saw, she spat on me. Sometimes—sometimes I scrub it 'til it bleeds," he whispered. "To git the feeling off. Her spit. It—"

Iliana kissed his knitted flesh. Her birds rustled. One of them lit on his calf.

He sighed. "I ain't talkin' 'bout that flesh. She ignored it."

"Your back?"

He fumbled with his trousers. Sweat formed along his upper lip.

"I can't make my body do everythin.' It's why I needed—why I need someone like us. Like you."

He slipped off his underclothes. "Please."

It wasn't quite a twin of her sex—too different, a thick reek of male—but more similar than she'd expected. A nub of flesh half as long as her finger, lurid pink. Swollen. It puffed out from under its hood. Coarse hair veiled the slit below it. Wet lips curled around the opening.

Low-pitched rasp. "Please, Iliana."

Oh. Thick air. Numb face. Her brain, working. She blinked.

Do I really care?

And all she could see were the wheat wafers of Host in their gilt box. Silent. Silent as she ran, and she'd never stopped running, had she?

God in heaven?

Heat and want. Shiner. The taste of him, the feel of his callused hands loving her.

"Love me," she said, and pressed into him.

He shuddered. She pecked his lips once, like one of her sparrows, and trailed down his weave of flesh, her lips and hands stroking him, tasting, enjoying. Warmth, wet and coiling in her innards.

"Does it feel—"

"Don't stop," he said.

God may do as He chooses, and I will do the same.

She kissed his nub. Sucked—*salt and sweat and skin, oh yes*—he moaned, a low rumbling moan. She played her usual parlor tricks, danced her tongue, and treasured the smooth silky nub of him, but different because *what if he didn't like them?* His hands laced behind her skull, pressed in, pressed her closer, yes—

(yes)

———◆◯◆———

In the dark, oil almost burned down. He embraced her under their blanket and murmured, "They're goin' to lynch me later tonight."

"Pardon?"

"You ever die before?"

She bit her lip. "I've lived a century and a half, Shiner. I shouldn't have. Old World flesh."

"Old World bodies."

"I quite like yours."

"I don't," he said, and heaved a sigh. "Iliana. Reckon I can ask you somethin'? I wasn't goin' to at first—I didn't think you'd—I didn't have the nerve to handle you rejectin' me. I'm sorry. Let me ask now."

Why can't we run?

But the question died in her throat. No. If it wasn't these townsfolk, it'd be others. No place would ever be safe.

"Tell me what to do, and I will do it," she said.

"How'd you feel about havin' a baby?"

She laughed. He didn't.

"Who'd ever want me to bear their child?"

He tsk-tsked, and he started talking. Death wasn't the end. Not always. There was a way. A way to unravel the mob. A way to form another body. He murmured about Odin, legends of the Tree of Life, the death and hanging, of metamorphosis.

"Yes," she finally said. "I'll do it."

———◦○◦———

Shiner was gone when she woke in the morning.

She didn't bother going outside.

Iliana dressed, sat on the edge of her bed, and waited. Something sick and metallic rang in her mouth. His smell clung to the sheets. She hugged them.

"*Rebenok,*" she said, caressing her sparrows. "We must stay hungry."

Chitter-chitter-cheep.

The knock.

The men dragged her out, and she didn't thrash. Didn't speak.

Thief, one of them said, and held up the trinkets they'd planted in her kerchief last night.

She nodded. They paraded her outside, sweat spreading under their arms, pellagra sores flaking around their mouths. Same malnourished men.

Shiner's body swayed on the gallows.

They left his clothes on. There's that, and the scream crescendoed up her throat—

Be calm. Good birds.

So limp. The black hood gathered flies, dark specks crawling over his hands, the ones that loved her and touched her—

A sob burst out.

Stay hungry.

They dragged her past the gallows. She didn't look back. Why give them the pleasure?

Nighttime.

Her cell had a pile of straw. She curled up on it.

A sheriff with a face charming as a boiled rattlesnake, and a goiter jutting from his throat guarded her. His dust-colored hair morphed to silver at his temples. He kept shoving hardtack through the bars, but Iliana shook her head. He threw in an apple. She ignored it.

Some man with a long grey face said she'd be hanged in the morning. More theft? Something about horse thieves? Murdering Earl Garrett? He droned like a mosquito breeding in bad water.

The sheriff led him out.

Chitter-chitter-cheep.

"Stay hungry," she said.

I unravel.

When the sheriff returned to gawk, she smiled at him. Her teeth gleamed.

"Would you like to feed the birds, sir?"

Chitter-chitter-cheep.

One of them fought out from under her corset.

"Ma'am?"

"They're very friendly, sir."

Chitter-chitter-cheep.

Gaze fixed on the birds, he slipped into the cell. "They soft?"

"Very soft."

Honey-sweet voice. Tilted head. She unpinned her hair.

"Come here," she commanded.

He did.

Think about Shiner. He needs this part.

Thrust-thrust-thrust, grunting and his fat old belly slopping as he thrust, *damn pig,* but she returned, wrapped her thighs around him, *My God, he probably tied the noose—*

Shiner.

She endured. The sheriff finished inside her. Warm tickle. Fluids dribbled down her thighs as she stood.

"Eat somethin,' miss," the sheriff said, fiddling his hands.

"I'm not hungry, sir."

Stay hungry.

——————◦◆◦——————

Thunder boomed over the dust. A bleak morning grayed without brightening. Static filled the pregnant air, and lightning gestated in the thunderheads, above the gallows they marched her towards.

Bird Lady.

Shiner's hand seemed to reach for her. Lividity purpled the tips of his fingers. Rot. An ache stabbed through her midsection. Hungry birds. Always her hungry birds. She and him. Old World flesh, too warped to exist here. Old World birds about to be hanged, hanging from their ropes, hungry and rotting and waiting for the New World to stop exterminating them—*because someday they had to*—because if they ran far enough, begged nicely enough, took the abuse—*we'll tolerate one Old World body, no more, God in Heaven*—maybe they could exist.

The long-faced man unfolded a black hood.

No.

Heat surged through her.

Unravel, my darling. He'd told her to sing. Sing for this part.

Iliana thickened her accent, "May I pray, sir?"

"Pray?"

"It's different in the Old World, I'm afraid. We don't kneel."

A terse look between him and the sheriff. The sheriff nodded, and released his grip on her wrists.

Chitter-chitter-cheep.

She'd laced her corset loose. Two sparrows squirmed out. The circle of towns-folk retreated a step. They wouldn't be walking soon. Three men carried re-volvers.

More sparrows. They flitted onto Shiner, chirping hellos.

She raised her arms to the blackening sky and *sang*—

Sing what, she'd asked Shiner, *Is it a spell? A prayer?*

The words don't matter. It's all feelin'.

And then?

He'd kissed her again. *Then, unravelling.*

—Singing in the Old World tongue, caterwauling to the heavens, throat raw and face stinging, the dusted faceless people backing away like she'd caught leprosy, because to them she *had,* but *damn it, she wasn't doing this AGAIN,* and her little sparrows, lovely little *rebenok,* gnawed at Shiner's noose with their sharp beaks, good birds, and maggots fell off his body.

Lightning flashed.

Birds exploded out of her. Somebody hissed, batting at the air.

Rope threads snapped under the weight. Sparrows attacked it.

Come here, come here, my Old World man, return!

Shiner's arm twitched.

Snap.

Dangling by a thread.

Return! Return and dance with me! Shiner!

Someone aimed a revolver at her—

CRACK!

Her ears rang. A sparrow fell dead. Blood dotted the ground.

Return with your love hands and voice and stubble, return and celebrate our flesh!

"Good Lord!"

Plunk.

Shiner hit the dust. It dirtied his shirt. *So limp, oh God what if it doesn't work— I will make it work.*

She continued. The body jerked. Then the elbow closed, moving like a rusty hinge. A man screamed. Blood-taste filled her mouth—*oh, they're eating after all.* A sparrow dug its beak into the sheriff's cheek, ripping. Delicious.

Shiner removed his black hood. He clambered to his feet. Swayed. Beckoned. Dead purple flesh rotted in patches. His neck couldn't straighten.

His lips split open as he grinned. "Iliana."

His voice was far-off, tinny, coming from the bottom of an invisible well.

The men backed away. She padded over to Shiner, wetness pooling between her thighs, pleasure, *oh yes oh yes,* and stopped singing.

"Shiner."

He extended his arm. Rot filled the air. "Shall we?"

She took his hand. Kissed him.

Putrid taste, but she slipped her tongue into him, slick and decayed, and it was still him, same motions, same soft rhythm. Energy. Heat curling down her thighs. He stripped. Ground himself into her.

Rain streamed down.

Throb. Throb.

He worked his hand into her almost-empty torso. "Your birds?"

"They'll come back."

"Unravel," he said, and rested his forehead against hers, his breath rattling out, "Focus."

Tickling warmth. A caress inside her. His knit flesh quivered—*touch me, yes, touch ME*—and no more Bird Lady, just him crooning *Iliana, Iliana.*

Screaming. One manic laugh.

A red, oozing line spiraled around their skins, fingertips to toes.

Silence.

Blood seeped through homespun weaves. Each face slackened. Life gone. Bleeding, pink muscle peeked through the slice line. They froze.

"Unravel."

Skin flew off in unbroken spirals like peeling apples. Went skyward. Coiled in mid-air, dancing. Cloth tore into strips. Muscle flayed open, floating with the rest, revealing pristine bone—*so white, so new*—and a keening sound split the air as bone cleaved into slices, flew up, orbited some unseen nexus, and wasn't it rather beautiful? Weren't they prettier this way?

Organs unraveled.

Floating, fleshy string. Peach-pale and pink and white and red—

Began twisting together. Braided into rope.

Flesh-twine pattered to the dust.

No sound but the soft rain. Thunder. Him.

"Did you?" Shiner asked.

"Yes," she said, and kissed him.

Yes.

His old body died. She let it.

Iliana's remaining sparrows roosted in her. Something else, too.

Iliana.

She found her mule, saddled it, and left the dead town.

She wasn't in the Old World anymore. The New World would be hers. And his.

And theirs.

Months later.

Hungry months, but she needed to eat more now. Iliana patted her corset. Her swollen feet ached.

She pursed her lips over the land deed. "I can do with it as I please?"

The man studied her. "Widow?"

"With a family. I like to farm, sir, and I don't hold with town life."

"You farm it, you git it."

Something moved in her, and it wasn't her birds. They were behaving right now.

"What a new world," she said.

Soft movement. Again.

Iliana, something inside her said. *Iliana.*

Shiner hadn't known whether he'd remember. Or if he'd look the same. *But still Old World, darlin', I'll still be me. I reckon,* he'd said, *I'll be a real man and that's that.*

You're a man to me, she'd said.

Will you help me?

Of course she would.

So she had.

Death and rebirth. Metamorphosis. All they had to do was wait a few decades. And Old World bodies had plenty of time.

Iliana felt Shiner quicken inside her, and she smiled.

Iliana.

I hear you.

Sedalia

BY DAVID J. SCHOW

DUE EAST OF NALGADAS Butte, Case could see dinosaurs silhouetted against a sunset the tint of a bruise. He snubbed his filter-less Camel against the instep of one boot and dropped it amid the scatter of dead butts at his feet. It smoldered cantankerously. He'd been standing for a long time, just watching.

As he watched, a Mamenchisaurus the length of two tractor trailer trucks eased up from relieving itself on the alkali hardpan. It switched a thirty-foot neck around to check its business, then promptly faded from view like a fuzzy TV image dissolving into static. The loose pyramid of million-year-old dinosaur shit remained completely corporeal. It was so real heat shimmer curled up from it. Case was accustomed to the stench. A professional, was Whitman Case.

While the big 'dine frizzed into vapor, a bug-eyed Coelophysis materialized not ten feet from where Case was loitering. The ostrich throat gulped in surprise as it attained solidity. It spotted Case, did a double-take like a cartoon character, and scampered away on spindly bird legs. It was the riotous color of an amoebic slide at an Iron Butterfly concert. It would be hungry for eggs or perhaps a bite-sized salamander, if it lasted long.

Good hunting, Case thought. He would not have tipped his hat even if he had been wearing one. Too damned hot.

If Whit Case resembled a Marlboro Man it was purely by accident; he felt as incongruous as the notion of a herd of ghost dinosaurs might have been, two years back. Nowadays people accepted the 'dines as part of the same world of betrayal, death and taxes as the one upon which they treadmilled the ole nine-to-fiver. Explanations for the phenomenon had not been instantly apparent, although a corral of academics fell all over themselves proposing theories. The sole halfway sensible explanation had been posited by a man named Seward, and he hadn't even been accredited. He told people why the 'dines had come back in simple language. All the rest had gone crazy with tabloid fever: Dinosaurs were skinks mutated by atomic radiation. From UFOs. From Russia. From Russian UFOs. They were automatons manufactured by corporations hungry to profit from mass panic. They were military biowar accidents.

They were almost overlooked in the mad dash for publicity. Case thought all the scholars and profs and degree chimps suffered from terminal vapor lock of the sphincter. Unlike the big momma 'dine that had just unleashed a megaton of extremely real — though antediluvian — reptile poop to the east of Nalgadas Butte. *A bilingual pun*, thought Case. *Christ, we've been hanging fire in one place so goddamn long the convolutions in my fucking brain are smoothing out.*

He wished he could be as smart as that Seward fella. Intelligent people probably weren't so bored all the time. He tapped out his next Camel. Nothing to do out here except wait, smoke, watch the sun ebb. Sentry the 'dines as they winked in and out, keep them grouped. Wait, smoke some more, cough, ask the drive mojo if they could press forward, onward with the dawn, and if the mojo said no again today, then wait some more, fuck your hand and try to make the day pass quickly so you could ask the mojo again tomorrow.

Aguilar had humped it up the geologic formation the drovers had named the Stirrup. Said he was searching for the limestone plateau where legend had it that a 'dine drover had scattered his mental marbles permanently by playing endless hands of twenty-one with the shade of Jack the Ripper, betting his soul or his life, Case had forgotten which. Aguilar had not stuck around camp, knowing that the mojo, whose name was Ernesto "Shack" Cocoberra, would just say no again today. So off he rode, without even asking.

Maybe Aguilar was going crazy waiting, too.

Droving had been a lost American craft until the 'dines had resurged. Who cared if they were totally real or not, so long as a profit might be turned from herding them?

The big beasts had rescued Case from the fallout of his third firebombed marriage and a coke habit which, fiscally speaking, had begun to resemble the jackpot of the state lottery on one of those days when nobody had picked the right numbers for awhile. He had not known how appealing a cold-turkey switchoff could be until his droving contract had been bonded. He'd been required to pass urine and blood tests, and had skinned past. Only just.

He had replaced the whoopee dust with Camels and contemplation. The hole left in him by Pearl never closed.

The hornet buzz of Aguilar's trailbike came razzing across the flats. Like Moses, he had come on down. Probably with no news of spirits. And at dawn Shack would gravely inform all hands that they had to stay right where they were for one more thrilling day.

If your honor was intact, the waiting wasn't so bad.

Case waited to swap the usual words with Aguilar. In about an hour there would be microwave chili and seven card stud, and a fire around which the oldest stories and the rawest jokes would be repeated one more time.

With a wet water balloon squeegee noise, a Triceratops pressed through into the real world, its golden disc eyes glazed from the transfer. It pawed dust and wandered off, making the earth tremble. Case sniffed the languid air. Nothing like fresh dino waft to hand-cancel your appetite.

Below, in the bowl of the valley, a thousand or so dinosaurs milled around in varying states of corporeality. Excreting. Mating. Waiting, like Case.

What started out as a *Time* Magazine cover screamer had become a growth industry. Case's current profession was a byproduct of the Sherlockian equations that had come out of that fella Seward's mind. And the happenstance that first set Seward to his brainwork had occurred at a rundown Texaco station in the middle of Riverside, California.

———————◆O◆———————

The best thing about Lloyd Lamed's antique pop machine was that it really kept the bottled soft drinks ice-cold. Lloyd had just taken a good swig off of his Dr. Pepper when the Tyrannosaurus Rex crushed his Texaco station. It jammed its grinning, leathery skull through the roof of the garage, nearly uprooting the entire building, and its confined thrashing took out louvered metal doors and cinderblock walls like toothpicks and cardboard. It kicked down the office. It wiped out the Ladies Room with its fat cable of tail.

Lloyd took three staggering backward steps away from the demolition, his dropped pop bottle disintegrating on the hot-topped drive. He never saw the pumps blow up because the devilish reptile snatched him high and segmented him with six-inch teeth. One swallow and most of Lloyd was gone. The fireball born of the exploding service station — two bays, four pumps and one hellacious overhead — billowed skyward, shoving the animal forward on a warm, concussive cushion. Its tail sent a fire hydrant spinning across the residential street. As it recoiled from the heat blast, it stomped on a canary yellow Corvette T-top parked at the curb, reducing it to a mashed tinfoil joke. A plume of water spewed twenty feet into the afternoon air. It bent over in a fashion never depicted in children's books and drank from the flow with a mottled crimson tongue.

Howie Raper, who had been larking on the crapper while Lloyd was stealing the Dr. Pepper from his own machine (Lloyd never paid and always used his key), lay buried from the waist down in a fall of shattered concrete, his left eye blinded by the flow of blood from his scalp. He was dying with his pants around his ankles. The vision flickered in his good eye long enough for him to witness the Rex's departure. It rampaged down the side street and into the twilight, away from the blaze, moving with huge, loping strides. Howie made one peculiar observation before he succumbed to smoke inhalation.

Jesus God, a purple dinosaur . . .

Here's Cal Worthington and his dog, Spot!

Seward's subconscious was obstinate. For some reason it kept repeating the seance. It was like a ride in Disneyland where each diorama of pirates or ghosts or whatever had its own tape loop, so as you rode past them in your little car you got an entire canned spiel in sequence. But if the ride broke down and you got stuck in one place, you'd keep hearing the same snippet over and over and . . .

"We call out to you now, Uncle Isaias, from our side of the veil. We are calling to you so that you may help us to contact the spirit of Murial MacKenna, dear, dear departed sister. Oh, Uncle Isaias, do you cleave with us this night? Can you heeeaaar me — ?"

When Seward thought of the robot playground that was Disneyland, he was able to fixate on the scam being perpetrated by the woman calling herself Madam Bathsheba Tyndall-Smythe. From behind draperies, an operative of Bathsheba's manned a video projector. Slanted beams bounced from mirror to mirror and recorded images manifested in the Madame's parlor as she held seance. It was taboo for her marks to leave the table. Breaking the circle of hands, she explained, would compel the visiting spirits to instantly depart. They sure as hell would, Seward thought. Worse, they might jump into fast-forward mode and embarrass the bereaved survivors.

Madame Bathsheba employed a Nubian to prevent customers from dashing through the key curtain in their grief. Seward employed a get-around he'd learned from a college pal who had been an All Star linebacker. As he liked to say, he "executed the reveal." The Nubian had almost executed Seward, trapping him inside a particularly stressful bear hug. But the hoax had been exposed.

The mirror gimmick was similar to an illusion Seward had seen in the late Unca Walt's Magic Kingdom. Actually, Unca Walt was supposedly freeze-dried in a cryonic fish tank somewhere, so he wasn't late, just postponed. Even after centuries of fakery, the best tricks were still done with mirrors. The glowering, turbaned sentry had turned out not to be a bona fide Nubian, either.

When Seward managed to slit his eyes, light, and inexplicably, sound flooded his head in a torrent. Fluorescent tubing, miles long and too brilliant. Linens so sterile they whisked away your breath. A mummy. A whipcord dude in a Stetson, stroking an American eagle. Banjo music going a few hundred RPMs too speedy. Seward lost his mental grip and tumbled back down to where the séance was still repeating. A woman's voice, soft and lugubrious, said *oh, I AM sorry mister (Seward didn't catch a name), but he's not out of it yet, poor man. Hm? It's major. Sorry.*

Mediums and necromancers of previous centuries had missed out on the advantages of video technology. Science, the so-called converse of the occult, had kept magic thriving by providing unscrupulous phonies with more efficient ways to bilk the gullible, almost as if some sort of gentleman's agreement existed between the fields of fraud and sorcery. The public was so eager to believe in the supernatural. They required very little prompting.

Well, now they'd *better* believe, Seward thought. Even if it puts me out of a job.

The good Dr. Falkenberg had taped up the damage done to Seward's ribs by the ersatz Nubian, and Seward got the usual admonishment on the physical hazards attendant to the profession of occult debunker. Falkenberg himself had begun to sound like a tape at Disneyland. Seward deposited the good faith check from Eloise MacKenna, sister of the dear, departed Muriel.

Next had come Marybeth's front porch.

He used his own set of keys to get in. The first thing she said to him had been: "Damn you, David Seward." It was her you-always-show-up-when-I'm-a-mess tone, which meant he could get his *own* drink while she polished off her af-ter-work shower. He knew his way around her five-room place. He poured a neat scotch and smiled at the thought of Marybeth in her terrycloth bathrobe. Her TV was on, playing to an empty room. As he emerged from the kitchen he caught the tail end of a very weird bulletin indeed.

Seward did not believe what he saw. It wasn't the first time.

He had abandoned Marybeth in the shower and run half a block toward Fareholm Drive when he realized he would need a car. He hurried back, scooped up his keys, and forced his aging radials to kiss the pavement with black stripes. Marybeth was still rinsing.

Just south of Sunset Boulevard the traffic had snarled on Fairfax. By then, he could see too well. He clambered onto the roof of his car to see better. He was so stunned by what he saw that he felt his body galvanized by an urban need long unexperienced: The need to have somebody in authority explain just what the hell was going on here.

Incoming automobiles had already closed off escape to the rear, the way litter piles up in a drainage grate after a storm. Seward leapt ungracefully from hood to trunk across a chaos of gridlocked cars. So few people yelled at him he almost forgot he was in Los Angeles.

Amid a clot of uniformed men on the sidewalk he spotted a major's gold oak leaves. He jostled closer through a riptide of gawking pedestrians and was three yards from enlightenment when the building wall folded down to bury them all.

His knees hit the sidewalk and he banged his forehead against a payphone carrel. Then a falling brick skinned his skull and severed his tie-lines with the real world.

. . . and his dog, Spot!

This time, Seward's eyes opened and did not deny the hospital room or the car commercial gibbering from the TV set. In an adjacent bed was the mummy, plastered limbs hanging from wires and slings. One eye was unbandaged. It moved from the TV to check Seward's status, caught him awake at last, and widened.

"Christ on a fudgsicle stick, boy, it's about time!" It was the major. It was partly the dogface brassiness of the voice, partly the eye, which Seward recognized because his job had always necessitated attention to minute detail. He remembered the major's eyes, watching the building come down to meet them.

"You've been out colder than a nun's punky for two days!"

This was verified by an RN who stopped by to make Seward swallow pink pills. He promised to marry her if she would bring more water. She was stocky, pretty, obviously fatigued.

Seward watched the major's visible eye follow the nurse out, and wondered whether the soldier's body cast could accommodate an erection. Then the major's eye came back to him.

"You need an update, am I right? Course I am." He let loose a chuckle that was more a cough. "Jeezus. You're gonna *love* this."

As he spoke, another Cal Worthington commercial screamed at them from the TV, assaulting their senses.

At the moment David Seward had been hastily introduced to various airborne portions of the law firm of Pratt, Bancroft, Keanau and Hudson in West Hollywood, Cal Worthington — southern California's emperor of automobiles — was busy down in Long Beach taping new commercials on behalf of movie insomniacs and potential customers up and down the entire Pacific Coast. All night, every night, on nearly every station, the worst Z-movie dregs and awful sitcom reruns the affiliates could get away with were punctuated by an endless barrage of ads for Worthington Ford, Worthington Dodge, Worthington Suzuki . . .

Time had marched. What once was Ralph Williams and his dog Storm was presently Cal and Spot. Cal's dumb gimmick was to feature a different Spot for each spot, so to speak. An eagle, a rhino, a shark at Sea World. Almost nobody remembered Storm the German shepherd anymore — except for old Firesign Theater fans — and as far as David Seward and millions of other co-Californians could recall, Cal had never stooped to using an actual dog. Something had been lost. Time had marched, and today Cal Worthington was Numero Uno.

His specialty was gang-buying leftover commercial airtime in the midnight-to-six leg, when the excitement of local TV slowed down a bit. If your set was on, you couldn't miss him, and cable had opened up whole new vistas for Cal to conquer.

The gangly car huckster had just hung a seven-foot boa constrictor around his neck when the Gorgosaurus rampaged in from frame left, flipping Hyundais and Daihatsus out of its path like cardboard boxes. Spot the boa panicked — maybe its reaction was racial — and slithered tight. Cal's eyes bugged. He took a header, clawing at the snake and hollering. The Gorgosaur flattened a Chevy Luv and spooned up its prey — cowboy hat, serpent, purple face and all. The audio track laid down the crunch of bones. Cal's final words were *keep shooting*. His cameraman, a UCLA film school grad, held bravely while his crew fled. Footage such as this could make him a star, he thought right up to the moment he died.

———◆○◆———

The mummified major was lecturing.

"Even small-fry artillery pulls their plugs, but what a friggin mess. Each one weighs *how* many tons? How much stinky, rotten goop all over the billboards and sidewalks if you blow them to hell? The sanitation crews threatened to strike right away. Yecch. You saw Fairfax Avenue."

Seward remembered.

He had watched a dreamy *banzai* wash along at strolling pace, its constituents nothing like the puppets of numberless Ray Harryhausen dino-operas, or flaccid iguanas in cosmetic jazz, or the honorable Godzilla. These monsters glistened and stank; bugs swarmed about them in clouds, riding the sour humidity of their advance. Thousands of beasts, walking north, massy and muscular, their shuffling strides emphasizing the sheer tonnage of living meat in locomotion, their metallic eyes afire with motility and hot, urgent life.

They were contrary to civilization. Their gigantism made them destructive quite apart from malice. Awkwardly they tipped over trucks and swept down streetlamps with their thick, switching tails. They blundered into each other, then backed into storefronts, demolishing them. Utterly unnoticed in the commotion, the odd screaming pedestrian got mashed into paté.

On the roof of his car, Seward had been transfixed by the shocking colors. The discordant clash of berserk pigmentation thoroughly contradicted the ho-hum deductions of decades of textbooks. The dinosaurs were vividly hued, bizarre, ultimately shocking.

The great industrial clockwork that was Los Angeles failed to command respect from these former tenants. The temblors of their footsteps pulverized the concrete; their basic hungers redefined highly-evolved citizenry as junk food. The crowding turned violent when an Allosaurus was gored by a Styracosaur the size of a Patton tank. The shrieking carnivore rolled through the entrance to a supermarket, taking out girders like jackstraws and shattering tons of glass. Its insufficient claws pawing for the puncture in its belly, the Allosaur's every thrash took lives. Gawking shoppers were summarily dismembered or squashed. The Styracosaur rattled its fringe of horns, agitating the flies that had come for blood. The rhinoceros-like forward horn was obscenely red and jutting, an up-thrust wet tusk. The east wall of the building was shrugged off by the thirty-ton Brachiosaurus walking through it. Its swanlike neck paid out like a vast orange ruler incremented in crimson hashmarks. The cutlass teeth of the Allosaur glinted off the supermarket fluorescents as it continued to die. In the parking lot, several tall, ostrich-looking reptiles nibbled at the tops of palm trees nurtured in this modern-day photochemical atmosphere, found the taste of the flowers brackish, and sent the trees plummeting down. Overhead, demoniac black shapes rode the thermals on wings of skin. An immense American flag tore loose from its mooring atop an insurance building and came drifting down, an undulating leaf of clashing colors, falling, falling.

In Seward's memory the descent of the football-field sized flag seemed the most terrible thing of all. The start flag for the apocalypse, perhaps. He saw billions of reptiles blacking out the concept of countries, casting entire continents into their shadow. This was no Army experiment gone haywire. This might be the end.

After being awakened by the comedy of the late Mr. Cal Worthington, Seward digested what the Major told him about the coming of the dinosaurs . . . and how they began to disappear as fast as they materialized.

"Tank crew zeroed in on a biggie," he said. "Poof — that dinosaur frizzed into static. They showed the tape on the news, slo-mo, instant replay and all that. You know when your cable service goes on the blink? Looked just like that. A monster the size of a construction crane just zapped into a cloud of blue-green vapor and swam away on the westerlies. And bam, bam, bam, there were dinosaurs appearing one second and disappearing a few minutes later, like they'd established some kinda beachhead but couldn't hold, you know? Well, militarily speaking, our problem shrank like a gonad in formaldehyde. For a second there it looked like this was going to be a disaster for property values, and now and again somebody got chewed up or squished."

The major's drone blended with the TV, and Seward let the medication sweep him away for a bit. An ebony shape with hungry bronze eyes scudded past their eighth floor window. He fell into a natural sleep and dreamed again of Disneyland.

<hr />

Aguilar had had himself a revelation up there on the Stirrup, or so he kept broadly hinting to Case. He squinted toward the valley of the 'dines, ciggie dangling from his sunburnt lips, an intense expression plastered across his face a hair too obviously. Aguilar rolled his own; the stench was similar to smoldering balsa wood.

"Nope. Just can't see him yet."

Case decided to humor him. "Moses, with a new, improved tablet?" He frowned. "Brontosaurus, green mottles, black saddle, alternating red and green on the tail. Black tail tip. You talk to the Shack?"

"What for?" Case dropped into his overblown imitation of Shack Cocoberra's chili pepper accent: "Chak, he say, pardone señor, we don't go no place today neether." Smoke and lees from the tepid tea in his thermos had congealed into an unlovely paste at the back of his palate. He coughed and spat uselessly. "I'm beginning to think he just wants to rack up overtime, is what I think."

"Naw. Shack's honest, at least."

"Overeducated, too." Case knew Shack's accent was mostly for atmosphere in the drive.

"Besides, it ain't worth it." Aguilar had made the argument before; this would not be the last time. "Easier to finish out, contract a new drive, get the sign-on fee upfront. When the drives move quicker he gets a faster turnaround on the fees."

"Yeah. Shack's honest." Mojos for authorized drives had to be licensed. In the beginning the licensing was akin to an emergency teaching credential, but the regs had been strengthened with the new administration. Taxes and prices always went up; wages chased but never caught them; with each preordained election came new rules. Always. These were the only facts of life with no ceiling. Today, mojos were just part of the paperwork.

"See Jack the Ripper?" Case said.

"What?"

"On the mountain top. Playing cards. Who told you to look for the green and black bronto?" Neither man could get his mouth around calling such a creature an Apatosaurus, which seemed just too-too.

"I saw it in a vision." Aguilar had been chewing peyote again. Case realized he was smoking the fetid, crematory hand-rolleds to deaden the smell of the buttons on his breath. Still dope-conscious but curious, Case had tried it with him once. It had tasted like turd-flavored Sen-Sen.

A Dimetrodon snapped to, displacing air with a pop. Case thought of a flashgun in reverse. The paper lantern struts of its spine rattled and the webwork of translucent hide refracted the setting sun into an instant rainbow before the two startled drovers.

"Dammit," said Case. "I wish they wouldn't come in so goddamn close." The big dinosaur belched and tromped away on skinny, bent legs, defying gravity.

"That's why we be here, amigo," Aguilar grinned. "Keep 'em off the expressways." Dinosaur gridlock was still an occasional problem.

"What about the green and black one — the one your vision said you were supposed to look for?"

"Just supposed to *find* him; that's it."

"And all will be revealed unto us . . . "

"Don't make fun." Aguilar's face went dead serious so fast it was hilarious. He could get religion at the most bone-tickling times.

Case felt too centered to argue. "Whoa, me friend," he said. And it *was* good — the view, the time of day, a smoke and a partner and breathing space and a dash of peace of mind. Wasn't that what all the Suits cried the blues for lacking?

In his lifetime Whitman Case had bailed out of a flaming bomber, survived seven serious auto accidents and three broken limbs, weathered eight muggings or robberies (two at gunpoint; another two during which he'd gotten the drop and walked away unrobbed), killed four men that he knew of in combat, missed catching a plane that subsequently crashed near Elkins Air Force Base due to pilot error, and nearly drowned once by getting his ankle tangled in a rope while white-water rafting down the Colorado. He had lowered his cholesterol and raised his fiber intake. He had lived through two surgeries — tonsils, and a detached cornea at forty-five. He had duly earned and spent several million American dollars, fathered no children, and married three times, beyond which he had "seriously" cohabited with seven women, not counting Iris, who was as crazy as a dung beetle in a hubcap, and counting Pearl, whom he still thought of every single day. He had smoked maybe five zillion cigarettes and tipped back an oil freighter or so of coffee, black. He had lived drunk and sober, rational and pissed off beyond sanity, benevolently then selfishly, and did not believe in supernatural deities. Ever since he had first seen a dinosaur picture book as a child he had trusted in what the scientists had said.

To wit: dinosaurs and human beings did not live at the same time. Despite all those great movies on Channel 11, the ones broken up by all the Cal Worthington commercials.

He recalled being saddened because it meant poor old humankind had missed the chance to know what thunder lizards *really* looked like. And that had turned out to be wrong, too.

Case would never forget the day he had found differently. It was one of those calendar junctures people commonly stored, like the JFK shooting or the Apollo moon touchdown or that time the space shuttle blew all to hell.

He remembered, without a smile, and when he remembered there was no need to ask whether Whitman Case believed in God, friend.

—————◄○►—————

"It took folks about twenty-four hours to learn how to stay out of their way," said the Major, meaning dinosaurs that materialized spontaneously. "Some say that the air ripples, just before. But once they got on the news, when they weren't knocking over buildings or eating people anymore, they were a huge hit. Some guy found out they'll eat dog food.

He got corporate endorsements. They'll eat garbage, hell, they'll eat crap we wouldn't touch for landfill. They shit all over everything. If they have enough time before they wink out, they build nests and lay eggs. Sometimes they eat each other, which is pretty funny when your lunch vanishes into thin air right when you bite." The Major chuckled self-consciously. "Nobody *cares* where they came from. They're famous."

"They're ghosts," said Seward. He did not look over from his bed. The quiet utterance made the Major's statistical monologue seem trivial. His unbandaged eye swiveled to. "Say again?"

"Ghosts." Seward watched the television, not seeing its ceaseless silliness.

He was reasonably sure the Major might ring for the nurse. Boy's finally tipped over, he'd say. Concussion has scattered his dice.

"How do you figure that?" The Major was honestly curious, not placating.

"They're *actual* ghosts. Shades. They emanate from places of the dead. *Their* dead, their graveyards. Remember all the dinosaurs headed north, up Fairfax? They were coming out of Hancock Park. They were materializing at the La Brea Tar Pits."

"Ain't no dinosaurs in the La Brea Tar Pits." The major was a local, and had toured the Paige Museum. "Just mammals. Mastodons. Sloths. Dire wolves. No dinosaurs."

"The fossil deposits and museum exhibits originated deep within the alluvial layers we now plumb for fossil fuel. Not from the pits, my good Major; they're coming out of the tar itself, which means they're also coming out of the oil wells and petroleum refineries, which *also* means they're coming from the plastics factories and whiskey distilleries and any plant that presses vinyl." His voice hitched down to a murmur in the extremely clean room, while logic forged links. "Even the air is full of petrochemicals, hydrocarbons. Supernaturally, it makes good sense spirits are literally coalescing out of thin air. Ghosts have been known to appear from thin air, you know."

Given that the dinosaurs were real, no foolin', then Seward's mind was magnetized toward the only sensible explanation . . . even though it was polarized against his life's calling.

And if they came out of plastic, that meant they were coming out of compact discs and cappuccino makers and toy stores and Gucci shoppes, and even that machine at the Griffith Observatory that injection-molded you a souvenir rocketship for fifty cents.

"Real, live ghosts." The Major pretended to chew it over. His mind naturally sought a logistical panacea. "So . . . how many dinosaurs would that be, then? T otal."

"How many centuries did the dinosaurs run the planet?" Seward asked back. "How long was the Mesozoic Era alone, ninety million years? Don't ask me what the lifespan of the average thunder lizard was, even given the bad living conditions and all. How many dinosaurs do you suppose could have been born in ninety million years? The human race has barely topped off its first million, and just look at us. All those dead dinosaurs, all back at the same time. All our smog is just calling back to its roots. Just think what it must be like in the OPEC countries right now."

The Major grinned. Patriotically.

Seward tried to find sleep; his mind, rest. He had a dream, not a nightmare, of ghost dinosaurs randomly popping up in Disneyland, where there were mechanical dinosaurs. His dreaming mind wondered if they would fight, already knowing which side would win.

All those dinosaurs. Where would we put them?

More than the end of the world, Americans dislike inconvenience. Accommodations would have to be made. Seward slept on it.

———◇———

In the 1980s the theory was advanced that dinosaurs had demonstrated herding behavior, and a pile of paintings were done depicting that which had never been considered before. The paleontologist who had posited this theory was among the stampede of idea guys seeking the government's ear. Grants and endowments awaited those whose unsolicited assistance proved useful in a time of crisis. Once it was realized that the ghost dinosaurs were easily herded, and would follow each other straight out of whatever American metropolis they were clogging up, Whitman Case found himself a new job: Ramrodding herds of ghost dinosaurs out to the open desert. They couldn't starve there because they were already dead.

Case, Aguilar and their fellow drovers rapidly became the experts who observed all the twists first. if a 'dine laid down a mound of shit, it remained real after the ghost phased out, having eliminated the remnants of digested intake millions of years old at long last. Academics were eager to dive into the dinosaur poop and analyze. If the 'dines laid eggs while corporeal, and those eggs got fertilized by other corporeated 'dines, the hatchlings did *not* fade out, ever. That wrinkle didn't seem to worry the companies that budgeted the drives too much just yet. It had only happened once or twice. Case had seen baby carnivores try to attack ghosts. Plant eaters munched on ocatilla stalks and prickly pear. The dinosaur equivalent of hoof and mouth, or rabies, could not lumber ghosts. The drovers guided them out past the dunes, where they congregated in broad valleys.

Or would, Case thought, if Shack the mojo would undent his buns and give them the blessing to press on with the drive for two more days of travel time. Then they could dump this herd in with the other 'dines and buzz home for the usual kinds of relief, another thing that had not changed much for anyone of a droving bent.

It had been that Seward fella, way back when, who had come up with the idea of having psychics predict fair or foul for the drives, since ghosts were involved. To put it simply, these dinosaurs were part-time ghosts, and the psychics started out as part-timers, too. Since Seward had suggested the idea to the government, he was appointed to sift applicants and weed out the phonies, in accordance with his former profession. He remained an occult debunker until his death, but after the dinosaur thing his heart just was not in his work so deeply.

Another Camel kissed Case's bootheel; Aguilar declined his offer of a smoke. Night was on in the desert and Jonas had a huge mesquite blaze crackling in a pit full of yesterday's embers. The drovers chowed down and tried to talk of things other than 'dines — lovers, the past, derring-do. Cars.

Ernesto Cocoberra trundled forth from his camper, a rotund, pasha-shaped man, small of stature, bright of eye, aware that his metaphysical dictates were preventing the drive from moving on, but good-natured enough that the drovers resented only the news, and not the Shack. He spoke their language without talking down or bullshitting them. It was inevitable that someone at dinner ask The Question, and tonight it looked like it was Case's turn.

Before Case could get whole words past his lips, though, Shack held up an oracle-like finger and said, "We're there already, Whit."

Aguilar made an *arrgh* noise, having none of this. "Aw, shit, Shack, we ain't moved nearly three weeks now. We ain't anywhere *already*. We're nowhere, is where we are."

You had to ask the question, Case knew. It was like a game. "Okay, Shack. But where are we?"

"Sedalia."

"Oh, great. What the fuck's *that* mean?"

"Quiet," Case said to Aguilar, who was pretty impatient for a guy who waxed so mystical a half hour previously. "What's Sedalia, Shack?"

"Crow, Whit — didn't you never watch no *Rawhide* on TV?"

Blank looks all around. Maybe the triple negative had them reeling. "Oh, yeah." Jonas scraped his dish over the fire. "Clint Eastwood. Some other actor who died."

"Man versus cow," said Shack. "A whole series about a cattle drive." Somebody sang *rollin' rollin' rollin'* sotto voce until Shack continued.

"Sedalia was the town they were driving the cattle to. Show was on the air seven years . . . and that goldanged cattle drive just went on and on, all seven years, and i t *never* got to Sedalia." He folded his arms, a buddha in his certitude, making pronouncements in the firelight.

"That's TV for you," Jonas grumped. "Makes its own timeframe."

"Wait — are you saying we're never going to get clear of this drive?" It was Bridges, the one who had been singing a second before. He was the youngest guy on the drive, full of sperm and not the right age to hear absolutes. "You're not saying that, man." He pitched a crumpled cigarette pack over his shoulder and Jonas glared at him.

"Aguilar had himself a vision up there on the Stirrup today," said Shack. "Why don't you share it with us?"

Aguilar hemmed and hawed and scuffed and blushed and finally cut the crap and told what he knew.

"I suggest y'all keep an eye peeled for that green and black Brontosaurus," concluded Shack. "It has to be an omen. If one of us spots it, then perhaps I could make an intelligent forecast for the drive . . . since I don't enjoy warming my ass out here for days on end any more than you guys do. I want to get back to Reno so I can do some serious gambling, goddammit."

The air displacement of a materializing 'dine nearly blew down the campfire. It was a big guy, a full-grown Trachedon, mud-colored with bright orange speckles like Day-Glo paint and a smell that reminded Case of the blowback from a sewage treatment plant. Most of the drovers hit the deck. Bridges did not. Bridges had not been on the June drive, the one where a Stegosaurus had untethered a volcanic fart into the campfire and nearly flash-fried them all in a flaming cloud of primeval methane.

The Trachedon saw them and made distance.

"You're right," Aguilar said to Case, looking up with dirt in his teeth. "I wish they wouldn't come in so close, either."

All through the night the dinosaurs came and went. Incoming, they sizzled with the sound of ripping cloth or the tearing of dry jerky. They roared and hooted and keened in the darkness of the valley, as prowls begun eons ago were resumed in the residual heat that leached toward the stars from desert dirt. Then they de-rezzed with a carbonated, fizzy noise, blurring, breaking up and fading out.

Near dawn, just as the snaggletoothed horizon grew bloodshot, Case shucked his sleeping bag and ambled over to his terrain bike to catch a smoke and work the sleepy seeds out of his eyes. When it came to the reasons men and a few women chose to embark on dinosaur drives, you usually never winnowed talk down to details. In that respect, the job was like Foreign Legion service. Case was able to keep most of his personal narrative tight to the vest. Each drover thought their reasons the most tragic or romantic — by god, it could be like one endless, over-dumb country & western ballad — except that everyone was too chicken to actually match for best.

Case held the draughts of good gray smoke deep. It perked his nerves and glands, and gradually, restored his definition of humanity.

The silhouetted dinosaur head interrupted the stripe of horizon light, stalking, a gargoyle marionette. The outline read Tyrannosaurus, and that was enough for Case to kick-start his bike and investigate.

The beast was one big trainfucker indeed.

Its architecture and fluidity sustained no comparison to the lumpen elephants or whales of modern times. Its musculature was woven tight as the braids on a bullwhip, girder tendons and cable ligaments tautly tuned beneath the stout mail of leather. Chatoyant eyes glinted in the predawn as it jerked its head around to fix the sound of Case's bike, speedy and alert, spoiling for trouble or some wet, carnivorous fun.

When something the size of a double-decker bus sneezed, a drover might become dino toe-jam in an instant. Case did not hit it with the bike's hot spot and make it bolt, all those crookedly-meshed six-inch teeth rushing down to macerate him. He checked it out, as he had checked all of them out for two years now.

An oilslick smell hung about it, like the rich clots of grimy black that vehicles excreted onto parking lots and driveways. The Rex whiffed Case but did not seem peckish or feisty. Case imagined the thermal pits on its snout processing the air itself. What did its ancient brain tell it about the morning? Was it chilly, warm? Just right? Did it aspire to any goals beyond the prowl, and food for the day? Did it apply any sort of personal style to its killing technique? The fixed grin on the sardonic reptile mask was certainly the visage of a hunter, and most hunters, thought Case, were driven by pride.

Over the bike's phones, he picked up an Arizona radio station kicking off a weekend celebration of the Beatles. That was safe and innocuous enough, yeah; happiness was a warm gun. Case's saddlebags included a .457 packed with heavy-grain slugs, but he rarely used it on drives and had not even taken it out once this trip. What for?

In an emergency, in case a 'dine got uppity or just plain needed to die in a hurry, the drovers had customized ordnance, usually sleeved in a special holster to the right of the terrain bike's gas teardrop. They were commonly called ass-kickers — two feet of scaled-down bazooka pipe with a pistol grip that discharged a canister of Plastique similar to the power-heads used by divers against sharks. The idea was to provide an immediate one-shot stop in a crisis; the only effective way to prevent a contrary shark from gobbling you on the spot was to blow its jaw completely off. The concept had been handily adapted to land use against recorporeated dinosaurs, and a balance of power had been swiftly inaugurated.

Case saw its violet eyes. I know you, oh yes I do.

He yanked the choke ring on the ass-kicker and flipped off the safety. Then he nailed the big Rex with his spotlight.

It was bright purple. One of its flanks was scorched and puckered from a burn — an earthly injury taken with it into the astral and brought back just now. In sum, that was enough for Case.

He shouted, and when the beast turned on him, he sighted through the red plastic grid.

Whitman Case's Corvette had been a thing of beauty to behold, a dream realized and a desire long coveted. It had been something in which he had invested the patience of a Russian consumer. Waiting for something gave you plenty of time to fantasize. Eleven coats of mirror-gloss canary yellow double-dipped in lacquer; chrome like the eye of a flame. A deadly serious 307 four-barrel carb and a police-chaser block. A wheel sleeve of buttery leather that matched the buckets. A total boner of a driving machine, new radials not even *dusty* yet and it had become history . . . because some numbnuts Tyrannosaurus Rex had waited a couple million years and an epoch or two just to step on it.

The fireball born of Lloyd Lamed's vaporizing Texaco station in Riverside had drawn Whitman Case to his front window just in time to see a purple dinosaur squash his 'Vette with no more effort than a hiccup required. Then the shockwave shattered the window and Case had other things to worry about.

He let out his breath; let the Rex eat a technological meteor. The explosion woke up the whole camp as thirty tons of Tyranno-casserole clouded the air with the reek of stale blood from another time, the dawn of time itself.

• • •

Two hours after breakfast, Aguilar spotted his own 'dine, the green and black one. The saddle markings on the Brontosaurus, he insisted, were unmistakable. It turned out to be a female.

Nobody spoke to Case. They figured him for drive jitters after he fragged the Rex. Shack got swamped once Aguilar reported the Brontosaurus. *Pardone señor, we go no place today neether.*

They watched the dinosaur all day. It got really boring really fast. By dinnertime most of the drovers had forgotten their noisy wake-up call and were mildly torqued at Aguilar.

"Big fuckin' deal!" snarled Bridges, throwing food and wasting it. He used fluorocarbon deodorant and owned a huge Jeep he used to modify the trails in national parks. Bridges had always been a litterbug; he didn't believe in much else. "Big revelation! Big mystical owlshit! Really pro, Aguilar, you asshole!'

Aguilar likened young Bridges to a behemoth phallus, and the other drovers had to wrestle them apart. The dust they'd kicked up hung around in the firelight, stubbornly. Shack shook his head sadly. Dumb mortals.

"You guys are so anxious to wrap the drive you can't hear the music for all the noise the orchestra is making," said Case. He'd been trying to use logic, like that Seward fella, whom he admired.

"See what?" Bridges was still aching for mayhem. He obviously hadn't had his butt kicked enough by living yet. "That fuckin' green and black 'dine? It's right over there, so what?"

"When did you spot it this morning?" Case said to Aguilar. It wouldn't do to tell Bridges to watch his language.

"About ten or so." Aguilar had coded a marker onto his digital watch to log the sighting. He was that bored.

"And our boy Bridges, with his keen eyesight, can still see it from here."

Jonas didn't get it. "And I hope it *stays* over there. Geez, don't you guys remember the farting Stego?"

Shack began to smile privately.

"Okay, Bridges." Case focused on the boy. "Maybe you can tell the class what time it is right now. You *can* tell time, right?"

Bridges was about to aim and fire when he went rigid, his yap stalling in the open position. "Oh. Jeezus . . . "

Everybody looked at each other. It was poignant, in its way.

Case rather savored playing oracle. This must be how Shack felt when he channeled some blast of psychic insight. "That 'dine, gents, has been solid for over twelve hours. Somebody better call the Guinness Book, because this is a first, as far as my experience goes."

Top end before the average ghost dinosaur frazzed out was generally two hours. They came back, but they never lasted long; that was why the hazard factor had dwindled so quickly. This female Brontosaurus showed no signs of going away, and it was an adult, not a newborn.

"A Maiasaur will be next," Shack said. "It will lay a full nest of eggs."

Case reviewed all. What had he accomplished? To cease the mad forward rush, the stampede of the simple day-to-day, that might actually be nice. He reconsidered all he had done, from losing his virginity to greasing the Rex that had wiped out his dream car, and realized right here, in the middle of nowhere, he had already found a valuable kind of peace. He had never thought in such terms before.

This really wasn't so bad, for a life.

The valley was full of milling dinosaurs. They were waiting and they had the patience of eons, because they had known — if only instinctually — that their time would again come 'round. Case wondered if he could be adaptable as that Seward fella had been.

"What do you reckon we oughta do?" Bridges asked Case. "Start shooting 'em? Is that why you bagged that one this morning?" The kid was actually worried.

Case grinned. Drovers never told all.

"Nope. I think we only need to do one thing, and that's find a way to welcome them home. No wars, no battles for dominance, all that useless military shit. You and I are the experts, Bridges. We oughta act like experts, and find out what the 'dines will need that we can provide, since they're coming home. Either we coexist, or *we* become the extinct ones. You get it?"

"What about civilization?" said Jonas. "No dinosaur could ever be a Magritte or a Blake or a Dali." His education was showing.

"Mm. More important, no dinosaur could ever invent Bic lighters or pop tops or bombs that suck away the whole atmosphere. Yes? That green and black Brontosaurus is the first one that's not just going to disappear. It's back to stay." Home again, he thought. The former tenants were resuming residence.

He knew it would take awhile for them all to digest the potential of their new roles. Not everybody was going to like it, but Case wasn't worried. There was time, and time marched.

Right now it was time to fire up another cigarette.

Rope and Limb

BY JEFF STRAND

"DARIUS BROWN, YOU HAVE been found guilty of an attempted bank robbery that left six innocent people dead. Do you have any final words before you are sent to the Lord for His judgment?"

"I have a few, yeah," said Darius. He cleared his throat and addressed the crowd of townsfolk. "I know I kept bringing this up in the trial—or, you know, what passed for a trial—but I think it bears repeating. I didn't kill any of those people."

"You were responsible for their deaths," said Mayor Wasser.

"Everybody keeps saying that, and I understand their perspective. I do. But I wasn't the one who shot them. It's not my fault that the bank teller pulled out a gun and kept missing me and hitting customers."

"If you hadn't been trying to rob the bank, he wouldn't have tried to shoot you."

"That's true, that's true," Darius admitted. "But he had a six-shooter and accidentally killed six people. That's *really* bad aim. One woman was on the complete opposite side of the bank from me. Like I explained during the trial, I'm not saying for sure that the bank teller was a madman who saw an opportunity to extinguish human lives and took advantage of it. I *am*, however, saying that it's disappointing nobody was left alive to testify about how much he was giggling while he was doing it."

"He's an upstanding member of our community," said Mayor Wasser, "and I will *not* have you suggesting that those half-dozen deaths made him happy. He promised to practice shooting targets in his backyard for no less than three hours a week. That's not the action of a thrill-killer. Shame on you for trying to disparage a fine man to save your own skin. I'm so angry that I could slap you in the face right now, but I won't, because that's not how mayors behave."

"That's right, they sure don't," somebody said. The townsfolk glared at him for not contributing anything substantive to the conversation.

"Anyway," Mayor Wasser continued, "you, Darius Brown, have been sentenced to death by hanging. Assuming that your cruel words about a bank teller whose only sin was that he cared too much weren't your final words, do you have any final words?"

"Yes," said Darius. "I see that there's a hangman's noose dangling from that tree, and there's a wooden box underneath it. It looks like you're going to have me stand on the box, and then somebody will put the noose around my neck, and then somebody will kick the box out from under me. Is that right?"

"Well, we were going to have you put the noose around your own neck so we wouldn't have to bring a second box, but yes, that is correct."

Darius frowned. "Really? That's how you're going to do this? The 'rope and limb' method?"

"How else would we do it?"

"A town that wasn't fifty years behind the times would use a trapdoor gallows. Walk me up there, pull the lever, and the trapdoor opens beneath me. My neck snaps immediately. Nice and efficient."

"Maybe we don't want it to be nice and efficient," said Mayor Wasser. "Maybe we want you to suffer for your crimes."

"I get that, but if I'm dangling there, choking and gagging, it reflects badly on you. It makes it look like you don't really know what you're doing. People will say 'Oh, the leaders of Grassy Point have no idea how to properly hang somebody.' It's embarrassing."

"I'm not going to go through the time and expense of building a trapdoor gallows just to avoid a bit of embarrassment. We don't do many hangings around here."

"That's all the more reason to take pride in the hangings that *do* happen." Darius said. He gestured to the crowd. "Don't they deserve a professional execution? If they've taken time out of their busy days to come out to the town square to witness a hanging, why should they have to settle for a cheap rope and limb show? It's disrespectful."

"You're the first hanging this year," said Mayor Wasser. "I'd be squandering their tax money if I commissioned a gallows."

"How much can a decent gallows possibly cost? It's some wood. You've got plenty of wood around here. Hell, you can cut down the tree you're about to use to hang me. Are you telling me that there's nobody in this entire town that can design a trapdoor?"

"I wouldn't know," said Mayor Wasser. "I've never asked."

A man standing near the front of the crowd raised his hand. "My name is Tom, and I'm the finest carpenter in the entire state of Oklahoma. I take personal offense to the suggestion that nobody in town can design a trapdoor."

"Are you mad at me or him?" asked Mayor Wasser.

"You."

"I never meant to suggest that you couldn't design a trapdoor. The troughs you've built for our town's horses are second to none. But you wouldn't build us a gallows for free, would you?"

"Well, no," said Tom. "I'd charge a fair price."

"Right. Which means that I'd be spending taxpayer money. Money that the citizens of this town have worked so hard to earn, on something we don't really need. And that would be irresponsible."

"It wouldn't be a difficult job," said Tom. "I could do it in an afternoon."

"I know what a trapdoor gallows looks like," said Mayor Wasser. "It's not a one-person job, is it?"

Tom didn't respond.

"I asked you a question."

"Well, no, I'd require an assistant."

"Oh, listen to that! He'd require an assistant! Now the price is going up a bit, isn't it?"

"Not by much. My assistants are poorly paid."

"Still, this luxury purchase isn't as inexpensive as you'd led us to believe. We don't need a goddamn gallows. We need a tree with a sturdy branch, and we need a rope tied into a noose, and that's it!"

"Does anybody around here even know how to tie a proper noose?" asked Darius.

"Yes, we know how to tie a noose! Now you're just trying to distract us, as if we'll get so caught up in the conversation that we'll forget to execute you! Well, it's not going to happen! I'm counting everything you've said so far as your last words, so if you'd hoped to exit this world with something more profound, it's your own fault."

Darius nodded. "Fair enough. By the way, over in Red Hollow, they have a twitch-up gallows."

"What the hell is a twitch-up gallows?"

"Oh, it's really impressive. So you know how you're using the caveman method of just dangling somebody from a tree? And you know how I'm encouraging you to use a trapdoor gallows, where the victim drops through the floor?"

"Don't call yourself a victim," said Mayor Wasser. "The victims are the six people who got shot in the bank."

"Right," said Darius. "Anyway, a twitch-up gallows is the latest in execution technology. Basically, instead of letting the evil-doer fall, you drop a counter-weight, which yanks the body *up*, breaking his neck immediately. The trap-door gallows are highly effective, but there are still the occasional setbacks. The twitch-up gallows get the job done right the first time, almost every time."

"Remember, I don't care about that. If you're dangling there and foaming at the mouth, that doesn't bother me one bit. If you don't die until your head pops off, oh well. I admire your effort, but you're not going to change my mind."

"I think Red Hollow actually had a double twitch-up gallows. You can hang two men at the same time. Now *that* is a show!"

"Is it, though?" asked Mayor Wasser. "You seem to think that this crowd wants it to be over quickly. That would be like the theater troupe coming through town and doing a Punch and Judy show with only one act of puppet violence. Why would the citizens of this fine town gather to watch your neck snap in half a second? I think they want the slow strangulation and gurgling that comes from a good old-fashioned rope and limb hanging. What does everybody else think?"

A woman raised her hand. "The people of Red Hollow do seem to have higher morale than we do."

"Since when?" Mayor Wasser demanded.

"Since always. Everybody knows that."

The townspeople all nodded and murmured in agreement.

"Well... if they do, and I don't think they do, it's not because of their double twitch-up gallows!"

"He's right," said a man. "It's because they have a much better whore-house."

The men all nodded and murmured their agreement.

"What the hell are you talking about?" asked Mayor Wasser. "The Grassy Point Pleasure Dome is the finest whorehouse for sixty-five miles! Those ladies will do things that would send our wives to the sanitarium! I reject your notion that the people of Red Hollow are happier because of their whorehouse! The diseases in that place are so thick that they squish through your toes when you walk inside. They should call it the Red Hollow *Crab* House, if you ask me."

"Well," said Darius, "if it's not the whorehouse, it's got to be their double twitch-up gallows, right?"

"No! It could be their clean drinking water!"

"Could be. But you don't know. All I'm saying is that there's enough uncertainty that you should take me back to my jail cell until we get this all sorted out."

"A double twitch-up gallows doesn't sound so hard to make," said Tom. "I can draw up a schematic and give you a quote by sunrise."

"We're only hanging one person!"

"True, but somebody will commit a heinous crime eventually. What about Doc Reed? Remember last week when he murdered a couple of the Grassy Point Pleasure Dome whores because they weren't as attentive as the ones in Red Hollow?"

"He apologized."

"But they were too dead to hear it."

"Enough," said Mayor Wasser. "He's trying to turn us against each other! How dare this outsider come in and criticize our executions and our fallen women! We should turn this from a hanging to a stoning! Everybody grab a rock and throw it at this son of a bitch! How does that sound?"

"That sounds positively horrific and I withdraw all of my previous comments," said Darius. "I'll take the rope and limb."

Darius stepped up onto the box. Mayor Wasser handed him the noose, which Darius placed around his own neck. Mayor Wasser took a deep breath, then prepared to kick the box out from underneath him.

"Uh, shouldn't you ..." said Darius.

"Shit," said Mayor Wasser. "Yes, yes, yes, I know." He looked out at the crowd. "Somebody needs to tie the other end of the rope to a branch."

"I'll do it if I'm rewarded with female company for my efforts," said Doc Reed.

"Never mind, I'm the mayor, I'll do it." Mayor Wasser looked at the tree, trying to figure out the best branch to grab to begin his ascent.

"Should I just stand here?" asked Darius.

"Yes." He raised his voice, speaking to the townspeople. "If he tries to escape, throw rocks at him! Sharp ones! Get him in the most sensitive areas!"

"I won't try to escape."

Mayor Wasser, with significant effort, climbed the tree and tied the other end of the noose to a large branch. He climbed back down, also with significant effort.

"I could've built a trapdoor gallows in the time it took you to do that," said Tom.

"Would you like to join him up there?"

"Looks like we might need a double—"

"Shut the fuck up!" shouted Mayor Wasser. He kicked the box out from underneath Darius.

Darius dropped, his feet dangling inches above the ground. He clutched at his throat and let out various gagging noises.

"Yeah, that's right, choke!" said Mayor Wasser. "Let that tongue loll out of your mouth!"

The branch above Darius snapped. He fell onto the dirt.

Before Mayor Wasser could say, "Son of a—" Darius glanced up just as the branch struck him in the face.

"Oh my goodness!" Tom wailed. "It got him right through the eyeball! Look at the blood and ooze spurting out of there!"

Darius screamed.

"I'm sorry, I'm sorry," said Mayor Wasser. "I should've picked a sturdier branch!"

"Pull it out! Pull it out!"

"You shouldn't do that," said the woman who'd made the earlier comment about how the people of Red Hollow had higher morale. "It'll make things worse!"

"How could it make things worse?" Darius shrieked.

"That branch is holding some of the blood in! If you pull it out, it'll be like yanking the cork out of a sideways bottle of red wine!"

"Should I shove it in more?" asked Mayor Wasser.

"No!" Darius yanked the branch away. "Fuck! It broke off in my eye socket!"

"He'll never get it out now," said Tom. "There's not enough for him to get his fingers around."

Darius desperately tried to pull out the piece of the branch.

"Stop that!" said Major Wasser. "Your fingers are making your eye socket wider! You're digging too deep!"

A frantic mother shielded the eyes of her two young boys. "I brought my sons to watch a hanging, not this grisly eyeball trauma!"

Gritting his teeth with the effort, Darius got the branch out of his eyeball.

"My God," said Tom. "It's so gooey that I can't even tell what's stuck to the wood!"

"This is why you needed a fucking trapdoor gallows!" Darius shouted.

"Make him turn his head!" said the mother.

"No! I will not turn my head away! Gaze at my disgusting eye socket, all of you! I presented a solution, and your mayor rejected it! Now every time each of you closes your eyes, you'll see what happened to *my* eye! This will haunt your dreams! You cannot unsee it! You will wake up in the middle of the night, bathed in cold perspiration, cursing the fates that brought you here today, forcing you to witness an image that will be forever imprinted on your mind's eye!"

"You're getting carried away," said Mayor Wasser. "It's gross but it's not *that* gross."

Darius vigorously shook his head back and forth, spraying blood on the mayor like a dog after a bath. Then he let out a deranged cackle and fled. Before he could escape, the mayor stepped on the end of the noose. As Darius reached the end of the rope, there was a loud *crack* and he dropped to the ground.

"That sounded like a neck-breaking crack," Tom noted.

"Yes," said Mayor Wasser. "It wasn't pretty, but in the end, it was a successful execution. Thank you for coming, everybody! Get home safely."

"Why is he still moving?" asked the mother.

"He's not."

"Yes, he is."

"Oh, that's just death twitches. It happens. If you died in front of your children right now, you'd twitch a little, too."

The mother shook her head. "He's alive."

Mayor Wasser knelt beside Darius. "Well, shit. Yeah, he's still alive. Looks like he's got a broken neck and he's paralyzed. At least he can't rob any banks in this condition. I think it's safe enough to still say it was a successful execution. He'll be dead pretty soon."

"How do you know that?" the mother asked. "What if he lasts for a few days?"

"The coyotes won't let that happen."

"I didn't traumatize my boys just to leave a paralyzed criminal to starve to death."

"Look how much blood is *still* coming out of his eye."

"It's not that much."

"It's not as much when it was spurting, but there's a solid trickle. He'll be dead in ten, fifteen minutes."

"What kind of lesson am I teaching these boys if you leave the job unfinished?"

"What do you want me to do?" asked Mayor Wasser. "Stomp on his head until it's nothing but mush?"

The mother nodded.

"Fine!" Mayor Wasser stomped on Darius' head a few times. He quickly discovered that stomping on somebody's head until it was nothing but mush was more difficult than one might expect. He needed better shoes.

"What if we dropped a big rock on his head?" asked Tom.

"Do you have a big rock?"

"No, but I'm sure we can find one."

"Climbing that tree really wore me out," said Mayor Wasser. "I don't want to deal with a big rock right now. What if we just marched all of the people in town past the body and everybody tore off a hunk?"

Tom shrugged. "Sounds good to me."

By the time the bloodied townspeople returned to their homes, Darius had been successfully executed. Mayor Wasser, who wasn't too proud to admit that he'd been wrong, commissioned a double twitch-up gallows the very next day. Sadly, his term ended with no violent crimes that required a hanging, and he regretted the unnecessary expenditure until his death of natural causes at the age of seventy-three.

Dread Creek

BY BRIANA MORGAN

DELILAH'S MOUTH WARMS AGAINST Jesse's as they kiss. He feels like the luckiest outlaw alive. Smiling, he pushes his new wife's dark hair away from her face.

"What are you looking at me like that for?" she asks.

"You look good," he says.

"Like a married woman?"

"Maybe."

Earl's whistle echoes off the surrounding mountains. Jesse's ears ring. He grins at Delilah and grabs his horse, Cleopatra's reins.

"Ready?" Jesse asks.

Delilah spurs her mare, Liberty. "Let's go."

Earl, Hosea, and Lily Anne have already ridden ahead. Their laughter floats back to Jesse on the wind. The cool air raises the hairs on his arms. He looks over at Delilah, only wearing a corset, a thin shawl, a long skirt, and boots—not near enough clothes for the desert at night.

It isn't exactly the honeymoon he promised her months ago. Then again, she knew what joining the gang would mean for her, and she still married him.

Once they make it to Ranch Ridge, he'll ask Delilah's father for her hand in marriage. They're already married, but her father doesn't know. Delilah is old-fashioned like that. Jesse wants to prove he means business.

Delilah's parents won't stick around Ranch Ridge for long. Their last letter to their daughter said as much. If Jesse can't meet them, his surprise for Delilah is ruined.

He feels bad enough that he hasn't gotten her a wedding band. Twine encircles both their fingers instead.

Jesse pulls his horse up to Earl's. Paco huffs at Cleopatra. Like their riders, they grew up together.

"Why'd ya whistle?" Jesse asks.

Lily Anne and Hosea hang back from them a little, letting Delilah catch up to them. Jesse hears them talking but can't make out what they're saying.

Earl's eyelids droop. He bends low over Paco's neck. "We all wanna stop for the night."

"We gotta get on," Jesse says.

"I know you have your sights set on Ranch Ridge, but we're just... we're goddamn shot. We all need sleep."

Jesse drags a hand down his face. If they don't press on, they won't catch up with Delilah's folks. He's exhausted, too, but they can't stop now.

"I'm sorry," Earl adds. "It's what the group wants. We can call a vote, but it won't go in your favor."

"Tonight?" Delilah says. She and the others have ridden closer. "We wanna bed down for the night?" she repeats.

Earl studies Jesse's face. He sighs. "Fresh start in the mornin'. Bright and early. We can make it."

Jesse isn't so sure about that. Hosea, Lily Anne, and Delilah are all looking at him, waiting for his reaction.

"If Delilah's all right with it, I guess I am too," Jesse says.

Delilah frowns. He knows that look. She's holding her tongue.

"Fine by me," she says.

Jesse nods. "It's settled. We're stayin' here tonight."

He doesn't like letting Delilah down, but the group wants to stop. Jesse can't very well go against them.

"We're close to Dread Creek," Hosea says. "Been down there once, long time ago. Decent source of water."

"We got plenty of food, but no water," Lily Anne chimes in.

Earl pats Paco's neck. "Jesse and I can tackle that. Y'all get everythin' else together."

"Won't take us long," Jesse says. Then, to Delilah: "You'll be all right, sugar?"

"I'll miss you is all," she says.

—◦—

Not long after, Earl and Jesse ride in search of water. Paco and Cleopatra carry them along in companionable silence.

"Been a while since it was just the two of us," Earl says.

Jesse nods. "Don't think we would've gotten this far alone, neither."

Earl gazes ahead, eyes scanning the horizon for water glinting in the sun. Jesse assumed Earl knew where it was since he's been there before. Maybe Jesse should've asked.

"Looks like a stream over yonder." Jesse points. A dark, shiny ribbon of water zigzags over the land.

"Could be," Earl says.

The two of them nudge their horses toward the water. As they get closer, Jesse realizes it is more brackish than he expected. Dirtier, too. He leans forward over Cleopatra's neck and sniffs. Sulfur.

"Not the best," Jesse declares.

Earl frowns. "Nothin' wrong with it."

"Stinks to high hell," Jesse says. "I ain't lettin' my wife drink that."

"Forget about her for a minute," Earl says. "I'm sayin' we ain't got a choice."

"Good water's worth the extra mile. I don't think we should settle."

"No, you never do."

A muscle jerks in Jesse's jaw. "What is that supposed to mean?"

"What do you think?" Earl asks.

It isn't worth the fight he might put up, Jesse knows. Earl is their unofficial leader. What he says tends to go.

Jesse can't suppress the urge to find more water, but he wants to keep Earl happy. So, he relents.

"You're right about the water," Jesse says.

"Thank you." Earl nudges Paco forward, closer to the stream.

Jesse dismounts Cleopatra and waits for Earl. They drop the reins and let the horses keep to themselves for a minute. Jesse and Earl have a metal canteen each, and Earl has two more for Lily Anne and Hosea.

They fill the canteens without further discussion and ride back to camp. Jesse's throat burns something fierce. His mouth is dry as dust.

———◦———

Delilah and Lily Anne stand outside the tents, pulling supplies off the horses and unpacking what they can.

Jesse ties up Cleopatra and heads on to Delilah. When she sees him, her face lights up.

"Didn't take too long," she says. "We thought y'all might be gone for a while."

Jesse bristles. "Water's not far. We got some from the creek."

"Dread Creek?"

"That's the one."

Delilah smiles at him. "Well, don't just stand there. Go get your wife a drink."

Jesse smiles back. Although he's still mad as a hornet at Earl, the sunset will dissolve it. There are issues between him and Earl that likely need resolving, but Jesse won't address them. He doesn't want to risk the loss of his best friend.

As soon as he fetches the canteen from Cleopatra, Jesse carries it to Delilah. He unscrews the cap and holds it out to her.

"Bottoms up," she says

He watches her drink, remembering how they met. She stood alone at the saloon, and Jesse bought her a drink. It feels like years since then, not months.

"Whatcha starin' at me for?" Delilah asks.

Jesse smirks. "Just think you're pretty."

"Yeah, well, you'd better. No goin' back now."

"We're stuck with each other," he says.

Jesse isn't convinced she won't tire of him, but they'll ride through that road when they come to it.

When Delilah finishes drinking, she passes the canteen to Jesse. Her cheeks are flushed.

"Penny for your thoughts," he says.

"Oh, you'd be so lucky."

Delilah's green eyes sparkle as she peers up at him. He really is the luckiest cowboy alive.

Earl's low whistle cuts through Jesse's thoughts. He'll have to return to them later.

"Let's get a fire going," Earl hollers. "Eat some food, sit a spell."

"Some wild evenin'," Delilah remarks. The corners of her lips curve upward.

Jesse shakes the canteen. "Lots of air in here. You drank nearly half."

"Maybe more than half," she says.

He sips from the canteen, shaking his head. "I'll let you get away with anythin'."

Delilah turns her head and her face catches the sun. Maybe it's a trick of the light, but something dark and unfamiliar flits across her features.

It's gone in a moment, like nothing's changed.

In its stead, she smiles.

———————————◄O►———————————

Jesse, Delilah, Earl, Hosea, and Lily Anne set up the tents and lay out their beds before sunset. Earl hammers posts into the ground for the posse to tie up their horses. When they finish working, Hosea builds a fire for them to enjoy. They sit around it talking long into the night—even though everyone is exhausted.

The contradiction nags Jesse, but he keeps it to himself. So long as they make it to Ranch Ridge tomorrow, everything is peachy.

Jesse sprawls on his bedroll kissing Delilah, when Hosea pokes his head through their tent's flap and whistles real loud with two fingers.

Delilah and Jesse break apart. Jesse groans and readjusts his trousers.

"Somethin' I can help you with?" he asks.

"Reckon you can," Hosea says. "We need to find somethin' to hunt."

"Get Earl to go with you. I'm busy here."

Hosea blows air out of his mouth. "See, I would, but Earl says his knee's actin' up again. I'd rather not fight him about it."

Jesse frowns. He reaches up and scratches the back of his neck. When they were kids, a stallion bucked Earl off. He landed with his right leg turned the wrong way underneath him. Since then, it's been a problem.

Delilah puts a hand on Jesse's arm. "Go on. You owe him for shootin' that snake yesterday."

Jesse's frown only deepens. Earl *did* save his life. Plus, they've seen their fair share of scrapes, and Earl gets him out of them all.

Delilah's fingers wander to the corners of Jesse's mouth. Groaning, Jesse gets to his feet and tugs at his trousers, willing his hard-on away. Hosea does him the favor of not mentioning it.

"See anythin' by that creek y'all found?" Hosea asks.

"Weren't really lookin'." Jesse kisses Delilah's forehead. "No clue how long this could take."

"Don't wait up for you?" she guesses. A smile turns her lips. "Me and Lily Anne got plenty to do. I won't even have time to miss you."

Jesse returns her smile. She makes smiling easy. "We'll leave y'all to it then. C'mon, Hosea. 'fore I change my mind."

The two of them duck out of the tent and into the cool night air. Distantly, a cicada whirs. Jesse is surprised to hear any signs of life—it feels like they've reached the end of nature altogether. The creek might be the only reason anything's alive.

Hosea turns his head and spits into the dirt. "Earl's just comin' up with excuses."

Jesse nods. "I've been sayin' so. Nobody listens."

They clamber onto their horses and ride out toward the creek. Hosea's horse, Scout, is Cleopatra's brother. Despite this fact, Jesse never spends time with Hosea. Out of everyone in their group, Jesse knows him the least. Hosea spends more time with Delilah and Lily Anne than he does with Jesse and Earl.

Maybe he gets along better with women because he relates to them. Not for the first time, Jesse suspects Hosea is into fellas.

Jesse likes the fairer sex. He always has. It's not something he has to question. Despite a drunken one-night tryst with a gunsmith years ago, he discovered men don't do anything for him. Then, he discovered Delilah, and the rest is history.

Or history in the makin', Jesse thinks.

"So, this creek," Hosea says. "That where y'all got the water?"

"Yeah," Jesse says. "Didn't taste too good."

"I'll bet it didn't. We ain't got much choice."

They scan their surroundings for signs of small game they could catch. Neither of them see footprints, feces, or the like. Maybe they won't find a thing.

At the water's edge, a snake slithers in front of Jesse's feet. He steps forward to get a closer look. Hosea grabs his arm.

"That's a mean one," Hosea says. "Venomous. Don't touch it."

For the second day in a row, Jesse nearly avoids death by serpent. If they make it to Ranch Ridge, he'll stop walking up to snakes.

Jesse and Hosea check the creek for fish. There are no signs of wildlife there, or anywhere near the water, other than the snake, the cicadas, and a few other insects lurking nearby.

Maybe the animals know something they don't.

Jesse's throat begins to itch, but it might be his imagination.

Defeated, Jesse and Hosea head back to camp sooner than they planned to. They say goodnight and part ways—Hosea going to his tent, and Jesse returning to his own.

As Jesse reaches to pull back the tent flap, Delilah's words stop his heart.

"Don't make me ask again," she says. "It's hard for me, you know."

"You sure ain't actin' like it," Earl replies.

Jesse freezes. Why is Earl in his tent? What is he doing with Delilah?

Jesse lowers his hand and lets it fall by his side. He needs to hear more. He has to know what's going on between the two of them. Anxiety constricts his chest.

Slowly, he creeps toward the side of the tent. The lantern inside throws Delilah's and Earl's silhouettes against the canvas. They're standing mighty close.

"I never wanted it to go this far," Delilah continues.

Earl scoffs. "C'mon, darlin'. You're the one who kept it goin'."

Jesse's blood simmers. Earl knows better than to call another man's wife *darlin'*, just as he knows he shouldn't be alone in a tent with the woman. Jesse and Earl have their share of disagreements, but they never hurt each other.

That's what Jesse thought, anyway.

He's too angry to process Delilah's response. All he can do is stand there.

"Well," Delilah says. "I'm puttin' a stop to it now."

Both of them go quiet. Jesse considers rushing in then, but he doesn't. He waits.

"You can't do that," Earl says.

"I believe I did," she answers. "I'm a married woman now. It ain't right for me to carry on like this with you."

"I saw you first." Earl's voice is tight and pained. "I saw you... I should've done somethin' about it. When Jesse went to talk to you, I didn't think—"

"Like hell you didn't," Delilah cuts in. "You weren't man enough to approach me. You didn't even want me until Jesse made me his."

"Delilah," Earl pleads, and for the first time in his life, Jesse hates his wife's name. In another man's mouth, it's poison.

Earl's sincere tone bewilders him. Jesse can count on one hand how many times he's heard his friend in pain. Earl has real feelings for Delilah.

Tough shit, Jesse thinks. *She isn't his wife.*

Jesse shifts his weight from one foot to the other as he listens to their conversation. Not for the first time, he wonders if he should've saved Earl's life at the river years ago.

Since childhood, they've traded lives between them. Jesse owes Earl for the snake and a hundred other incidents.

Then again, Earl has been fucking Jesse's wife.

Jesse's hands tighten into fists at his sides. *Never should've been this way,* he thinks. Another, darker thought crosses his mind: he could make sure that the bastard never fucks his wife again. All it would take is a shot to the head or the chest, and that would be the end of it. Jesse and Delilah could go back to normal.

Normal. If there is such a thing for men like him.

Jesse's fingers scrabble against his chin, scratching the stubble. Rough on his skin, it burns, but Jesse barely notices.

Hot, liquid rage burns a hole in his stomach. He knows he could storm in there and demand an explanation. Maybe skip the explanation since he knows that they've been fucking. He can shove Earl, ask him what his problem is. Maybe haul off and punch him in his smug face.

Every fight Earl has been in, he folds like a card.

Again, the lure of the gun at his hip and the promise of all-encompassing relief is almost too strong to resist. His thumb brushes over the butt of the gun in its holster. He sucks in a breath. He pauses.

If Jesse kills Earl, Delilah won't love Jesse anymore. Hell, she might not even like him. The possibility of losing her is so much worse than anything else his mind can conjure. He has to abandon the urge to kill for now.

He exhales in a rush. His hand goes to the tent's flap. All at once, Jesse slips inside and Delilah and Earl's heads swivel in his direction.

Delilah has the decency to step away from Earl. Unlike Delilah, Earl doesn't move.

When they make it to Ranch Ridge, he'll beat the shit out of Earl.

Delilah tucks a strand of hair behind her ear. She does this when she's nervous, Jesse knows. *Good*, he thinks. *At least she has an* ounce *of shame.*

"Jesse," Delilah says.

"I'm back," he replies.

"We were just talkin'," Earl says, like Jesse is a moron. They might've been *just talkin'*, but they've been *just fuckin'*, too.

"Nice talk?" Jesse asks.

Earl doesn't answer him. His gaze shifts to Delilah, but hers won't move from Jesse's face. Jesse's jaw tightens. A vein pulses in his forehead.

"I'd best be gettin' some sleep," Earl says. At last, he looks at Jesse. His face is draped in shadow. In the scant light, he looks ghoulish.

The corner of Jesse's mouth twitches. "Seems your leg ain't so bad anymore, is that right?"

Earl forces a smile. It doesn't reach his eyes. "Yeah, I reckon so. Well, I'll get out of y'all's hair. Have a good evenin'."

"You, too," Jesse says. His eyes lock on Earl and track his movements as he leaves the tent. Once again to her credit, Delilah only has eyes for Jesse.

She must think he's stupid, too. Maybe he should punish her.

Jesse takes his hat off and sets it on the end of his bedroll. He doesn't say a word to his wife. She doesn't say anything, either. Maybe she doesn't trust herself to.

They climb into bed. Jesse turns his back to Delilah, facing the wall. Delilah presses herself against him—or rather, she tries to—and Jesse wriggles away until they aren't touching.

Once they get to Ranch Ridge, Jesse will confront her. He'll ask her what the ever-loving fuck she's been thinking. He'll ask Earl how the fuck he could do this to him.

What Jesse *won't* ask, though, is the question he already knows the answer to. It's the one he can't voice because then it's all real:

Does she really love me?

"Jesse," Delilah's voice reaches out to him in the dark. For a moment, Jesse tenses. Is she going to come clean? Is she going to apologize?

Instead, she just tells him, "Blow out that lantern."

Jesse does. The tent dissolves into darkness. All Jesse can hear is the cicadas and some bugs he doesn't recognize. Not even a coyote howl to make him anxious. No camp sounds, either, like crackling wood or Hosea singing off key while Lily Anne plays the guitar.

Everyone else is asleep.

Except Earl. There's no way he can fall asleep that fast.

Delilah doesn't even wish Jesse goodnight. She doesn't kiss him. Jesse closes his eyes and tries to sleep despite the anger buzzing in him like a stirred-up swarm of bees.

A scream tears Jesse from his sleep. Drenched in cold sweat, he twists his head to check on his wife. Delilah sits upright staring out of the tent. Her dark eyes are wide with terror. Otherwise, she looks all right.

Who's screaming, Jesse wonders? Maybe the *why* of it matters more than the *who*, but it's all he can focus on.

Jesse wants to find the source of the screaming. Hell, he *needs* to find it. If someone in the camp is screaming, maybe there's a coyote or something else tearing through the tents. For all Jesse knows, they might be next.

"Fuck," Jesse says.

Delilah reaches for his hand. He's too unsettled not to give it to her. His skin crawls as the dread closes over his heart.

Whatever's happening out there, it isn't good.

Jesse reaches for his gun, but it's not there. He looks down. His whole belt is missing. He can't be certain, but he could've sworn he went to bed still wearing it, like he does every night.

"Need my guns," he whispers.

Another scream rips through the air, followed by a piercing wail.

Delilah scoots close to Jesse, pressing into his side. "Somethin' bad out there," she says.

"Need my goddamn guns," he repeats.

"Go without," Delilah says.

Jesse scowls. He has no clue what he's walking into, and he's not about to head out there unarmed.

If Earl's the one in danger, Jesse doesn't care. Problem is, at least one of those screams came from a woman. *Lily Anne.* Earl isn't suffering alone.

"*Jesse,*" Delilah hisses. "You gotta go on out there."

"You stay put," he says.

Jesse's heart hammers against his ribcage. He stands and checks for his belt once again, out of habit more than anything. Of course, it isn't there.

When he exits the tent, he's not sure what he's seeing. Dawn stretches its pale pink fingers across the sky, but it's not enough light to see much else. All Jesse knows is there are two people there. He has to get closer, though he doesn't want to.

Hosea lies on the ground with blood pooling underneath him like the sky at sunset. Jesse can't quite wrap his head around what's happening. As Jesse creeps closer, he sees blood pouring from Hosea's ears, eyes, and mouth. Judging by the stain on the sand beneath him, blood leaks from *every* orifice.

The less Jesse thinks about that one, the better.

Hosea's eyes and mouth are closed. The scream hadn't come from him.

Turning, Jesse notices Lily Anne lying on the ground, too. She must have crawled out of her tent—her feet are still inside the flap. Either she just came out, or she tried crawling back in.

Jesse's pulse gallops like a wayward stallion. He wishes he had his guns.

"Where's Earl?" he asks Lily Anne. "Thought I heard him screaming."

Lily Anne's face is white. Her eyes are wide and wild, and her voice is high and tight. "He's dead," she says. "Hosea... he's dead! I heard him mutterin' outside the tent and came out here to help him..." She looks toward Hosea and shudders. "He's bleedin' everywhere. Nothin' I could do."

For the first time, Jesse realizes that the front of Lily Anne's dress is covered in blood. It's hard to tell in the scant light. In the preamble to sunrise, he assumed her dress is red. Now, he knows better.

"All that his?" Jesse asks, nodding toward her dress.

"I don't know," Lily Anne says. She looks down at her dress and groans. She opens her mouth to tell Jesse more. She touches her hair, and her left ear falls off. It lands on the ground beside her.

Jesse steps backward. "Jesus."

Lily Anne frowns, not understanding the reaction. She looks down at the ear and shrieks, although she appears too weak to move or do anything about it. A ribbon of fresh blood cascades down her neck and over her shoulders.

"Jesus!" Jesse says again. Whatever happened to Hosea must be happening to Lily Anne, too.

And still no sign of Earl, despite Jesse hearing his scream.

"We need help," Lily Anne moans.

Jesse isn't sure who the *we* is, since Hosea has passed, but he agrees. Their best bet for medical help is Ranch Ridge. Nothing else around for miles.

Then again, maybe it's safer to wait. Lily Anne's in no condition to travel. Jesse still doesn't know what's ailing her—what ailed Hosea—and it makes Jesse pause. If they're the only two people sick, maybe it'll pass. Hosea hasn't been in the best health, anyway. Maybe he died due to his lack of fitness.

Jesse looks over at Hosea, then returns his attention to Lily Anne. Inspiration dawns on him.

"Were the two of y'all sleepin' together?" he asks. He hates to ask her this, especially since he knows she used to be sweet on Jesse himself, but Lily Anne has a tendency to jump the camp beds. She'd even been with Delilah. It almost ruined her and Jesse's relationship.

He should've been more wary of Earl than Lily Anne.

"It ain't anythin' like that," Lily Anne insists. Somehow, she manages to sit up against the tent. She presses a hand against the place where her ear was. She doesn't scream again. Maybe she's in shock.

"You fuck him today?" Jesse asks.

"No." Lily Anne's eyes narrow. "Not that it's any of *your* business."

That rules out any venereal cause. Jesse's arm tingles. He swats it, expecting to kill a mosquito, but when he lifts his hand, there's nothing. Not even a bite. He scratches the spot.

"What did y'all eat?" Jesse persists.

"Same as everyone else."

"Y'all brew your own booze or somethin' like that?"

Lily Anne scowls. "What the hell would I know about brewin' some booze?"

She doesn't drink. Jesse forgot. She's never said why, but she's stuck to it.

"All I've had to drink is water," she says.

Jesse's other arm itches. He scratches it, too. They all drank the water. He's never known water to make body parts fall off. Worst they've been through was getting sick from some bad water, vomiting and shitting themselves empty.

Never nothin' like this, Jesse thinks.

Another wail pierces the desert night air. It's Earl's.

"I gotta go get him," Jesse says. "Reckon you'd better stay there."

"Don't have much choice," she answers. "I ain't said, but... well, I can't move my legs."

His concern for Earl muffles the alarm in Jesse's mind. Despite Earl's betrayal, he's the closest thing Jesse has to a brother. He can't help fearing for him.

Jesse swallows the lump in his throat. He pokes his head inside their tent. Delilah is fast asleep, He has no idea how she does that.

"Earl!" Jesse calls. It echoes off the distant mountains. He tries again. "Earl! Where the hell are ya?"

"Jesse!" Earl hollers.

Jesse thinks it's coming from down by the creek, the one they filled their canteens and watered their horses from that evening. Jesse looks for Cleopatra but she's nowhere to be found. *All* the horses are missing.

Just like his guns.

"Shit," Jesse mutters. He wets his lips and whistles for Cleopatra but she still won't come running.

Jesse takes off. He can't remember the last time he ran like this, the wind whipping his hair and whistling past him. He's going as fast as he can and it still feels like moving in a dream, like wading through water so thick that if he stops it will pull him under.

He has to get to Earl. He has to see what's wrong..

He knows he should be more concerned about Lily Anne and Hosea. But Hosea doesn't need help anymore. For all Jesse knows, Lily Anne might not need it when he gets back, either.

Jesse's lungs burn like they're filled with hot coals. A stitch knifes his side. He swears and keeps going.

He finds Earl with the horses down by the water. All the horses lie on their sides along the riverbank. Fear quickens Jesse's breath.

Earl sits on the sand with Paco's head in his lap. Blood oozing from Paco's mouth darkens Earl's trousers. Paco's eyes are glazed. Unseeing.

Panicked, Jesse doesn't speak to Earl. Instead, he goes to Cleopatra. Her body looks wrong, her legs splayed out and her neck reared back. Her eyes are open, t oo.

Jesse kneels by Cleopatra's head and puts his hand in front of her nostrils.

Nothing.

Tears prick Jesse's eyes. Grief overrides the panic.

When Jesse pulls back Cleopatra's lips, blood oozes over the teeth and tongue and splatters onto Jesse's hand, syrupy liquid seeping through his fingers.

Jesse recoils. He looks back at Earl. He almost forgot about him.

"What happened?" Jesse asks.

"I couldn't sleep," Earl says. "I decided to take 'em down here to drink. I fell asleep with 'em. When I woke up, the horses were already gone and all of 'em were bleedin'."

"So are you," says Jesse.

Blood drips from Earl's nose. He pinches his nostrils and tilts his head back. The blood floods the back of his throat and he gags. He lets go of his nose and spits the blood on the ground. His nose won't stop dripping.

Again, Jesse realizes that the blood underneath Earl might not all be Paco's. Maybe Earl's just as sick as the others.

"Did they drink before you fell asleep?" Jesse asks. Liberty, Scout, Vixen—he knows they're dead, too. None of the horses have moved. Jesse's brain feels like it's on fire, heat curling over his eyebrows. His arm itches again but it's too easy to ignore it with everything else going on.

"We all did," Earl says. "Same water we put in the canteens. Same water everyone drank."

Delilah, Jesse thinks. *And me. We're shit out of luck.*

A fly hovers over Cleopatra. It settles on her eyeball. Jesse's stomach burns like someone poked it with hot iron.

Earl coughs again. Three teeth fall out and scatter on the sand. More blood falls with them, making abstract red shapes in the dirt.

"I gotta go back," Jesse says.

"No!" Earl lunges for him, barely missing Jesse's leg. He doesn't try again. "You can't leave me here," Earl says. "You can't leave me to die alone."

"No one's dyin'," Jesse says, but he doesn't even believe that. All he's certain of is that he needs to find his wife. He needs to do everything in his power to fix what's wrong with them.

"I'd never leave you like this," Earl says.

Anger flares in Jesse. "You'd fuck my wife, though, wouldn't you?"

He doesn't stick around to see Earl's reaction. He doesn't need to. He already knows.

Vengeance doesn't matter to Jesse anymore. Earl's getting his, and so will they.

Back at camp, Lily Anne is slumped against the canvas of her tent. Her eyes are half shut. Anxiously, Jesse creeps over to her and touches her neck. She's cold. He doesn't feel a pulse.

Jesse's hand comes away tacky with blood. He curses and wipes it off on his pants.

He needs to get to Delilah.

Someone is crying. Muffled sobs drift through the air. Jesse hasn't heard that sound often, but he'd know it anywhere.

"Delilah," he says, stepping into their tent. It's still too dark to make out much. The sun will come up soon, but maybe they don't have much time.

Jesse's stomach churns again. It feels like he's swallowed burning nails, and maybe it's all in his head, but his legs are trembling, too, and he can't get them to stop.

His wife lies on the bed.

He kneels beside her and stretches out his hand to settle on her stomach. It rises and falls, but her breathing is shallow.

Jesse trails his hand up her chest and neck to touch her face. She's warm but slicked with cold sweat. Her face is sticky, but he doesn't think it's blood.

Delilah moans, scooting away from him. When she opens her eyes, her long eyelashes tickle Jesse's fingers.

"I don't feel too well," she says.

"Me, neither." Acid crawls up Jesse's throat. He swallows hard, but the reflux burns. The water is coming for him. It will come for all of them, in time.

"Who screamed?" Delilah asks.

"Earl," he says. "Hosea. And... Lily Anne." Jesse isn't sure how he should proceed. What good will stressing out Delilah do when none of it will matter in the end? Assuming they all drank the water—which, really, is not an assumption—and assuming they're all going to share the same fate, they don't have too much to look forward to.

"They all right?" Delilah asks.

Jesse hesitates. "Yeah. There's... there's nothin' wrong with 'em now."

It's not an outright lie, but it might as well be for how bad it makes Jesse feel. He doesn't want to meet his maker wracked with all this guilt.

Jesse stretches out on the bed beside Delilah. Even though the desert is cold at night, his wife radiates heat. He wishes he could see her face.

"Don't get up," Jesse says. He stands and walks over to grab the lantern, lighting it with some matches. It burns bright, filling the tent with an amber glow. Jesse relaxes. The light makes everything feel more manageable, at least for the time being.

But then he swings the light around and sees the ruins of Delilah's face. He almost drops the lantern.

The tip of Delilah's nose is gone. A raw, bloody mass marks its place. Blood spills like tears from her eyes.

Jesse's stomach roils. It's all he can do not to vomit or scream, but he doesn't want to frighten her.

"Sugar, we're gonna be fine," Jesse says. "We're gonna be just fine."

His teeth feel loose, like they might all fall out. He thinks of Earl. He tries to think of something else. His mouth tastes like copper, and his throat is so *dry*.

Delilah coughs up bloody phlegm that spatters on the bed. She gapes at the mess, her jaw dropping open, both hands fisting the blankets. Every muscle in her body tenses.

"Delilah," Jesse says. His head feels like it's full of cotton. He wants to say more, but the words refuse to come. His tongue sits useless and behind his ill-fitting teeth. If he could move his tongue, he could push the teeth out.

Delilah sits up. More light diffuses through the canvas tent. Must be sunrise. Jesse can see all of Delilah now, although he wishes he couldn't.

Blood streams from her exposed nostrils, slithering down her chin and neck. More blood drips from the corners of her mouth. Her eyes are wide, unfocused. Jesse can't see her ears to tell if they're bleeding, nor does he want to check.

His ears burn. He doesn't want to touch them, either.

"I need water," Delilah says. Her words come out garbled. Jesse isn't sure if she's having trouble speaking or he's having trouble hearing, or both.

Water's what got them all into this mess. Still, they're damned already.

And he'd give her anything.

Jesse's bruised heart breaks for her. It breaks for all of them. He reaches over and picks up the metal canteen, passing it to Delilah. There isn't much left. He doesn't think it matters.

Delilah's hands tremble as she unscrews the cap and lifts the canteen to her lips. As she drinks, some of the water dribbles down her chin.

Jesse debates whether he should tell her about the water. About overhearing her talking to Earl. They don't keep secrets from each other—at least, he thought they didn't. Maybe there's another one she's taking to her grave.

He sits up a little straighter and stretches his legs out in front of him. Each inhale hurts, and his lungs feel like they're full of poison, but that's because they are. His belly, too. His blood. Every bone in his body.

Jesse's tired. Fatigue has crashed into him like a train. He's not sure whether that's from running or drinking from Dread Creek. He shouldn't close his eyes. That much he's sure about.

The canteen falls from Delilah's hands, landing on the bed. Water soaks the blankets. Delilah's top lip sticks to the mouth of the canteen, still pink and healthy.

Jesse looks at her and wants to scream, but he doesn't. Even with her face torn up, he loves her.

Until death do us part, he thinks.

A ray of sunlight peeks through the front flap of the tent. Delilah coughs hard and wet, the effort jolting her body. Jesse scoots close to her and pulls her into his arms. He wants his face to be the last thing she sees, and for hers to be his.

"What are you lookin' at me like that for?" she asks. Tears of blood drip down her cheek. Jesse brushes them away with his fingertips.

"You look good," he says.

Delilah doesn't respond. Her eyes fall shut, and she suffers through each rattling breath she takes. Jesse's fever boils his brain. He knows he won't have long now.

When Delilah's eyes don't open again and her breathing stops, Jesse touches the twine around her finger. He envisions a gold band there, glinting in the light. She deserves a wedding ring.

His left ear falls off, but he barely notices the pain. The other falls off, too.

Jesse closes his eyes. Soon, everything stills.

It Calls

BY PATRICK R. MCDONOUGH

NIGHTFALL BROUGHT WITH IT a bitter air, which slunk across the snow-covered Montana prairie and through every hair-thin crack. That air was the type of numbing force that worked while you slept. It wasn't created by a vengeful lord or fallen light from the heavens; it just was. The arctic nip blued flesh, muddled the mind, made basic movements clumsy, weakened breath, and overpowered internal heat, matching body temperature to ambient air, forcing every nerve to shiver.

That was why Constance and Effie Glass often slept in the parlor, wrapped in the warmth of the fireplace—a comfort they always looked forward to. But now, the large fiery mouth made Effie whimper, confused, and clutch her Mama under a shared blanket.

It terrified Constance too, creating a tic, a trembling hand with fingers that pulled themselves into claws. She concealed the spasm outside of the blanket, away from Effie's view.

The light can't hurt us. Can't hurt Effie. Can't hurt me.

Within the center of the bright white fire, lines formed into the eyes, face, and *smile* of her love, Emmett Murdock Glass. That face tilted and the smiling mouth whispered, "Run."

"I'll find you," she muttered to herself.

A little hand tugged at the sleeve of her nightgown.

"Mama."

Constance looked down into those cornflower blue eyes, worried she'd reveal her own terror.

"It's alright, Mama. I'm scared too."

Effie was four. Some would say *only* four, but it doesn't take someone of Nikola Tesla's intellect to know she was old enough to understand the weight of what was happening.

Constance relaxed. A quick check revealed the flame to be just a flame—no premonition of her missing husband. She sniffled, ignoring the frozen tear clinging in the corner of her eye.

"Are you okay?"

"Yes, my little star." She pushed the tear away.

Effie giggled. "That's what Papa called me."

"Mm-hmm," Constance said, nodding. "And I'm his shooting star." Fire crackle filled the air. "As long as I have you by my side, I'll be okay."

"I'll be your protector." Constance's throat tightened, almost to the point of suffocation. Effie felt her Mama's hand squeeze her own extra tight.

She was the one who should be the protector, not the other way around. The fear and anxiety that loomed over her and Effie was something new. It wasn't until earlier that day, when a light burst through the sky—so intense that it made the sun appear petroleum black—that she felt hopeless in shielding her daughter from harm's way. So profound was the anomaly that it stole conventional sight from mother and daughter. The light trapped them in a world made of shades of white. It stole their sense of touch or smell, and apart from a celestial chorus from above, all sound deadened, as if they were underwater.

Dancing at the edge of her vision, outlines of colossal beasts—leviathans—swam around. Fibrous roots covered their bodies like thick fur, and trailing behind were the silhouettes of humans. Amongst the people came the agonizing scream of a man: desperate, scared, and familiar.

Familiar...it was incredibly familiar.

It was the same scream she had once heard from her husband.

Crack-POP!

A yelp escaped Effie. It took a moment to slow everything down, to realize the sudden pain came from her little girl gripping onto her stomach.

"It's okay, my little star," she whispered. "Just loosen your grip, alright?"

"That wasn't me, Mama." Effie pointed to Constance's belly.

Constance shook her head, wanting to speak but unable to. She didn't know how or why *her* thumb and pointer were the ones pinching her belly fat. Madness claimed her mind. That had to be it. All she could envision, hoped for, prayed for—*wished* for—was to look out the window and see Emmett, homeward bound on their trusted mare, Grit.

She yanked the cord of the window shade, up enough to witness a desolate, snow-covered prairie. A prairie that should have been blanketed by night. Instead, light gleaming up and through the icy pond, tinted the entire grassland and the bordering forest in shades of yellow, green, purple, and white.

It violates the dark sacred night.

"Mama." Effie's voice pulled Constance back to reality again. She released her hand and with it, the shade fell back into place.

"Yes, my heart?"

"Can you read to me?" Before Constance could answer, Effie held up a book.

A smile broke over Constance's face, followed by an unexpected laugh. Effie laughed too. "*All Around the Moon*, huh?"

"Uh-huh." Effie nodded vigorously. "Jules Verne makes me happy."

"He makes me happy too."

Effie flipped the cover open to an illustration of the moon and traced her fingertip along the outline. "It really worked," she said to herself.

Constance's left hand gently guided hair behind Effie's ear and leaned in. "What worked?"

"My wish."

"I don't understand."

"I wished to the stars. To help find Papa."

The next morning, Constance found Effie staring out the same window she had looked through the previous night.

"What are they doing, Mama?" she asked, without turning around.

"What are who..." Constance's jaw hung open in awe, unable to produce another sound. Deer, groundhogs, foxes, birds of varying breeds, and even a massive grizzly bear, gathered around the ice-covered pond, statue-still. Flames flickered from their charcoal eye sockets, like distant glimmering stars. Waves of light danced above the pond. Somehow, someway... the light's power only grew stronger since it crashed into the pond.

It crashed and there's no hole.

Even in her state of disbelief, Constance couldn't figure out how something so powerful and large could end up in the pond without breaking the icy surface.

She locked on Emmett's fishing hut, and the familiar crescent moon he carved into the closed door. Her heart pounded his name, telling her to run to it.

A constant hum emanated from the heavens. The celestial orchestra created strange music that aided the even stranger pattern of lights and gathering woodland creatures. Was Emmett going to pop out of his hut? Or was all of this the result of starvation and exposure to extreme cold? She had heard of such things, of people going mad. She wondered if she was trapped in the dream world of Verne himself. Then the answer came to her

"This is the wish come true!" exclaimed Constance, not realizing she spoke out loud. She didn't hear her daughter's question, and repeated the sentiment of the wish coming true. It all made sense now. That's when the ice hut's door swung open, revealing a silhouette.

The light did that!

The light brought him back, because the light wasn't malicious. The light didn't possess ill intent and never tried to intimidate her. Rather, it was their savior, their protector, an angel. This was why the animals were brought to the pond. It was all for the reunion!

Love hammered her heart like the stomping hooves of a Pony Express Thoroughbred, and vibrated her flesh making it impossible to sit still.

Constance looked down, surprised to find her boots on. "When did that happen?"

"It's Papa!" Effie exclaimed, shoving her feet in her boots too. "It's really him!"

Light suddenly beamed from Emmett's eyes, locking with Constance's.

Fear not, my shooting star.

The voice skittered into her mind only to leave in a nauseating reverberation.

Her stomach acid churned, and her guts felt like they plummeted through her anus, splattering the floorboards. A blinding storm in her mind created a haze of chaos and confusion.

"That—" a battle ensued in her mind— "that's a fake." The realization crushed her, making it difficult to breathe.

None of this made sense. It just was, and the light wasn't good, it wasn't an angel, but something horrible, something her heart knew to be evil in its purest form.

Grab Effie and run like hell, you asshead

But she couldn't do that. All she managed was to witness Effie's feet kick up snow as she raced toward the pond.

"Papa! Papa!" Effie shouted.

Constance could hear the tears in her daughter's cries, her pleas to be wrapped in her father's arms once again.

"No, no, no, no!" Constance shrieked, pounding her fists against the glass window. "Stop! Just... STOP!"

Effie couldn't hear her Mama. She was too focused on her father, the one person in this world, other than Constance, that made everything else invisible. But that wasn't her father.

She ran toward the thing with glowing eyes. The thing that called from the light.

Fake Emmett bent down like always, arms spread as wide as angel wings, ready to collect his child. A creepy smile spread across his face, and the light in his eyes didn't hinder the little girl's progress.

The vibration from the celestial chorus intensified, their voices pressing into the crown of her skull. Effie had to be experiencing this too, right? Constance would never know by Effie's excited giggles and flapping arms.

"Effie!" Constance shouted. The few feet that separated mother and daughter felt like miles. Effie was so close to the shanty. Any second now, Fake Emmett would wrap her in its arms and pull her beneath the ice.

Into the brightest bright.

The void of Hell's Light.

Constance extended a hand toward Effie, reaching and missing once, twice. On the third try her pointer and thumb pinched the fabric of Effie's nightgown. She yanked back as hard as she could, feeling Effie's head slam into her sternum a second later.

"Leave us ALONE!" Adrenaline took over. Her left hand clenched into a tight ball, cocked back, then thrust forward with the weight of an anvil, just how Emmett taught her. His mushy flesh stuck to her knuckles and peeled from its angular cheekbone, splintering like dried twigs. Next, her knee drove into his crotch.

Fake Emmett didn't react. Didn't even move. It was as if something or someone were holding him up.

"My shooting star." His breath came out in a puff of blue smoke, and with it, a strong odor of rotting flesh and feces that molested all sense of taste and smell. That stench wormed through every hair-thin passage, snuffing out the fire in her belly. Frost coated Fake Emmett's once thick black beard, his swollen lips were discolored, a chunk of his nose rotted off, and sections of translucent flesh, revealing a network of sparkling black veins, were divided by gashes filled with a coagulated amber secretion, reminding Constance of tree sap.

A part of her brain demanded she listen, that everything could be explained by extreme Montana winter conditions, and the light she saw in his eyes was false. Sanity vanished the moment Fake Emmett opened his mouth. The teeth that weren't rotted had turned into icy fangs, some jutting at odd angles. Flickering stars, along with planets—*actual* planets—and lights similar to the one in the pond, replaced where his throat should have been. Appendages of the universe wrapped around Constance, pulling her in like a hungry beast.

A scream broke through. A scream that called for her Mama.

———◦❖◦———

Suddenly, stellar sound and light vanished, and Constance was back in the ice shanty.

Emmett turned to expose his profile, revealing root-like tendrils syphoning his blood, inserted throughout his back, an abominable bastardization of a porcupine. His tattered hunting frock exposed charred flesh, iced-over fat, coagulated sap-blood, and in some places, burnt bone. Emmett nodded at something behind her. An ice saw hanging on the wall, its sharp teeth begging to bite into something.

"Help...me." Emmett's voice was raspy, but it was *his* voice. The light in his eyes turned back into their familiar steel grey color.

"Emmett... it's really you."

"Hurry." His eyes slowly closed. She raced to grab the cast iron handle, spun on her heels, and slammed its big teeth into leathery flesh. Black gritty chunks of gunk flowed out of the meaty tendrils. The earth trembled and bursts of light filled the shanty, forcing every action to appear like a series of photographs.

Emmett screamed and intense rays shot out of his eyes. He grabbed for Constance but she was too determined. The appendages gave some resistance but the saw teeth sliced through. Blood sprayed out, covering Constance's face, hands, and nightgown. Grimy maggots with illuminating bodies like fireflies flailed in the ichor.

"Mama!"

How the fuck did she forget about her little girl?

To her right, near the hole Emmett used to fish out of, were more tendrils, wrapping themselves around Effie. Strangling her legs and arms, forcing every part to remain still with the exception of her face, she called for her mother again. Emmett grabbed Constance's hair and tried to yank her head off, but that only intensified her blood-splattering sawing. Moments later, the blade separated Emmett from squirming blood gushers that retreated back into the ice hole. Emmett fell back with a thud. Black gunk dribbled out of his back, and with more of those squirmy light worms, releasing high-pitched screeches. Constance couldn't help him now. She raced to Effie, fell on her knees and tried digging her fingers into the appendages but they were too tight. There was no blood in them yet; they just looked like black worms.

"LET HER GO! LET HER GO!"

Instead, they began to drag her toward the hole, toward the world of light.

Panic set in. She wanted to grab onto the only free part of her daughter—her head. Flaring nostrils and tear-filled eyes would be the last thing she ever saw of her little girl.

"AH!" Emmett screamed, jumping atop the section of appendages between Effie and the hole. He opened his mouth lion-wide and bit down into the tendrils. As he jerked his head back-and-forth like a rabid mutt, blood spilled over onto ice and the world shook. Constance saw one of Effie's hands break free and pulled. There was little resistance. The wrigglers had turned their focus on Emmett.

Effie could stand. They hadn't taken that away from her yet. Constance and Emmett locked eyes.

"Don't look back," Emmett said. A crystal formed in the corner of his eye. She tried to swallow a wad of spit down but couldn't. She looked at Effie, who returned her gaze, and they ran like hell. The second they crossed the threshold of the hut, light launched the icy foundation, along with Emmett and the shack, into the heavens.

———◆———

Between the cracking ice and slippery surface, every footstep promised to be their last. A gasp from Effie compelled Constance to look down. Palms pressed against the ice, as did a face or two..

"Mama!" Effie screamed.

"Focus on our house!" she said, right before jumping over a gap that dropped into a bright white void. She peripherally spotted creatures watching from the shore. All she wanted was to hug Effie and be safe. She squeezed Effie's hand extra tight, wishing she could throw her ahead, into their home.

Constance stepped on solid ground, a few long strides away from safety.. Something massive shot out of the ice—leviathan. Then another explosion followed by another. Ice shards crashed into the open water and smashed all around them. An ice block slammed into her upper-back, sending her forward, nearly tripping, but refusing to fall.

"Almost there, Effie!" They shot through the opened doorway, an escape from oblivion. "Safe, we're safe, Effie!" She couldn't catch her breath or slow her mind. The returned adrenaline jittered nerves and peeled back her lips, forming a hysterical smile.

We're safe, safe...

She could give Effie that reassuring hug now. Let her know nothing bad would ever happen again. Not ever! Constance spun on her heels; arms spread angel wing wide. They hung there, even as her smile became a frown, breath trapped in her throat, eyes widened, locked on the thing she gripped white-knuckle tight. It was what remained of Effie.

Her hand.

———◦○◦———

Constance hadn't moved an inch—not a goddam inch—from the door. For an hour? A day? A week? Time no longer meant anything. Her little girl's smile, the things wrapped around her, Emmett, the light, her fucking hand, they haunted her like lamenting wraiths. The images gutted Constance, leaving her hollow and accepting of a silent death.

Tap-Tap-Tap!

Pecking against the window scrambled her nerves.

Tap-Tap-Tap!

Her fists clenched.

Tap-Tap—

Constance shot up and screamed, "GOD DAMNIT!" White clouds frothed from her mouth. She looked down, no more than a foot away was Effie's hand. White tendons trailed out of the wrist like flat earthworms. That couldn't be the last memory of her baby.

Tap-Tap-Tap!

"SHUT—" she raced toward the sound— "UP!"

The rapping beak of a deranged-flames-for-eyes woodpecker fractured the window. An owl suddenly rammed into another section, leaving half of its bloody skull poking into the house, black gunk dripped onto the hardwood floor.

The front door creaked open. Effie walked into view. Her right arm dangled, crystalized meat ribbons draped from where her hand should have been. Her head tilted, spotting her motionless hand, and she giggled.

"Mama." That wasn't her voice.

Constance knew if she peeked around the door, she'd see tendrils slithering into her daughter's back, controlling her like a puppet master. Glass shattered turning into sloppy wet thumps. The birds broke through, the owl hobble-running toward Constance. Black watery fluid sloshed out of its busted skull.

Constance ran across the room, grabbed a mounted rifle above the fireplace, cocked it, pivoted on her heels, and prayed it was loaded. Deer, groundhogs, snakes, wolves, and other woodland creatures with flashing lights for eyes filled the open room.

"Stay the *fuck* back!" She stared at Effie. A warm fetid breath brushed the nape of her neck.

"Don't fight it," Emmett's grime-and-frost-covered hand reached from behind, gripping the mouth of the rifle's barrel. His other hand firmly planted on her shoulder.

A deafening bang filled the room. Fake Emmett's stump of an arm remained beneath the barrel. Arm muscles contracted, trying to command a hand that was no longer there. He stared at the black gritty fluid gushing out of him, like a fleshy geyser.

Constance turned and ran for the backdoor.

"Mama, don't leave!"

Effie's dead.

A brown fur-covered body blocked the egress, stuck its head in, and bellowed. Constance roared back, charged, and rammed the barrel down the bear's fucking throat. She pulled the trigger, grizzly war paint splattering her face. It wobbled and fell to its side taking the rifle with it. She pushed her way through a narrow space, stepping into an open field.

She wasn't fast enough to make it to the woods. She wished Grit was still here. She wished *something* fast could sweep her up and away.

As if answering that wish, a braying came from the barn. Standing in the barn's open doorway was Grit. Its eyes matched that of the other creatures. She didn't dare run towards her. Grit was no longer hers. No longer in control of her own facilities. Constance ran for the woods.

The grizzly flopped around trying to claw at the pulpy exit wound in the back of its neck. From above, crows, woodpeckers, ravens, and owls flew toward her. On the ground, a pack of snarling wolves, grunting deer, and hissing serpents.

Snow shot upward at one end of the prairie, in a trail that was directed toward her. Massive antlers gave it away to be a moose. Her mind said run, but her legs refused.

She turned toward the incoming behemoth. "You win."

One deep inhale, closed eyes, and arms extended, as if she wanted to go out like Jesus.

Ready to accept what was to come.

Her heart slowed, her breathing too.

My shooting star.

Emmett's voice rasped in her mind.

We'll protect you

. The sky rumbled, washing over every other sound and motion, forcing a temperature drop. A light so bright that it blotted out the sun forced Constance to shield her eyes. That wasn't good enough. Stark white stung her eyes and warmed her body, warming everything else around her too.

Puke-green and tar-black coated every tree, the ground, and house. Steam rose from the rancid stains, coating Constance's tongue and nasal passage. She couldn't understand if this was the infinite hell she deserved for not protecting her daughter. Or maybe everything ripping into the sky was real.

The moose floated far above her, tiny as a sparrow now. Blood rained down from every single creature that had dared chase her. She couldn't follow the moose or other animals all the way up, for that was where the light shone the brightest.

The light sent a searing pain through her eyes and straight into her brain. She fought it for as long as possible, because two figures captured her focus. Two people dangling at the ends of celestial umbilical cords.

Effie...Emmett...

We'll protect you.

Their limbs flailed like ragdolls. Blood rained over the prairie and surrounding woods, resembling a story from *The Old Testament*. Some stray creatures fell from the sky, softly swaying, and covering sections of red snow. Soon the ground was littered with fur husks. Bodies so dehydrated that not even the worms or maggots would touch them.

The sky had a pink tint to it she'd never seen before. Constance wondered if it was a stain the light left behind. If the leviathan left a mark, so to speak. She wondered how to continue living. Time meant nothing again, and she remained frozen in place until her brain returned to reality.

That light transformed her family's safe haven into a desolate wasteland. No longer would the cheerful chirps from a sparrow, or the comforting song of a robin, or the soft whoosh of a deer fleeing through tall grass, be a thing. As for the pond, it was now a massive pit too deep to explore. Emmett's shanty was now splintered lumber, spread across the muddy puddles and frost-bitten trout and perch.

Constance Glass had survived an anomaly that stole her life. The leviathan of light abducted her husband and little girl. Her entire world. Effie's smile, a kiss from Emmett, holding Effie's hand...the severed one, and father and daughter being pulled up into oblivion, would forever haunt her.

There was no reason, no understanding to any of it.

It just was.

Old Habits

BY L. M. LABAT

A STILL, DEAFENING SILENCE enveloped the night air. Deep within the midnight hour, as the last breaths of summer awaited the inevitable chills of autumn, a faint amber light flickered in a small kerosene lamp. As it sat in its glass chamber on top of an aged table, the withering flame danced its weary light upon the weathered veneer. In the dense quiet, a man sat with his back flush against his seat. He stared at his notations with wide eyes and a ghastly pallor. His thin lips quivered as he kept his mouth shut tight and tiny droplets of cold sweat dripped onto the scribbled pages of his journal.

The tired bones of the house popped and creaked while the man's muscles ached. Though his throbbing muscles screamed inside his neck, he turned to look at the dusty beams upon the ceiling and walls. Then, as the noises ceased, he steadied his quickening heart and peered through the window.

Across the vast stretches of dry land, the brown, prickled grass of prairie and cracked earth succumbed to relentless darkness underneath the pitch-black sky, as it swallowed all remnants of nature. As he averted his eyes from the encroaching void, he glanced at the pile of stained sheets on the cabin floor, before returning to his papers. After rubbing his heavy eyelids, he grasped his fountain pen with his long fingers and wrote.

September 3, 1852. It's been four months since our departure from Indian Territory. From his acquaintances, father told me all the great things he heard about Utah Territory, with its open air and vast mountain ranges. But unfortunately, I've not yet found solace in those rumors. Even long after we crossed territory lines, the grass remained as rough and dry as my last resting place. However, as we rode deeper into unknown fields, the ground felt colder, less welcoming.

He paused his hand and leaned back in the chair. Looking over to the empty seat beside him, the man passed his fingers over the arm of his chair. He straightened his back and picked up the pen. Memories saturated his mind and flung his consciousness back into the past.

Even now, I can still see her.

A woman, covered in sweat and a thin film of filth, lay stretched on top of a thin mattress. Her obsidian hair stuck to the sides of her face and neck as heat radiated from her desiccating body. As each clock tick-tock echoed louder into the night, an apprentice searched through their bags of instruments. The numerous bottles of tonic and sedatives clinked together, making an irritable racket.

"Stop messing with those bags and help me, boy," the physician said. The man continued to sort through the materials. "William!" the doctor shouted.

"Yes, Dr. Lester?" William shuddered.

"Get over here," Lester ordered. William returned the vials to their compartments and stood alongside his mentor. He handed William a wooden rod, "Go on over there and open that mouth. Make sure you get this in there, so her tongue stays secured," he grumbled. "Don't need no more shit happening tonight."

"Yes, sir," William replied as he grabbed the bar. The uneven wood bore scratches and imprints from teeth marks. Every dent served as a constant reminder of past patients. Even after a decade, the sounds of weakened grunts and choking cluttered his head. He walked to the bedside and sat next to the woman to open her mouth.

A putrid, sour odor wafted over her cracked lips from days of vomiting. William gagged at the pungent smell and covered his nose. "We don't get time for your stalling!" Lester barked. "Now, stop wincing and get that damn bar in there! Keep that airway open."

Tears welled in William's eyes as he covered his nose with his shirt. Leaning closer to the patient, he grabbed her chin. After holding her mouth open, he slipped the small rod between her pale lips and readjusted her head. "What do we do now, Les—"

Lester slapped William across the back of his head. "Dr. Lester."

William closed his eyes and sighed, "Sorry, Fa—" He corrected himself, "Dr. Lester."

"Good." Lester placed his tools back into the bags. He handed William a few vials of tonic and a couple of sedatives. "Bring this to the others and collect the payment. We've done all that we can do for tonight."

"W-We're going now?" William stuttered. "But, she's still—"

"What more do you expect?" Lester interjected. "This sickness isn't going nowhere anytime soon. Alleviating the pain is all we can manage right now. Besides"—he said, closing his bags—"we need to keep moving before this gets us, too." He grabbed the lantern from the table and gestured to the woman, "That'll be you if we stay."

William furrowed his brow and looked toward the patient. He parted her hair away from her face. Her shallow breaths warmed the tips of his fingers. "But," he whispered, "We could still do something. Can't we?"

Lester kicked the door open. The old, iron hinges creaked as a gust of wind almost blew out the lantern's flame. Lester called out to his son, "Well?"

William sighed and stood up from the bed. He grabbed his coat and secured his boot laces. "I'll go get the horses ready."

"Good boy," Lester grinned, handing the bags to William. "Remember, get the payment before those bottles leave your hand," he said, patting the side of William's face. "Yeah?"

William averted his eyes and glanced back into the house. Covered in shadows, the woman stared at them from the shallow bed. William gasped.

"Hey!" Lester shouted. He grabbed William's ear, "You listening to me, boy?"

"T-The woman!" William replied. His voice trembled, "The woman! She—"

"What?" Lester asked. He peered back into the house. The woman remained still in her bed. Beads of sweat glistened over her face, dotting her eyelids as she slept. Lester turned to William and snatched the vials from his hand. "Never mind the money. Leave that to me. Just get the damn horses ready." He dropped the heavy bags on his son's foot. William bit his tongue and let out a sharp exhale.

The rugged leather soles of Lester's boots scuffed the floor of the small farm-house. As he exited the premises, his burly steps shook the brittle wooden steps. He looked over his shoulder at William.

"Anything else you need me to do, sir?" William asked. "I can get the payment if you need me to do it."

"No," Lester replied. He shook his head and walked off towards the barn. "I should've never left you at that homestead," he sneered. "I swear your mama raised a bitch."

William bit his bottom lip and looked down at his delicate feet. Even well into his young adulthood, his frame never matched the solid build of his father. He coiled his nimble fingers around the handles and hoisted the cumbersome bags onto his narrow shoulders. "Damn it."

Hot breath blew past his ear. "William."

A foul odor drifted past him. He spun around and halted. The young woman stared at him from the shadowed farmhouse entrance. Her ghoulish face wors-ened in the waning moonlight.

Frozen at the sight of her dry lips stretched tight over rotting teeth, William's heart sank into his quaking chest. Her pungent breath reeked as a white film covered her swollen, reddened tongue. The woman gripped the doorframe and crept over the threshold. Her raspy, frail voice carried over the wind, "William."

William gasped as his throat tightened with fear. He tripped and hit his head on the cold ground. When he stood back on his feet, she vanished.

He dusted his clothes and coughed hard into his hands. Speechless, he stared wide-eyed at the house. His knees quaked as he shifted his feet to run. "No," he sputtered. "S-She was right there." He steadied himself and wiped the dirt from his cheek. "She was right there. I—"

"William!" Lester shouted as he made his way back from the barn. He held a small pouch of coins in his palm. "Pick up the damn bags and ready the horses!" William shook at his father's booming voice, grabbed the equipment, and hurried toward him. After securing the saddles and reigns, the two men took their leave into the night.

William stopped writing. The flame quivered in the lantern beside him. His neck tensed as the walls creaked behind him. Shivering in a cold sweat, he placed his fingers on the back of his neck and rocked in his chair. "Keep it together," William whispered to himself. "You know what this is. Just keep going."

The fire's dance stood still. A dark shadow stretched across the floor. William stopped himself from looking over his shoulder and focused on his journal. "The following days sank in the true devastation of the tragedy. From small towns to long-standing homesteads, scarlet fever showed no mercy. Children fell the hardest to the illness." William shook his head, "I never thought I'd see so much heartbreak."

The scarlet fever epidemic ravaged his homeland during the mid-1800s. "Children, especially newborns and toddlers, remained the most vulnerable to the disease. Panting from the overwhelming heat, the babies writhed in pain as blistering, red lesions littered their frail bodies. As they coughed and wailed for relief, the infants strained to swallow any form of nourishment that sat atop their swollen whitened tongues," William recalled. "As the high fever continued to spread death across the regions, schools, markets, and other public gathering places emptied in droves. Due to the rampant nature of the vile bacteria, medical professionals of all degrees urged civilians to refrain from meeting in close quarters with others. The sickness utilized the air and direct contact was its primary pathways for infection. While the isolation increased, the months bled into one another. The everyday clamor of innovation was hushed under the quarantine. However, no amount of distancing muted the crescendoed cacophony of tortured laments."

"My father and I knew some of the families from previous visits and deliveries," William remembered. "After a bit, everywhere we went asked for Johnathan Lester." As a well-respected physician, Dr. Johnathan Lester gained the attention of many from humble backgrounds and affluent social circles across the plains. At the height of his popularity, he garnered more audiences after creating his unique brand of tonics and other remedies. "He helped plenty of people," William sighed. "A lot of women we treated survived hard pregnancies." He frowned. "Neither of us knew we'd be burying those same babies."

A dark figure loomed in the distance. As its shadow reached and touched the nape of William's neck, its elongated body glided closer and appeared in his peripherals. Faint whispers seeped into his ears. William closed his eyes. "No," he said.

"Even though he knew," the voice whispered, "he didn't stop." The voices grew louder.

"We," William corrected. "We didn't stop. We kept going." A tear ran down his cheek, "But, what could I do? I couldn't say no to him. I--"

A shrill screech pierced through the silent room. The sound rattled William's brain. He screamed and lowered his head. "You're right!" he cried, burying his face in his palms. "You're right. I could've done something! I didn't!" He wiped his eyes, "I didn't."

William peeked over his hands at the clock. He forgot how many hours had passed since his father left for supplies. He steadied his breathing and returned to his journal. William continued jotting down his memories.

After leaving the farmhouse, William rode alongside his father to various towns and sold a series of his homemade concoctions. No matter where they arrived, the two men received a welcome from a sea of sallow faces. As their weak bodies trembled, they held their arms wide open for their favorite doctor. Although clients kept their distance from loved ones, the crowds dismissed their fears of scarlet fever amongst each other, all for obtaining diluted hope from their favorite miracle worker.

While the morale declined, the saloons, though tending to fewer patrons, provided whatever they possessed to locals. Lester granted most of his attention to these establishments. The women gathered around the windows and steps upon hearing the familiar jingle of his bottled tincture and the thud of his heavy boots.

Lester strolled through the saloon doors and sat at to the bar. His broad shoulders bumped against the long wind chimes strung up around the threshold. The polished metal clanked and twinkled against the outer walls. William followed him and sat alone, one table behind his father.

The scent of chewing tobacco, cigarette smoke and watery beer polluted the cluttered room. Under the beef tallow candles, the rich amber light masked the faults and blemishes while illuminating everyone's skin with an ethereal golden glow. As with every visit, William watched a small crowd clap with joy and packed every section surrounding his father. Every barkeeper waited for their chance to serve him. The women did, too. In taking preventive measures, William bore the task of holding all the money in case someone dared to pickpocket his father. Until the late hours, William remained vigilant for Lester's signal to pay the barkeepers and fair belles.

"More like scarlet ladies," William mumbled under his breath. He took a quick swig from his dented flask and sat back in his seat. The taste of alcohol never agreed with him, but it proved as the only thing to numb the constant loneliness. He reached down into his satchel and retrieved his journal.

The laughter from the bar rumbled through the building and drowned his thoughts. "Howling bastards," he said, gathering his items. "I can't think in this mess." He moved from the table to a small couch in the back of the saloon. Sitting on the stiff cushions, he took out his journal once more and recorded the events. He peered across the room and watched his father for any gestures between finishing his paragraphs. After realizing that the crowd failed to dwindle, William rested his feet on top of the table, stored the coin purse deep into his vest, and prepped himself for a long night.

Throughout the night, Lester entertained his hypnotized listeners with tales of his ventures and medical marvels. William watched, as woman after woman passed him over and strolled towards his father. Lester coiled his arms around each lady, young and old, as they melted from his embrace. William took another sip from his flask. "It's like mama never existed." He grimaced as the dark alcohol burned his throat. "Like he never even cared about mama anyway."

"Mama."

William froze as a hot breeze wafted across his face. A nauseating, sour musk stung his nose. He stood up and coughed into his sleeve. "Oh, my God," William choked. He looked down at the floorboards and covered his nose with his arm. In many of the saloons he visited with Lester, he discovered that rodents and other small critters sheltered themselves under the gaps in the buildings. Sensing that some creature found itself trapped beneath his feet, he searched for the source of the foul fumes. The reeking stench of bile grew stronger with every gained inch. "Oh, God," he recoiled, gagging. "What is that?" As he backed away from the couch, he heard the wind chimes clattered outside the front door.

"William." A hollow voice called to him from the far end of the saloon. William turned towards the entrance. His brow furrowed in watching a tall, shadowed figure standing beyond the threshold. As its gaunt, cloaked body blocked the pale moonlight, it wrapped its spindled fingers around the frame and pushed its crooked body through the doors.

William gawked at its mass. The others kept laughing and talking in their boisterous, drunken stupor. Lester and his sycophants carried on with their late-night amusements, oblivious of what creature stalked the night.

As it lowered itself under a splintered archway, the hood of its blackened cloak tore free from its crown. Candlelight revealed a long, weathered doe skull covering a human face. It turned its head towards William.

"Dr. Lester," William whimpered. In panic, he flailed his hands above his head. "Dr. Lester!" he repeated. His heartbeat pounded faster as he tried to catch Lester's attention. "Father!" he yelped with a raspy breath. He failed to project his voice over the drunken fools.

Though slow, the hulking beast seemed to glide across the floor. The abyssal eye sockets of its decayed doe skull echoed like vacant graves. However, William sensed the looming entity staring back at him. The beast made its way past the bar. He pushed his shoulder through the masses and reached out toward Lester. He grabbed Lester's shoulder, "Father!"

The ruckus dimmed. A handful of people snickered as they looked back at William. They muttered to each other. Lester slid his eyes towards his son. Sinking into his shoes, William halted under his father's glare.

"What's this?" a woman said, swishing liquor in her glass. "Father?" she giggled. "Say, sugar," she said, nudging Lester's arm, "You never said you had a boy of your own." She smiled as she eyed William. "Well, maybe not a boy," she twittered. William blushed. She poked Lester's arm, "But why didn't you say anything?"

"Something else you want to tell us?" asked another woman. "You still single, huh?"

More jokes passed through the crowd. Some of the men patted William on his back. As his worried eyes darted around the room in search of the creature, he chuckled and nodded in response to the playful taunting.

No sign of the entity remained.

"Dr. Lester!" one man exclaimed. "What's his name?" He grabbed William's shoulder. Booze wetted his yellowed beard. "What's your name, son? You a doctor, too?"

"He's not a doctor," Lester answered. He stared at William from his bar stool. The cold, unwavering disappointment hanging in his eyes, contrasted with the faint smile held on his face. He finished his drink. "He's my apprentice." He pushed the glass aside and stepped away from the bar. Lester gestured for William to pay the barkeeper and made his way towards the exit. "He's not my son."

⸺◆⸺

William slammed his pen down. Ink splatted onto his hand from the broken tip. The lantern shook as the candlelight flickered. William's heart cracked. In reading the entry, his innards twisted at the memory. "Why?" he sobbed. "Why does he have to be so..." He pitched the fractured pen across the room, "Damn it !"

The chair moved beside him. William's hands shielded his face. The temperature dropped. A horrid wheeze circled him. From the back of the room, the cloaked entity made its way to the table and sat in the vacant seat. Its large ribcage expanded with each ragged breath as it looked down at him.

"Please," William said. Tears poured through his fingers and onto his chest, "Just do it!" He blew his nose into his shirt. "Stop haunting me and end this already." The creature sat still and continued to watch him squirm beneath its shadow. "I can't sleep. I can't eat. I'm losing all my wits!" He shook his head, "My father doesn't believe me. Like he'd give a damn anyway. He wouldn't care if I disappeared or not." Lester's glower burned in his mind. He scoffed, "He'd probably want that."

The figure decreased in stature but remained ever motionless. As the clock ticked, the silence grew. Harnessing his strength, William exhaled and lowered his hands. "Mama raised you better than this," he whispered. The spirit tilted its head. He straightened his back and forced himself to lock his gaze with the eldritch skull.

"I just wanted him to like me, you know?" he admitted. "I took note of everything I could with hopes that I would be able to recreate the things I saw." He glanced at the open journal. "Mama always encouraged me to write. She helped me make it all sensible, whenever things turned sideways." He placed his hand on the book. "Old habits, I guess."

The creature raised its hand, reaching for his head. William closed his eyes. He balled his fist on the journal in hopeless defeat, "I'm sorry."

It stopped. In silence, with its hand hovering above William's head, it waited for him to speak. "I knew what he was doing with all those people. All the lies. Babies. Women. It didn't matter, so long as he could peddle his tonics." He chewed his tongue. "And, I know what I did... nothing. I kept my head down and answered every order he barked. I thought that if I just followed him, he'd..." William dismissed the thought. "Never mind."

William adjusted himself in the seat, closed the journal, and faced the cloaked figure. "Wherever I'm going," he said, "It's too good for something yellow, like me." He wiped his face, "If I may, can I please be buried with this?" He lifted the journal to its eyes. "It's all I've got left of her."

The creature stood and inched towards him. William held the journal against his chest, struggling to keep his gaze fixed on the entity. His eyes widened with fear, as the faint glimmer of a darkened sclera peered back through hollow sockets. Its hands moved towards the sides of his head. Its cracked, elongated nails touched the ends of his wild hair.

"I'm sorry, Mama," William exhaled. A tear ran down his face. "I'm so sorry."

The creature's hand clasped William's face. He shuddered and yelped at its frigid grasp. Its neck bent down—cracking and popping like burning wet wood—stopping when a familiar warm breath coated his forehead.

"Go."

William looked up at it. "What?"

A sudden warmth radiated from the creature's palms and pulsed against William's cheeks. Its hardened, wax skin's dismal, icy chill faded into a soft and gentle touch. It grabbed the bottom of the doe skull and lifted the mask free. With dewy, tan skin, shrouded in raven-black hair, a woman's face appeared from the darkness. Her eyes remained hidden, but William saw her full, plush lips form a delicate grin.

"Go," she repeated. Her comforting smile reassured him. "Take the reins of your horse and leave."

"Leave?" William asked. "What about my father?"

The woman's lips thinned. Within moments, a row of decayed teeth lined a gaping maw. William yelped and retracted his words. "I'll go! I swear it!" He vowed to depart the cabin. "I'll leave without him."

The woman's face returned to its youthful beauty. She pulled down the mask. "Think of your father no more," she instructed William. The cabin door creaked. As he peered at the egress, William's heart dropped. The last patient. Though still frightful with a stark pallor, the young lady's face and body bore no red lesions. She held the door open for him. The creature released his head. "Go."

William grabbed his satchel and ran out of the cabin. Panting as he entered the night air, he crashed into Lester on the bottom step. "What the hell's your problem, boy? Running out in the dark like that?" He dropped his collection of kindling and pieces of wood.

Lester shoved him. "I'm talking to you, boy. What's your deal?" William refused to respond. Lester shoved him again. William fell backward and toppled hard onto the ground, hitting his head on the edge of a rock.

Lester scoffed and picked up the items. "Useless little shit." He hoisted the materials over his shoulder. "You know what? Don't even bother getting back inside. You can stay your dumbass there for the night." With his head ringing in pain, William lay dazed as his vision doubled, looking towards his father.

William tried to warn Lester of what lurked in that cabin, but his agony rendered him speechless. "Just shut it, William," Lester ordered. "Don't want to answer me? Fine. Like I need to hear you start sniveling again." He walked past the entities standing in the threshold and dropped his haul on the table.

William's eyelids grew heavier. As his vision blurred, he watched the sal-low-faced woman and the rotten doe skull close the door. Finally, weary and worn, his eyelids were impossible to lift.

Autumn clouds drifted overhead. As the darkness dispersed and gave a wide berth to dawn, the sun's warmth beamed on William's body. The winds blew cool over the lands and carried dust over his head and clothes. William slept deep into the late morning.

The two horses neighed in the distance. The vibrations from their feet alerted him. Upon awakening, the bright light stung his eyes, while his head still ached. Aside from the rushing winds and playful whinnies, the cabin and its prairie surroundings lay quiet. After regaining his balance, he stabled his stance and looked at the cabin. "Empty?"

No sign of Lester or the spirits that engaged him. With the door wide open, nothing inside the small cabin showed evidence of previous inhabitants. As he examined the threshold and surrounding grounds for his father, he discovered a line of deer tracks imprinted in the dirt. During his travels to the location, William viewed no wildlife in those vast meadows. As he followed the hoofprints, he saw them stray away from the property and vanish into the vivid wetlands.

A small voice wisped passed his ear, "Go." Steadying his pace, he stumbled back towards the horses and secured the saddles. Then, with his journal strapped tight to his person, he rode deep into the West.

Hungry

BY JESSE ALLEN CHAMPION

LAU TSAI-TAN CAME DOWN the mountain with his pickaxe on his shoulder, silent among the mass of chattering men. Ahead of him, two hundred Chinese workers celebrated the end of a long day of breaking rock for the railway. They all walked down the slope between the tall trees, the air smelling of fir and spruce.

"I'm glad we won't be moving camp for a few days," said Man Gen-ge. "I'm going to take a half-barrel down to the lake, fill it up, and have a good soak."

Ping Gui waved a hand in front of his face. "Good thing," he said. "Another night sharing a tent with your stink, and I will lose my sense of smell forever!"

"Hah," Song Fei-Han said, good-naturedly. "That's your own upper lip you're smelling, Dog-Breath!"

The others laughed. One man pointed to a row of tree stumps. "How strange! Why are those stumps so tall?"

Lau glanced where the man indicated, then slowed to a stop. Indeed, the stumps were all about ten or twelve feet high, stark and pale, marking the edge of the forest, which covered the mountain flank down to the valley's edge.

"Stupid white men." Ping spat. "To cut down a tree, *gwai lo* stand on a ladder!" Laughter greeted this as well.

The men walked on, but Lau remained in place. A feeling of deep foreboding crept through him.

This morning he had waked in a camp ten miles away, high in the Sierra Nevada mountains. While he and his gang hammered and dug along the surveyed line of what would be the Central Pacific Railroad, another crew moved the workers' gear to a new site in a high valley. Between them, the mountains cradled a sparkling blue lake, where even now the patched tents of the Chinese camp, and the dingy tents of the white men's camp, were rising on opposite shores. Smoke spiraled up from cook fires, and a pleasant breeze danced over large meadows blooming in the high frenzy of summer.

Mountain, lake, earth, and air—all the elements of auspicious *feng shui* were present. Yet Lau felt sweat break on his brow, and knew something was wrong. Staring at that bizarre row of tall stumps, a shudder ran down his spine.

"Hey, Lau!" Song waited below him. "Why so slow? Is your foot bothering you again?"

Lau shook his head, reluctant to voice his misgivings. Song climbed back up the slope towards him, his long black queue swinging forward over his shoulder. Like all the men, he wore loose denim trousers and a much-faded denim work shirt. He was as stocky and muscular as Lau was lanky and wiry, as talkative as Lau was silent. The two had been friends ever since they met on the ship from Canton, two years ago.

"No, Cousin," he said, using the polite term. "My foot is well healed."

Song peered closely. "You look unwell. Is your *ch'i* disturbed?"

"Perhaps the sun has shone too brightly on my head."

Song grinned, revealing two missing teeth. "Now, if we were at home, I would have my wife weave you a good straw hat to keep the sun off. Maybe you can buy one of those round-top hats the *gwai lo* wear."

Lau shrugged. "I wouldn't want anyone to mistake me for Tight Hat." Tight Hat was the name the Chinese gave the gang boss of their section, a florid Irishman who insisted on wearing a fashionable bowler too small for his head.

Song laughed loudly. "Mistake *you* for Tight Hat? Not likely. But what ails you, that you stand here when there is hot food and a bath waiting?"

Lau had no answer. *This was a bad place.* He did not know how or why he knew this, but it was a bad place. But how to explain this to Song, without sounding like a fool?

"Let's go, before Ah Sam gives away our dinner," Song said merrily.

Lau reluctantly followed his friend down the mountainside and through the camp. They ducked under lines of laundry strung between tents and kicked roaming chickens out of their way. Smoke from a dozen cook fires curled through the camp, obscuring the occasional pile of boots. Men called greetings as he passed, but Lau did not return them.

They do not feel it. We are like men who sleep on the edge of a cliff, unknowing.

Laughter erupted as he passed one campfire; farther along he heard men chanting a harvest song. Lau found his tent—which he shared with Song and three other men—pitched at the very edge of the encampment, close to the lake. Ah Sam, the senior member of their tent, ducked out of it carrying a bag of rice.

"There you are," he said. "I need some water. Can you fetch it please, Junior Cousin?"

The term was mere courtesy, but Lau appreciated even that much consideration. All the other men in the tent, including Song, came from the same village. The white men had stupidly assigned four men to one tent, and to avoid the disastrous bad luck that would follow such an unlucky number, the four had invited Lau to join them and make five. Still, even after a year, he felt like a hanger-on. Silently, he picked up the wooden bucket and headed for the lake.

The meadow was thick with grass; Lau thought again of the wasted space here in America, land that back home in Canton would long ago have been planted with crops. A grasshopper leaped away as he approached—a good omen. The lake was so clear that he could see every pebble below the surface. It was utterly unlike the roiled, muddy waters of the stream near his farm; Lau thought it must be what a lake looked like just after the gods created the world. He plunged the bucket into the water. *Cold water on a hot day,* he thought. Like the cooling drinks his wife would bring him in the middle of the day during planting season. Lau wondered how she was doing, and whether his brother-in-law was helping her with the planting this year as he had promised. *Soon,* he thought. *Soon I will be quit of this Gold Mountain, and go home where I belong.*

He hefted the dripping bucket and started back, thinking of his home, and the leak in the roof he had not patched before he left, and whether his old aunt, the last member of his father's family, was still living—

Cold fingers brushed across his face, and between one step and the next it was as if a veil fell across the world. Lau gasped, frozen in place. A cold, dirty feeling seeped into him. Only a few yards away, the camp bustled with life and activity, but it was as if he saw it through a pane of smoked glass. The bucket in his hand trembled, slopping water on his leg. A low, trembling sob threaded through the half-silence. Almost too low to be heard, it keened of loss and deep despair. And were those *words?* Babbling at the edge of understanding?

"Who... who's there?" Lau said, although most of him did not want to know. "Song? Is that you?"

The light dimmed; there was a grey tint to the air, as if it were the middle of winter, rather than the middle of summer. "Ah Sam?" Lau croaked.

Something brushed his hand, almost a caress. He yelped as invisible fingers pinched his arm. He dropped the bucket. "Get away from me!" he cried. "Don't touch me!"

His paralysis broken, Lau leaped for the camp, driven forward by panic. He tripped and fell to his hands and knees. A young voice near his face said something he could not understand, crying out in words he did not know. A sharp pain in his arm shocked him and he threw himself to his left, rolling to his feet. In a dozen steps, he was at his tent, gasping and looking back over his shoulder.

"Where is the water?" Ah Sam looked up from the fire, where he was stir-frying onions and cattail shoots. "Didn't you get it?"

"Someone's out there!" Lau cried. "Look!" He pointed towards the meadow, where the setting sun now threw the shadow of the mountain across the valley. "Don't you hear it?"

Ah Sam shrugged. "You've been drinking Leung's rice wine, haven't you? I warned you, he puts fish guts in it."

"I heard voices! Someone pinched me! And someone was crying—"

"Is supper ready? I want to go watch that wrestling match over at Yee's." Song ducked out of the tent. He stared at Lau, who stood trembling and looking over his shoulder at the lengthening shadows.

"Lau is hearing voices," Ah Sam said, disgusted. "Oh, look! My onions are burning! This stupid *lan yeung* dickface can't even fetch water!"

"There is someone out there! Someone invisible!" Lau said, his voice trembling. But he knew as he spoke how crazy he sounded.

The other members of his tent entered the firelight. Wai Teng was the second oldest of the men, thickset and heavy-featured, with hair already greying. Yang Han-Lee was wiry and bent from carrying heavy loads all his life, and his face was pockmarked by disease. Both had wet hair, having gone to the lake to bathe. "Is dinner ready yet?" Yang said. "Ah Sam, you idiot, you're burning the onions!"

"I keep getting interrupted by visionaries and layabouts," Ah Sam said testily. "And no one will fetch me water. Do you want tea with your dinner or not?"

Yang jerked his head at Wai. "Big Man, can you bring water for this poor, weak woman who cooks for us?"

Ah Sam snorted, but since Yang was his sister's husband, he said nothing. Wai also said nothing, but strode past the fire, past Lau, into the meadow. It was almost full dark now, and Lau quickly lost sight of the man's broad back. He could hear him swishing through the grass, heard him stop (*picking up the bucket,* Lau thought), and then the diminishing sounds of his steps. Lau ignored the men murmuring behind him, tensing for a scream or a shout. But in a few minutes, Wai trudged back into camp bearing a brimming bucket.

"Put it next to that log," Ah Sam said, pointing with his chopsticks.

He did as he was told. Song sat down on the log, patting its smooth surface. "Where did you snag this?" he said. "This is a good bench."

"It was right here," Ah Sam said. He waved at the fire. "Lots of half-burned logs here. I think there used to be a cabin nearby. The *gwai lo* left empty huts all over the place, while they were looking for gold." The others nodded, having come across many abandoned miner's huts over the two years of building the railroad. "It's one reason I picked this spot." He glared at Lau. "That, and the fact that it's close to the water."

Yang dipped a tin cup into the bucket and used it to rinse his hands and face. "Long day on the line," he said. "Min Guo-Hong says they've reached the cliff face; tomorrow they start blasting the new tunnel."

Lau stood on the edge of the firelight, ignoring the conversation. He could not make himself turn his back on the empty meadow, the lake, and its looming darkness. The moon was rising, and across the clearing he could see the pale trunks of the tall stumps gleaming in its light. *Who would cut trees so high off the ground?* he wondered, distracted. Giants? Flying men? Devils? He shook his head. *This was stupid,* he told himself. He was sick, or sunstruck. These thoughts were for children's stories, or drunken tales in a tavern.

Ah Sam lifted the rice pot off the fire and set it aside. "Junior Cousin, can you fetch our bowls from the tent?"

Lau nodded and stepped through the flaps. Each man's bedroll lay carefully in its assigned spot, according to his status and relationship to the rest of the men. Lau, as the lowest ranking member, was closest to the door (and the drafts, in winter). Ah Sam had piled utensils in the middle, and Lau sorted through them. He listened to the camp settling around them—laughter, singing, distant voices raised in argument or debate, a barking dog. Normal, orderly, familiar.

Something brushed against the back of the tent, the side away from the fire pit. Lau jumped and dropped a bowl, which clattered when it struck a wooden box.

"What are you doing?" Ah Sam called. "Are we to eat hot rice from our bare hands?"

Lau stared at the tent wall. Something pressed inward from the other side, trying to force a way through the canvas.

The canvas is old. It will tear, thought Lau. *It must not get in. Don't let it in! Don't let it in!*

"Lau!" called Ah Sam.

It was pressing harder now, and a shape molded itself out of the fabric—a point, two curves above it on either side. A face! Fear cascaded through him.

"No!" Lau cried. "You can't get in! Go away!"

"Lau! We're hungry out here!" Yang called.

Then the face was gone, the tent wall smooth and unbroken.

Anger filled Lau. He turned and lunged through the tent flap. "Who did that!" he said. He looked from one face to another. "Ah Sam? Wai? Who's playing tricks on me?"

Song blinked, Ah Sam scowled and the other two stared blankly at him. "What are you talking about?" Yang said.

"One of you is trying to make a fool of me," Lau said coldly. "Hiding in the grass by the lake to trip me. Brushing against the tent wall just now, while I was inside. Which of you was it?"

Ah Sam stared at him, then spat into the fire. "You make yourself a fool by such talk."

The other men avoided his eyes, all but Song. He looked bewildered. "We have all been sitting right here together," he said. He looked around at the others, then back at Lau. "Perhaps someone else is playing a joke on you?"

"Or the *gwai lo*," Yang said. "You know they like to mock us."

"Foolishness," Ah Sam snapped. "The *gwai lo* bosses have better things to do than to play tricks."

Yang shrugged. "Remember how they cut off Chin Kee's queue in his sleep? And they got Lo Yung-Chee drunk and made him dance naked?"

The others nodded. "They do not respect us," growled Wai in his deep voice.

"Perhaps we should hang a mirror outside the tent," Ah Sam said. Everyone knew that demons were afraid of their own faces, so mirrors were a good defense. "But then, it might keep Lau out of the tent!" The others laughed.

Lau knew he was losing face. Bowing low, Lau said, "I apologize for my shouting and my disturbance earlier. Please allow me to clean up after the meal."

Yang Han-Lee, whose turn it was to clean up, bowed back. "It would be an honor," he said politely. "I will lay out the bedrolls, as I am anxious to sleep."

Lau filled his bowl, but could not bring himself to eat. The others finished their meal, leaving a few grains of rice in the bottom of each bowl to show that they were not greedy. Wai grunted something and marched off towards the center of camp; Ah Sam announced he was going to the lake to bathe. Yang ducked into the tent, and Lau soon heard him bustling about as he arranged the sleeping mats. Song stretched, nodded to Lau, and said, "I'm going to bet on that wrestling match." He strolled away.

Lau heated water in the rice pot, then scrubbed the dishes. He cleaned the firepit, puzzled by the many pieces of half-burned wood sticking out of the sand. Had they camped on an old bonfire? Faint snoring came from the tent; Yang was already asleep. Lau filled the pot with water and set the tea box beside it. He felt hungry, but something inside him refused the very idea of food. As if the idea held danger, or contamination.

"What do you want?" he whispered to the darkness. Nothing answered, and yet a feeling of shame crept over him.

It was waiting for him. Lau did not know what stalked him, but the cold and the voices and the face pressed against the tent were real. He pushed up the sleeve of his jacket and saw the bruise where he'd fallen in the meadow. He peered closer. That wasn't a bruise; there were tiny marks in an oval... he drew in his breath sharply. Bite marks? In the shape of a *human* bite?

The water boiled, and he reached for the tea.

A thin, high scream broke from the tent. Lau's hand jerked. "Yang?" he cried. "Yang, are you—"

The scream again, and something ripped and scrabbled at the canvas wall near Lau. Lau dropped the pot of boiling water, ignoring its blistering hot splash across his shins. The tent wall bulged outward, billowed inward again as something struggled and fought. Lau felt as if he had turned to a statue carved of ice.

"What's that noise?" Song ran up, looking around wildly. "Lau? Is someone hurt?"

The scream once more, fading, hardly human, and then a gurgling sound. Song cried, "Yang!" and dove for the tent.

"No!" Lau grabbed his friend's shoulder and held him back. "Don't go in there!"

Song stared at him. "Are you crazy?"

Behind them, men poured out of tents, some holding axe handles or clubs.

"What's that noise?"

"Who's screaming?"

"Are we under attack?"

The sounds from Lau's tent had stopped, but the wall nearest the fire showed a dark, wet stain that dripped down to the ground.

"What's going on here?" Ah Sam ran into the firelight, a towel around his neck. He looked from Lau to Song, snorted, and pushed into the tent. Other men crowded near, looking at Lau and the tent. Wai shoved his way to the front, glaring at Lau as if he had done something wrong.

Ah Sam burst from the tent, his eyes staring, his hands bloody in the firelight. "Yang..." He fell to his knees, retching. "No, don't go in there. Demons!"

Cries and whispers echoed through the mass of men. "Is someone dead? Is it the *gwai lo?* Or the red barbarians?"

Song pulled from Lau's grasp. "Are we cowards?" he hissed. "Yang is our tent mate. We must see to him!"

Lau let him go in alone, knowing he would forever curse himself for it. He did not know what Song would see, but he knew that Song would never forgive him for letting him see it.

All fell silent as Song entered. All heard his shocked gasp, then his whimper of fear. They remained hushed as he stepped slowly back through the entrance, a stunned expression on his face. "Something..." He stopped, gulped, shook his head. "Maybe a tiger? Yang is dead. Something tried to *eat* him—" Then he turned away, hiding his face.

The crowd parted, and voices murmured, "The doctor... the doctor is here."

Chan Jun-Fan pushed his way through the men. He wore white men's under-clothes, the single garment called 'long johns' for some reason, and a fine silk top hat. His queue was mussed, and his eyes were rimmed with red from drinking. "What has happened here?" he asked, his voice authoritative.

Lau bowed respectfully. Chan held no certificates from the Imperial Registry, but he was the most educated man in camp and owned two books, so the title of Doctor had settled on him. He was the camp's chief liaison with the whites, having lived amongst them long enough in California, to learn some English. "A man, Yang, has died," Lau said, his voice hoarse.

"A fight?" Chan asked.

Song gasped. "No, sir. A... beast of some kind. Or a demon."

The crowd murmured and drew back. Chan pushed past Lau to enter the tent. Lau made no move to stop him; Song was his friend, but Chan was a respected elder. Of the two, Song's shock was more worrisome.

Lau stepped back, nearly tripping over the burnt log that had been his dinner seat earlier in the evening. Another man stepped closer, so Lau stepped further back, and suddenly realized he was on the edge of the light, with his back to the empty meadow. He spun around, ice froze over his nerves, and beyond the bright firelight, a void. A sheet of stark darkness.

He knew something was watching him. Something... *hungry*.

Chan emerged from the tent, visibly shaken. He gestured to the crowd. "We must remove him from the tent," he said. "I need two men, perhaps three."

There was a long silence, and no volunteers. Finally, Song straightened and stepped forward. "I am not afraid," he said, though the tremor in his voice proved him a liar. Chan nodded, and Wai stepped forward, and the three went back into the tent.

What they brought out, they brought out in pieces. Cries of horror shimmered through the crowd as legs and arms and a stripped torso emerged, carried in slings of blankets that Lau knew no one would ever touch again. The pieces were laid on the ground near the fire, more or less in order.

Men stumbled into one another in their haste to back away. One or two stood their ground, peering closely in morbid fascination. Ah Sam knelt, trembling, beside one of Yang's legs. With a quivering finger, he pointed to a dark oval mark.

"There. That is a bite mark." He snatched his hand back, though he had not touched the body. "And here! And over here! See there are bite marks, and here, where the muscle is torn. He turned his head, stood, and stumbled away, his hand to his mouth. Other men pressed forward, looked, then turned away.

Ah Sam wiped his mouth. "You!" He pointed an accusing finger at Lau. "You were here all alone with him. When all the rest of us were eating, you refused. Then you stayed behind all alone. Were you hungry for human flesh?"

Chan straightened quickly from his stooped posture. "Nonsense," he said firmly. "No man did this."

The crowd did not listen.

"A demon!" A skinny man wearing a cotton robe cried out and bent to pick up a rock. "Get away! He's a demon come to eat us all!" He hefted a rock and flung it at Lau, but it missed and hit the log next to his feet.

Others stooped for rocks, but Chan raised his hands. "Friends, let us not lose our composure. This is not a time to act like frightened women. We must—"

"Aiee!!!" A man cried out and jumped, turning around to look behind him. "Someone pinched me!"

"No, Kwok," his neighbor said, pointing. "Something *bit* you!"

Kwok, a fat man with heavy jowls, pulled up the cuff of his pants. Sure enough, a bloody bite mark showed on his leg. Kwok released a high scream and slapped at his leg, flailing. "Get away from me!" He lunged backwards, toppling into another man, and they fell heavily to the ground. Both men cried out, beating their clothing, writhing, and twisting to get away from something invisible. Other men yelled and twisted, bite marks appeared on hands, legs, even faces. One man screamed and held up a hand, blood spurting from the stump of a finger.

Lau stared in horror, his feet moving in a frantic drunkard's dance, putting distance between himself and the crowd. He stumbled over the burned log, scrambled upwards, and found his arm caught in a hard grip. He cried out and thrashed, but calmed some, when he saw the hand holding his elbow belonged to Doctor Chan, and the two retreated from the frenzied mob.

"What is it?" Lau panted. "What can this be?"

"A ghost of some kind. Or many ghosts," Chan said grimly. "I do not understand. What has brought them here?"

"A ghost? But no one has died. At least, not until Yang." Lau looked around, aware that once again, they were on the edge of the camp, almost in the meadow. Shame, regret and grief sliced through him, but more painful than those were the feeling of cold, deep rage.

Behind them, a low moan sighed through the grass. Chan spun around, staring into the darkness. "What is that?"

Lau looked at him, at the dark meadow whose grasses bent silver under the moon. "You hear it also?"

"Someone crying. A child?"

The sobbing again, and words just under the threshold of meaning. "I cannot understand the words," Lau said.

"Speak to me!" Chan called into the dark wind. "What do you want?"

A high, thin wail. Lau thought it sounded like a child, an exhausted one, perhaps. Or a dying one. But what child would be here?

Chan bent low, in a listening posture, and now Lau saw something move, something that was silver mist in the moonlight, like watching a shadow move under water. Thin, distorted, but human-like. The skin on his neck crawled. Behind him, the men scattered, fleeing the biting, invisible teeth. Lau sensed, but could not see, shadows gathering around him. He smelled blood and despair, heard the grinding and chewing of jaws crunching bone and stripping flesh.

"Doctor Chan?" he said softly. "What are they?"

Chan turned to him slowly, and Lau saw bloody marks on his cheeks and hands. "They are hungry. Very hungry."

"Who are they?"

Chan shook his head. "Children of the *gwai lo*, I believe. They are whispering in English."

"*Children?*" Lau clutched his hands together. "What shall we do?"

Chan staggered backward as something struck his arm. "We must feed them, of course."

Lau spun around; Song stood behind him, teeth marks on his jaw line, holding one bleeding hand in another. "Come, we must get away."

Chan hissed in pain and jerked his leg away; blood seeped through his cotton leggings. "No," he said. "They will only pursue. There is only one way to appease a hungry ghost."

Lau frowned. "Yu Lan?" Yu Lan was the Festival of Hungry Ghosts, usually held in the seventh month. "But it is the wrong time of year."

"Ghosts do not care," Chan said with authority. "How much food do you have in your tent?"

Lau looked at Song. "Three days' supply, like everyone else. Do you want us to go back in there and get it?"

Chan shook his head. "No—aiee!!" He flinched, and blood streamed from a wound on his forehead. "Quickly! Bring all you can. Tell everyone to fetch all they have and bring it here."

"What about you?"

Chan turned and shouted something in a loud voice. Lau could not understand the words.

Song leaned in close. "I think he is speaking in English." He tugged on Lau's arm. "Come. Do as he says, quickly."

They ran from tent to tent, spreading Chan's order through the camp. Most men backed away in alarm, bleeding from a dozen bites, their eyes black with terror, while others gathered bags and boxes of food. By the time Lau and Song returned to their tent, piles of food were stacked around it. Yang's body lay where they'd left it, next to the fire. Chan stood over it, holding his bleeding arm and shouting in English.

"Is he saying charms?" Ah Sam crept closer. His face was drawn and sweaty.

Chan gestured Lau over. "Throw all the food into the tent. Don't bother to stack it."

Lau and Song tossed bags of rice, tins of tea, and rashers of dried beef into the tent. When all the food was inside, Chan reached down and picked up a brand from the fire. He stood at the entrance to the tent, shadows flitting near the opening. He smelled the charnel stench, felt rage and shame wash over him, but as if it wasn't *his* rage and shame. And he felt something else: guilt.

Chan tossed the torch into the tent. It disappeared into the dark interior, until light sprang up, and for a moment, revealed the silhouettes of children creeping around. The light threw shadows of the stacked food, and the child horde leaping onto the shadow food; hunched over shapes ravaging salt beef, and stuffing illusory rice into their mouths. The light grew, the fire licked up the sides of the tent, and the heat and smoke drove the men back. The rear wall collapsed, sending a shower of sparks high.

"More food!" Chan shouted. "Feed them more!"

Ah Sam objected. "This is more than we burn at the Ghost Festival."

"Yes," Chan said. "But I think maybe these ghosts starved to death."

Men brought more food and tossed it into the flames. The sides of the tent collapsed, leaving only the front to stand, flames licking along the flap.

And for one blink of an eye, almost too quick to see, Lau saw a young *gwai lo* girl standing in the entrance. She stared at him with sunken eyes, her yellow hair lank and dirty around her face, and dress faded and stained with the same blood that ran down her chin and coated her hands. Her eyes burned large in her white face, and they held such terror and rage and shame that Lau looked away, unable to meet them. When he looked back, she was gone. The tent wall crisped, folded, collapsed into another shower of sparks.

Men gathered all around now, no longer afraid. This was a ritual they understood, the feeding of spirits. One by one, they stepped forward, bowed, and added to the offerings. Bags of onions, an entire leg of pork went into the fire. One man tossed his bag of tobacco into the flames. Chan stood straight, the firelight dancing across his solemn features, speaking in English. Although he could not understand the words, to Lau they sounded like a dismissal.

Hoofbeats, a shout, and three men rode up on horses. One man nearly flung himself off his mount. Lau recognized him; the workers called him Red Boss for his fiery hair. He strode foreword, shouting.

Most of the men melted away into the shadows to avoid trouble. Red Boss ran his hands through his short, thick hair, leaving it standing up. Chan bowed to him.

"What does he want here?" Ah Sam whispered behind Lau. "Why is he interfering in our business?"

"I think he wants us to get buckets and put out the fire," Song said.

"No," Ah Sam said. "If the fire dies, the hungry ghosts will attack us."

Chan bowed again, shook his head firmly at Red Boss. The Irishman ranted and waved his arms and shouted at the men. All stood firm, and the fire crackled and burned, and in the flames, Lau saw smoke that looked like thin children. He took a deep breath and stepped forward.

Red Boss stopped when he saw him. Chan bowed, but said sternly, "What are you doing, Lau? I will speak to him."

"Ask him…" Lau found words sticking in his dry throat, and cleared it. "Who are the children?"

Chan stared. "Ask a *gwai lo* about ghosts?"

Lau remembered that *gwai lo* meant 'ghost man', but held Chan's gaze. "Ask him. Please."

"Yes, Doctor," Song said, and ranged himself next to Lau. "Who are they?"

Reluctantly, Chan bowed again, and spoke in a low voice to Red Boss. Red Boss froze, then turned, looking around at the men's faces. He spoke to Chan again, and then Chan stepped aside so that Red Boss could see the body of Yang that still lay before the tent.

Red Boss stood over it for a long time. He looked around at the faces of the workers, at the flames eating the tent, at the boxes and barrels smoldering inside it. He spoke in a low voice.

Chan bowed and turned to the workers. "Red Boss says this valley was once known as 'Emigrant Pass'," he said in a loud voice. "Many *gwai lo* families came through here to get to California."

Men nodded. Of course, the railroad they were building followed many old roads already much used by whites. Everyone had seen the abandoned cabins and settlements along the way. This much was clear to all.

"One winter, a party was snowed in," Chan continued. "Red Boss says the snow was deeper than two men's heights. There was no food, and the lake was frozen. The people ate their dogs, their horses. They ate bark from the trees."

"The stumps," Song whispered. "Those tree stumps, so high. Now I know why they were so tall; the snow was so deep the men were standing high above ground when they cut the trees."

Chan continued. "The people were starving. Many of them died. Men, and women, and children. When there were no more dogs or horses, they ate their shoes. And when still no one came, they ate the dead."

Utter silence met this pronouncement. Each man knew stories of war, of famine, knew rumors of cannibalism. To have it starkly presented like this, in blood and firelight, was to hear death whispered in one's ear.

"They're hungry," Song said.

"They're ashamed," Lau said. And perhaps mad. "To eat your own parents? They are damned, and they know it."

Red Boss said something else to Chan, gesturing at the fire. Chan told the assembly, "This tent is where one of the cabins sat. Red Boss says the rescuers found half-eaten corpses in it. The rescuers burned it to the ground."

"And Ah Sam picked it for our camp because the logs were handy," Song said, disgusted.

Lau watched as Red Boss walked to his horse and got on it and rode away without looking back.

One by one, men turned away. Ah Sam and Lau picked up the log that had served as a bench. They tossed it into the flames.

Chan came over to stand beside Lau, wiping sweat and soot and blood from his face.

"Will this be enough?" Lau asked.

"I don't know," Chan said. "How hungry do you have to be to eat your parents? How can you find peace after death?"

Lau shuddered; such an abomination was unthinkable.

"I am going to round up more food to feed that fire," Song said. His voice was full of grief. "If it goes out, if they get hungry again…" He didn't have to finish the thought.

"Did they have names?" Lau asked. "Did Red Boss know them?"

Chan coughed as smoke floated their way. "He said they were known by the name of their leader, a man named Donner."

"He knew of this story, yet the *gwai lo* let us camp here?" Lau felt disgust and anger.

Chan shrugged. "They are *gwai lo*. They are barbarians. They pretend that what they do not understand does not exist. They do not believe ghosts are real." He looked around, gazing at Lau with narrow eyes. Chan strode away, a black silhouette against the firelight.

Lau felt a cold breeze touch his cheek. He didn't have to turn; he knew a shadow stood behind him, a shadow of a young girl with hellfire eyes and a hungry expression.

He knew it would be there all his days.

The Redheaded Dead

BY JOE R. LANSDALE

In memory and tribute to Robert E. Howard

REVEREND MERCER KNEW IT was coming because the clouds were being plucked down into a black funnel, making the midday sky go dark. It was the last of many omens, and he knew from experience it smacked of more than a prediction of bad weather. There had been the shooting star of last night, bleeding across the sky in a looping red wound. He had never seen one like it. And there had been the angry face he had seen in the morning clouds, ever so briefly, but long enough to know that God was sending him another task in his endless list.

He paused on his horse on a high hill and pushed his hat up slightly, determining the direction of the storm. When the funnels were yanked earthward and touched, he saw, as he expected, that the twister was tearing up earth and heading swiftly in his direction. He cursed the God he served unwillingly and plunged his mount down the hill as the sky spat rain and

the wind began to howl and blow at his back like the damp breath of a pursuing giant. Down the hill and into the depths of the forest his horse plunged, thundering along the pine needle trail, dashing for any cover he might find.

As he rode, to his left, mixed in with the pines and a great oak that dipped its boughs almost to the ground, was a graveyard. He saw at a glance the gravestones had slipped and cracked, been torn up by tree roots, erosion, and time. One grave had a long metal rod poking up from it, nearly six feet out of the ground; the rod was leaning from the ground at a precarious due west. It appeared as if it were about to fall loose of the earth.

The pine needle trail wound around the trees and dipped down into a clay path that was becoming wet and slick and bloodred. When he turned yet another curve, he saw tucked into the side of a hill a crude cabin made of logs and the dirt that surrounded it. The roof was covered in dried mud, probably packed down and over some kind of pine slab roofing.

The Reverend rode his horse right up to the door and called out. No one answered. Reverend Mercer dismounted. The door was held in place by a flip-up switch of wood. The Reverend pressed it and opened it, led his horse inside. There was a bar of crudely split wood against the wall. He lifted it and clunked it into position between two rusted metal hooks on either side of the doorway. There was a window with fragments of parchment paper in place of glass; there was more open space than parchment, and the pieces that remained fluttered in the wind like peeling, dead skin. Rain splattered through.

Down through the trees swirled the black meanness from heaven, gnawing trees out of the ground and turning them upside down and throwing their roots to the sky like desperate fingers, the fingers shedding wads of red clay as if it were clotted blood.

The Reverend's horse did a strange thing; it went to its knees and ducked its head, as if in prayer. The storm tumbled down the mountain in a rumbling wave of blackness, gave off a locomotive sound. This was followed by trees and the hill sliding down toward the cabin at tremendous speed, like mashed potatoes slipping along a leaning plate.

The Reverend threw himself to the floor, but just before he did, he saw gravestones flying through the air, as well as that great iron bar, sailing his way like a javelin.

All the world screamed. The Reverend lay flat, his back wet from rain flashing through the window. He did not pray, having decided long ago his boss had already made up his mind about things.

The cabin groaned and the roof peeled at the center and a gap was torn open in the roof. The rain came through it in a deluge, splattering heavily on the Reverend's back as he lay face down, expecting at any moment to be lifted up by the wind and drawn and quartered by the Four Horsemen of the Apocalypse.

Then, it was over. There was no light at the window because mud and trees had plugged it. The roof was open at the top, and there was a bit of daylight coming from there. It filled the room with a kind of hazy shade of gold.

When the Reverend rose up, he discovered the steel bar had come through the window and gone straight through his horse's head; the animal still rested forward on its front legs, its butt up, the bar having gone into one ear and out the other. The horse had gone dead before it

knew it was struck.

The only advantage to his dead mount, the Reverend thought, was that now he would have fresh meat. He had been surviving on corn dodgers for a week, going where God sent him by directions nestled inside his head.

In that moment, the Reverend realized that God had brought him here for a reason. It was never a pleasant reason. There would be some horror, as always, and he would be pitted against it, less he thought for need of destroying evil, but more out of heavenly entertainment, like burning ants to a crisp with the magnified heat of the sun shining through the lens of a pair of spectacles.

The Reverend studied the iron bar that had killed his horse. There was writing on it. He knelt down and looked at it. It was Latin, and the words trailed off into the horse's ear. The Reverend grabbed the bar and twisted the horse's head toward the floor, put his boot against the horse's skull, and pulled. The bar came out with a pop and a slurp, covered in blood and brain matter. The Reverend took a rag from the saddle bag on the horse and wiped the rod clean.

Knowing Latin, he read the words. They simply said: And this shall hold him down.

"Ah, hell," the Reverend said, and tossed the bar to the floor.

This would be where God had sent him, and what was coming he could only guess, but a bar like that one, made of pure iron, was often used to pin something in its grave. Iron was a nemesis of evil, and Latin, besides being a nemesis to a student of language, often contained more powerful spells than any other tongue, alive or dead. And if what was out there was in need of pinning, then the fact the twister had pulled the bar free by means of the literal wet and windy hand of God, meant something that should not be free was loose.

For the first time in a long time, Reverend Mercer thought he might defy God, and find his way out of here if he could. But he knew it was useless. Whatever had been freed was coming, and it was his job to stop it. If he didn't stop it, then it would stop him, and not only would his life end, but his soul would be flung from him to who knows where. Heaven as a possibility would not be on the list. If there was in fact a heaven.

There was a clatter on the roof and the Reverend looked up, caught sight of something leering through the gap. When he did, it pulled back and out of sight. The Reverend lifted his guns out of their holsters, a .44 converted Colt at his hip, and a .36 Navy Colt in the shoulder holster under his arm. He had the .44 in his right fist, the Navy in his left. His bullets were touched with drops of silver, blessed by himself with readings from the Bible. Against hell's minions it was better than nothing, which was a little like saying it was better than a poke in the eye with a sharp stick.

The face shad sent a chill up his back like a wet-leg scorpion scuttling along his spine. It was hardly a face at all. Mostly bone with rags of flesh where cheeks once were, dark pads of rotting meat above its eyes. The top of its head had been curiously full of fire-red hair, all of it wild and wadded and touched with clay. The mouth had been drawn back in the grin of a ghoul, long fangs showing. The eyes had been the worst; red as blood spots, hot as fire.

Reverend Mercer knew immediately what it was; the progeny of Judas. A vampire, those that had descended from he who had given death to Christ for a handful of silver. Christ, that ineffectual demigod that had fooled many into thinking the heart of God had changed; it had not, that delusion was all part of the great bastard's game.

There was movements on the roof, heavy as an elephant one moment,
and then light and skittering like an excited squirrel.

The Reverend backed across the room and found a corner just as the thing stuck its head through the gap in the roof again. It stretched its neck, which was long and barely covered in skin, showing a little greasy disk of bone that creaked when its long neck swayed.

Like a serpent, it stretched through the roof, dropping its hands forward, the fingers long and multiple-jointed, clicking together like bug legs. It was hanging from the gap by its feet. It was naked, but whatever its sex, that had long dissolved to dust, and there was only a parchment of skin over its ribs and its pelvis was nothing more than bone, its legs being little more than withered gray muscle tight against the bone. It twisted its head and looked at the Reverend. The Reverend cocked his revolvers.

It snapped its feet together, disengaging from the roof, allowing it to fall. It dropped lightly, landed on the damp horse, lifted its head and sniffed the air. It gazed at the Reverend, but the dead animal was too inviting. It swung its head and snapped its teeth into the side of the dead horse's neck, made a sucking noise that brought blood out of the beast in a spray that decorated the vampire's face and mouth. Spots of blood fell on the sun-lit floor like rose petals.

It roved one red eye toward the Reverend as it ate, had the kind of look that said: "You're next."

The Reverend shot it several times.

The bullets tore into it and blue hellfire blew out of the holes the bullets made. The thing sprang like a cricket, came across the floor toward the Reverend, who fired both revolvers rapidly, emptying them, knocking wounds in the thing that spurted sanctified flames, but still it came.

The Reverend let loose with a grunt and a groan, racked the monster upside the head with the heavy .44. It was like striking a tree. Then he was flung backwards by two strong arms, against the window packed with limbs and leaves and mud. The impact knocked the revolvers from his hands.

It came at him like a shot, hissing as if it were a snake. The Reverend's boot caught the skin and bone brute in the chest and drove it back until it hit the floor. It bounced up immediately, charged again. The Reverend snapped out a left jab and hooked with a right, caught the thing with both punches, rocked its rotten head. But still it came. The Reverend jabbed again, crossed with a right, upper cut with a left, and slammed a right hook to the ribs. When he hit the ribs, one of them popped loose and poked thought the skin like a barrel stave that had come undone.

It sprang forward and clutched the Reverend's throat with both hands, and would have dove its teeth into his face, had the Reverend not grabbed it under the chin and shoved it back and kicked it hard in the chest, sending it tumbling over the horse's body.

The Reverend sprang toward the iron bar, grabbed it, swung it and hit the fiend a brisk blow across the neck, driving it to the ground. His next move was to plunge the bar into it, pinning it once again to the ground in the manner it had been pinned in its grave. But he was too slow.

The creature scrambled across the floor on all fours, avoiding the stab, which clunked into the hard dirt floor. It sprang up and through the hole in the roof before the Reverend could react. As the last of it disappeared, the Reverend fell back, exhausted, watching the gap for its reemergence.

Nothing.

The Reverend found his pistols and reloaded. They hadn't done much to kill the thing, but he liked to believe his blessed loads had at least hampered it some. He worked the saddlebag off his horse, flung it over his shoulder. He tried the door and couldn't open it. Too much debris had rammed up against it. He stood on his dead mount and poked the bar through the hole, pushed it through the gap far enough that he could use both ends of it to rest on the roof and chin himself up. On the roof he looked about for it, saw it scuttling over a mass of mud and broken trees like a spider, toward a darkening horizon; night was coming, dripping in on wet, dark feet.

The Reverend thought that if his reading on the subject was right, this descendant of Judas would gain strength as the night came. Not a good thing for a man that had almost been whipped and eaten by it during the time when it was supposed to be at its weakest.

Once again, the Reverend considered defying that which God had given him to do, but he knew it was pointless. Terror would come to him if he did not go to it. And any reward he might have had in heaven would instead be a punishment in hell. As it was, even doing God's bidding he was uncertain of reward, or of heaven's existence. All he knew was there was a God and it didn't like much of anything besides its sport.

The Reverend climbed down from the roof with the rod, stepping on the mass of debris covering the door and window, wiggled his way through broken trees, went in the direction the vampire had gone. He went fast, like a deranged mouse eager to throw itself into the jaws of a lion.

As he wound his way up the hill it started to rain again. This was followed by hail the size of .44 slugs. He noticed off to his left a bit of the graveyard that remained; a few stones and a great, shadowy hole where the rod had been. With the night coming he was sure the vampire would be close by, and though he didn't think it would return to the grave where it had been pinned for who knew how long, he went there to check. The grave was dark and empty except for rising rainwater. It was a deep hole, that grave, maybe ten feet deep. Someone had known what that thing was and how to stop it, at least until time released it.

The light of the day was completely gone now, and there was no moon. With the way the weather had turned, he would be better off to flee back to the house, wait until morning to pursue. He knew where it would be going if it didn't come back for him. The first available town and a free lunch. He was about to fulfill that plan of hole up and wait and see, when the dark became darker, and in that instant he knew it was coming up behind him. It was said these things did not cast a reflection, but they certainly cast a shadow, even when it was thought too dark for there to be one.

The Reverend wheeled with the iron bar in hand. The thing hit him with a flying leap and knocked him backwards into the grave, splashing them down into the water. The bar ended up lying across the grave above them. The Reverend pulled his .44. It was on him as he fired, clamping its teeth over the barrel of the revolver. The Reverend's shot took out a huge chunk at the back of the thing's head, but still it survived, growling and gnawing and shaking the barrel of the gun like a dog worrying a bone.

The barrel snapped like a rotten twig. The vampire spat it out. The Reverend hit him with what remained of the gun. It had about as much effect as swatting a bull with a feather. The Reverend dropped the weapon and grasped the thing at its biceps, attempting to hold it back, the vampire trying to bring its teeth close to the Reverend's face. The Reverend slugged

the thing repeatedly.

Using a wrestling move, the Reverend rolled the thing off of him, came to his feet, leaped and grabbed the bar, swung up on it, and out of the grave. Still clutching the bar he stumbled backwards. The vampire hopped out of the hole effortlessly, as if it the grave had been no deeper than the depth of a cup.

As it sprang, the Reverend, weary, fell back and brought the rod up. The sky grew darker as the thing came down in a blind lunge of shape and shadow. Its body caught the tip of the rod and the point of it tore through the monster with a sound like someone bending too-quick in tight pants and tearing the ass out of them. The vampire screamed so loud and oddly the Reverend thought the sound might knock him out with the sureness of a blow. But he held fast, the world wavering, the thing struggling on the end of the rod, slowly sliding down, its body swirling around the metal spear like a snake on a spit, then bunching up like a doodle bug to make a

knot at the center of the rod. Then it was still.

The Reverend dropped the rod and came up on one knee and looked at the thing pinned on it. It was nothing more now than a ball of bone and tattered flesh. The Reverend lifted the rod and vampire into the wet grave, shoved the iron shaft into the ground, hard. Rain and hail pounded the Reverend's back, but still he pushed at the bar until it was deep and the

thing was beneath the rising water in the grave.

Weakly, the Reverend staggered down the hill, climbed over the debris in the cabin, and dropped through the roof. He found a place in the corner where he could sit upright, rest his back against the wall. He pulled out his .36 Navy and sat there with it on his thigh, not quite sleeping, but dozing off and on like a cat.

As he slept, he dreamed the thing came loose of the grave several times during the night. Each time he awoke, snapping his eyes open in fright, the fiend he expected was nothing more than a dream. He breathed a sigh of relief. He was fine. He was in the cabin. There was no vampire, only the pounding of rain and hail through the hole in the roof, splashing and

smacking against the corpse of his horse.

The next morning, the Reverend climbed out of the cabin by means of his horse foot-stool, and went out through the hole in the roof. He walked back to the grave. He found his saddlebags on the edge of it where they had fallen during the attack. He had forgotten all about them.

Pistol drawn, he looked into the grave. It was near filled with muddy water. He put the revolver away, grabbed hold of the rod, and worked it loose, lifted it out to see if the thing was still pinned.

It was knotted up on the rod like a horrid ball of messy twine.

The Reverend worked it back into the grave, pushing the bar as deep as he could, then dropped to his knees and set about pushing mud and debris into the hole.

It took him all of the morning, and past high noon to finish up.

When he was done, he took a Bible from his saddlebags and read some verses. Then he poked the book into the mud on top of the grave. It and the rod would help to hold the thing down. With luck, the redheaded dead would stay truly dead for a long time.

When he was done, the Reverend opened his saddlebags and found that his matches wrapped in wax paper had stayed dry. He sighed with relief. With the saddlebags flung over his shoulder, he went back to the cabin to cut off a slab of horse meat. He had hopes he could find enough dry wood to cook it before starting his long walk out, going to where he was led by the godly fire that burned in his head.

Seeking A Grave In Canaan

by Wile E. Young

UTAH, 1866

The wind blew from the west, carrying salt on the breeze, falling like drops on the desperate people living here. It had been a long path since the battlefields of the war, where I'd killed my brother. I'd felt the wound still etched on my soul and had filled it killing for the Cheyenne, but I'd only run into old reminders of my brother there.

Now I'd come to fight for the Ute.

They called this place Last Water, the final stop to quench your thirst before the trail transformed into endless salt flats. The distant black mountains loomed over the infertile white, stretching to the horizon. I saw distant figures trying to make for a better life beyond. The land would drink them dry

I hitched my horse, patting his neck as I retrieved the bundle of greenbacks from my saddle bags. There were no soldiers here, no Nauvoo Legion attempting to press their claim on this land. I just needed my trail fixings; Mormon blood could wait.

There were three wagons in the street, their possessions strewn out in the dirt. The families stood over them, offering all they had for food and water. I watched them from the porch of the general store, feeding my curiosity. They gave away everything but their clothes, skins sloshing with water offered in return. Their haggard children cried as their toys were taken from their hands, more water given. When it was finished, they turned west to the great emptiness. I watched them until they were small black specks trailing dust.

"Don't like your horse, partner."

There were three men on the porch, Latter-Day Saint ranch hands herding cattle to civilization's last gasp. I heard the Gun whisper, waking at the sound of these like a hound sniffing blood.

The middle one stepped forward, gesturing with his shooting iron at my horse. "You an Injun lover, boy?"

I was on the warpath, had been ever since Virgil and I came home. I'd painted my horse with the adornments of my adopted people, Comanche symbols for war and protection. These men couldn't discern the markings of one tribe from another. It didn't matter to them. Black Hawk and his warrior killed them, they killed in return, and they looked to fight any who sided against them and their church.

I watched and wondered the best way to end them. I could haul their bodies out into the salt, dedicate their blood to good fortune for the Ute in this war. But I could just as easily let them live. It was their choice.

I made to move past them when I heard the flick of a pistol hammer pulled back. I spun on my heels and let the Gun sing; the bullet split the man's head open like kindling on a chopping block. Bits of his brain splattered over his companions, both watching with wide eyes and trembling guns, then they ran. I listened to the footfalls as they fled and crouched over the twitching corpse, staring at the eye dangling from its socket, and I wondered if his soul flitted away to the promised land. I placed a boot against the meat that used to be a man and rolled it into the dirt, watching it sprawl next to my horse. Then I went and bought my provisions.

The shopkeeper accepted my money, his gaze drawn to the corpse barely seen through the storefront window. "If I were you, son, I'd be moving along. That man you killed had plenty of friends in this town."

I opened the pouch, storing the wafers, beans, and other bits of food I'd need along the trail. I caught the man staring at the brand under my eye and took in his ivory hair and the cracked, dry skin that had seen its share of hardship. I didn't answer him, just left the money on the counter for him to collect before I returned to my horse. Flies already settled on the running red river seeping into the ground.

My eyes drew up to the saloon and I felt the need for a drink, a bit of whiskey to warm me before I set out again, stalking the Nauvoo Legion as they chased the Ute.

My shadow stretched across the ground and a few heads turned, most of them carrying the money they took from the departed pilgrims. The low but cheerful talk vanished just as quick when I walked past, a black poison against the day.

I took a seat at the bar; the few men present taking their money to other watering holes. There was a distant commotion, expected it to be about the town's freshly departed. The bartender paused as I sat, reaching down to find whatever nerve he could muster. "You hear those shouts, mister? They're coming to hang you."

I tilted my head, looking into his brown eyes. "Undertaker will eat well this week then. Give me a shot of whiskey."

The man didn't move, only straightened his apron. "I won't serve murderers or injun lovers."

I slipped the Gun from my holster, gripped the barrel, and swung in a wide arc. I heard the soft crack of his jaw, a few teeth skittering across the bar like rattling stones.

The bartender moaned, hands scrabbling to hold his mouth together, blood leaked through clenched fingers, and I pressed the Gun's barrel between his eyes.

"Whiskey." I repeated.

He cried out as he let his jaw drop, distending, and his hands went to work making my drink. I kept track of him as he left the bottle and disappeared into the back of the saloon to lick his wounds.

Outside, I counted a half dozen men, all of them heeled. One of the dead man's friends pointed to the interior of the saloon. I turned back to my drink as the doors swung and I heard rustling leather as a few pistols cleared their holsters.

I watched the whiskey swirl at the bottom of the glass, gave them my only warning "Word of advice? Leave."

There were footsteps and I turned to see two women push through their men. The older one shook her head. "Not until you hear us, sir."

I leveled the Gun at her and the younger woman gasped, holding her hand to her mouth. The men straightened, focusing their irons. The older woman frowned at them. "All of you are wasting yourselves. You've heard the stories from the east."

The younger woman reached forward, grasping at her companion's hand. "Zimrah, we cannot trust a savage—"

Zimrah shrugged out of her grasp, staring hard at me. "Quiet, Lael. This man is exactly what we need."

Their gun hands looked uncomfortable, their pistols shaking like pebbles next to the railroad. They were Mormons, couldn't be anything else in Last Water, and they were desperate. The scent of need was strong.

I reached and finished the last of my drink. "Willing to listen, but then I'll be leaving."

The older one, Zimrah, walked towards me with her head high. Her eyes looked at the Gun in my hand, and I heard it wonder what her blood would look like running across the floor. She tucked a single grey strand of hair back into her brown locks, her other hand gesturing for the younger woman, Lael. There was assurance in that summoning, the quiet command that a gun couldn't give you. She was used to her will being heeded.

The young woman came and placed a hand on Zimrah's shoulder, while the men waited at the door, eyes watching me like resting wolves. I thought the two had familiarity that went deeper than friendship, could be kin by the way their spirits fed on the comfort they drew from each other.

"I will be direct, Mr. Covington. Our husband has been taken from us."

Wives to the same man, it made sense. I nodded to the men they'd brought with them. "Your family?"

She nodded. "My brother, Lael's cousins—" She hesitated, and her eyes flicked to the youngest. "My son, Dannon."

I looked at the kid, still clothed in the ill-fitting air of manhood. Old enough to begin to make his way in the world, but too young to know how to do it. He seemed to shrink under my eyes as his mother spoke. "Our husband, Tollen, he stood righteous, upright. He gave the water from our well to any travelers who came this way."

I tapped my finger hard against the Gun, silencing her as I turned my back. Then I decided to give her the hard lesson that the past six years of my damnation had imparted to me. "No one is righteous, the fire calls for all of us." I brought the barrel of my Gun close and tapped it against the brand seared into my flesh. "I've seen you there."

I saw Lael whimper, but Zimrah didn't hesitate to correct me. "Lies. You may be damned, Mr. Covington, but Tollen has just been led astray. Taken in by a false promise, the same as those unfortunates that left here this morning."

I moved around the bar, feeling the men's eyes follow me, holding their rifles like it would protect them. I reached for the abandoned bottle and poured myself another shot. "And what do they believe?"

Lael's hand grasped at her sister-wife's shoulder and the men shifted uneasily. I knew it for what it was, common knowledge that people of Last Water would rather ignore than acknowledge.

"We have heard stories, Mr. Covington. Strange stories from the lips of half-dead men, dying from thirst. And stranger claims from those who come here giving everything they have for water. Stories of a city, and a man, a prophet preaching blasphemy."

I took a drink, feeling the burn. "This prophet have a name?"

This time it was Lael who answered. "Strato Cobb. They say he grants miracles."

My grip tightened around the glass. I knew why they had come to me. They couldn't know that I knew the name, but to them, Strato Cobb was a nightmare walking out of the worst pages of their holy book. And they needed another nightmare to kill him.

Zimrah continued. "Lael's son, Selwin... he's sick. Tollen refused to hear the Lord's word, and His will to call him home. He left two days ago, carrying Selwin across the salt. Trusting his own understanding!"

I could see the fury uncoiling in her like a rope. Tollen had given into fear and sought to undo his pain in the whispered promises of something else, and his first wife hated him for it.

Lael pursed her lips, touching the bar across from me like it was some feral animal. "We can pay you for your services, to help kill this man and rescue my husband and son."

I shook my head. "You aren't willing to pay my price. I don't shine to money or riches." I looked into the younger woman's eyes. "My price runs red, and I offer it up to hell."

Locked in her gaze, I dove deep and swam in the crevasses of her soft soul, then I asked her the all-important question. "Are you willing to pay that for your child?"

The younger woman paled. She closed her eyes and began to whisper something that I thought was a prayer. I looked past the two women to the men. "One of you? Your blood and soul for kin?"

But it was Zimrah who spoke up. "I'll pay it."

I turned to the woman, but she didn't flinch from my gaze. "I don't believe in whatever tricks you can conjure. My God protects me." A notion I aimed to dissuade her of at the end of this. I'd listen to her soul scream, joining the shrieking calls of the rest begging for succor from their eternity.

The men parted before me as I walked towards the door. I wondered if they could hear the Gun urging me to tear their innards from them and water the salt to make death grow.

"Saddle your horses then."

<hr />

The townsfolk of Last Water watched us go, pitying eyes that turned to fear when my shadow passed over them. There was a woman crying over the fly-ridden corpse of the man I'd killed, a sweetheart by the look of her. I saw her eyes but left her to grieve, her sobbing intermingled with the prayers offered for us, chanting platitudes for their brethren they never expected to see again.

The salt billowed in clouds around my horse's hooves, and after a few miles, Last Water was nothing but another mirage lost in the haze. I watched my comrades on horseback surrounding me. Lael held a hand against the salt, coughing as she fumbled with her shawl. Zimrah had wrapped herself tight, but I could already see the sheen of sweat on her pale skin.

The eight of them came to a stop as I hollered, "Stay close! Easy to get lost in this country, this land isn't kind!" It was the only warning I would give before we continued the journey.

I could already feel it, in the salt that snuck its way into my water when I drank, in the illusions of things moving like specters in the great clouds blown everywhere around us. This place was more.

To them accompanying me, it would feel like a chill or a sickness. They didn't know the touch of a true working. They didn't have the knowledge of secret things and how places like this thirsted to drag men into death.

We passed shallow pools of water running bluer than the sky from the salt in them, and it wasn't long until we started passing the bodies. They were face down in the water, the rags still clothing their withered husks bleached. They'd died going soft in the head, thinking these pools would offer relief to their yearning bones. They were pilgrims; there were no rusted pistols or dead horses, just dry wood from walking sticks and empty canteens. I marked them as we passed, the men and the women dried and left to bake under the sun. A few children were with them, curled in on their stomachs like an insect that had met the bad side of a boot.

All of them had gambled on the journey, but they'd lost, and now the only thing that filled them was salt. I saw some of the men pause, looking down at the bodies, little more than leather and kindling.

Zimrah made to dismount, and I called to her. "You get off that horse and you might not find your way back to us."

She shook her head. "It isn't right to leave them here, they need to be buried."

I gestured at the landscape. "Land takes its own."

She looked like she wanted to argue, to call my chips and see if I was as stone cold as the stories said. If they left their horses to attend the dead, it wouldn't be a cruelty to indulge the Gun's hunger. Better a bullet than the dry death they'd face.

I couldn't say what I would have done, fate has a way of intervening in things like this. And this time, it appeared in the form of a man praying for life. One of the bodies twitched, then breathed deep, a coughing fit spitting wet chunks of something red into the salt.

One of the men froze when he saw him, calling back to the rest. "He's alive!"

I dismounted from my own horse, never letting go from the reins as I knelt next to the man, looking at the wretch's tanned and dried skin. His chest rose and fell weakly, and his eyes reminded me of bright stones down a well; bottomless and empty. A rattling whisper came from him, "Wa-wa-ter…"

The Mormons made to offer him reprieve, uncorking their canteens. I made sure that their mercy was unneeded.

I fired. The bullet found its home between the man's eyes, his last pleading dying away on the sharp breeze. I heard the shouts, the threats, the pulled guns, but ignored all of them. There was no blood from the wound, just salt running like fleeing insects, the familiar satisfaction of a taken life denied me. The Gun didn't whisper its usual joy.

There were screams and scrambling footsteps when the corpse took another gasp, but whatever life he had been clinging to was gone from him and replaced by whatever grievous miracle had taken root here.

The salt-encrusted bones cracked as the dry man stood, then came the rifle shots. The bullets sprayed tufts of salt; brown blood as thick as sap rolled out of the wounds. I fired twice more and watched the outstretched hands reach around the rifle of the closest man.

The rifle rotted, the metalwork tarnishing like it had spent years beneath the sun. Then the withered hands found healthy flesh. The dry man's tongue darted out, lapping at the sweat glistening along the live man's throat.

The man's skin desiccated and flaked away. Dark blood ran as he fell with the dry man on top of him, sucking at the wound. It wasn't water, but a dried-out husk didn't care; wet was wet.

The gun hand gasped for help, his voice hoarse. I aimed at his head and pulled the trigger. There was the familiar feeling of a soul departing, unbound, blood calling for vengeance. Then I focused on the dry man.

Bullets from a gun, even mine, had done nothing. This required more, and fate was gazing strong today. The cursed thing in front of me was focused entirely on its kill. I reached into my saddle bag; there were plenty of workings I could have called on, but sometimes all you needed was a good fire.

I found my tinderbox, and scraped the flint, sending a shower of sparks across the dry man. Bones more arid than old brush nurtured the flame, and then the salt flat saw the birth of new heat. There was a hiss of steam escaping joints and the pile of searing remains collapsed on another corpse, one that looked like it had been in the desert for years.

The salt reclaimed its own.

———————◄O►———————

The storm came after the sun hid behind the mountains. The wind picked up, and at the horizon of shadow, I saw a wave of salt and dust. It covered us, and in the dark, lives were lost.

The Gun whispered to me, and I aimed it warily. There were dry mouths in the darkness eager to soothe their torment. I found an outcropping, like some spirit had reached down and built an altar in the gloom, and at its head was a yawning opening, a cave. There was a branch on the ground close to the entrance, and it didn't take long to light a flame on the dead wood. I waved the burning sign and watched a fraction of those who traveled with me come from the dark.

Zimrah came, supporting Lael, both women coughing despite their coverings, and Dannon followed. Zimrah handed Lael to Dannon, who took her deeper into the cave, he lead our horses with her, and the older woman stood with me, hollering for the others. The burning branch sparked from the blowing salt, glowing orange embers tumbling away into the black.

The wind continued to howl, and I thought I heard something else, faint screaming that came and was swallowed by the oncoming night. I glanced to Zimrah, still shouting the names of her kin in defiance of the world. I left her with the torch and took my place against the stones, watching the woman until she had screamed herself hoarse. Then I listened to the terrified breathing from the two who had lived.

———————◄O►———————

Daybreak came. I hadn't slept, thoughts of dry things finding our camp stole rest from me. The temptation of the Gun was strong, urging me to spill the lives of these people. It would be a fine offering; their souls would feed my weapon and their bodies would feed the salt. But I had a notion of what was coming: Strato

Cobb and his blasphemous miracles. I had borne witness to his work before. Always better in those times to have sacrifices at hand.

We didn't wait for the sun to get high before departing. I urged my horse on, hearing his panting. Despite giving them water, the stinging salt and heat would drive the beasts to death today.

The stone outcropping was the only visible landmark other than the brown smudge of distant peaks. But to our north, I could make out a line of dark figures. We broke into a full gallop, salt erupting in little tufts to mark us.

A few heads turned at our approach, hollow gazes that seemed to pass through us. It was a line of pilgrims trudging west, from one horizon to the next. Men raised their canteens and found nothing, as women shrouded in their salt-caked hair carried their dead babes...

It was Dannon that spoke. "Who are they?"

A man stopped at the sound of his voice; the bones of his neck audibly cracking as he turned to look at us. "Are... you... the prophet?"

Zimrah shook her head. "Travelers, sir. Looking for my husband."

I watched the man's skin crack around the edges of his smile. "Then... he... rests... with God." He turned away and continued the journey he'd never complete, but it was a path that we followed. More desperate folk appeared as we trod the pilgrim road, coming from all directions across the endless white, all of them in need, all of them blind to what was waiting.

We kept our pace through most of the day, wandering among the travelers, eyes rooted on the western sky. I could kill them, it was tempting, such a meal of pious souls around me. It reminded me I had a debt to repay. The hunger rose, the coaxing I'd sated in blood the past years raising its hackles. Only, the city appearing ahead saved them from the death I wished for them.

It appeared like a mirage from the heat, shimmering haze becoming white sandstone and adobe. The path was well trod, tufts of feeble grass somehow finding purchase in the salt. There weren't gates, and I didn't see gun hands ushering the throngs, all of them were going one direction. I took my horse into the shadows between *kivas* and huts, and the others followed. They looked at each dark doorway as we passed, grips tightening on their shooting irons, fearing what could be lurking.

We secured the horses, and I made sure that I had enough ammunition. Zimrah cradled her rifle, putting a comforting hand on her trembling sister-wife. "Come, let's do our heavenly father's work."

I ignored the Gun's guidance then, the urge to tell the woman that her god's work was all around us.

The salt was wet in the main street, water carved furrows through until it met the dirt. The pilgrims found it, falling to their knees and lapping like dogs. Every gulp slaked their thirst even as it dried out their soul. Soon, they would be like the dry man we had met, parched and hollow.

I lashed out to grab Dannon, who'd gone to his knees. "Don't drink the water."

I saw his cracked lips, desperate eyes already wandering back to the stream, so I killed the nearest pilgrim. My knife slid across the withered throat and the red blood mixed with the clear water, muddying it. None of the pilgrims stopped drinking.

We followed the brook, moving with the crowd, all of them streaming to the source. There wasn't anything like saloons, banks, or anything else that civilized folk had built with their hands. It was massive and ancient, a temple raised to savagery and blood. The water flowed down its steps, running to the four winds, and into the mouths waiting below.

At the top was a woman nailed to a cross.

She was naked, a bloody cloth wrapped around her eyes, wrists and feet crippled and bleeding, and she was pregnant. Strato Cobb stood under her, preaching to his flock. His wild eyes danced over the masses. "Brave souls, welcome. Blessed are you who have endured, for you shall be pure!"

I moved forward, marking his appearance: grey shaggy hair and beard, bare chest scarred with the symbols of his faith, torn priest raiment covering his legs. Imagined he prided himself on looking a mad prophet crying in the desert.

And every miracle worker needed disciples. There were a dozen that I could see standing guard and helping those who'd managed to ignore their thirst. I was close enough to hear them, promising living water that would quench them.

I realized that the crucified woman's belly quivered with every soul that drank.

A woman called for her husband, who remained behind lapping at the water. One of the men conducted her up the steps and Strato watched her come. "Do not weep for those who perished, those who chose the river of death over the water of life."

The woman was pale, shivering despite the sun bearing down on this place, a lunger from the look of her. Strato pulled her to her feet, shouting to those standing at the base of the temple. "All of you bear witness. This is the miracle that has been prepared for you."

The crucified woman bled from her feet, her wrists, between her legs... Strato reached up and soaked his hand in her life. He brought it back to the lunger. "All who drink this will never thirst again."

The sick woman didn't hesitate; she nursed at the offered hand. Her skin flooded with new color, the patches of hair on her head coming alive, then she stood whole again.

Strato smiled and pulled her up. "Come sister, sing a new song." She went to her place on the temple and her voice joined with the rest of them.

I could see Zimrah, Dannon, and Lael, easy enough in the crowd, they were the only ones cradling rifles. But when you came like wolves among the sheep, the shepherd had a way of spotting you. One of the disciples suddenly froze, and then shouted, pointing at Zimrah. She cried out in return, pushing through the crowd towards the man, Dannon and Lael dogging her heels. For the first time, I saw the boy clinging to the disciple's leg... Tollen and his child.

I watched Lael fall to her knees, sobbing, hugging her son close. Zimrah embraced her husband who returned it, reaching out for Dannon to join them. I saw her look for me in the crowd, eyes unseeing as I whispered a working, drawing symbols in the salt to hide me from the world. It was strong magic, but the thing growing in the suffering woman's belly fed Strato something stronger. He had eyes to see, and hands to shed blood. And he had seen his disciple's family.

I watched him descend the steps, his hands wide. "Welcome, weary souls."

Lael watched, afraid, while Zimrah glared. But Tollen smiled, his devotion unwavering. "It's ok," he said. "Don't be afraid. He has come to make the whole world clean." Wonderful lies, but what Strato sowed would never grow.

Zimrah broke from Tollen's grasp, speaking up to the prophet. "I'm taking my husband back to the heavenly father and righteousness."

Strato gestured to the woman hanging from the cross. "My lady, he has drank from the blood, from the body broken for him. He sings a new song and is a servant of a new god."

The woman's belly quivered at the words, and all the folk drinking the water around the temple cried in ecstasy, slaves to the will of whatever was growing inside.

Tollen joined his prophet, holding his young son high. "How long has heaven remained silent for us, Zimrah? This isn't unanswered prayers and toil. This place was supposed to be the promised land, and we still fight for it."

Strato gestured to the crucified woman. "And when he is born, he will wipe this land clean for us, for those who forsake their thirst."

Tollen reached out his hand and Lael took it, Dannon following, guiding them both up the steps to the cross. I could have stopped it; a swift bullet and I could adorn the temple with new blood. But far be it from me to judge folk damning themselves, nailing the scales to their own eyes and calling it righteousness.

Zimrah shouted for them, held back by Strato's other penitents, watching her husband take her son and younger wife into the fold, helpless unless she wanted to shed blood. She wouldn't make that decision, she wasn't me, and I watched her family pay the price. Dannon followed his father's instruction like a good son, drinking from the blood. Lael hugged her little boy close, then she too sucked at the bleeding feet of the false Christ. The marks of the journey faded as their health was restored and their minds were lost to blasphemy.

Tollen had taken his son's canteen, filling it with the blood, and he brought it back to his first wife. "My love, this is what we've been waiting for, communion with a true god."

A single tear spilled from his wife's eye, running its way down her cheek, and she wrenched her arms away from her captors. "It's too late for that. I brought the devil with me."

I stopped my words, scraping the symbol in the salt with my boot, then I aimed the Gun at the nearest disciples. It sang death, blood spraying across the steps of the temple, joining with the water.

A few were armed. I saw Tollen reach for Lael's pistol, but it didn't matter. No gun could kill me. The salt sprayed out around me as the few armed men fired, and my feet met the temple steps. I ignored the disciples; the Gun only cried for the blood of the prophet.

"Strato... been awhile."

The man had lost his fervor. He held his hands out like they could save him from the death I'd prepared. "You can't stop it, Salem. My god is born this day, and those who drink his water give their essence to him. Those who drink his blood live through him!"

His eyes fixed on the Gun held in my hand. He knew as well as I the power in the perdition's iron, and the price I had paid for it. He spit, shaking his head. "I proved my power to you and your brother. You were the wicked seed of your father, the devil, and I hoped—"

I pulled the hammer of the Gun, chambering the bullet. "You hoped what, Cobb? That we'd turn aside? Told you then that my thirst ain't quenched in salt or water. I quench it with death."

Strato watched as I let the barrel drift from him, following, trying to put himself between the Gun and what was behind him. I decided to dig the knife as deep as it would go into his soul. "And I'd wager that until it's born, whatever you're growing in that womb can feel death."

I turned faster than a snake struck, firing quick, and watched the crucified woman's belly shudder, her blood erupted like geysers. She screamed with each new wound and then sagged on the cross.

The nails couldn't hold her anymore, the unforgiving metal tore through her skin, and she fell. Her corpse smashed into the ground, and her belly burst like a rotten watermelon. I watched the blood run, entrails laid out for the world. But there was something else in the offal, something that bled salt and possessed four faces. Malformed wings sprouted from its back like a baby chick, and small arms that tried to clasp the wounds I'd given it.

Just as the penitents clutched at themselves as they lost their lives.

It began at their mouths; they sneezed salt, grasping at their throats as their skin to dry, whole patches replaced with white.

I listened to their death cries like a fine song, watching the new pillars of salt form across the mound. The dry folk watched their betters suffer and die before returning to their thirst.

When it was finished, only Strato and Zimrah were still living, and the prophet had sunk to his knees, staring at the dead thing come loose from the womb. "This... this isn't..." He wasn't listening to the clinking of my spurs and didn't react as I reloaded. I pressed the Gun to his head.

"I... I saw a world free from sin."

The Gun whispered its triumph, and I shook my head. "Ain't free from sin as long as I'm living in it."

I fired and let Strato join his god.

Zimrah barely resisted as I took her from the temple. I placed her on her horse, waving my hand to clear my vision from the sharp wind. A storm was coming to bury this place, and the dry folk would go with it. Imagined that the towns around this desert would find a dead man sucked dry of moisture every now and again, but they'd explain it away, a bad dream. Strato Cobb and his preaching would become a memory, a story only I remembered.

I made sure the damned place was far behind us before I brought us to a halt. The sun hung in the late afternoon like a wound, bleeding its light. Zimrah knew what was coming and she didn't resist as I laid her on the ground. She'd promised to pay my price and it had come due.

I took a jar from my saddlebag, placing it at her head, drawing the symbols around her. She barely turned to look at me as I sat. "What will happen?"

The Gun was in my hand, and it thirsted. "A brief pain, then I'll take what I can carry."

Her blood sprayed like a sneeze when I fired, and the salt drank from her end. The light left her eyes, and I murmured the words, gathering up her life as it ran. There was power in such things. Then I butchered her, hanging her head from my saddle, fingers dangling like a trophy. I made fresh red symbols on my horse. What organs I didn't need, I left.

And the buzzards ate well.

An Exploration of the Weird West: An Afterword

BY PATRICK R. McDONOUGH

HOWDY, READER—

I'm Patrick McDonough: writer, podcaster, lover of all things horror, and now—editor. If you've made it this far, then maybe you're wondering how *Hot Iron and Cold Blood* came to be. Let's jump all the way back to the beginning.

Earlier in 2022, I wrote a short story titled "It Calls" for Silver Shamrock Publishing's submission call for splatterpunk westerns. *Midnight in the Stagecoach* would have been the fourth volume in their annual *Midnight* series. My submission for the last two received a rejection, but I knew *Stagecoach* was going to break that losing streak.

Unfortunately, with only three weeks to go until submissions closed, the press shut down.

I spoke with the previous owner of Death's Head Press, Patrick C. Harrison III (PC3), asking if DHP had considered publishing their own splatterpunk western anthology, and if he would be willing to read "It Calls". He kindly said he'd be happy to take a look.

The next day, an email containing good news, bad news, and a dash of hope, arrived.

"You have come a LONG way since that story I read a few years back. This one is great. Very well written and extremely unique... As far as publishing, we don't currently have any anthologies in the works. That's the issue... If that were to happen, this story would certainly make the cut." – PC3

A few days later, not only was the anthology a go, but Patrick was true to his word. My story was the first accepted to Death's Head Press's yet-unnamed western anthology. It also turned out to be the only story edited by Patrick C. Harrison III (my unofficial co-editor), the notes were attached to that initial email.

Once the tumbleweed got rolling, the focus on splatterpunk shifted to a broader range, covering all subgenres of horror, set primarily in the Old West. After devising the guidelines, sifting through the submissions, sending out acceptances and rejections (I don't think I'll ever get used to that last one) and reading through the invited stories, the anthology's architecture began to take form. Through that framework, I discovered that there is narration within sequence itself. For the *Hot Iron* story order, I wanted to start with a straight western, ease into the weird until we hit the queerest one, and gradually transition back toward grittier westerns, with an epic finale.

Jill Girardi's "Ruthless" is a love letter to S. Craig Zahler's *Bone Tomahawk*, while Owl Goingback's "Texas Macabre" feels like a westernized salute to Washington Irving's *The Legend of Sleepy Hollow*. "Holes", by Brennan La-Faro, gives readers a taste of his Buzzard's Edge mythos, and Vivian Kasley's "Soiled Doves" plants a desire for more brawling brothels.

"About her Given Name" is Kenzie Jennings's second story involving the Lady in Red, and Ol' Ronald Kelly's "The Night of El Maldito" is an original tale, while offering something to satisfy his most ardent of readers. To date, "The Deviltry of Elemental Valence" is Edward Lee's only story set in the West (present or past), and I'd love to see him write more. The zenith of oddity comes in Drew Huff's "Old World Birds", a fantastical tale that addresses a universal message: love is love and it comes in endless forms.

David J. Schow's "Sedalia" exemplifies how a writer's back catalog can be just as exciting as the latest and greatest, with its clever ability to weave poltergeists with dinosaurs. I hope everyone who reads Jeff Strand's "Rope-and-Limb" laughs as much as I did. "Dread Creek" by Bri Morgan shows one of the most fucked up ways to die. Several times over. Then there's my spun yarn, "It Calls", the origin story of a character I have big plans for, one day.

"Old Habits" by L.M. Labat hits hard and makes me hope she writes more short fiction. "Hungry" by Jesse Allen Champion is the only story featuring Chinese railroad workers that I read during open submissions, an exciting topic tailor-made for Old West horror fiction. "The Redheaded Dead" isn't the first time I've read one of Joe's Reverend Mercer stories. "The Hungry Snow" is just as good, and both show how a seasoned wordslinger uses their almighty pen. We end with Wile E. Young's "Seeking a Grave in Canaan", which reminded me of the original *Doom* and *Silent Hill* videogames. With a Salem Covington adventure, you'll find intense gunplay, terrifying creatures, and an unnerving atmosphere.

It's worth noting how important forewords are. They are quite literally the first voice the reader experiences. They set the tone, which is why I wanted RJ Joseph to be that person, and boy did she ever do a phenomenal job. She's as kindhearted as she is intelligent with crafting a concise and powerful sentence. When I called to ask if she'd be interested, I felt like a little kid inviting my friend over to watch horror movies. Her reply was an excited 'yes!'. That's how I view *Hot Iron and Cold Blood*, a fun time with friends who love horror.

I'd also like every reader who enjoyed this book to be aware of and thankful to the following people: First and foremost, Ken McKinley, if he never had that open call for *Stagecoach*, I would never have written my story, thus having no reason to pursue Death's Head Press; Brennan LaFaro and Kenzie Jennings, without their in-depth beta notes, my story would have been a jumbled mess of potential, they helped to shape the story into something dreadfully chilling; the founders of Death's Head Press: Jarod Barbee and Patrick C. Harrison III, for accepting "It Calls", and granting me all the opportunities I never thought I'd have.

Then, there's the new team behind Death's Head Press: Steve Wands, Jeremy Wagner, Kristy Baptist, and Anna Kubik, they stayed true to my original vision in its entirety, and Steve kept me in the loop and my head above water throughout the company's internal changeover; to Julia Borcherts and Jordan Brown of Kay Publicity, for spearheading the promotion of this strange little book; to the fifteen incredible contributors, for making a first-time anthologist feel loved, respected, and proud as ever for their stories; to Robert Sammelin, his cover alone is going to sell copies, but seriously, it's a remarkable piece of art, bravo!

Joe R. Lansdale and Ronald Kelly, whenever I had an obstacle to address or any doubts in myself or what may come of this book, those two *always* made time to listen and offer feedback. Without any of those people, this book would not be in your hands today. To all the aforementioned, thank you for keeping good faith in me, I have no words to express just how touched and thankful I am. We made something really god damn special.

Last, but certainly not least, I am thankful for you, dear reader, for taking a chance on this brutal and diverse anthology, consisting of up-and-comers and legends in the field.

We'll meet again, somewhere out in the dark country... sooner than later.

—Patrick R. McDonough
New Jersey, February 22nd, 2023

About the Authors

R.J. Joseph

Rhonda Jackson Garcia, AKA RJ Joseph, is an award winning, Stoker Award™ nominated, Texas based academic and creative writer/professor whose writing regularly focuses on the intersections of gender and race in the horror and romance genres and popular culture. She has had works published in various applauded venues, including the 2020 Halloween issue of *Southwest Review* and *The Streaming of Hill House: Essays on the Haunting Netflix Series*. Her debut horror collection, Hell Hath No Sorrow like a Woman Haunted was released in August 2022 by The Seventh Terrace. Rhonda is also an instructor at the Speculative Fiction Academy and the co-host of the Genre Blackademia podcast.

When she isn't writing, reading, or teaching, she can usually be found wrangling her huge blended family of one husband, five adult sprouts, six teenaged sproutlings, four grandboo seedlings, and one furry hellbeast who sometimes pretends to be a dog.

She occasionally peeks out on Twitter @rjacksonjoseph or at www.rhondajacksonjoseph.com

Jill Girardi

Jill Girardi is the award-nominated, internationally best-selling author of Hantu Macabre. A film based on the book with the same title is currently in the works (directed by Aaron Cowan, a senior member of the visual effects team that won four Oscars for Avatar and Lord of the Rings.) Jill is also the founder of Kandisha Press, an independent publishing company dedicated to promoting women horror authors around the world. She is currently working on Hantu Macabre 2, a short story collection, and a novella titled "Mangrove Jack." Her favorite published stories to date are "One Every Year" which appears in the Dark Murmurs anthology by Silent House Press, "Mister Olivelli" from Lunatic Lullabies by Pyke Publishing, and "The Ecstasy of Gold" from 25 Gates of Hell by Burwick anthologies. She mainly writes dark humorous creature features and still believes in twist endings.

Find her on Twitter/Instagram: @jill_girardi

Owl Goingback

Owl Goingback has been writing professionally for over thirty years, and is the author of numerous novels, children's book, screenplays, magazine articles, short stories, and comics. He is a three-time Bram Stoker Award Winner, a Nebula Award Nominee, and a Storytelling World Awards Honor Recipient. His books include *Crota, Darker Than Night, Evil Whispers, Breed, Shaman Moon, Coyote Rage, Eagle Feathers, The Gift*, and *Tribal Screams*. In addition to writing under his own name, he has ghostwritten for Hollywood celebrities.

Twitter: OGoingback

Brennan LaFaro

Brennan LaFaro is a horror writer living in southeastern Massachusetts with his wife, two sons, and his hounds. An avid lifelong reader, Brennan also co-hosts the Dead Headspace podcast. Brennan is the author of Noose, as well as Slattery Falls and its forthcoming sequels. You can read his short fiction in various anthologies and find him on Twitter at @brennanlafaro or at www.brennanlafaro.com. For the most up to date news, sign up for Brennan's newsletter, Postcards From the Falls at http://brennanlafaro.substack.com.

Vivian Kasley

Vivian Kasley hails from the land of the strange and unusual, Florida! She's a writer of short stories and poetry which have appeared in various science fiction anthologies, horror anthologies, horror magazines, and webzines. Some of her street cred includes Grimscribe Press, Ghost Orchid Press, Diabolica Americana, The Denver Horror Collective's Jewish Book of Horror, Kandisha Press's Slash-Her, Death's Head Press, and poetry in Black Spot Books inaugural women in horror poetry showcase: Under Her Skin. She definitely has more in the works, including her very own first collection. When not writing or subbing at the local middle school, she spends her time reading in bubble baths, snuggling her rescue animals, going on adventures with her other half, and searching for seashells and other treasures along the beach.

Twitter handle: @VKasley

Kenzie Jennings

Kenzie Jennings is an English professor residing in the sweltering tourist pocket of central Florida. She is the author of the Splatterpunk Award nominated books *Reception* and *Red Station* (Death's Head Press). Her short horror fiction has appeared in *The Avarice, Baker's Dozen, Slash-Her: An Anthology of Women In Horror, Slice Girls, Worst Laid Plans: An Anthology of Vacation Horror, & Dig Two Graves, Vol. 1.*

Twitter: @kenzieblyjay

Ronald Kelly

RONALD KELLY was born November 20, 1959, in Nashville, Tennessee. He attended Pegram Elementary School and Cheatham *County* Central High School, and, during his junior and senior years, had aspirations of become a comic book artist before his interests turned to writing fiction. Ronald Kelly began his professional writing career in the horror genre in 1986 with the sale of his first short story, "Breakfast Serial" to *Terror Time Again* magazine. Specializing in tales of Southern horror, his work was widely published in magazines such as *Deathrealm, Grue, New Blood, Eldritch Tales,* and *Cemetery Dance.* His first novel, *Hindsight,* was released by Zebra Books in 1990. He wrote for Zebra for six years, publishing such novels as *Pitfall, Something Out There, Father's Little Helper, The Possession, Fear, Blood Kin,* and *Moon of the Werewolf (Undertaker's Moon).* His audiobook collection, *Dark Dixie: Tales of Southern Horror,* was included on the nominating ballot of the 1992 Grammy Awards for Best Spoken Word or Non-Musical Album. Ronald's short fiction work has been published in major anthologies such as *Cold Blood, Borderlands 3, Dark at Heart, Shock Rock, Hot Blood: Seeds of Fear, The Earth Strikes Back,* and many more,

In the mid-1990s, the bottom dropped out of the mass-market horror market. When Zebra canceled their horror line in October 1996, Ronald Kelly stopped writing for ten years and worked various jobs including welder, factory worker, production manager, drugstore manager, and custodian. In 2006, Kelly returned to the horror genre and began writing again. In early 2008, Croatoan Publishing released his work *Flesh Welder* as a stand-alone chapbook, and it quickly sold out. In early 2009 Cemetery Dance Publications released a hardcover edition of his first short story collection, *Midnight Grinding & Other Twilight Terrors*. Also in 2010, Cemetery Dance released his first novel in over ten years, *Hell Hollow*, as a hardcover edition. Between 2011 and 2015, Kelly's Zebra horror novels were released in limited hardcover editions by Thunderstorm Books as *The Essential Ronald Kelly series*. Each book contained a new novella related to the novel's original storyline.

After his comeback to the horror genre, he has written several additional novels, such as *Restless Shadows, Timber Gray,* and *The Buzzard Zone,* as well as numerous short story collections: *After the Burn, Mister Glow-Bones & Other Halloween Tales, The Halloween Store & Other Tales of All-Hallows' Eve, Season's Creepings: Tales of Holiday Horror, Irish Gothic,* and *The Web of La Sanguinaire & Other Arachnid Horrors*. In 2021, his collection of extreme horror stories, *The Essential Sick Stuff,* published by Silver Shamrock Publications, won the Splatterpunk Award for Best Collection. He is currently publishing two new horror series: *The Saga of Dead-Eye* and the EC Comics-inspired *Southern-Fried* story collections with Crossroad Press.

Ronald Kelly lives in a backwoods hollow in Brush Creek, Tennessee, sixty miles east of Nashville, with his wife and young'uns.

Edward Lee

Edward Lee is the author of over 50 books in the horror, suspense, and sci-fi genres. He has also had comic scripts published by DC Comics, Verotik Inc., and Cemetery Dance. Many of his novels have been reprinted in Germany, Poland, Japan, Italy, Romania, Greece, Russia, Spain and other countries. He is a Bram Stoker Award Nominee; his Lovecraftian novel *INNSWICH HORROR* won the 2010 Vincent Price Award for Best Foreign Book (Austria), his novel *WHITE* ovel *WHITE TRASH GOTHIC* won the 2018 Splatterpunk Award for Best Extreme Horror Novel, and his collaborative novella *HEADER 3* (with Ryan Harding) won for Best Extreme Novella. In 2020 Lee won the J.F. Gonzales Lifetime Achievement Award. In 2009, the movie version of his novella *HEADER* was released by Synapse Films. Lee is a U.S. Army veteran and lives in Seminole, Florida.

Drew Huff

Drew Huff is the author of *Free Burn*, coming out on March 2024. Born and raised in eastern Washington, she enjoys writing stories that explore the intricacies of trauma, body horror, and fear. Her short fiction, "Word of Nellie," is the closing story in Darklit Press's "The Sacrament" anthology. Another short story was included in Hungry Shadow Press's anthology, "It Was All a Dream," and another short story, "Old World Birds" is being featured in Death's Head Press's anthology, "Hot Iron and Cold Blood." Her short story "Same as it Ever Was" is being featured in Night Terror Novel's charity anthology, and also a flash fiction piece, "The Bird, Frozen in Time". She is currently editing her other novel, *The Divine Flesh,* and drafting another novel, *The Exodontists.*

Website: drewehuff.com
Twitter Handle: @dreadnought_dru

David J. Schow

DAVID J. SCHOW is a multiple-award-winning American writer. Ten novels, thirteen short story collections, comics (*John Carpenter's Tales of Science Fiction* — "*The Standoff*" and "*HELL*"), movies (*The Crow, Leatherface: Texas Chainsaw Massacre III, The Hills Run Red*), television (*Masters of Horror, Mob City, Creepshow),* nonfiction (*The Outer Limits Companion, The Art of Drew Struzan*), and can be seen on various DVDs as expert witness or documentarian on everything from *Creature from the Black Lagoon* to *Psycho* to *I, Robot.* Thanks to him, the word "splatterpunk" has been in the Oxford English Dictionary since 2002. Google him.

Twitter: @DavidJSchow

Jeff Strand

Jeff Strand is the Bram Stoker Award-winning author of over 50 books, including *Pressure, Clowns Vs. Spiders,* and *Twentieth Anniversary Screening.* He has never participated in a railroad heist or been thrown out of the front window of a saloon, but he did visit Tombstone. Several of his books are in development as motion pictures...a slow and maddening process. He won the Splatterpunk Award twice and lost one other time, but the loss was to Jack Ketchum, so it's all good. He also lost the Bram Stoker Award to Peter Straub, Jonathan Maberry, and Stephen King (twice) before his eventual victory. He loses to cool people. He is wanted dead or alive in seventeen counties. You can visit his Gleefully Macabre website at www.jeffstrand.com.
Twitter: @JeffStrand

Briana Morgan

Briana Morgan (she/her) is a horror author and playwright. Her books include *The Reyes Incident, The Tricker-Treater and Other Stories, Unboxed: A Play*, and more. She's a proud member of the Horror Writers Association, the Science Fiction & Fantasy Writers Association, and the Alliance of Independent Authors. When not writing, Briana enjoys gaming, watching scary movies, and reading disturbing books. Twitter: @brimorganbooks

Patrick R. McDonough

Patrick R. McDonough is an editor, writer, and the producer/co-host of the Dead Headspace podcast. His penchant for horror and history leads him down endless paths, growing his interest in forgotten stories. He's a New Englander currently living in South Jersey with his wife, son, and pets. You can find his short fiction in various anthologies through Silent Hill Press, Cemetery Gates Media, and Crystal Lake Publishing. Twitter: @Prmcdonough

L.M. Labat

As a native of New Orleans, author and illustrator L.M. Labat weaves her artwork into horror, occult, and historical fiction stories. With accolades and origins stemming from biology, psychology, and fine art, she continues to fuse her collective knowledge and skills into her work. She debuted with her novel titled "The Sanguinarian Id." Visit her at http://www.lmlabat.com Twitter: @LMLabat

Jesse Allen Champion

Jesse Allen Champion is a native Texan and writer of frequent western-themed stories. From Texas to California, Jesse has worked at dude-ranching, theatre management, technical writing, and editing. As comfortable on a horse as a keyboard, Jesse's fiction remembers the Old West, with the tumbleweed going wherever it will and a man on horseback as the ultimate arbiter of good and evil.

Joe R. Lansdale

Joe R. Lansdale is the author of forty-five novels and four hundred shorter works, including stories, essays, reviews, introductions and magazine articles. His work has been made into films, *BUBBA HOTEP, COLD IN JULY,* as well as the acclaimed TV show, *HAP AND LEONARD.* He has also had works adapted to *MASTERS OF HORROR* on SHOWTIME, and wrote scripts for *BATMAN THE ANIMATED SERIES*, and *SUPERMAN THE ANIMATED SERIES.* He scripted a special Jonah Hex animated short, as well as the animated Batman film, *SON OF BATMAN.*

He has received numerous recognitions for his work. Among them THE EDGAR, for his crime novel *THE BOTTOMS, THE SPUR,* for his historical western *PARADISE SKY,* as well as ten BRAM STOKERS for his horror work, and has also received THE GRANDMASTER AWARD and the LIFETIME ACHIEVEMENT AWARD from THE HORROR WRITERS ASSOCIA-TION. He has been recognized for his contributions to comics and is a member of THE TEXAS INSTITUTE OF LITERATURE, THE TEXAS LITER-ARY HALL OF FAME, and is WRITER IN RESIDENCE at STEPHEN F. AUSTIN STATE UNIVERSITY.

He is in the INTERNATIONAL MARTIAL ARTS HALL OF FAME, as well as the U.S. MARTIAL ARTS HALL OF FAME, and is the founder of the Shen Chuan martial arts system.

His books and stories appear in over twenty-five languages.

Wile E. Young

Wile E. Young is from Texas, where he grew up surrounded by stories of ghosts and monsters. During his writing career he has managed to both have a price put on his head and win the 2021 Splatterpunk Award for Best Novel. He obtained his bachelor's degree in History, which provided no advantage or benefit during his years as an aviation specialist and I.T. guru.

His longer works includes *Catfish in the Cradle* (2019), *The Perfectly Fine House* (2020), *The Magpie Coffin* (2020), *Shades of the Black Stone* (2022), *Clickers Never Die* (2022), and *Dust Bowl Children* (2022). His short stories have been featured in various anthologies including the *Clickers Forever* (2018), *Behind the Mask- Tales From the Id* (2018), *Corporate Cthulhu* (2018), *And Hell Followed* (2019), *Splatterpunk Bloodstains* (2020) and *Bludgeon Tools: A Splatterpunk Anthology* (2021).

Twitter: @TexasCthulhu.